The Scrolls of Prophecy

Book One of the Sacred Scrolls Saga

Robert C. Andrews

Visit the author's storefront for other material and updates on the continuing Sacred Scrolls Saga at:
http://stores.lulu.com/store.php?fAcctID=720243

ISBN: 978-0-6151-7437-2

~~ The Eastern Province of the ~~
~~~ Kingdom of Coleraine ~~~

The Scrolls of Prophecy

Book One of the
Sacred Scrolls Saga

Robert C. Andrews

For the Girls of Excelsior Youth Center

From our collective reality comes my need

for fantasy

Author's Forward

Dear Reader,

First of all, I'd like to thank you for choosing to read my book. Writing this story was quite an experience; I'm pleased to be able to share it with you.

I also need to thank some of the people who helped bring this adventure to life, either by stimulating my imagination or cleaning up my written work. Takako, Lucy, Darrell and Terri – the EYC Writers' Group – you fall into both categories. Without the support of the group, this book would be just one more unfinished project to add to my pile of lost dreams. I owe you all more gratitude than I can properly express here. Sharon, Patrick, Jera, Emily, Mom and Dad, and the countless others who encouraged me to keep at it: thank you. Lastly, a special thanks to Sarah Fenston for drawing a beautiful map for use in the Lulu editions of the book and to Pam Worthen and Patrick Partin for the internal artwork. Your talent brought my vision to life.

With regard to the organization of the narrative: I wrote this story with an eye toward the parameters of Dungeons and Dragons or Roll-Playing Games. While I don't bother the reader with ideas such as 'hit points' or 'mana capacity,' those themes are present in the undercurrent of the story. Likewise, the characters will procure magical items as the plot progresses and they will tend to get more capable as their experience grows. That is not true in all cases, but it is a general trend to look for.

Also, I invite you to look for the philosophical or literary references that are sprinkled throughout the book. I won't give examples of them here, but I would love to discuss them with you on the Lulu web page. Check out my storefront for discussion topics, news and updates on the continuing Sacred Scrolls saga (http://stores.lulu.com/store.php?fAcctID=720243).

Lastly, dear reader, since you've come this far, perhaps I could impose upon you a bit further and ask you to do something unusual. Flip to the back of the book, please, and read the prologue to the second book in this series "Mark of the Crescent Moon." Don't worry, it doesn't give away the ending of the first book. I ask you to do this simply because it provides scope and perspective that might prove beneficial as you start to explore the kingdom of Coleraine and the world of the Sacred Scrolls.

In conclusion, thank you for taking the time to read this forward and thank you, again, for choosing to read my book. I hope you have as much fun reading it as I did writing it.

Sincerely,
Robert Andrews

Contents

Prologue

The fortress had stood for nearly three thousand years. Built by the masons of King Adbar the Second during the Third Age, its huge stone bulwarks withstood siege and flame when the king was overthrown and his city burned to the ground. Though the city could be rebuilt, the greatest treasures of its people could not be replaced and so were ferreted into the fortress. Unfortunately, only a select few of the king's inner circle knew the secrets of opening the vaults under the mountain. When they died in the siege and ensuing last stand of the king, the secrets of the vaults died with them. The treasures within the fortress survived untouched for centuries, a lasting legacy to a vanquished people.

Over time, the tide of humanity ebbed and flowed over the outcropping of rock built into the mountainside, the fortress now known as Citadel Adbar. Various forms of civilization were built, wiped clean and rebuilt around the citadel, with tales of the treasures held within growing more fantastic at every retelling. Citadel quests became common and over the years robbers, marauders and other treasure-seekers had breached many of the outer vaults, but the inner core of the fortress remained intact and utterly inaccessible.

When at last the reign of the de la Ponce lineage brought stability to the region, the Citadel was adopted as the royal depository and the guarding of its secrets was entrusted to the Brotherhood of Callamore. The Brotherhood outlived three royal families, evolving into a reclusive band of scholars whose names were largely unknown and whose eyes seldom saw the sun.

Their singular knowledge of the fortress made the Brotherhood indispensable and their usefulness was matched only by the maniacal fervor with which they undertook their duties. Their devotion to the vaults and the secrets held therein had become their religion, practiced with measured exactitude and reverent rituals.

On this day, within the depths of Citadel Adbar, a ritual was beginning. The most prized article in the entire fortress was being extracted from its vault for maintenance. This ritual was performed only once every five hundred years; whole generations of the Brotherhood had practiced for the event.

The bald crown of Brother Albus shone with perspiration as the old man marched in timed steps to the vault's door. The chanting of his Brothers swelled around him. The walls of the corridor were lined with the dark-cloaked men, each holding a single candle. Their feet stamped upon the floor to keep the meter of the chant and the footfalls now echoed through the cavernous fortress. As Brother Albus neared the door, he could no longer discern between the beat of his heart, his blood pounding in his temples and the resounding *boom* of the chant swirling around him.

With a trembling hand the man withdrew five jewels from a pouch on his belt. The vault's huge stone door had five slots cut into a circle. Albus placed a jade into the topmost slot and a garnet in the slot on the bottom left. The top right took a diamond and the bottom right a ruby. Albus held the last stone, a brilliant blue topaz, between his thumb and forefinger. He lifted the stone above his head and the chanting ceased with the echoes running away through the tunnels. The old man wiped the sweat from his eyes and lowered the topaz to the door.

Upon insertion of the last jewel, a click within the door was followed by the sound of sliding stone and then a blazing light poured through the holes. Each jewel sparkled in its unique beauty. Two of the younger Brothers stepped forward and heaved open the door. Into the vault stepped Brother Albus. Through some ingenious design, sunlight refracted through the hulking mountain and streamed into the chamber through a portal in the ceiling. The shaft of light illuminated a golden chest in the middle of the room. Brother Albus kneeled before it and uttered a small prayer, and then he lifted the lid.

The old man shrieked and fell backward out of the vault, clutching at his chest as if stricken. Several of his brethren rushed forward to help him. They lifted Albus to a seated position and the old man tried to speak, but could not find his voice. His eyes reflected utter terror.

"Gone," the old man finally managed to gasp. "They are gone!"

The Brotherhood of Callamore rushed forward and pressed into the tiny vault. A collective gasp went up through the dust-flecked shaft of light. The golden chest was indeed empty.

Part One
~ *Corpus Delicti* ~

The Heart of the Matter

Chapter One

~ **Aurora** ~

Aurora Daelin watched the old elf nobles descend the steps from the counsel chamber. They had been in conference with her father and the experience left them all fatigued. Their shoulders were slumped and their faces dark as they passed her. Only Shorlen Hycaen, her uncle and the captain of her father's personal guard, had managed a feeble smile. His eyes betrayed the gesture, however. Seeing the anguish on such a beatific face sent shivers down Aurora's spine. She knew perfectly well that Shorlen alone amongst the nobles was in favor of ending the seclusion of their people, this self-imposed quarantine.

For eight hundred years the elves had remained hidden deep in the shadows of Westwick Forest. Their line having been tainted by breeding with humans, many elves were no longer immune to the ravages of time. Those who were not of the purest blood were beginning to age. They became feeble and weak. Their hair turned gray and their skin became leathery. Eventually, they died. Those families whose blood remained pure had fled into the deep dark of Westwick, their strong magic and symbiosis with the living world allowing them to remain hidden deep within the forest.

The half-elves who were left behind, however, those whose blood was mixed with human ancestry, became pariahs, mongrelized outcasts shunned by the remaining peoples of the kingdom. The term 'elf' became an affront, hurled in insult with disdain and contempt. There had even been a brief effort to eradicate the half-elves, but that effort was spawned in ale-induced boast and bluster and it soon faltered. Even so, the eradication efforts had resulted in a cataloguing of heritage. Peasants who had lived for thousands of years in a land where noble blood was exalted now had a reason to trace and praise their own family line. Every family known or suspected to have elven blood was identified, labeled and stripped of their possessions and lands. Year upon year, decade upon decade and century upon century of hatred, distrust and oppression had reduced half-elves to the status of beggars and miscreants. The continued existence of a majestic race of full-blooded elves was unknown to all but a precious few, and the elves of Westwick took great pains to keep it that way.

But change was stirring in the land. The Fifth Age was drawing to an end. There was disagreement within the Westwick hierarchy regarding differing interpretations of the Sacred Scrolls. A minority of the scholars, those who had served as advisors to the ruling family for the past millennium, believed that the time of the prophecy was at hand. Other scholars, by far the majority, claimed that the precursor events foretold in the Scrolls had not yet occurred and, therefore, the time of the prophecy had not yet come. Most of the nobles had chosen to believe in the latter interpretation of the Scrolls, as it allowed them to maintain the safety of their seclusion.

The debate had raged for nearly a year. The Jarlaeth, the counsel consisting of the heads of each of the noble families, had been meeting almost daily. Aurora's father, Talos Daelin, was the Jarl. As the head of the ruling family, it fell upon his shoulders to preside over the counsel. The stalemate in the Jarlaeth was beginning to weigh heavily on Talos. Divisions were beginning to form. Rumors of subterfuge and illicit alliances against House Daelin were becoming prevalent. Though it was true that elves would never resort to assassination or any form of aggressive move against the ruling family, the Jarlaeth could, by unanimous vote, place a new family at the helm of the Westwick kingdom. So it was that a sense of foreboding had been growing in Aurora's heart for several weeks now.

The hollow smile that her uncle offered her as he passed out of the counsel chamber sent Aurora's feet into motion. As she lightly and quickly ascended the steps and entered the first hall, her high brow was furrowed with worry.

"Father?" she inquired from the doorway of the dark counsel chamber.

"I am here, my dear," her father's voice came from the left of the long room, where the remains of a fire burned low in the hearth. "Come and sit with me awhile and tell me of your day."

"I would much rather hear news of the Jarlaeth," Aurora responded as she took a seat near her father.

The faint, red glow of the dying fire made the lines of worry upon the Jarl's face seem many and deep. Aurora could see him replaying the last counsel in his mind and she took his hand in both of hers. The touch of her smooth skin broke his dour recollection and he squeezed her hands, offering a valiant smile.

"Do not worry yourself with such unpleasantness," he said. "It is not befitting of an elf-maiden of your beauty."

"Truly, Father, I wish you would stop trying to protect me from matters of such import," Aurora responded curtly.

"Intrigue at court should not occur in Westwick!" Talos fumed, though his eyes and his tone softened almost immediately as he looked into his daughter's beautiful face. Her white hair gleamed with a rosy hue in the light of the failing fire. Her deep blue eyes were pools of concern. "There is much I have not told you." He sighed deeply. "But perhaps it is time that you learned of our peril." Aurora waited patiently as her father looked back into the coals in the hearth. A look of great pain came over his face. "The Sacred Scrolls are missing from Citadel Adbar."

Aurora felt the blood drain from her face. From her earliest days she had heard tales of the Scrolls, yet she knew nothing of their origin other than legend and myth. Though she was considered young by elf standards, still she was over three hundred years old. For the past several decades she had been growing increasingly impetuous and frustrated by her father's refusal to include her in matters of government. With one sentence, however, her father had quelled all of her selfish desires. *The Sacred Scrolls are missing from Citadel Adbar.* She recalled the pallid faces of the nobles as they left the counsel chamber. If before she had been concerned, now she was truly petrified. She looked back at her father to find him watching her intently. He was testing her, she realized, measuring her response. She knew in that moment that her childhood was over. Sitting tall and resolute, she returned her father's gaze and asked, "What more do I need to know?"

Satisfied with his daughter's response, Talos looked back to the fire and began a tale that few had heard since the passing of the last age.

The Sacred Scrolls had been kept safe in Citadel Adbar for over two thousand years, since the War of the Haunted Isle ended the Fourth Age. Saint Constantine, the monk who served as personal advisor to King Andred de la Ponce, accompanied the royal army to the island of Banthus in search of a traitorous sorcerer by the name of Kendrid the Red. Kendrid was the king's cousin, but his lust for power could not be sated in that role. The sorcerer became enthralled with the black art of necromancy. He began researching and conducting experiments in the hopes of raising an army of the undead. When he unearthed the Rites of Renivaar, a tome from the Second Age that gave him incredible dark powers, Kendrid tried to usurp the throne.

Utilizing his years of research and empowered by the tome of evil incantations, Kendrid forged a necromantic poniard. *Saewol Etanae* he named it, the Soul Eater, and any human whose life was taken by the blade was condemned to the existence of a bone warren, an undead abomination of the human form that is forever servile to the will of Soul Eater's wielder.

That night, Kendrid stole into the rooms of eight of the ten men who comprised King Andred's personal guard. The remaining two guards were serving out the night standing vigil at the door to the king's quarters. Quietly, Kendrid slid *Saewol Etanae* through the hearts of the slumbering men. A last escaping breath of agony was all that could be heard as each body yielded to its grotesque transformation.

As dawn broke on Kendrid's night of evil deeds, the traitor and his ghastly new minions converged on the bedchamber of Andred de la Ponce. The two guards in the passageway had a rotating system: while one stood at attention, the other rested in a chair set back against the door. The man standing guard was taken wholly by surprise, the threat hardly registering on the edge of his conscious thought as the shadows lengthened and then rushed in on him. Before he could even begin to counter the strike, his head fell to the floor and his blood was sprayed back into the face of his comrade. The sitting man sprang to his feet, toppling the chair against the door and waking the king.

"Alarm!" the guard yelled as he pulled his sword.

Roused from his slumber and somewhat confused, Andred de la Ponce struggled to gather his senses as the sounds of battle rang outside his door. The guard fought valiantly and desperately, parrying blow after blow as he tried to maneuver in the narrow doorway. Scrambling out of the tangle of his sheets and rushing to the door, Andred engaged a thick metal bolt.

"Back fiend! Your shadow shall not fall over..." the guard's last word turned into a gurgle and his body slumped to the floor. A puddle of blood ran under the door and the king nearly swooned. *Thump! Thump!* The intruders threw themselves against the door and shrieked an unearthly wail at the barrier. Andred recoiled in fear, stumbling backward until he fell onto his bed. *Crack!* The door began to give way and the king scrambled back to the head of his bed, cowering in fear. Just as the door exploded in a shower of splintering wood and the bone warrens rushed in, bright light flooded the chamber from the doorway to an adjoining room. The creatures shrieked again, but this time their wail resounded of pain and shock mixed with their anger and bloodlust.

"*Con sarné dol annolon*!" boomed a thunderous voice. "Be gone from the light!" The king looked over to see Arcanis Rhu, one of the youngest yet most powerful mages in his court, stride into the room. Arcanis held forth his staff, the magical light pouring from it with such force that the entire room was thrumming with the energy. The bone warrens shrieked again and fled from the chamber. Arcanis advanced toward the door as the creatures departed, but stopped in his tracks when he saw the doorway blocked by the form of Kendrid the Red. The evil mage stood with hands folded over his waist-high staff, leering at Arcanis from under his cowl.

"Your spell holds no sway over me, fool!" Kendrid spat.

"What treachery is this?" whispered Arcanis.

"Do not concern yourself with matters that are beyond you, my young friend," the red wizard sneered.

"I am no friend to one who would attack the king," Arcanis replied.

Kendrid issued a low, sinister laugh, "The throne shall be mine, Arcanis, and your king will serve me from beyond his own grave." With that, the sorcerer threw back his hood and summoned a magical barrier, the purple globe enveloping him and protecting him from magical attack.

"Scildori affélo!" shouted Arcanis Rhu as he slammed the bottom of his staff upon the floor. The young mage conjured his own barrier while maintaining the spell of Holy Light to keep the undead creatures at bay. Those two spells, however, were all he could muster at one time. Purely defensive, he was merely buying time until more help arrived.

Kendrid gave a wave of his staff and unleashed a bolt of searing lightning that crackled and sparked as it met the glittering blue globe of Arcanis's protective barrier. The acrid smell of electricity permeated the room, but Arcanis Rhu was unhurt and held stubbornly to his two active spells. Roaring in frustration, Kendrid changed tactics and reached into a pouch, pulling forth six small bones from a wild beast. He dropped them on the floor and fell into another spell. Using the bones as a medium, he summoned forth six snarling dire wolves.

Their eyes glowing red with evil intent, the creatures sprang toward Arcanis Rhu. Though utterly exposed to the summoned animals, the young mage held onto his defensive spells, knowing that certain doom awaited them all if he should falter. At the last moment, just before the beasts fell upon the wizard and tore him apart, soldiers of the royal army emerged from the side passage and surged past Arcanis to intercept the wolves.

Outnumbered now and unable to utilize his necromantic spells in the face of the Holy Light, Kendrid retreated. Though the chase was taken up almost immediately, the sorcerer and his undead minions managed to escape the castle through its labyrinth of hidden passages.

Kendrid fled to the island of Banthus where he inhabited an abandoned castle and made good on his dream of summoning an army of the undead. Three separate attacks by armies of men were repulsed, not a single survivor returning from the island. The fourth invasion found the fortress, indeed the island as a whole, deserted. No trace could be found of Kendrid or his ghastly army. Banthus, or the Haunted Isle as it became known, had remained deserted ever since.

In an effort to learn what had become of his traitorous cousin, King de la Ponce sent his personal advisor, a monk named Brother Constantine, on a mission to the Haunted Isle several months after Kendrid's mysterious disappearance. That mission met with disaster, however, as every member of the party fell victim to a terrible illness and perished. In the last days of his life, as the delirium of his illness wholly consumed him, Brother Constantine locked himself in his room and wrote what came to be known as the Sacred Scrolls. They included predictions of minor future events, all of which had come true. But the Scrolls also contained a prediction for the return of Kendrid the Red, a tale that became known as The Prophecy.

The fire in the counsel chamber was nearly extinguished by the time Talos Daelin finished his story. He looked at his daughter to find her deep in thought, staring into a corner but looking far into the past. After a few moments the silence became palpable and

Aurora broke her train of thought and looked back to her father. "So Brother Constantine was sainted and the Scrolls were placed in Citadel Adbar," she prompted.

"Yes," he confirmed, "but no one has seen the Scrolls since the last time they were taken from the vault for cleaning and application of preservative agents. That was five hundred years ago. Earlier this year, when they were due for maintenance, the vault was opened to find the Scrolls missing."

"But there are copies of the Scrolls, correct?" Aurora reasoned.

"Yes, but their power and purpose has never been fully understood. It is quite possible that the Scrolls themselves will play some part in the fulfillment of the prophecy. Constantine was deep in the throes of his illness when he wrote them. The language is often jumbled and incoherent. Thus, there are differing interpretations as to their exact meaning. One interpretation, which I believe to be the most accurate, asserts that five precipitating events will occur to announce the return of Kendrid the Red. The first is the birth of a human avatar for his spirit. The child will have a red birthmark on his back in the shape of a crescent moon. Of course, we have no way of knowing if such a person has been born. The second signature event was to be a drought across the human kingdom of Coleraine."

"Such a drought occurred fifteen years ago," Aurora broke in.

"Indeed it did," Talos nodded somberly.

"What is the third event?" Aurora asked quickly.

"The death of a king with no heir."

"Why, King Umberley just..." Aurora's voice trailed off as the full weight of the information hit her. The human king of Coleraine had just died, less than a year after his only son and heir had been ambushed on the road and his entire entourage wiped out. Umberley took the news hard; his health failed rapidly in his grief. Now the human kingdom was in turmoil with cousins, nephews and other relations vying for possession of the throne. Open war was a possibility. Though the elves of Westwick usually took only a passing interest in the affairs of humans, this development, in light of the drought and the disappearance of the Scrolls, truly held implications for their entire way of life. Aurora's voice was shaky when she continued, "The fourth event?"

"Plague," Talos replied, "though the type and severity are unclear."

"And the fifth?" Aurora asked quickly, truly desiring an end to this conversation.

"The fifth?" Talos echoed, surprised that his daughter needed to ask. "The fifth event is invasion, Aurora, an invasion by a monstrous horde of the undead that the plague-depleted humans will have no hope of countering. This end has been foreseen. That is why our people went into hiding and have maintained our seclusion here in Westwick. Our role in the coming conflict cannot be known with certainty, but it is clear that if the prophecy is to be thwarted and Kendrid the Red defeated, we must render aid to the humans. Not aid in battle, for we are too few. Indeed, if the fifth event occurs and the horde breaks upon this land, then any battles we might fight will be futile."

"What, then, is to be done?" Aurora asked.

"I cannot act openly without the support of the Jarlaeth." Talos gave a great sigh. "And I fear that support will not be forthcoming." He leaned close to his daughter, taking her hand and looking her hard in the eyes. "We must learn what has become of the Scrolls, and we must try to discern if Kendrid's human avatar has been born. Only then will we know if the prophecy is truly at hand. Only then will we know how best to proceed. With the disagreement in the Jarlaeth, there are few I can trust."

"I will do it," Aurora responded before he could ask the question.

Talos brushed a hair back from her soft cheek and put his hand upon her shoulder. "My beautiful daughter," he said. "You are worthy of the noble blood that flows in your veins." He smiled and rose, pulling her up with him, and together they began walking from the hall. "You must keep your heritage secret. No one can know that you are elf-kind until we are ready to end our seclusion, and that time has not yet come. Now, let us plot your course to Citadel Adbar."

Chapter Two

~ A Thief in the Night ~

"Bah! Are ye calling me a cheat, then, ye scurvy-bent dog?"

"Aye, I am at that, ye flea-ridden dwarf!"

Timmen O'Hook sat comfortably amidst the dark rafters of the Wyvern's Tail Inn, watching the argument unfolding below him with keen interest and a good deal of amusement. The Wyvern's Tail was his usual haunt. The large meeting hall and tavern was always teeming with sailors and travelers passing through the busy coastal city of Pilas Antum. With politicians and soldiers of the Royal Guard frequenting the Tail for the brothel that lent a nice twist to the establishment's name, Timmen was never lacking for pockets to pick.

"If ye're thinking ye been cheated, maybe ye be wanting to discuss the matter further out in the lane," coaxed the thick dwarf.

"Me and me mates'll be glad to join ye and teach ye to mind yer manners when the *Tide Runner* puts into port," replied the gangly-limbed sailor. Timmen smiled as he watched the dwarf and the three sailors move through the crowd and push through the Tail's large double-doors. He already knew what the outcome of this brawl would be; there would be three fewer hands on the *Tide Runner* when she set sail in the morning.

The spry halfling walked along a beam and quickly shimmied down the wall to drop to the ale-soaked floor. Darting nimbly through the crowd, Timmen passed by the bar and reached up to accept a scrap of paper from Cane Shanney, the owner of the

Tail and a friend of the halfling thief. Timmen glanced at the paper as he climbed the stairs to the living quarters of the Inn. He stopped at the third door on the left and looked behind him to assure that he had not been followed, then he lit a match and carefully inspected the door, the handle and the lock. Once convinced that the door was not booby-trapped, he quickly picked the lock and slipped into the room.

Timmen produced a candle from his pocket and lit it with the match. He cupped his hand to project the light away from him and began carefully looking through the room. The thief was familiar with all of the rooms in the Tail and knew there were no hidden compartments, so he looked through all of the existing furniture before moving on to the sailors' baggage. He took a few coins from a heavy wool coat and a gold ring from the dresser.

"They'll not be needing these," he said softly to himself. He chuckled and shook his head. What fools to have picked a fight with Dorak Shale! That dwarf's heart is as black as the stone that is his namesake, and twice as hard. Timmen continued searching the room, taking his time to look carefully for traps. He had all night, after all, since the sailors would not be returning. He soon discovered a small trunk hidden under a bed. Timmen cursed at their choice of hiding places for the trunk. It would take him the better part of an hour to ensure that there were no traps on or about the bed, or under it, or holding the trunk in place.

"I hope Dorak kills them slowly," he muttered spitefully as he set about his work, though he was fairly certain that the fight in the lane was already over. Timmen doubted that the sailors would be able to set any complex or cleverly disguised traps, yet he still went through the tedious process of searching very slowly and deliberately. Carelessness, he knew, could be disastrous in his line of work. He checked the perimeter of the bed, the sheets, the headboard, the four legs, the feather mattress, under the mattress, under the bed and all about the trunk. Finally, he extracted the trunk from its hiding place and began inspecting it in detail.

The trunk had two hinges, each with eight intersecting teeth joined by a pin. The teeth were tightly joined, which meant that a needle or other trigger device could not be hidden there. The seal of the lid was true, with no bulges or crevices to indicate that the wood had been bored. The lock was a common pin and tumbler, its depth not sufficient to house a dart or some other weapon that might be sprung upon the careless or unwary. Timmen tapped all of the walls and the lid, listening for the deeper *thud* that would indicate a coiled spring was in place. Hearing none, he inverted the trunk and tapped the bottom. *Tink, tink, tink, thunk.* Timmen smiled. Sometimes it was just too easy.

The halfling reached into his coat and extracted a leather-lined booklet from which he pulled a small hand-auger. After a short series of taps revealed the center of the spring, he quickly drilled a small hole in the bottom of the trunk. He then pulled from his hat the long tail-feather of a cock pheasant. Some people thought he wore the feather in his cap in an effort to look dashing, but it was, in fact, a tool of his trade. He inserted the feather into the hole and used it to explore the inside of the trunk, the black bands across the feather serving as a natural ruler. The details of the trap's design flowed down the feather's quill to the thief's trained and sensitive fingers. The trunk had a false floor with a hole in the center, under which there was a dagger loaded on a tightly coiled spring.

Timmen put the feather back in his cap and pulled a clamp from his kit. The top of the clamp was on a hinge so it could be extended straight to maneuver through narrow places and then dropped to clamp down upon its target. Once the coiled spring was clamped, Timmen turned the trunk upright and picked the lock. As he opened the lid, he heard the telltale click as the trap was loosed, but the spring merely groaned against the clamp. The thief snorted derisively and snapped his fingers at the trap. He hesitated a moment to savor the anticipation and then pulled back the thin velvet coverlet to reveal his prize. His eyes sparkled in the candlelight as he beheld a jewel-encrusted dagger.

"Where did those swabbies get a blade such as this?" Timmen wondered aloud.

"From the Countess," came an unexpected answer.

Timmen spun around to see a lean and dark stranger reclining in the shadows by the window. The halfling was so surprised that he dropped both the dagger and his thieving kit.

"Who, who are you?" he stuttered.

"An emissary of darkness, Timmen O'Hook," the stranger sneered wickedly, his eyes glinting and teeth glistening in the candlelight. "Or shall I call you Timmy the Crook?"

Timmen staggered back a few steps. Only his friends called him Timmy, and only his closest friends teasingly called him Timmy the Crook. "How do you know me?" he asked.

"The Countess has taken note of your work, my little friend, and she is most impressed," the stranger said and leaned forward into the light of the candle. "That is not to say that she is pleased, however."

Timmen got his first good look at the stranger's face when the man leaned forward and a spark of recognition sent ice water tumbling down his spine. "What should the Countess want of me?" he asked nervously.

"Respect," the stranger replied, his visage stern and ominous, "and tribute. Your operation here in the Tail has grown profitable. Why, look at the treasure you have just procured." Timmen followed the stranger's eyes to the jeweled dagger on the floor at the halfling's feet.

"How did three lowly sailors come to possess . . ." he began to ask.

"That is none of your concern," the stranger broke in. "You need only concern yourself with what the Countess requires of you." The man stroked his dark goatee and smiled as he continued. "She can ensure continued prosperity, but she requires tribute for her protection."

The threat was thinly veiled and was not lost on Timmen O'Hook. "What tribute does her Excellency require?" he asked.

"A pittance, I assure you." The stranger leaped forward with cat-like grace. Before the startled halfling could flinch, he was face to face with the dark man crouching before him. Timmen felt hot breath on his face as the man spoke. "Let us begin with this," he said, holding the bejeweled dagger before the halfling's eyes. His penetrating gaze narrowed on the little thief and he grabbed Timmen roughly by the hair, pulling him close. The tip of the blade danced lightly across Timmen's exposed throat as the man continued, "Do not mistake yourself for one who can disregard a mandate from the Countess. You will restrict your trade to the Wyvern's Tail and you will deliver thirty omani to the Countess every week. Take the money to Madame Olivier at the Copper Dram. Do not fail in this, little one, or you shall find our next meeting to be profoundly unpleasant." The assassin accentuated his last statement with a flick of the blade, opening an inch-long gash on the halfling's chin.

A flurry of shadow and the stranger was gone into the night, the shutter of the open window left creaking in the wind. Timmen tore a length of cloth from the bedding and held it to his chin to stem the flow of blood. The thief gathered his tools, gave a last spiteful glance out the window, and then left the room.

"What the hell happened to ya, boy?" Cane Shanney was wiping his hands on a greasy towel as he walked toward the halfling. Timmen had to fight him off like he was swatting flies to keep the big man from using the same greasy towel on his bloody chin. He offered only a sour look as he pushed past the bartender to get at the wash basin where he dipped a rag and held it to his chin. Dripping bloody, soapy water, he trudged to the keg and stood directly below the spigot, which was three and a half feet from the ground and just the right height for the halfling. Timmen tilted his head back and opened the keg, drinking at least a pint of the strong brew before closing the spigot and wiping down his entire face with his rag. He walked to where Shanney stood watching and climbed onto a shelf under the bar.

"Them sailors didn't come back, did they?" Shanney asked in his thick brogue. Timmen offered no response. The big man started wiping down the bar with his dirty towel as he continued. "I didn't think so. Dorak came back inside only a few minutes after they left. Sure'n that dwarf cleaned the lane with 'em."

"They got off easy," Timmen mumbled.

"Eh? What's that? Easy, you say? Never heard it called easy to be diced by Dorak Shale."

"They got off easy," Timmen repeated. Cane Shanney stopped his work and stepped back to regard the little thief curiously. It was a long moment before Timmen looked at him. "They had Zakarus Rinn on their trail."

"Hey? Rinn? Bugger me!" Shanney squatted to face the halfling perched under the bar. "Was it the assassin that touched up your chin?"

"It was him alright," Timmen replied. The words were so bitter in his mouth that they made his stomach turn. "And I won't forget the slight, or forgive the scar he's left me." Timmen looked at the bloody rag with disgust and threw it past his friend into a wastebasket.

"Now Tim, don't go getting bullheaded," Shanney warned. "You're gonna get yourself in a world o' hurt. They don't call Rinn the Shadow Wolf for nothin'."

"He's a shadow when he's sneaking up on people," Timmen replied, "but when he's not prowling around he's just a man."

"And you expect to catch him with his guard down?" the bartender asked incredulously. Timmen offered no reply but looked straight ahead into the shelf, his gaze seemingly on the verge of boring a hole through the wood. Shanney had a sinking feeling in his gut. He knew the answer before he even asked the question, "What are ya planning on doing, Timmy?"

The halfling locked the big man with an ice-cold stare, "I'm going to break into Tavora Manor and take back what is mine."

The manor of the Countess of Westbury had fortifications nearly as strong as Citadel Adbar itself. The mansion was ancient, one of the oldest structures in all of Pilas Antum. Even the architecture was imposing, with sharp angles of jutting stone that cast odd shadows in the moonlight and tall, narrow windows that promised of hidden archers and ever-vigilant watchfulness. Built upon a tall outcropping of rock on the very edge of the Andaluric Sea, the monolithic building commanded a prominent view of the sea-lanes to and from the city. The cliff-face was sheer, dropping five hundred feet to the rocks below and the ceaseless, eternal seething of the tide. Access to Tavora Manor from the cliff was impossible.

The manor's walls were tall and thick, starting at the edge of the cliff on the northern side and curling around the structure to meet the southern precipice. Atop the walls were sentries dressed in the dark blue raiment of the Royal Guard, the Countess's heritage adding an official veneer to her fortified stronghold. Her true power, however, did not come from status or nobility, but rather from her control over Pilas Antum's seedy underworld. The brutal manner with which she maintained that control was well known and so whatever enemies the Countess acquired did not fear the sentries patrolling the manor walls. Instead, they feared the unseen watchers who would not sound an alarm and haul a trespasser to court and stockade. Those who guarded the Countess from shadows unseen promised torturous death to anyone caught inside the manor grounds without permission.

Timmen knew he had his work cut out for him. He had never attempted anything even remotely as dangerous as breaking into Tavora Manor. After he left the grumbling Cane Shanney and retired to his room, he spent the remainder of the night deep in thought. He came to the conclusion that he could not simply break into the fortified mansion. He had to come up with a plan to sneak in by more subtle means.

He fingered the new scab on his chin and thought of the Shadow Wolf. Tribute, indeed! Thirty Omani was no pittance, and the thought of doing business with that fat Madame Olivier was not an appealing one. Timmen put his hands behind his head and gazed up into the darkness. The manor's guard would be doubled in the coming weeks as the Countess hosted the Council of the Eastern

Province. Timmen gave a start and sat up straight. An idea began to form in his mind. A thin smile appeared on the halfling's face as he leaned over and blew out the room's only candle. Finally he knew what had to be done. At last he could sleep.

Timmen sat uncomfortably in the dark anteroom of Lady Curry's second-story apartment, which was nothing more than a converted loft above a butcher's shack down on the docks. The stench was overwhelming, and not all of it was coming from the fish.

"The Lady will be with you shortly," said the skinny and very ugly young girl whom Lady Curry had taken as an apprentice. The girl bowed and disappeared through a curtain of hanging beads. Timmen made a face. *What is that stink? Smells like a free-range kobold smeared itself with excrement and then crawled in the corner and died.* The halfling looked around the loft and snorted with disgust. *'Lady' Curry, that sure is a gentle euphemism. She's as much a Lady as I am a knighted paladin. And that kid sure is ugly. Good thing she caught on with Curry because she'd starve if she had to make a living off her look, even down here on the docks.* Timmen chuckled at the thought, but his smile was quickly replaced by a sour grimace as he took his next breath. The smell from the other room was getting worse, if that was possible.

"The Lady will see you now."

Timmen looked up to see the girl smiling self-consciously and holding the bead curtain open for him. She looked away as he passed and Timmen felt a pang of remorse for making fun of her. The girl disappeared behind him and he made his way into the darkened room. Lady Curry was sitting in a large, billowing piece of furniture that could loosely be called a chair. There was a small round table in front of her and a large bearskin rug in front of that. Timmen approached, but stopped short of stepping onto the rug.

"What do you desire of me, little one?" the woman rasped in a voice that sounded like pebbles scraped across cobblestones. It may have been his imagination, but Timmen thought the air became even more pungent when the woman spoke.

"I desire a potion, my Lady," Timmen answered through a tightened throat. He was trying desperately to breathe only through his mouth. The woman inhaled deeply and seemed on the verge of speaking again when she erupted into a fit of coughing that brought spittle bubbling to her lips. After several long moments, the fit passed and the woman's voice was much clearer and somewhat melodious when again she spoke.

"This is a large city; there are many places to find such things. What brings you to bother an old woman with such matters?"

"Two things bring me to you, my Lady," the thief answered. "First, the potion I desire cannot be found within street-front shops or trade caravans. It is rare and potent, and great skill is required in its creation." Timmen paused to measure the effect his compliment had on her. She smiled faintly.

"And your second reason?" she prompted.

"Secrecy, my Lady. Merchants ask questions. What is more my concern, they tend to answer them as well. My endeavors are my own, and rumors are bound to circulate in my wake. I desire to employ one who has acquired the wisdom of humility."

The old woman threw her head back and laughed heartily. Timmen waited patiently until her cackle ebbed and she asked, "What have you got planned, little thief? What makes you seek the aid of an old woman on death's door?" When Timmen refused to answer the question, the woman tried another. "What potion do you desire?"

Though he knew they were alone, Timmen couldn't stop himself from looking around the room before he whispered, "I desire Carambine's Potion of Occupancy, my Lady."

The old woman's smile was replaced by a look of utter shock. Indeed it appeared as though she had been slapped across the face. "You know not what you ask!" she suddenly blurted and again the spittle flew from her lips. "That potion has been outlawed, and for good reason. Occupancy of another person's body poses great danger. What could a little thief such as yourself hope to accomplish . . ."

"The Countess," Timmen broke in. He was playing his last card and he knew it was a winner.

The old woman went silent and sat up straight. She pulled her old, matted gray hair back from her face and locked the halfling with the eyes of a huntress. "What did you say?" she asked.

"You heard me," Timmen replied quietly yet firmly, his eyes refusing to cower from her gaze.

The old woman studied him for a long moment and then she closed her eyes and sat back into her cushions. She tried to take a deep breath, but another fit of racking coughs seized her and her body trembled. When the fit passed, she seemed thoroughly exhausted. She waved her hand in dismissal and with a wheezing voice she said, "You shall have it in the eve of the morrow. Bring one hundred Omani as payment. Now, leave me."

Timmen turned and left the room on wobbly legs. He pushed brusquely through the bead curtain and passed quickly through the outer room, refusing to look at the young girl as she leaped up from her seat. Once out in the cool night air, Timmen quickly descended the steps from the loft down to the street. He walked hurriedly down the block and around a corner, then sat down on a bench and put his head in his hands. He fingered his chin and listened to the sounds of the ships gently rocking in the marina, the riggings clanging softly against the masts. *There's no turning back now*, he thought. *There's no turning back now.*

Chapter Three

~ A Court with No King ~

Dunk Worley walked as fast as he dared over the uneven stone flooring of the remote and little-used passage in Tavora Manor. The cup of tea he was bringing to his master, Lord Thrain Wyndam, had spilled half of its contents onto his hand, burning him and making him stifle expletives under his breath. The day was still an hour from dawning and Dunk shivered against the cold. He heard a cow bawling in the distance and wondered aloud, "Why in the name of all the Saints must we hole up in this dingy and stinky wing of the Manor?" He plodded on for a few more steps and then answered his own question with the words that had been hammered into him since he was a lad, "Master Thrain is a wise man, Dunk. Don't be substitutin' your own judgment for his."

Dunk crept down a last long hallway. The corridor had one torch burning halfway down the outward wall and tall, narrow portals on either side of it. He glanced out the first portal as he passed and saw the third-quarter moon hanging in a clear, cold sky. Dunk muttered another expletive at the cold draft that swept through the portal. The torch flickered and faltered in the wind. As Dunk passed underneath it, he could not see beyond its small circle of illumination into the dark passageway beyond. Before his eyes could re-adjust to the dark, a chambermaid came upon him heading in the opposite direction. She gave a small, high squeal of surprise and Dunk spilled the remainder of his master's tea down the front of his shirt.

"Stinkin' pig tits!" Dunk yelled in pain. He immediately covered his mouth and his eyes went wide in embarrassment. The flustered porter cleared his throat, "Er, excuse me, miss," he said and blushed furiously. The girl giggled as she continued on her way. Dunk wiped off his tunic and pants and stumped down the corridor, shaking his head and muttering under his breath. He did not notice the shadow that followed him down the passageway toward his master's bedchamber.

"My lord?"

"Enter, Dunk." Lord Wyndam's strong baritone voice set the porter's knees to shaking. He dreaded failing his master, not for fear of reprisal, but for fear of disappointing the man whom he had come to love almost as much as his dear departed Dad. Dunk entered the chamber and closed and locked the door behind him. Rounding the corner to the small side-room that served as an office, Dunk found Lord Wyndam already awake and at work at the desk.

Dunk stood forlornly behind his master, toeing the ground and hanging his head. Lord Wyndam noted the silence and stopped writing, raising his head to address the young man behind him, "What is it, lad?" he asked.

"I'm afraid I've lost your tea, my Lord," Dunk said ashamedly.

"Lost it? Do you mean you have misplaced it? Or has it escaped you?" Lord Wyndam turned to face his porter. "Perhaps we should assemble a search party."

Dunk blushed and smiled. He knew that his master was making light of the situation to dismiss his failure, to show him that it was a small thing and that he should not feel bad. He looked into his lord's warm eyes and loved him truly. "I could get you some more, my Lord," he said.

"That will not be necessary," Lord Wyndam replied as he turned back to his work. "I am almost finished here." The old nobleman folded a letter, dabbed it with wax and sealed it with a signet hung about his neck. "Take this outside of the manor and into the city to find a courier. It is to be taken directly to my son." He gave a great sigh as though a burden had been lifted from his shoulders. "Now, I believe I would like a ride before breakfast. Kindly go to the stables and ready Ashton before taking my letter."

"Yes, my Lord," Dunk replied. He accepted the letter from Lord Wyndam's hand and then turned and left the chamber. As he hurried down the corridor he shook his head and wondered aloud, "I thought I had locked that door on the way in." He walked past the portals and shivered again, "I don't know where your head is this morn, Dunk Worley," he said. He shook his head and muttered to himself all the way down to the stables.

"Tell me of Lord Thrain Wyndam," the Countess of Westbury spoke the man's name with contempt.

Zakarus Rinn reclined comfortably in a chair set before the Countess's large oak desk. "He is an impressive man, to be sure," the Shadow Wolf replied. "Though I fail to see why you sent *me* to look in on him. It seems a rather menial task for one of my abilities. I am hardly a common spy."

"Must I forever stroke your ego, Zakarus?" the Countess sighed.

"Stroke what you will, Madame," Rinn replied with a slight bow. The Countess smiled faintly but did not respond. She looked at the assassin through narrowed eyes and the smile faded from her porcelain face. Rinn saw that their banter was over and returned to business. "Lord Wyndam has brought no security or guards with him. To do so, of course, would have been a public affront to your Highness. His insistence on quartering in the remote wing of the manor, however, puzzles me. It would seem that staying in a more heavily-populated part of the building would afford more safety to a man whose aspirations for the throne are not in accordance with your wishes."

"That man will find no safety within Tavora Manor or the whole of Pilas Antum," the Countess sneered. "Lord Wyndam is an astute man and he knows this to be true. He is staying in the servants' quarter to insult me, so it does not appear that he is staying here as my guest."

"He has brought only one servant, his porter," Rinn continued, "Though more may accompany young Master Wyndam when he arrives."

"Ah yes, Master Alishane Wyndam," the Countess's face brightened and she tapped a delicate finger upon the arm of her chair. "I am eagerly awaiting the arrival of such a promising young man. I understand that he has just completed his third year at Rue Mortelei."

"He has indeed, Highness. Two more years at the school and he will graduate as one of the finest clerics in the land, from what I hear."

After a long moment of contemplation, during which Rinn noted a sparkle in the old woman's eye, the Countess broke her train of thought and looked back to the assassin. "Mark the movements of Lord Wyndam. The time may soon come when I make use of your considerable talents. Now, leave me. I must make ready for the Council."

The Council of the Eastern Province was a meeting of the higher nobility in the eastern quarter of Coleraine. Its purpose was to find agreement among the region's nobility as to who would represent the Eastern Province at the Council of the Kingdom, where the next king would be crowned. In days past, this was accomplished by a tournament of jousting, sparring, archery and various other feats of knighthood, the tournament taking the place of open conflict and warfare. Though the Council was still accompanied by the Tournament of Knighthood, the balance of power was determined in the meetings of the Council, which were dominated by underhanded politics and treachery. In these endeavors, none surpassed the Countess of Westbury. Thus, most people believed that the Council would have two primary contestants: the Countess, with her marionette Lord Fence Winningham pinned firmly under her thumb and ready to do her bidding should he attain the throne, and Lord Thrain Wyndam, whose noble blood traced back beyond memory and was rumored to include direct descent from ancient royalty. Before the Council had even commenced, however, the Countess had put her machinations into motion. Lord Thrain Wyndam would not live out the week.

Timmen O'Hook sat under the great canopy of Cane Shanney's mead tent on the common grounds outside of Tavora Manor, where Shanney had moved his operation away from the Wyvern's Tail for the duration of the coming festivities. Though the Council of the Eastern Province had not yet officially commenced, the Tournament of Knighthood was set to begin on the following morning and the drinking and merrymaking had been in full swing for several days now. Timmen was finding it increasingly difficult to keep his hands busy and out of the pockets of the people thronging about the grounds.

Shanney had finally given up trying to talk Timmen out of his plans to break into Tavora Manor; he had known enough halflings in his time to know that it was senseless to pursue an argument once one had made up his mind. Now, Shanney stood behind his bar under the large tent and watched Timmen with great concern; the halfling had coins dancing back and forth across his nimble fingers and was clearly anxious. Though the bartender had no inkling as to the thief's plans, he feared that the time was nearing when Timmen would put those plans into motion. And he feared that his days of enjoying the halfling's company were drawing to an end.

As the brooding Cane Shanney turned to serve a pair of drunken and slobbering patrons, Timmen's restlessness finally got the better of him. He abruptly got to his feet and walked from the shade of the tent out into the hot midday sun. He kept looking around at the people who were talking and eating without proper regard for their coin purses and belongings. He found himself scouting out the Royal Guardsmen, who were lazing at their posts completely disinterested in anything except conversations about the coming tournament. *It would be SO easy,* Timmen thought as he watched a particularly fat noble woman devour a roasted turkey leg while her purse, like her skin, dangled loosely from her arm.

Timmen forced himself to turn and walk away with the reminder that he couldn't afford any trouble whatsoever if he were to pull off his plans. He decided to busy himself by looking for Lady Curry and her ugly little assistant.

Lady Curry had given him quite a shock when he showed up at her loft to pick up the Carambine's Potion of Occupancy he had commissioned her to create for him. After he dropped his payment onto her desk the old woman produced two vials, smiling wickedly as she explained that one was for him but the other was for herself.

"I am sure that you've heard tales of my hatred toward the Countess, else you would not have told me that your plans involve her," she had said before erupting into a fit of coughing. "The tales are only half the story. There are other, very personal reasons for me to seek revenge upon that woman. My illness leaves me with little to lose and your plans, whatever they be, provide me with an opportunity."

"But, but…" Timmen had stuttered in his shock.

"I'll not ask you any details of your plans, nor will I answer any inquiries into my own. Good day, little halfling, and may the fates smile upon us both." He had been ushered hastily out of her loft and down into the street, where he sat in stunned silence before wandering away.

Now Timmen found himself scouring the crowd and trying to spot the old hag. Not that he planned on asking her any questions, he knew that to be a fruitless endeavor. But he would love to follow her around for awhile and glean what he could about her intentions. If she acted before he did, then getting into Tavora Manor would be twice as difficult, and it was nearly impossible already.

These thoughts were driven from Timmen's mind in the next moment by a blaring of horns down the lane. The crowd began to frantically push each other to get out of the way as a host of heavy cavalry lumbered into view. Timmen was caught in the moving throng of people, which is not a good place for a halfling to be. Timmen O'Hook, however, is spry even by halfling standards and he quickly darted in and out of the legs, swinging bags and walking sticks of the people jostling around him. Just as the thundering hooves bore down upon him, Timmen glanced back momentarily and ran face-first into the soft, fat rump of a very round man. With a muffled *oomph,* the air was driven from his lungs and he was flung down into the dust.

Timmen rolled himself into a tiny ball and waited to recover his breath while expecting to be trampled to death at any moment. What happened next, however, came as a complete shock. Timmen felt himself being lifted from the ground and carried away from the horses and the crowd of people. His eyes were watering from the blow that knocked the wind from him and the tears were mixing with the dust to form a sticky goo around his eyes, but as Timmen looked up at the woman who had rescued him, both his eyes and his mouth opened wide in astonishment. The woman wore the dark blue chain mail and helm of a soldier of the Royal Guard. Her face was unmistakably beautiful, but what caught Timmen's attention was her right ear. Her helm had shifted in the tussle to expose several tresses of whitish blonde hair and a pointed *elven* ear. The woman noted his astonishment and the direction of his gaze and abruptly dropped him onto his feet. Before the startled halfling could recover his breath or utter a single word, the elf-woman straightened her helm and disappeared into the crowd. Just then, Timmen's lungs responded to his mind's urging and he took a great inhale of breath. He stood there for several moments gasping and looking after where the woman had disappeared. When his daze finally ebbed, he began looking around him to collect his wits.

"That damn Lord Winningham!" roared a man at Timmen's left. "He'd 'a trampled ever' last one of us an' not blinked an eye." Several grumbles of agreement echoed through the crowd, but no sustained complaints against Lord Winningham would be voiced this close to Tavora Manor. The crowd began to move along again with mutterings of mead and ale. Timmen looked up the lane at the retreating host of Lord Winningham's mounted escort. He began entertaining thoughts of ale himself when a flicker of movement caught his eye. He looked up at the rooftops skirting the lane just in time to see a dark figure flanking Lord Winningham's entourage. Timmen knew the man and would never forget him. He had found the Shadow Wolf.

Dunk Worley raised his mug and took several large gulps, spilling as much mead down the front of his shirt as he managed to swallow. Dunk had been in Cane Shanney's makeshift tavern since early afternoon. Now, an hour or so after the sun had set, he was finally approaching his limit of Shanney's Marauding Maven Mead. Dunk enjoyed celebrating whenever given a reason and leave from his lord's service. Tonight he had leave and an excellent reason to celebrate: young Master Alishane Wyndam had arrived to join his father at the Council of the Eastern Province.

Master Wyndam was in a dour mood when he arrived but Dunk assumed that was merely because of the long road he had traveled from Rue Mortelei. Dunk wasn't the sharpest arrow in the quiver and he had ultimate confidence in his lord, else he might have thought that the contents of the letter he sent early that morning was the cause of young Alishane's bad mood. All the porter knew for sure was that father and son Wyndam had been in council in Lord Wyndam's quarters since shortly after Alishane's arrival and that he had been given leave to go down to the manor grounds and enjoy the festival. Dunk had no way of knowing as he ordered another mug of mead that both his confidence in and his loyalty to his lord were about to be tested as they had never been tested before.

"Still, Son, I would rather you had heeded my warnings and gone back to the school to finish your education," Lord Wyndam was voicing this opinion for the tenth time since their conversation had begun.

"Father, how can I return to Rue Mortelei knowing that your life is in danger here in Pilas Antum?" Alishane responded.

"It is nothing I cannot handle, Al. The Countess would not dare make an overt move against me during this pivotal time. We are all under intense scrutiny. I do not fear for my life. Not yet, anyway. What I fear is a move to undermine my standing and reputation. The Council will meet for perhaps five days, starting tomorrow. I believe the Countess is waiting to measure the mood and inclinations of the Council before deciding how best to assail me. There is no doubt in my mind, however, that she will act in some manner to prevent my ascension to the throne. Whatever happens, you must not be involved. I will not allow this business to mar your reputation or damage your chances of becoming an ordained cleric."

"If I were to abandon you in your time of need, Father, I would be contradicting everything I have learned at Rue Mortelei."

"And have they taught you how to be a stubborn ass, as well?" Lord Wyndam's voice boomed in his exasperation.

"No, Father, I believe I learned that from you." Alishane answered, smiling. "And quite an excellent instructor you have turned out to be."

"And you are an excellent student," Thrain Wyndam replied as he draped an arm across his son's shoulders. "I am merely trying to protect your future and all for which you have labored to attain."

"I know that, Father, but at some point you must stop trying to protect me."

"Only when I lay in the cold, hard ground, Alishane. I swore that at your birth and I will hold to that always. Now, since you cannot be swayed, let us sit and plan our course of action. The Countess is shrewd and we must work together at the Council tomorrow."

As the elder and younger Wyndam sat by the fire and continued their conversation, the Shadow Wolf watched through the window while clinging to the side of the outer wall. *'Cold, hard ground,' Wyndam?* he thought and his lips curled in a wicked smile. *The Earth is waiting for you. And you shall be joined with her sooner than you think.*

Timmen sat beneath the makeshift bar under Cane Shanney's mead tent. Not that he was in the mood for company or merrymaking, he was sleeping under the bar while the Tail was deserted and he had to wait for the patrons to leave before he could try to find some sleep. Unfortunately, he knew that sleep would not come easily this night.

Timmen had followed Zakarus Rinn from rooftop to rooftop along the lane as the Shadow Wolf mirrored Lord Winningham's mounted procession. They had finally come to a halt atop a building overlooking the manor gate. Timmen sat watching Rinn, who was himself watching Winningham's cavalry entering the manor proper. When the last of the horses had passed through the gate and it had shut with a loud *clang,* the Shadow Wolf had slipped over the edge of the roof and disappeared from sight. Timmen crept to where Rinn had been and cautiously peered over the edge. The assassin was nowhere to be found. It was a three-story drop to the street below, but the Wolf was not clinging to the wall or creeping along a ledge. He could not be seen walking along the street. Timmen crawled back from the ledge and sat for a few moments. He was stunned and more than a little impressed. The thought crossed his mind, not for the first time and not for the last, that maybe he was biting off more than he could chew.

Timmen had wandered the grounds of the manor common for an hour or more before returning to Shanney's tent. He knew the time was approaching when he would have to act, but he didn't know if he had the resolve to do it. The fear that boiled up when he considered his plan bothered him greatly. He didn't like to think of himself as lacking in fortitude. In the end, his stubbornness won out. He wanted to recover the dagger that he felt was rightfully his, and he wanted to repay the Shadow Wolf for the scar he would bear for the rest of his days. He was sure he could accomplish both once he made his way into the Manor.

It was with renewed resolve that Timmen emerged from under the bar to scope out the crowd and try to discern how much longer he had to wait before some quiet and sleep. He sat on an empty keg in the corner and leaned back against one of the tent poles, scanning the crowd. He was looking quickly from one face to the next, with very little concern and more than a little resentment. He had passed by one face and gone on to three others when his brain registered that the girl had been looking right at him. He quickly looked back to the girl, who was still looking at him. She smiled and winked. Then he recognized her. It was Lady Curry's assistant.

"Oy!" Timmen cried and he leaped up from the keg. The girl quickly turned and began dancing through the crowd, heading for the edge of the tent and the darkness beyond. Timmen lost sight of her quickly as he entered the forest of people towering over him.

He made for the spot where she had been and began looking frantically around. After a few moments, he saw her through a gap in the swaying crowd. She was looking back at him, still smiling, and then she turned and headed away from him again.

Timmen tore after her, darting around, under and between the legs of the people in the crowd. When he reached the spot where he had last seen her, again he found that she had disappeared. Growing frustrated and angry, Timmen looked around and spotted her once more, looking back at him and smiling wider than ever. Scowling darkly, Timmen started after her, but when she turned and took off again, Timmen changed tactics. He found a tall man standing near him and climbed nimbly up the man's back, looking quickly over the heads of the people in the crowd until he saw the girl and marked the direction in which she was heading. Before the drunken man whom he had climbed could reach around and grab him, the halfling dropped to the ground and swiftly cut widely to the left of where the girl had last been. He moved quickly through the crowd but slowed as he neared the spot where he expected her to be. Weaving between people and peeking around legs, he spotted her. She was giggling and looking back at where she had just been, expecting him to appear there.

Timmen came up behind her and said, "Game over" as he swatted her firmly on the rump.

The girl squealed and jumped a foot in the air as she turned to face him. She laughed boisterously and then she said, "Forgive me, master halfling. 'Twas just a bit of fun." Timmen's face remained stony. The girl gave one more giggle and then, with a sigh of disappointment, she said, "All right. Let us leave these drunks and speak in private." She turned and made her way through the people and out from under the tent into the darkness. Timmen tailed her very closely the entire way. When they reached the security of darkness and seclusion, the girl sat on a low stone wall and motioned for Timmen to have a seat beside her. The girl sat looking at him brightly. The smile had returned to her face.

"Well?" Timmen asked.

"Well what?" the girl responded.

"Why did you find me?" Timmen growled.

"Because you were not having much success in finding me," the girl answered. "And I thought it best that we have a word."

"I would much rather speak with Lady Curry. Kindly take me to her."

"Oh, I should think you'd have had your fill of pointless chases tonight," the girl said and giggled again.

Timmen was becoming aggravated. "What do you mean?" he asked more loudly than he intended.

"What I mean is," the girl said with an air of superiority that made Timmen's face flush red, "that it is quite pointless to search for something that you have already found." Timmen looked at her quizzically. She gave another giggle and then a muffled, exaggerated series of coughs. She sat there beaming and winked.

Timmen's eyes widened as he understood. "You!" he said in a hoarse whisper.

"Me," Lady Curry confirmed.

"Why are you . . ." Timmen began to ask.

"Because this body provides greater freedom of movement than my own," the girl said, "and, quite frankly, because the child is unattractive enough to pass through crowds without drawing a second look. I, like yourself, prefer not to be noticed."

"But how are you able to occupy her body for so long a period of time?"

"Kami, that is her name by the way, is a psionist. She can read people's thoughts and even control the actions of some small animals," answered the girl. "She is combining her power with mine to extend the effects of the potion. I will be here as long as I need to be, unless a counter-spell is performed, of course."

Timmen's mind flashed back to his derogatory thoughts about the girl and the look she had given him afterward. A moment of embarrassed regret swept through him, but he stifled it and returned to business. "Why do you desire to speak with me?" he asked.

"It is best that we coordinate our efforts," she answered. "Though we act with separate purpose and will likely split up once inside the manor, acting in concert greatly increases our chances for success. Have you not thought the same?"

"I have," Timmen answered.

"And I trust that we can work together while respecting the secrecy of our individual plans once inside the manor walls?"

"Of course."

"Excellent," the girl replied. After a long pause, she continued, "I believe it to be imprudent to wait much longer."

"I'm prepared to go in tomorrow night, if that suits you," the thief replied.

"It does," the girl answered.

"An hour after sundown," Timmen said. "Where will I find you?"

"I will await you at the end of Mr. Shanney's bar," the girl answered with a glint in her eye. "Remember, once you have taken the potion you have less than a minute to enter your target's body."

"I'll remember," Timmen answered.

The girl looked away into the darkness and her voice trembled as she spoke. "All these long years I have waited for my revenge."

"Tomorrow night," Timmen said as he got up and left. "We go in tomorrow night."

Chapter Four

~ Of War and Warfare ~

Dunk Worley sat behind Lord and Master Wyndam on the raised platform overlooking the sparring pit, which stood to one side of the common grounds where the Tournament of Knighthood was taking place. The Tournament had just commenced with an opening ceremony consisting of a proclamation of sportsmanship, a lengthy reading of the names of the contestants, and a brief comic skit put on by an acting troupe from the Canterbury Theatre in Pilas Antum. Now the crowd was sitting with bated breath, awaiting the entrance of the first two contestants into the pit.

Dunk felt privileged to be sitting with his lord on the platform; these seats were few and thus very expensive. Looking about him, Dunk saw nothing but nobility. None of the other lords or ladies had paid for one of their servants to accompany them onto the raised platform. Lord Wyndam had said nothing of it; he merely handed Dunk his platform pass as though it was expected that a lord should buy his porter an exalted seat to a once-in-a-lifetime event.

Dunk suddenly felt very embarrassed. He looked around him expecting to find everyone looking at him, but most were looking instead at Lord Wyndam. They glanced at him repeatedly and would whisper to each other while doing so. A wave of anger and suspicion swelled in the servant. How dare these people whisper rumors about his lord! How dare they show him such disrespect! He looked back to Lord Wyndam to see if he had noticed the staring faces and hushed voices carrying his name on the breeze. The old man seemed perfectly at ease. He sat scanning the grounds in front of him, occasionally tilting his head to the side to make a casual remark to his son. Dunk felt his muscles relax. If his beloved and trusted lord was not concerned, then certainly Dunk Worley need not be.

Dunk looked back to the pit just as a blaring of horns and raucous cheers from the crowd announced the arrival of the first combatants. Each man walked toward the center of the pit from opposite sides, trailed by attendants and streaming banners with the symbols and colors of the noble families they represented.

The knights could select their own armor and swords to compliment their fighting style. One of the men was very large; he was wearing full plate-mail armor with gold trimming that shone brightly in the sunlight. The big man was carrying a huge two-handed broadsword that was longer than most men are tall. The smaller man walked with a light, quick step that told of great agility. He wore dark red chain-mail armor that hung down to his knees and was girt about his waist by an emerald green belt. Bronze bucklers were strapped to both forearms. In his right hand he carried a thin and graceful sword, in his left a dagger. It was clear even to those who were unknowledgeable in the ways of combat that these two men would employ very different fighting styles. The crowd began to murmur with excitement.

The combatants met in the middle of the pit and their attendants spread out behind them. A hush fell over the crowd. The tournament crier took a few steps out into the pit and his high, shrill voice rose out of the dust.

"The Tournament of Knighthood is thus commenced. These men, being of high valor and honor, shall fight in the name of their lord to bring glory unto their houses." The crier paused as a cheer erupted from the crowd. When it died down, he continued. "Hailing from the county of Devonshire, fighting under the banner of Lord Addenbrook, the Tournament officials recognize Sir Connor Sonnegut." The smaller man turned to the gallery, raised his sword vertical before his face, and swept it quickly back down to his side in a traditional salute. Again the crowd cheered, then the crier continued. "Hailing from the Argon Vale, fighting under the banner of Lord Chelleman, the Tournament officials recognize Gor Barahd." The large man turned to the gallery and swung his huge sword over his head, giving a great roar that brought loud cheers from the onlookers. "The combatants shall fight under the rules of tournament sparring until incapacitation or surrender," the crier said and then paused. During that brief silence, the tension in the arena built to fever pitch. Then, to a great explosion of cheers, the crier finally shouted, "Let the fighting begin!"

The two combatants turned and walked back to their attendants, who began busily checking their knight's armor and weapons one last time. A horn blared and the attendants scurried from the pit. The knights turned to face each other. The horn sounded a second time and the two men advanced. Sir Sonnegut, being the smaller of the two, stopped first and allowed the bigger man to close the final distance between them. Barahd came in with a sudden charge, his two-handed sword extended in a straight thrust. Sonnegut parried with both sword and knife while stepping quickly to the side. Barahd went with the momentum of Sonnegut's parry, continuing his sword off to the side then spinning quickly about and bringing the weapon back around in a mighty horizontal swing aimed at the smaller man's midsection. Sir Sonnegut, however, had quickly retreated, having decided to weather the larger man's early offensive maneuvers and wait for him to tire from wielding his heavy sword and moving around in the thick, plate-mail armor.

Staying well outside the range of Barahd's large sword, Sir Sonnegut danced nimbly from side to side, trying to entice the big man into chasing him around the pit. "Come, my brutish friend," Sonnegut taunted, "the bull is only dangerous when it charges." Gor Barahd took his two-handed sword in both hands and began weaving it before him in startlingly quick figure-eight motions. His huge, powerful wrists rotated to bring the blade up diagonally, then down, and then up diagonally in the opposite direction. The blade became a twinkling blur before him as Barahd advanced steadily on the smaller knight. The crowd gave a collective "ooohhhh" of appreciation at the big man's display of strength and swordsmanship. Sir Sonnegut retreated, unable to interpret the maneuver to see how the next strike would be launched.

Sonnegut skittered straight back, but soon ran out of room for his retreat. He feigned a motion to one side and when Barahd angled in that direction to intercept him, Sonnegut skipped quickly in the other direction and circled back out into the open center of the pit. There was an audible exhalation of breath as the crowd resumed breathing. Barahd stopped whirling his blade in front of him and instead held it straight out as he turned and resumed his offensive.

Sir Sonnegut continued a slow retreat, then suddenly advanced and gave two quick taps with his sword to Barahd's blade, forcing it out wide to Sonnegut's left. Barahd countered by bringing his blade back in to a defensive position, but that was exactly what the smaller man had hoped he would do. Sonnegut continued his attack by ducking down and to the left, advancing in under Barahd's weapon and raising his own sword in his right hand to pin his adversary's blade while his left hand flashed forward with the dagger. Sonnegut's aim was true and the dagger found a crease between the plates of the larger man's armor. The blade of the dagger sliced easily through the leather jerkin worn under the plate armor and glanced off of a rib bone before slicing across, opening a six inch gash in Barahd's side.

The big man howled in anger and pain. He dropped his left hand off of his sword and punched the smaller knight as Sonnegut danced away, but the exchange had not been equal. Sonnegut resisted the urge to press his advantage. He knew the big man was bleeding now and that would make him tire all the quicker. Gor Barahd also knew that his energy was slowly draining from him and that time was now in the smaller man's favor. Barahd needed to open a new offensive quickly before his size and strength turned from an advantage to a hindrance.

The crowd could now see the blood seeping through the armor at the big man's side as he resumed his dazzling figure-eight swordplay. Again Sonnegut retreated. Barahd waited until the smaller man glanced behind him to see how much space he had left in his retreat, then the big man set his feet and leaped forward quickly. Sonnegut turned back around to find himself suddenly within range of his opponent's large, two-handed sword. Barahd's blade was slashing upward from right to left as he advanced; he rotated his wrists and brought his sword all the way down to his right, pinning Sonnegut's blades down and creating an opening in the smaller man's defenses. Barahd kicked out with his left foot, his huge boot connecting with Sonnegut's right shoulder and sending the smaller man sprawling back into the dirt.

Barahd lumbered after the prostrate Sonnegut. He lifted his huge sword over his head and brought it crashing down at the smaller man. Sonnegut rolled to the side, narrowly avoiding the blade as it crashed into the dirt sending dust into the air and bringing a gasp from the crowd. Again the big man slashed his sword down in a mighty chop, and again the smaller knight rolled to the side just in time to avoid a crushing blow.

"Somebody help him!" screamed a woman in the audience, but help would not come. Barahd chopped again, purposefully going wide this time to force Sonnegut to roll to one side. Barahd was already moving as Sonnegut rolled right to him to avoid the falling sword. He kicked the smaller knight brutally in the head, then raised his weapon high in the air and hesitated a split second to make sure his aim was true. After taking measure of his target, Gor Barahd brought his heavy sword crashing down into the ribs of Sir Connor Sonnegut. The knight's chain-mail armor prevented the blade from cutting him in two, but the sheer force of the strike shattered his ribs and rendered him completely incapacitated. Barahd hovered over him for a moment to ensure that he would not rise, then turned and staggered out of the pit.

The crowd was stunned into silence. Many of the women were silently weeping. Sir Sonnegut's attendants rushed to his side, where the stricken knight was now quivering and spitting up blood. Lord Wyndam turned to Dunk to find his porter's mouth hanging open in shock and his face pale. "It is a brutal business," Lord Wyndam said, "and not to be undertaken for sport." The old nobleman shook his head sadly as he rose. He dropped a comforting hand upon his porter's shoulder and said, "Come, Dunk. Let us away."

The crowd slowly dispersed, but the grounds remained eerily silent. No one spoke above a whisper. Later that day, a large and exuberant throng of people would witness the first jousting match. The sparring matches, however, drew sparse crowds for the remainder of the Tournament.

The Great Hall in Tavora Manor was large and extravagant. Tall, carved pillars of marble rose to buttress an intricately painted ceiling. Hundreds of candle sconces lined the walls and cast a pleasant glow throughout the room. In the middle of the hall, long tables had been brought in and placed in a large rectangle to seat the nobility in attendance for the Council of the Eastern Province. The Countess of Westbury sat at one end of the rectangle, flanked on her left by one of her advisors and on her right by Lord Fence Winningham.

The Countess had devised to have Lord Wyndam seated at the opposite end of the rectangle from herself, the seating designed to clearly show the adversarial nature of the meeting. Lord Wyndam, however, had politely traded places with Lord Garrett Finneran of Anderton halfway up the length of one side of the rectangle of tables. "The light in this seat will make it easier to read my notes, you see," Wyndam had explained. By the time the seats around the table were filled, the Countess was already scowling.

As the last of the nobility in attendance settled into their seats, the Countess rose to her feet and the room fell into an expectant hush. "Ladies and Lords of the surrounding counties and the outlying reaches of the Eastern Province, good afternoon," she began. "We are gathered here today for the time-honored tradition of the Council, so that we may find agreement and peace and avoid the even more time-honored tradition of violence and bloodshed." Many of the two hundred in attendance chuckled uneasily at the Countess's mirth, but their eyes darted to Lord Wyndam at the reverential manner in which she referred to violence and bloodshed. Lord Wyndam smiled pleasantly, his eyes revealing nothing as he sat watching the Countess. She continued, "I am most pleased that you all could make it. I cannot remember the last time Tavora Manor was this busy. I trust that everyone's accommodations are acceptable?" The Countess let her cold eyes sweep the room. Many cowered from that gaze; even Alishane Wyndam found strength to return it only after looking first to his father. After a pause, during which no one uttered complaint against the accommodations, the

Countess swept up her long, billowing gown and sat down. "Well then," she smiled, "let us begin."

A long and uncomfortable silence ensued. No one seemed eager to be the next to speak. A cough echoed through the hall and a cheer erupted off in the distance from the jousting pit. Eyes were turned uneasily about the hall, and then they all made their way imploringly to the Countess. She sat looking coolly over the assembly, a thin smile curling the corners of her mouth. *Let them know who is in control here,* she thought to herself. *Let them know how much they need me.*

When the Countess felt that she had complete control of the room, she looked briefly at Lord Horacio Smythe. Smythe immediately rose to his feet and declared in a loud, officious voice, "The assembled nobility of the Eastern Province extend our gratitude to our revered and gracious host, Lady Morna de Lorraine, the Countess of Westbury." Smythe ended his statement with a deep bow to the Countess, then he sat down and looked around the room expecting his peers to be applauding their agreement. He received only blank stares and silence. Smythe was flustered and he faltered in his prepared speech. He looked quickly to the Countess, who locked him with a dark stare. "If… if it please her Highness," he stuttered as he continued, "I nominate Lord Fence Winningham as our Royal Ambassador to the Council of the Kingdom."

The Countess looked quickly to Lord Talmus Colb, who jumped to his feet. "Highness, I second the nomination of Lord Winningham," Colb stated before any mutterings among the crowd could commence. "His heritage can be traced from his father, Brant Winningham, to his grandfather Alba Winning…"

"I believe we all know the tale of Lord Winningham's lineage," Lord Finneran cut in, interrupting Talmus Colb and drawing a gasp from the crowd and a murderous glare from the Countess. Undaunted, Finneran continued, "as I'm sure we all know of his family's debt to the Countess."

Fence Winningham jumped to his feet and shouted, "Many parts of the kingdom were hardstruck by the drought, Finneran. Landholding families must do what is necessary to maintain possession of their lands when the peasants entertain thoughts of revolt."

"And we remember how your family maintained possession of the lands," Finneran retorted. "The smoke from the funeral pyres of the dead leave a reek in the sky to this day."

Lord Winningham went very red in the face and his hand was straying toward the hilt of his sword when the Countess held up her hand. Winningham paused and looked at her thin, white finger extended before him. She pointed slightly at his chair and he sat down. "Lord Finneran," the Countess said softly yet with a definite edge to her voice, "your family's holdings in the remote wooded vales of Anderton were largely untouched by the drought. Others were not so fortunate. Perhaps you should reserve judgment on matters you do not fully understand."

"What I understand, your Highness," Finneran replied evenly, "is that the men who purged Winningham's lands of dissident peasants were wearing the blue armor of the Royal Guard and can now be found skulking among the shadows of Tavora Manor."

"You know nothing of Tavora Manor or any of the inner workings of Pilas Antum!" the Countess said, her voice becoming threatening. "If you did you would be more mindful of your tongue, lest you should lose it." A murmur went through the gathered nobility. Thrain Wyndam smiled faintly. The Countess quickly regained her composure and continued, "It would seem that the great distance between Anderton and Pilas Antum has caused us to lose touch with one another, Lord Finneran. Our differences in geography have given rise to differences of opinion. Perhaps we should increase trade between our lands to ensure future accord."

"I do not desire trade with Pilas Antum, Countess," Finneran answered. "Nor do I desire to be in accordance with your empiric aspirations. It is quite clear that Lord Winningham is your toy in this matter and that he is here only to do your bidding. I do not want the same to be said of this Council. The Eastern Province must send a representative to the Council of the Kingdom who is untainted by association with criminals. For that reason, I nominate Lord Thrain Wyndam for Ambassador of the Eastern Province."

Murmurs of agreement rippled through the great hall. "Here, here!" shouted one noble. "Yes!" shouted another. Garrett Finneran took his seat at the end of the rectangle opposite the Countess. Alishane Wyndam, looking upon the man with wonder and admiration, saw Finneran look briefly to the Countess, then look about the room at the results of his words, and then look back to the Countess and smile. Something in that smile sent ice water tumbling down Alishane's spine. He looked to his father to find the old man studying the Countess intently. He followed his father's gaze and saw the woman sitting perfectly still, her face blank as her eyes darted around the room.

Fence Winningham again leaped to his feet. "Thrain Wyndam is as crooked as ever a man was!" he shouted. The room fell silent and every eye turned to Lord Winningham. Alishane tensed, his hands gripping the arms of his chair. The Countess made no move to stop Winningham's outburst. "He maintains control of his own lands through threat and larceny. His supposed piety and contributions to the church are but a ruse to throw off suspicion."

Again the buzz of murmuring voices rose throughout the room. Most seemed skeptical of Winningham's claims. "What proof have you?" asked Lord Danshing, who was a known supporter of the church.

"I have proof by Lord Wyndam's own hand," answered Winningham. He held aloft a piece of rolled parchment.

"Let me see that," said Lord Danshing, who took the parchment and began to read. The man's face went pale a moment later and he looked up at Lord Wyndam in a mix of shock, disappointment and pain.

Lord Winningham took the parchment back from Danshing and held it forth triumphantly. "It is here!" he cried. "The proof that you request is here. That man," he pointed accusingly at Thrain Wyndam, "is responsible for the death of Prince Umberley!" A gasp went up from the crowd of nobles. Lord and Master Wyndam both sat with mouths open in utter shock. Winningham continued, "This parchment is a letter to Lucius Porveux, whom we know is the Baron of Lower Meade. It was written by Lord Thrain Wyndam and it clearly shows complicity in the murder of the Prince in exchange for large tracts of land from the Wyndam estate." The crowd began to murmur excitedly. Dark eyes were turned upon father and son Wyndam.

"Why?" asked Lord Danshing in a shaky voice. "Why would Porveux risk an attack on the royal family simply to gain more lands?"

"That is a question only Lucius Porveux can answer," Winningham said, looking through narrowed eyes at Lord Wyndam. "I'm certain he was promised more than land once our new king is seated." He turned back to address the room at large, "Regardless, the proof of Thrain Wyndam's guilt is before you." He again held up the letter. "It is signed in the Lord's own hand," Winningham shouted above a rising clamor, "and was sealed by the Lord's own signet."

The murmuring from the crowd escalated into a full-blown frenzy. "Show!" demanded one man. "Show!" repeated another. Soon the assembled nobility was chanting as one, "Show, show, show."

Talmus Colb walked before Thrain Wyndam as the shouts echoed off the walls. Lord Wyndam was still sitting in shock and had gone very pale. "Your signet, sir," Colb demanded, holding out his hand. Lord Wyndam looked at his son. It was the first time in his life that Alishane had seen true fear on his father's face. Alishane felt utterly helpless as he watched his father draw the chain over his neck and put the signet in Colb's hand.

Lord Colb walked to the head of the rectangle of tables where Winningham stood waiting. The two men flanked the seated

Countess, one on either side of the woman who sat looking directly into the eyes of Lord Wyndam. Colb and Winningham joined signet and seal, holding them up above the Countess's head for all to see. "They join," the two men declared in unison, and the Countess smiled into the face of the doomed Thrain Wyndam.

__Chapter Five__

~ For Sport and Retribution ~

"I have no idea how they got my signet, Al," Thrain Wyndam said to his son. "Perhaps they created a duplicate using wax from a discarded seal."

"Possible, but unlikely," answered Alishane. "I've never heard of such a thing being tried before."

"Anything is possible with the Countess," Lord Wyndam growled. The two had been in Lord Wyndam's room with guards posted outside the door since the Council had disbanded late that afternoon. Night was now falling rapidly and father and son sat talking as darkness seeped into the room. Lord Wyndam looked about at the darkness and suddenly moved closer to his son. He looked him hard in the eyes, his voice taking on a note of urgency as he spoke, "Alishane, I want you to leave this place tonight. The Countess's proof is sufficient in this place and time, while we are in her Manor and without a King's court for trial. She will act quickly to secure her victory while she has the advantage."

Alishane was already shaking his head in refusal. "No, Father," he said stubbornly. "I cannot leave you alone when the wolves are circling."

"If the wolves are circling it is because I am already hamstrung and helpless," replied the older man. "If you stay you will suffer the same fate as me."

"What would you have me do?" Alishane yelled. "Go back to our estate and sit idle as an old maid while my father is executed? I can't go back to the school in the face of these charges."

"No, you cannot," said Lord Wyndam, leaning forward to grab his son by the shoulder. "I need your help, Al, like I have never needed it before. You must go to Lower Meade and attempt to speak with Lucius Porveux to arrange our defense. I do not know what the Countess plans for Lucius, but I fear for his safety. She will not allow him to answer to these charges."

Alishane sat in silent thought. The Countess's net seemed without flaw, and it was closing about them both. The seal of wax undeniably matched his father's signet; he had seen it himself as it was passed around the room. The Council had degenerated into a shouting match between those who believed the charges and those who remained loyal to Thrain Wyndam. But as the parchment, seal and signet made their way around the room, Lord Wyndam's supporters fell to silence. At last, Lord and Master Wyndam had been ushered out of the Hall and into this room by the Countess's guard. As he considered what had happened and what was apt to happen in the next few days, including the likely execution of his father, Alishane Wyndam began to see the wisdom of his father's words. The Countess's plan still relied on two things: the silence of Lucius Porveux and a quick execution of Thrain Wyndam. "How much time do you think you have?" he asked his father.

"Tomorrow, perhaps the day after," answered Lord Wyndam.

"Then I'll go tonight," Alishane declared.

Cane Shanney's mead tent was crammed with people talking about the day's events. As Timmen moved through the crowd, he heard talk about many different subjects, each of which would be worth a month's gossip under other circumstances.

"Me lady was saying that Connor Sonnegut may not live out the night," said a dirty and fat woman with more chins than teeth.

"I heard that Gor Barahd isn't even a proper knight, but rather a mercenary hired by Lord Chelleman," responded the equally dirty man seated opposite her.

Timmen moved away a few steps and then overheard two nobles speaking. "I never would have thought it possible," one was saying.

"Ah, but you can never tell about those who yearn for power," the other answered.

"True enough," said the first. "And the seal was unmistakably made by Wyndam's signet."

"Now what about young Master Wyndam?" said the second. "Surely he's between the kettle and the flame."

"Yes, and he'll soon be run through and hung over that flame to cook." The nobles chuckled and knocked their mugs of ale together.

Timmen continued pushing through the crowd. He had been at the Tournament of Knighthood and had already heard about the apparent fall of Thrain Wyndam. The next bit of news he heard, however, stopped him cold. A man came running up to the tent looking hysterical and frightened. "Lucius Porveux is dead!" the man yelled in a shrill and panicked voice. The entire crowd went silent and turned upon the bearer of the ill news. "Dead," the man repeated. "Dead in the night."

"How?" "When?" "What more do you know?" asked voices from the crowd.

"Last night in his bed," the man answered shakily. "Woke up this morn with his throat cut."

"Impossible!" scoffed one man. "You been tiltin' the jug again Scurvy?"

"Heard it meself from the rider come into the stables, I did," said Scurvy indignantly. "Rider come in hard with the news for the Countess and the others at the Council. Upper *and* Lower Meade are shut down tight and the Baron's men are out scourin' the countryside lookin' for the killer. Ask me, they won't find a thing. Anyone who can get in and kill Porveux in his bed ain't about to be caught."

The crowd under Shanney's canopy began talking excitedly. Timmen shook his head in disbelief. He knew, perhaps better than anyone else, the skill that must have been required in executing the Baron. Given recent events, he had a strong suspicion of who the killer might have been. "The Shadow Wolf," he whispered to himself as he made his way toward the bar.

The girl was seated at the end of the counter, waiting for him as she had promised. Unlike their last meeting, however, the girl was not smiling. She had a very dour expression on her face as

Timmen took the stool next to her. "Ill tidings," she said in a hushed voice. "There is evil in the air tonight."

"I'm still going," Timmen said with as much determination as he could muster.

"As am I," said the girl, "but our task may be more difficult. Security may be tighter with Porveux's killer on the loose."

"Unless I am very wrong," the halfling answered darkly, "Porveux's killer is in the Manor as we speak."

The girl turned to look at him and a flicker of apprehension crossed her face. She looked down at her hands folded upon the bar. "We should get going," she said.

"Yes," Timmen agreed. He got up from the stool and looked at Cane Shanney to find the bartender watching him. Timmen smiled faintly and nodded to his friend. Shanney did not return the smile. The man stood watching the halfling as Timmen turned and followed the strange girl into the night.

"Welcome back, Zakarus," the Countess said as the assassin slid into the chair opposite her desk.

"Highness," Rinn answered with a slight nod. "You look resplendent as always."

"I trust your journey was fruitful?" she asked.

"Lucius Porveux will not hinder your plans, Madame," the Shadow Wolf answered with a wicked smile. He began polishing the dust off of his black leather boots as he continued, "And have they gone well? Your plans, that is?"

"Remarkably well," the Countess smiled and turned to look out of a window toward the remote wing of the Manor where Lord and Master Wyndam were being held under lock and guard. "Even Wyndam's staunchest supporters were unable to argue against a parchment sealed by his own signet." She turned back to regard the assassin and a flicker of warmth flashed briefly across her face, "You have proven most useful, my old friend."

"Old friend?" Rinn asked, looking up from his boots and sitting back in the chair. "There was a time when we were more than friends, as I recall."

The Countess's face again became stony as she replied. "You made your choice, Zakarus. I let you choose between power and passion and you chose power."

The Shadow Wolf gave a wry grin. "'Twas no choice at all Madame, for power *is* my passion."

The Countess returned his smile. "We have always had that, at least, in common," she said. The smile disappeared from her face as quickly as it had come and the woman returned to business, "I hope you are not too tired from your journey to perform one more service for me tonight?"

"Whatever you require, I shall see it done," Rinn answered with a small bow.

"Good," the woman said and turned once more to gaze out her window. "I will not risk the scrutiny of a public execution. I want this situation resolved tonight. Make it appear as though the

Wyndams were trying to escape," Rinn noted a sparkle in the woman's eye as she turned back to him and finished the sentence, "and then kill them both."

Timmen led the girl through back alleys and over darkened rooftops until they sat peering around a corner at a back entrance into Tavora Manor. They could see two guards standing outside the gate.

"You intend to occupy a guard?" the girl asked in a whisper.

Timmen nodded and took the vial from his vest pocket. "It will get us into the Manor and should afford me some freedom of movement once inside."

"How do you intend to get me in?" asked the girl.

"Wait five minutes and then walk up to the gate. After that just follow my lead," the halfling answered. He took a deep breath and removed the stopper from the vial. Timmen hesitated a moment and looked at the girl. She nodded once and Timmen took another deep breath, then he swallowed the potion in one large gulp.

The potion burned his throat all the way down. When it reached his stomach, it felt as though his internal organs were being sucked inward, compressing in upon themselves and being turned inside out. Timmen hunched over in pain. Just when he felt that his stomach must be the size of a pea, the potion exploded through his arms, legs, feet and fingers. Timmen's body tingled and then went numb. Looking down, he could no longer see his physical form.

"Go! Now!" the girl whispered urgently.

Timmen tried to walk forward but found that he could not. His body, if he still had one, was not responding to his mind's urges. Taking a moment to calm his rushing nerves, the thief looked inward and found the steadying peace that had served him so many times before. He sent his will forward and his presence surged out of the shadows and over the cobblestones of the street. A few moments later he was hovering before the two guards. In deciding which of the two men to occupy, he started thinking about which one looked cleaner and would likely have better breath. *What a strange thing to worry about,* he thought to himself and almost laughed. Suddenly he realized that he was running out of time. He chose the cleaner of the two guards, which was still repugnantly dirty, and willed himself into the body.

The guard's eyes went wide and his body stiffened when he felt the intrusion. He tried to resist, but the element of surprise, the potency of the potion and the force of Timmen's will were too overpowering. Timmen suddenly found himself in the body of the human, standing six feet tall and looking back out into the street. He felt the weight of the armor and the helm upon his head.

"You all right?" the other guard asked him.

"Eh?" Timmen asked, astounded at the gruff sound of the voice coming from his mouth.

"You had a bit of a shiver," said the guard.

"Must have caught a breeze," Timmen replied.

"Or thinking about Sally Ann again, hey?" the guard asked and poked him with his elbow.

Timmen only grunted, trying to end the conversation. He didn't think it prudent to talk too much. The guard went back to watching the lane and did not speak again. After what seemed an eternity to the halfling in the human body, Timmen saw the girl emerge from the shadows and start walking warily toward them. "Oy there, girl, what took you so long?" he asked her.

"Um, I was a bit delayed, I'm afraid," the girl answered, trying to pick up on where he was leading her.

Timmen leaned over to the other guard and whispered, "I've an appointment with this lass here. Mind if I take a few moments to myself?"

The guard looked the girl over a few times and grimaced. "With her?" he asked. "You aren't paying her are you?"

"Aye, I am," Timmen answered. "She's a professional, she is."

"This one?" the guard asked in a loud, astonished voice. "What would anyone pay her for?"

"That's the point, isn't it?" Timmen gave a lecherous grin. "It's what she does that you've got to pay for."

The other guard shot Timmen a disgusted look. "I don't even want to know," he said. "Just don't be too long about it."

Timmen winked at the girl and they walked through the gate toward the inner manor grounds. When they were out of earshot, the girl punched him in the arm. "A prostitute?" she whispered angrily. "You've made me out to be a bloody whore!"

"It worked, didn't it?" Timmen grumbled. "Besides, I owed you one for not telling me how much it was going to hurt to swallow that potion."

Dunk Worley was trying not to look hurried or desperate as he approached the guards outside Lord Wyndam's room. He had been busying himself with menial tasks all evening to keep his mind off what was happening to his lord. He felt as though his world was crashing down upon his head and he was utterly helpless to stop it. Dunk had been in the stables looking after Lord Wyndam's horse Ashton when a rider came in bearing terrible news. Now he was trying to bring that news to his lord.

"Hold!" shouted one of the guards. "What is your business?"

"I bring Master Wyndam's bedclothes and personal effects so that he might stay the night with his father," Dunk replied meekly. The guard searched through his clothing and the gear he was carrying and then unlocked the door and motioned the porter inside.

Dunk entered and found Lord and Master Wyndam packing a bag. The porter pulled a long dagger from his boot and placed it on the bed near Alishane, then he stepped up close to his master and asked in a hushed voice, "Are we leaving, my Lord?"

"Alishane is not under arrest," answered Lord Wyndam, "and he is riding out tonight for Lower Meade."

"Meade?" Dunk asked tremulously.

"He must get word to Lucius Porveux about what has happened here and arrange our defense," Lord Wyndam said as he continued packing the bag.

"My Lord," Dunk's lip quivered as he spoke, "that is why I came to speak with you." Lord and Master Wyndam both stopped their work and looked at the porter expectantly. Dunk's voice was squeaky and cracked as he continued. "Lucius Porveux is dead."

*   *   *   *   *   *   *

Timmen and the girl had parted ways out in the yard and were each making their own way into the manor's main building. She went in through the kitchen posing as a servant and he through the large front door; in the body of the guard he did not need a ruse, but simply saluted the duty guards and walked right through. Though he had never been inside the Manor, he had spent many hours over the last several days studying the building from rooftops in the surrounding area. The architecture was old and unlike anything he had seen before, but it was still fairly obvious that the main living quarters were in the upper levels of the center of the building. Thus Timmen knew the general direction in which he wanted to move.

The thief was standing just inside the front door in a sparkling marble entrance hall with lush tapestries and large portraits adorning the walls. The largest chandelier he had ever seen hung from the high ceiling. In front of him were two staircases, one on either side of the room, each curving about the outer walls to meet at the far end of the hall. Hung from the banister on the second level were flags bearing the Countess's colors and the Crest of Westbury. Timmen crossed to the staircase on the right and began climbing. Though he could feel the strength in the human body, he winced at the noise being made by the armor he wore and longed for his own lithe, little form.

Upon reaching the top of the stairs, he was faced with a decision. Off to his right he saw a long carpeted hallway with doors on either side. Turning to his left, he saw another long carpeted hallway with doors on either side. Up and down each hallway milled the nobility being quartered in the manor for the Council. Looking behind him, he found that the staircases spiraled for the height of several men and then climbed the same walls in the opposite direction from which they had ascended from the lower level. Looking around quickly, he decided to climb the stairs to the next level.

The next two floors each resembled the one he had just left. They were followed by a parlor. The three after that appeared to be servants' quarters and they were followed by another parlor. Next came a sort of museum with many old suits of armor and the heads of strange beasts lining the walls. The problem was that the staircases ended here on the ninth floor. Timmen knew from counting windows that there were ten floors in this section of the building. He was fairly certain that the Countess's living quarters would be found on the tenth floor, and that's where he wanted to go.

If he didn't find the jeweled dagger there, then perhaps he would find some other treasure to steal. *The staircase leading to the next floor must be hidden somewhere among the artifacts,* he thought to himself as he entered the museum.

Timmen began looking about the room for signs of a hidden door, taking care to also look for traps. The process was extremely slow. The thief had just finished inspecting a large gargoyle head when he heard a noise from the other side of the room. Timmen quickly darted behind a suit of armor and tried to hide. He wanted desperately to be back in his own halfling body. A door opened at the far end of the room and a man dressed in black emerged. Timmen knew the man at once; it was Zakarus Rinn.

Timmen felt his heart begin pumping violently in his chest. He was certain that Rinn would be able to hear it thumping as the man walked down the length of the room toward the spot where Timmen crouched behind the suit of armor. Sweat began to drip into the thief's eyes as the Shadow Wolf drew nearer. Timmen held his breath as Rinn came upon him. Fortunately, the assassin was focused on his own thoughts and he walked right past the hiding thief. When the man in black had passed by and his footsteps could be heard descending the stairs, Timmen gave one last look around the museum and then turned to follow the assassin.

Chapter Six

~ The Hunt and the Hunted ~

The girl had followed much the same course as Timmen once she left the kitchen and entered the central wing of the Manor. But whereas Timmen was going by intuition in finding his way, Lady Curry had been in Tavora Manor before and knew exactly where she was going.

Years ago, Lady Curry had been a friend of the Countess, but then the Countess took Curry's husband as a lover. When Lady Curry found out, she confronted the Countess. Her mistake was doing it in private. Were it done in public, the Countess could not have been so swift and brutal in ridding herself of the nuisance. Thieves raided the Curry mansion and the entire family was killed, but Lady Curry's body was never found. She escaped and lived in obscurity for twenty long years, her life on the docks taking a heavy toll on her body. Then she became ill and could feel her life waning. But as her strength diminished, so did her fear of the Countess. When the halfling came to her with a plan to break into Tavora Manor, her own opportunity for revenge had been too great to resist.

Now she found herself in the body of an ugly teenage girl, dressed as a housemaid and walking up the steps of the manor toward an end that had been in the making for twenty years. She was on the sixth flight of stairs, between the servants' quarters and the parlor, when she met a man dressed in black descending the stairs toward her. One look into his eyes sent a chill coursing through her and made her knees weak. She shrank back against the wall and looked past him, trying to avoid his gaze. Apparently the man was used to getting such a reaction from the house staff because he paid her no mind and continued on his way. She had just started climbing the stairs again when a guard came down following the dark man. Again she tried to be inconspicuous and it wasn't until he reached out and grabbed her by the arm that she recognized the guard as the one Timmen had occupied.

"You can't get through that way," Timmen whispered.

"I can," the girl replied. "I know the secret passage."

Timmen regarded her briefly and then nodded. "Good luck," he said and walked past her, following the man in black.

The girl climbed the rest of the stairs and strode straight through the museum. When she came to a statue of a knight slaying an ice salamander, she pulled down on the tip of the spear and a door appeared in the wall and swung silently inward. The inky blackness was complete as she walked inside and pushed the door closed. After a few moments, an odd green light began to glow from a line of emeralds set in the wall. She saw a spiral staircase and began to climb. When she got to the top, she found another door and paused. She felt out of breath and her fingers were tingling. Lady Curry looked down at the young body she was occupying and felt more hale and strong than she had in many years. A memory filled her mind of her youngest child impaled and hanging from a shining blade. The woman's anger swelled and she opened the door and entered the dimly lit office.

"I did not summon a chambermaid," the Countess said airily. The girl gave no response, but stood glaring at the woman sitting behind the desk. The Countess looked up from her work.

"Did you not hear me, girl? I have no need of your service. Leave me," she said. The girl's only response was a slight curl at the corner of her mouth. The Countess rose from her seat and began to circle her desk.

"You've aged well, Morna," the girl said.

The Countess stopped in her tracks and regarded the girl suspiciously. "How do you know my first name?" she asked. "And how dare you address me so informally!"

The girl gave a wicked smile. "I should think formalities would be unnecessary between women who have shared a lover," she said.

The Countess knew then that the girl was not who she seemed. "Who are you?" she asked icily.

The girl's smile disappeared and her eyes narrowed. "An old friend," she replied, "and an old enemy."

"I care not for the prior and have many of the latter," the Countess snapped. "Declare your name and your intentions."

"Do not worry, Morna, I'll not keep you in suspense," the girl's eyes flashed as she spoke. "I have waited too long to see you face to face again." The girl's body began to tremble. A low, painful moaning resonated from deep in her throat, rising in pitch and volume as her body began to jerk more violently. Soon her body was shaking so hard and fast that it was a blur, then it was two blurs as a second form began to remove itself from the first. The girl's loud, painful moaning was joined by a second voice cackling maniacally. The two voices were distinct, yet they combined to form a grotesque, demonic harmony. The Countess watched in stunned fascination, unable to move from where she stood. Gradually, the cackling grew louder while the moaning waned. Suddenly, there was a flash and a snap of energy as the two forms were thrown apart. The girl lay sprawled on the ground and Lady Curry stood facing the Countess.

"Gwendolynn Curry," the Countess sneered. "The years have not been kind."

"I see your charm has not diminished," Curry stated coldly.

"I had thought you dead long ago," the Countess continued as she slowly and deliberately placed an opal ring upon her finger. "You come now to seek your revenge?"

"Not to seek it. To claim it!" Curry exclaimed and she reached inside her cloak, pulled forth a dagger and advanced.

But the Countess was not defenseless. She extended her bejeweled hand and shouted, *"Immobiliary Totalus!"* Lady Curry was rendered motionless. She was stopped in mid-stride with her arm raised and the dagger poised to strike. Only her eyes moved and they registered her shock and fear. "Did you think me a helpless old hag, Gwendolynn?" the Countess spat venomously. "I have not maintained my power through shrewdness alone," she continued. "Your skill with potions was always well known and may have grown stronger over these long years, but you are no match for me."

The Countess slowly approached the helpless Lady Curry and took the dagger from her hand. Standing face to face, the Countess looked directly into the tortured eyes of Gwendolynn Curry. "Few people know of my power as a sorceress," the Countess said, "so you may count yourself privileged to witness it, though I doubt you will find the experience pleasant." The Countess walked past the immobile Lady Curry and closed the door to her private chambers.

Gwendolynn Curry had stolen twenty years away from death, but her debt would be paid in full tonight.

Timmen followed the Shadow Wolf as quietly as he could, considering he was occupying a large and bumbling human body. Fortunately, it seemed as though Rinn was in a hurry for he walked quickly and did not look behind him. It wasn't until Rinn turned down a long hallway and Timmen stood in the corridor watching that he grew concerned that the Shadow Wolf knew he was being followed. The assassin had unlocked a door and was about to walk through it when he looked back at Timmen for a long moment. Timmen was about to turn and run when Rinn abruptly entered the room and closed the door behind him.

The thief knew that his disguise was no longer any use to him. He looked around and found a servant's closet, which he entered and released his hold on the human. It was more difficult than he had expected to leave the body and he worried about the racket being made as the guard fought to expel the invasive presence. After a minute of struggle, however, the halfling walked from the closet and looked around the deserted corridor, leaving the exhausted and barely conscious guard behind.

Zakarus Rinn exited his room a few minutes later. He had changed into a short-sleeved black tunic that exposed the silver and gold gauntlets upon his forearms. A sword dangled from his belt. The assassin had expected to see the guard who was following him, but the man was nowhere to be found.

Rinn began walking toward the remote wing of the manor and a meeting with Lord and Master Wyndam. He did not notice a halfling perched in the shadows atop a statue, watching his every move.

"Porveux is dead?" Alishane asked Dunk incredulously.

"Aye, Master Wyndam," Dunk answered. "A rider came in with the news an hour ago. He said Porveux was killed last night in his bed." Dunk looked nervously at Lord Wyndam. The old man had a pained look on his face. "What does this mean, my Lord?" the porter asked.

"It means Alishane's destination is no longer the Horn of Meade," answered Lord Wyndam.

"Am I still to leave?" Alishane asked his father.

"Yes!" Lord Wyndam's deep voice boomed. "And I don't want an argument this time. You *must* leave, Al. Go home and protect our estate. If you are caught up in this any more than you are then the Countess will dispose of you as well and declare our lands forfeit. Being a lord means looking out for the interests of those under your charge, Alishane, not just your own wants and desires."

"I do not desire lordship," Alishane said bitterly.

Lord Wyndam sighed. "I know," he said and put a hand on his son's shoulder. "But fate never asked us what we wanted."

"This is not an act of fate, Father!" Alishane exploded and pulled away from his father's touch. "The Countess has moved against you because you stood in the way of her aspirations. I remain a threat to her as long as I am alive. She will not allow me to reside in peace on our estate."

"You will be able to defend yourself much more effectively from our own lands and surrounded by those who are loyal to you," Lord Wyndam replied. "There are many who will never believe these charges, no matter how much evidence is leveled against me. And there are many more who do not like or trust the Countess. You must weather this storm, Alishane, and then you will get your chance at revenge."

The last statement pacified the younger man. "Revenge," he whispered. Alishane Wyndam returned to packing his bag. "I shall have my revenge or my soul will burn from the effort."

Timmen followed the Shadow Wolf down several flights of stairs and along increasingly dark passages. They were moving into a remote wing of the manor, which made it easier for the halfling to follow the assassin. Soon they came to a door guarded by two members of the Countess's guard. The corridor was poorly lit so

Timmen was able to creep up close and listen as the Shadow Wolf addressed the two guards.

"You are relieved," the assassin said shortly. One of the guards began to question the order, but quickly held his tongue at a glare from the dark-eyed man. Timmen hid in the shadows as the two guards walked toward him. The first guard looked very confused at being relieved from his duty. The second guard, however, made Timmen's breath catch in his throat. It was the elf woman who had saved him down in the street. She had almost passed him by when she turned and looked right at him through the shadows. She smiled faintly and nodded. Timmen was absolutely stunned, first at seeing her again and second at how she could see him in the dark. He sat watching the two guards walking down the corridor until they were lost in the darkness, then he shook off his surprise and returned to his purpose.

Timmen crept forward and saw the Shadow Wolf standing with his ear pressed against the door. After a moment, the assassin was apparently convinced that the inhabitants were not standing by the door because he leaned down, picked the lock and cracked it open. In a blink the Shadow Wolf was inside the room and Timmen was alone in the corridor. He crept to the door and pulled a small reflecting glass from his thieving kit. Crouching down near the floor, he pressed his own ear to the door to listen while he used the glass to look underneath. He heard a muffled conversation from the far end of the room and he saw three men: two looked like nobility, one old and one young, and the third appeared to be a servant.

"Yes!" the older man yelled. "And I don't want an argument this time. You *must* leave, Al." The man's voice lowered and again became muffled

A few moments later the younger man raised his own voice. "This is not an act of fate, Father!" he said loudly.

Timmen now knew that they were father and son and that they were having an argument about the younger man leaving. He also knew that they were apparently enemies of the Countess, which would explain why they were locked in the room under guard. What he didn't know, however, was why the Shadow Wolf had come here. Then the younger man turned toward the door and started stuffing articles of clothing into a satchel. He muttered a few more words, but the only one Timmen could make out was 'revenge.'

It was at this moment that the Shadow Wolf stepped from a darkened corner near the door. "And on whom would you seek revenge, young Master?" he asked. Dunk and Lord Wyndam jumped to their feet, but then froze when the Wolf's hand moved to the hilt of his sword. "Would you seek it upon the Countess for the damage she has done to your reputation?" The Shadow Wolf taunted as he continued to advance. "Or would you seek it upon *me* for killing your father?" The assassin suddenly flicked his wrist outward and a dagger appeared from his sleeve. Before anyone else in the room could move, he threw the dagger at Thrain Wyndam. Alishane and Dunk turned as one to see Lord Wyndam's eyes wide and his face suddenly ashen. His hands groped helplessly at the hilt of the dagger protruding from his throat. Blood was seeping freely from the wound. He sank to his knees, looked briefly at his son, and then fell facedown on the floor.

The next few seconds were a blur of frantic motion. Dunk went to Lord Wyndam and hovered over him protectively, trying to stem the flow of blood from a man who was already dead. Alishane Wyndam seized the dagger Dunk had left on the bed and leaped at the Shadow Wolf with an ear-splitting roar. Zakarus Rinn pulled his sword and stepped forward to meet the oncoming cleric. Their blades came together with a resonating *clang* that made Dunk Worley jump and issue a slight squeal. Alishane stabbed wildly in his anger, but Rinn parried every blow with ease. After his initial charge, Alishane Wyndam began to retreat frantically. The fear showed on his face as he realized that he was severely overmatched.

Timmen watched at the door. He didn't know what else to do. Suddenly, he felt a presence surge up behind him in the corridor, but before he could turn to see who it was the person heaved against the door and burst it wide open. Timmen looked up to see the elf woman standing in the doorway. The light from the room flowed over her and Timmen took a large inhale of breath at the sight. She had taken off her helm, releasing her white hair to shine brilliantly in the torchlight. Her pointed ears stood out starkly from her beautiful face. She slowly pulled her own sword and it rang in a melodic song as it was freed from its scabbard. The torchlight glittered along its length.

The Shadow Wolf glanced quickly over his shoulder and his surprise showed clearly, but he did not lose his fighting edge. He turned back to Alishane Wyndam and brought his blade down, then quickly back up to force the cleric's knife straight out in front between the two of them. Alishane's weapon was now vulnerable and Rinn hit hard to the side, driving it out wide and creating an opening in the cleric's defense that the Shadow Wolf did not miss. He lunged forward and drove his sword deep into Alishane's shoulder. The young man turned slightly at the last moment, avoiding a fatal blow. Alishane slumped stricken to the floor and the Shadow Wolf turned to face the advancing elf.

No one said a word as the two slowly closed the distance between them. The only sound was Dunk sobbing softly over Lord Wyndam's body. The elf and the Shadow Wolf stopped at the same moment and each stood regarding the other.

"I had thought your kind extinct," Rinn said in an even voice.

"We are still here," the elf answered; her voice was airy, her accent sharp and angular.

"And what is your business in Tavora Manor?" Rinn asked, his eyes falling to survey her guard uniform.

"Protection of innocence," the elf replied.

The Shadow Wolf sneered and his eyes flashed red. "Enemies then," he said and raised his sword.

"Enemies," the elf confirmed and raised her own weapon.

The Shadow Wolf darted forward and their blades clashed. The ring of steel on steel echoed off the walls as each stepped back and they began to circle.

"Halfling!" the elf called over her shoulder. "Gather the servant and take the nobleman out!" Timmen entered the room and quickly darted behind the elf. It seemed to him the safest place to be.

The Shadow Wolf's lips drew back over his teeth in a terrible snarl when he saw Timmen. "You!" he said.

The elf launched an offensive, which Rinn defended with ease, and again the two circled. Timmen followed, staying behind the elf. Soon their movement brought him close to Dunk Worley, who was still lying over the body of Thrain Wyndam and sobbing.

Timmen went to him and shook him frantically. "Come to your senses, man! We must be away!" he said.

Dunk looked up with teary eyes and stared dumbly at Timmen. He looked over at Alishane Wyndam, who lay moaning on the floor a short distance away, teetering on the edge of consciousness. Dunk looked back at Timmen with a lost, vacant look in his eyes. A flurry of swordplay and the ringing of steel drew Dunk's attention to the elf standing guard above him, her bright hair flowing with her graceful movements. His eyes went wide in shock at the incredible sight. He looked back at Timmen with his mouth hanging open just as the halfling slapped him hard across the face.

"Your new lord needs your help!" Timmen growled, pointing at Alishane. The truth finally registered on Dunk and he gently laid Thrain Wyndam's head upon the floor. They moved to Alishane and roused him, struggling to lift him to his feet. Timmen looked toward the elf to find that her back was once again to them, her feet dancing lightly upon the floor as she fought the Shadow Wolf.

"We're ready!" Timmen yelled and the elf immediately went on the offensive, her blade flashing and driving the assassin back and to the side of the room. Dunk struggled to support Alishane as they crossed to the door. Timmen could hardly help at all since he stood only half as tall as the two men. When they made the door, Timmen looked back to see the elf and the assassin still locked in mortal combat. She looked diminutive yet graceful and deceptively powerful. He turned and left the room, the ringing of steel following him down the corridor.

When Timmen caught up with Dunk and Alishane, the nobleman had recovered more of his strength and was supporting his own weight as he limped along. Timmen knew there were few guards in this part of the manor, but the wall would still be guarded. He decided to make for the same small gate he and the girl had entered with the hope that only one guard would still be posted there. He was surprised to find himself wishing that he were still in the human body.

They encountered no other people as they hurried through dark corridors and down several flights of stairs. A few frantic minutes later, Timmen peered out of a door almost directly below the room in which the battle was taking place. He saw no one in the yard and motioned for the others to follow him out into the night.

In the next moment, as they scurried across a large, open courtyard, a blinding light erupted above them and they stumbled to their knees. The three of them turned to see a shaft of purest white light pouring out of the window to Lord Wyndam's room.

"Elf magic!" Dunk whispered breathlessly.

"Elf?" Alishane croaked. Timmen pulled them away and they sprinted to the shadows of the wall.

They walked more slowly now, stopping whenever they heard voices or footsteps high on the wall above them. They made their way along the base of the wall toward the gate. When they got near it, Timmen motioned for them to halt and he sneaked forward to scout the situation. Two men were again guarding the gate. Timmen cursed under his breath and turned to rejoin the others. Just as he came upon them and began to tell of the guards, the elf appeared out of the shadows and silently joined them. Alishane Wyndam turned and saw her for the first time. His eyes widened in his surprise and he began to speak. Dunk covered Alishane's mouth with his hand to keep him quiet.

"You made the light?" Timmen whispered.

The elf nodded.

"To blind your foe," he reasoned.

Again the elf nodded.

"So the Shadow Wolf is dead?" the halfling asked.

The elf shook her head. "No," she answered. "I cannot use my magic in an offensive way. My powers would leave me if I had killed him. He has been… subdued." She smiled faintly.

Timmen looked worried. "If he's still alive then he will soon be on our trail. We must be on our way." They all nodded and listened to him intently, though Alishane glanced repeatedly at the elf. "There are two guards at the gate," Timmen continued. "If they raise an alarm we'll never make it."

"I will take care of it," the elf said. She reached behind her and unhooked her helm from her belt. She swept her hair up on top of her head and tucked her ears inside the helmet as she put it on. The halfling and the two men watched her walk up to the guards and converse with them briefly. With a shrug and a cordial wave, the guards turned and walked away toward the front doors. When they were out of sight, Timmen ushered Alishane and Dunk through the gate.

The streets of Pilas Antum were dark and deserted as the group fled from the manor. They had not gone far when Alishane's strength faltered and he swooned. The elf rushed to his side and helped him to keep walking. As they hobbled along, Alishane could not help but stare at her.

"How is it that the men of the guard do not see you for what you are?" he asked her.

She smiled. "A gift of my people," she answered. "The human mind is fairly open to the power of suggestion."

"But I did not imagine the bright light that blinded the assassin," Alishane continued.

"No," she confirmed and her smile remained. "That gift is mine alone."

They walked a few more steps and Alishane presented his hand. "My name is Alishane Wyndam," he said.

The elf took his hand and her blue eyes sparkled as she looked upon him. "I'm Aurora Daelin," she replied.

Zakarus Rinn entered the private chambers of the Countess to find the room packed with her personal guard. He looked at a bloodstained pile of clothing on the floor and a young girl being held up between two guards. He turned inquisitively to the Countess.

"We have had intruders tonight, Zakarus," she said.

"More than you know," the Shadow Wolf replied while rubbing the sizable knot on the back of his head. The Countess regarded him darkly as he continued. "Alishane Wyndam has escaped."

The Countess's eyes flashed in anger. "We will speak in private, Zakarus," she said to the assassin and then turned to her guard. "You all will leave me. Take that mess out of here and dispose of it," she said, indicating the remains of Lady Curry. "Take the girl to the dungeons. Burn out her eyes and cut off her thumbs, but leave her tongue so that she may bear witness of what happens to those who assail the Countess of Westbury."

The girl's legs buckled and she slouched between the guards who were holding her. She cried uncontrollably as they dragged her from the room. The Countess watched her go with no expression on her pale face but a slight narrowing of her merciless eyes. Late into the night, the girl's agonized wails could be heard emanating from the dungeons of Tavora Manor.

Part Two
~ *Spondet Peritiam Artis* ~

Each to His Art

Chapter Seven

~ **Arcanis Rhu** ~

A deep haze of low clouds shrouded the land as the old man slowly made his way along the narrow wooded path. Forest creatures of all shapes and sizes eyed him suspiciously and then darted deeper into the wood. He had the distinct impression that they were running off to announce his approach. Turning a bend in the path, the old man saw a black squirrel with large pointed ears sitting on a low, overhanging branch. He stopped and leaned on his staff, regarding the squirrel who sat watching him closely.

"Be at ease, little one," the man said to the squirrel, "you have nothing to fear from me." The squirrel turned and chattered into the trees, then turned back to face the old man. Its tail twitched back and forth nervously. The man smiled. "Your friends need not fear me either. Kindly go ask them if I might have a word with them. I am an old man and I grow tired of walking endlessly in these woods." The squirrel's twitching grew faster. After a moment, it turned and scampered from one tree to another, deep into the woods and out of sight. The old man found a moss-covered rock and sat down, laying his staff across the knees of his battered brown cloak. He sat for a long time stroking his short, white beard and listening to the sounds of the forest, which still seemed nervous and expectant.

"What brings a wizard to Westwick Forest?" asked a voice from behind the old man. He jerked slightly in his surprise, then slowly turned to address the three elves behind him. Two of them had bows drawn, the arrows trained on his heart.

"Oh, I assure you, you'll not need your weapons," the man said with a warm smile.

"Humans do not have permission to wander Westwick Forest at will," responded the elf. "Just because you are able to see through our enchantments does not mean you have been extended an invitation. Your presence here renders your life forfeit, so I believe I will keep my own counsel on the necessity of weapons."

"As you will," the old man said with a chuckle as he slowly got to his feet. He stood facing the three elves, supporting his weight with his staff. "But if I am indeed a wizard, as you have surmised, and I have proven able to defeat your enchantments surrounding the forest, then wouldn't your weapons prove useless against me as well?" He smiled slightly as the two elves with the bows looked nervously at their leader. "Fear not, fear not," the old man said as he rounded the rock to approach the elves. "As I told your little friend there," he nodded toward the squirrel, who had returned and sat watching from a very high branch, "I have come to talk to the Jarlaeth, not to cause trouble." His eyes twinkled and he smiled merrily.

The elves were stunned into silence at his mention of the Jarlaeth. This old man seemed to know a lot about them. The leader of the three raised his hand and signaled for the others to lower their bows. "What business have you with the Jarlaeth?" he asked.

"One thing at a time, my friend," the wizard scolded. "It is not a subject to be discussed out in the open forest, not even a forest as well-guarded as this one. Take me to the Jarl, then my tale will be told in full."

The three elves looked at each other with uncertainty, then the leader turned and began walking into the deep darkness of the forest. "We will take you to the inner sanctuary, where you will wait while I confer with my superiors. Let us hope that you do not have to test your magic."

"Slowly, if you please," the wizard said lightly as he began to follow. "I am an old man and I have not yet learned how to fly." He chuckled at his joke, but the elves did not laugh.

Talos Daelin stood on the steps outside his front door, waiting patiently with his hands held behind his back. His keen eyes scanned the forest about him. The symbiosis of the woods was askew; he felt it and knew that his scouts would be coming to him shortly to report. Elves walked gracefully about the square, looking occasionally at their leader. They felt the disturbance as well, and while some were appeased to see Talos standing calmly, tall and regal, some were embittered because they believed that his meddling in the affairs of humans was surely the cause of the disturbance to their home. Talos noted their expressions and smiled warmly to each of them. The divisions in the Jarlaeth were now almost impossible to control. His time was running out, and he knew it.

Presently one of the scouts from the outer ridge walked purposefully through the village and directly to Talos. "My Jarl," the scout said with a nod of respect, "I must report a trespasser within Westwick." The scout paused for a response from Talos, but the Jarl did not answer; his deep gray eyes did not even flicker. A crowd of elves now began to gather about the square to learn what they could. "I believe him to be a wizard, for he saw through our enchantments and carries a staff," the scout continued.

Something flashed in the Jarl's eyes at the word 'wizard,' their depth suddenly disappeared and they focused acutely into the eyes of the scout. The elf trembled and cowered from that gaze. He turned slightly in preparation to leave and his voice shook as he said, "I have left him under guard in the inner sanctuary. I thought it best to consult you before taking any other action. Right this way, my Jarl, I will show you." The scout started back the way he had come with Talos Daelin on his heels, but while the scout looked harried and unnerved, Talos strode through the watching throng with purpose and his head held high. The crowd parted before him.

A short while later Talos followed the scout into a clearing, where he saw an old man in a very worn brown cloak sitting on a large rock with an ornate wooden staff across his knees. The man's flowing gray hair hung clean yet untidy down his back, with twigs sticking out here and there. The wizard, for Talos certainly agreed that he looked like a wizard, had a tidy white mustache and beard, though his cheeks and neck showed days-old stubble.

When Talos approached and stood looking at him, the old man said nothing; he merely sat returning the elf's gaze with a sparkle of great mirth in his eye. After a tense minute of silence, both men spoke at precisely the same moment.

"What business have you…?" Talos began to ask.

"You are the Jarl?" the wizard queried.

The Jarl's face grew stony and the wizard's smile grew wider. After a long moment, Talos confirmed, "I am the Jarl."

"Excellent!" replied the wizard, getting to his feet. "Let us find some privacy. We have much to discuss."

The old man moved past Talos and started down the path, but the scout jumped over and barred the way. Talos turned slowly to regard the old man, his visage hinting at irritation. "You presume to be welcomed as a guest after trespassing on our lands?" he asked.

"You presume to own the forest simply because you reside here?" the wizard retorted. He turned slowly and laboriously to regard the elf, though his eyes still twinkled. "That is not the way of the Elves, as I remember them."

The Jarl frowned. "Change spawned through necessity can be harsh," Talos answered as he moved to join the wizard on the path, "and unwanted."

"Travel spawned through necessity can be harsh, as well," chuckled the wizard, "and equally unwanted. Yet here we are."

"Indeed," Talos answered. He stood appraising the old man for a few more seconds and then said, "Very well, follow me and we shall speak."

Seated in a small study in the back of Talos Daelin's home, the elf and the wizard sipped tea and quietly gathered their thoughts.

"I appreciate your hospitality," the old man said softly.

"Though the circumstances are unusual, certain customs must still be observed," answered the Jarl.

"The tea is very good," the wizard continued, "I don't believe I have ever tasted anything like it."

"I should think not," Talos smiled slightly. "It is made from berries, herbs and roots that are found only in this forest."

"And what effect will it have on me?" the wizard asked wryly. "Other than on my taste buds, that is."

The slightest flicker of surprise flashed over the Jarl's face. This man showed some nerve to accuse him, but the man also possessed great knowledge and insight, for the accusation was correct. "It opens the mind and loosens the tongue, thus encouraging useful discourse," he answered.

The old man laughed heartily, trembling so much that he nearly dropped his staff. Talos looked at him incredulously. He had not spoken directly with a human in such a long time that he wondered if they had all gone mad. At last the old man's laughter ebbed and, wiping a tear from his eye, he said, "We are not so different, you know, your race and mine. We each have our suspicions and misgivings, and yours are well founded. Let us get on with our discussion then, so that I might put yours to rest." The old man put down his teacup and leaned forward on his staff. "I am Arcanis Rhu," he said with a wide smile, "and I have come a long way to speak with you, good Jarl of Westwick."

"Arcanis Rhu?" whispered Talos Daelin. "I know that name. Were you not the favored mage of King Andred de la Ponce?"

"And several of his heirs after him," replied the wizard.

"So you must be…"

"Very old, yes," Arcanis confirmed, "by the standards of humans. And yet I am but a child in your eyes, I am sure."

"These are strange days, indeed," Talos marveled. "What brings you to Westwick?"

Arcanis Rhu sat back in his chair and heaved a great sigh. He looked truly weary as he took a deep breath and began his tale. "After my service to the royal family ended, oh I guess it must be around twelve hundred years ago now, I went into business for myself. I was at the peak of my power, you see, and I wanted to travel the wide world. And that is what I did. I wandered far and the tales of those days are so many and fantastic that I sometimes wonder if they are true or merely the confused fabrications of an aging mind." The wizard smiled inwardly as his memory soared back over the years of his life. "Regardless," he continued, "I have been retired for over three hundred years now, living in quiet solitude and trying to hold onto my powers." He winced and tried to straighten his bent back. "Recently, though, it is such a struggle just to retain some clarity of mind and continue to draw breath."

Again the wizard paused. It seemed he needed to regain some strength before he went on, for he closed his eyes and appeared to meditate for awhile. When at last he opened his eyes and focused them on the Jarl, they were much clearer and very deep, like the sharp, bare peaks of mountains whose roots ran to the foundations of the earth. "As you can see," the wizard spoke evenly as those deep eyes narrowed on the Jarl, "I have ended my retirement and sought you out, and it is no small matter that brings me."

Suddenly Talos knew why the wizard was here. He leaned forward earnestly as Arcanis Rhu continued. "I was there, Talos Daelin. I was there when Brother Constantine returned from the Haunted Isle and I watched as every one of his fellow travelers perished from the mysterious illness. It was I who counseled the King in his angst when Constantine also took ill and locked himself away in his chambers. A week passed, during which time we heard deranged ranting and rambling, singing and chanting coming from within. Then it ended. Two days passed and we heard nothing. It fell to me to enter Constantine's chambers and confirm what we already knew. The man was dead. But beside his emaciated corpse I found something incredible. The Scrolls, Talos Daelin. *I* found them. *I* was the first to read them. I know their meaning, perhaps better than anyone, and the time of their destiny has come. The Prophecy is at hand, my good Jarl. The time has come for your people to end their seclusion and fulfill their role as foreseen and written in the Sacred Scrolls."

Talos Daelin suddenly realized that he was sweating. He sat back in his chair and frowned, "My spies in Pilas Antum tell me that the Scrolls are missing."

"What?" the wizard asked in alarm. "I had not heard that. As I have said, my retirement left me in seclusion." He closed his eyes and rubbed his temples. "This is dire news indeed. The Scrolls are vital to the fulfillment of the Prophecy. Kendrid the Red's avatar, the body into whom his spirit has been reborn, cannot know the truth of his soul. To his mind, he is but an ordinary person and, in fact, an ordinary boy he is. But his soul is corrupted. If the resurrection ritual is performed upon his flesh, a ritual only the Scrolls can reveal and only when they have been bathed in the avatar's blood, then the poor boy's soul will be ripped asunder and Kendrid the Red will return."

"Why were they not destroyed years ago, if they held the power to return such evil to the land?" asked the Jarl.

The wizard was a long time in answering. A shadow seemed to pass over him before he spoke, "I tried to have them destroyed, but the King feared that destroying the Scrolls before the birth of the avatar would free Kendrid's spirit to return in some other way. King de la Ponce believed that if Kendrid's spirit were bound to both the Scrolls *and* an avatar whose birth could be known when the foretold events unfolded, then we would have a much greater chance of countering the Prophecy and destroying Kendrid the Red forever."

A long silence ensued. All that could be heard was the chirruping of birds and the wind in the trees. Finally, the wizard looked up from his thoughts and peered darkly at the Jarl. "They must be found," he said. "We *must* find the Scrolls and place them in safe keeping."

"I have concluded as much," Talos agreed, "and I have taken action to that end. My position as Jarl is threatened. I cannot promise the support of my people. In fact, there are few I can still trust. Thus, I have sent my daughter to Pilas Antum to investigate. She has found no information whatsoever as to the whereabouts of Kendrid's avatar, for surely the boy has been born and is walking Coleraine as we speak. He should be about fifteen or sixteen by now if his birth preceded the drought, as we suspect." The wizard nodded in silence and the Jarl continued. "As for the disappearance of the Scrolls, my daughter reports that she believes the Countess of Westbury is involved. Her power in Pilas Antum is unrivaled, and if anyone has the ability to breach the security of Citadel Adbar, she is the one."

The Jarl paused briefly to allow the wizard to comment. Arcanis was still sitting with his fingers to his temples. He muttered a soft 'hmm' and Talos continued.

"My daughter, Aurora, has infiltrated Tavora Manor in the guise of the Royal Guard. She reports to me through our spy network in the city, but I have not heard from her in weeks. I would worry for her safety if not for my faith in her abilities."

"She is prepared for the trials that may befall her?" The wizard asked.

"She is the daughter of the Jarl," Talos answered soberly. "She is as prepared as any elf could be, which I believe says a lot. And yet," the Jarl hesitated and looked troubled, "she is young and impetuous. She is very headstrong and brash. I fear she will need assistance in this matter before the end and I know not where she shall find it." He looked hard at the wizard. "She will need counsel, Arcanis. She could use your wisdom and knowledge of the Scrolls."

The wizard did not stir. He seemed to have returned to his meditative state. At last, he opened his eyes and addressed the Jarl,

"My knowledge runs deep, my friend, very deep. I have learned many things only to forget them and learn them again. But I am only a mortal man, and I am very old. It takes all of my strength to draw breath and sit here before you. I cannot wield my power as I once could; even small expenditures of magic drain me greatly. No," he shook his head; "I cannot be the force that drives us through these trials. I fear that if I were to join your daughter on this journey I would be more of a hindrance than an aid."

"There is no single power that can drive us through these trials, so fear not your own frailty," Talos answered. The Jarl stood and walked to the window, holding his hands behind his back while surveying the forest. "I had always thought," he said in a troubled voice, "that the role of the Elves in this tale would be in healing the humans of the plague that is foretold to be coming." He shook his head and his proud shoulders sagged. "But now I believe that my people will not have a role in the coming struggles, not collectively anyway."

Talos Daelin was silent for a long while, absorbed in his own tumultuous thoughts. At last he turned back at the old wizard. "Do you know how Elves receive their names, Arcanis?" The wizard shook his head and sat patiently as the Jarl turned back to the window. "Every elf has a personal magic that is unique. Some are gifted smiths who can imbue enchantments into their works. Some have speed of movement, even by the standards of elves." The Jarl turned from the window and returned to his seat in the blink of an eye. The wizard smiled indulgently. "It is believed that the magic we are given reflects the nature of our soul," Talos continued. "My daughter came into the world shining like a thousand suns." Talos's voice quavered and he put his face into his hands. "She is the purest soul I have ever known, and now I have thrust her into this." The Jarl wiped his eyes and looked back at the wizard. He appeared almost desperate as he continued speaking. "Help my daughter, Arcanis, I beseech you. Find her and be her sage."

The shoulders of the old man seemed to sag under a great weight as the duty was laid upon him. When he answered, he looked very old and tired and his voice cracked, "My powers are waning, Jarl Talos Daelin, as I have said." He closed his eyes briefly and took several deep breaths. When he opened his eyes and continued, he sat taller and his voice no longer faltered. "But I have enough strength left in me for one good fight. If it is to come, then it will be at your daughter's side. She will have my counsel and she will have my aid, and when the time comes, if it should prove necessary, she will have my life."

Chapter Eight

~ Respite Lost ~

"Forgive me, but I must stop for a rest," Alishane Wyndam grunted through gritted teeth.

"Your pain has worsened?" Aurora asked as she helped the man to sit.

Alishane nodded. "My healing skills stemmed the flow of blood and will heal me in time, but the wound was grievous."

"I heard you were being schooled at Rue Mortelei," Aurora said as she searched through the little pack she carried at the small of her back. "Cleric is a noble calling."

"Speak not of nobility," Alishane wheezed as he struggled to sit. "It is a curse I tried in vain to avoid, and it doomed my father to a terrible death."

"Your father represented all that is right and decent in nobility," Dunk Worley said sharply as he moved closer.

Alishane kept his eyes on the ground and his voice measured and controlled as he addressed the servant, "You served my father faithfully, Dunk, and he loved you. But do not lecture me on the man's qualities, for no one knew them better than me."

"We can all see that you're grieving, Master Wyndam," Timmen now joined the conversation, "but this is not the time to dwell on the past, or to remind a servant of his place." The thief looked quickly around the dark alleyway. "We must get off the streets."

"The halfling is right," Aurora said. "We have decisions to make and much to discuss, but we cannot do it here." She pulled a strange-looking leaf wrapped tightly around an unknown object from her pouch and handed it to Alishane. He looked at her inquisitively and she answered, "Belithia root, or what you might know as Thorn's Bane. It will ease the pain. Chew it slightly and then tuck it between your cheek and gums."

The cleric nodded. "I'm familiar with the root, though not with this leaf."

Aurora smiled. "The leaf is native to my home." She closed her pouch and fastened it to her back, then turned to Timmen. "Do you know the city? Have you anyplace we can hide?"

"I've been leading us toward the Wyvern's Tail Inn. I know it well and it is deserted during the Council and Tournament," answered the halfling.

"And you can get us in?" Aurora asked. Timmen shot her a look of indignant disgust. The elf gave an elegant laugh. "That's good enough for me, master thief. Lead the way."

The Countess and the Shadow Wolf sat in silence at her desk, waiting for the servants to finish scrubbing the floor where Lady Curry's blood had pooled. When they were at last alone, he turned to her and waited for her to speak.

"Tell me of the escape," she said.

"I entered the room and listened to a bit of their talk," Rinn began. "Alishane Wyndam was preparing to leave and go back to their estate to rally support. I disposed of the elder Wyndam with ease and was making sport of his son when I encountered... interference."

The Countess raised a thin eyebrow in concern. "Interference of what kind?" she asked.

"An elf," the Shadow Wolf answered. He found it strangely satisfying to see the look of utter shock register on the woman's face.

"Surely you were mistaken," she gasped.

"I fought hand-to-hand with her, Highness. Trust me when I say that I got a good look." Rinn's eyes got a faraway and somewhat wistful countenance as he continued, "Never have I encountered my equal with a blade. And she played me like a cat with a mouse."

He looked back at the Countess to find her smiling wickedly. "You have great affection for this elf-woman," she observed. The Shadow Wolf's eyes narrowed, but he said nothing. "Ever has your heart leaned toward women of power and consequence."

"My interest in her is that she is an enemy and a hindrance to our plans, nothing more," Rinn spat with more emotion than he had intended.

"Your interest in her will be whatever interest I instruct you to take, Zakarus. Do not mistake the woman with whom the true power lies." The Countess's eyes flashed, but her voice was ice cold. The two stared at each other for a long moment before she continued, "So she defeated you."

"She kept me occupied," Rinn corrected, "while a halfling came in to spirit away the servant and young Wyndam."

The Countess pursed her lips in thought. "A strange alliance," she concluded. After a moment of reflection, she pointed at the assassin's forearms and inquired, "Did you use the gauntlets?"

"No," the Wolf answered, "I did not have a chance. She blinded me with some form of Elvish magic and then was gone."

"And you didn't pursue?" the Countess asked. The Shadow Wolf did not answer. "Well," the woman concluded, "in any event, do not use the gauntlets until you have no other choice. That side of your nature must remain secret."

The assassin glared at the Countess before giving a quick nod of consent and then he changed the subject. "The halfling is known to me. He is a thief who works the Wyvern's Tail. I caught him pilfering the jeweled dagger that was taken from the *Wind Runner*."

"Do you think he will return to the Tail?" the Countess asked.

"It is closed for the duration of the Tournament; the owner has set up a tent outside the grounds." Rinn considered for a moment. "I believe the halfling would make for the Tail, yes, but if the elf knows the city then there is no telling where they might go."

"How could there be elves in this city without our operatives reporting it?" the Countess asked rhetorically.

"It is more than that, Highness," Rinn said, shaking the Countess from her thoughts. "The elf was dressed in the raiment of the Royal Guard."

The Countess stood from her chair and turned behind her, ripping open the curtains and looking out at the courtyard of the manor. "In my home!" she stormed. She turned back on the Shadow Wolf with a savage look in her eye. "I have built this empire by *always* knowing more than my opponents. And now this, under my very nose," She looked frantic, almost desperate. "We must find them, Zakarus! You must find them for me!"

Rinn gave his customary small bow. "I am at your service, as always, Highness," he said.

The woman was pacified. She returned to her seat and sat thinking for awhile, looking at the faint bloodstain that remained on her office floor. "I must get a rug," she said absently. Zakarus Rinn sat patiently, waiting for her to collect her thoughts. At last, she reached a conclusion and looked back at the assassin. "We must take further action to ensure that Alishane Wyndam remains an outlaw. Do not conceal the fact that he has escaped. On the contrary, make it widely known. Go at once to the quarters of Lord Fence Winningham. You will find no guards as the Lord considers himself safe here in my care. Kill him. And do so in clumsy fashion so that it does not look like the work of a professional, but rather the act of a vengeful and desperate Alishane Wyndam."

The Shadow Wolf nodded slowly. He knew that the nobleman had left his dagger behind when he had fled from Lord Wyndam's room. "I will frame him adequately," the assassin promised.

"Good," replied the Countess. "Then to the trail of the elf and halfling." She picked up her quill and began writing on a roll of parchment. "You are dismissed," she said without looking up. "And send for Lord Finneran on your way out. I desire a word with him."

Zakarus Rinn rose and left the office. As he descended the spiral staircase his mind told him that he needed to sleep, but his body did not feel tired. He was invigorated by the thought of hunting the beautiful elf. He smiled wryly to himself. *The Countess was right,* he thought, *I am drawn to powerful women.*

The elf, the halfling, the nobleman and the servant sat quietly to one side of the large central fireplace in the meeting hall of the Wyvern's Tail Inn. They had started a fire for light and warmth and to cook the food they scrounged from the cellar, but upon instructions from the elf they kept the blaze small enough so as not to emit noticeable smoke from the chimney. They each sat chewing their food in silent thought. The elf had pulled her gleaming white hair back and tied it in a loose knot; her fair face was pale in the feeble light. The halfling wore a deep scowl upon his face; a coin danced back and forth across his knuckles. The nobleman was in obvious pain, both physical and emotional. For all of it, he stole occasional peeks at the elf sitting next to him. The servant was the sorriest by far, having lapsed into muffled sobs that made his shoulders quake.

Aurora Daelin was the first to break the silence. "Now we must speak," she said. "Though we each have a tale leading us to this meeting, it would be most prudent to discuss only those parts of our past that will impact our future." She looked around the motley group and only the nobleman met her gaze. "For my part I will say only that my people are not extinct, but we are in hiding. We have a network of spies throughout Coleraine who have reported disturbing events and I have been sent to gather information firsthand. I went first to Citadel Adbar where I confirmed that the Sacred Scrolls have gone missing. Nobody seems to know what happened, but the Brotherhood of Callamore is preparing an Inquisition." She paused and the nobleman's eyes widened. The halfling looked up in surprise. The servant took no notice and continued to sob. "I have no direct evidence to suggest that the Countess is responsible for the disappearance of the Scrolls," the elf continued, "but her guild of thieves and extortionists is the dominant criminal presence in the area and I find it unlikely that she is not involved."

A long moment of silence passed. The halfling scowled and looked back into the fire; the nobleman stared at the elf; the servant sniffled and wiped his eyes.

At last, with his eyes still narrowed into the blaze, the halfling spoke. "What do you know of a vessel named the *Wind Runner*?" Timmen asked.

"Nothing," the elf answered simply. She waited for the halfling to volunteer more information, but his scowl only deepened and he chewed on his lip. Finally the elf prompted, "Why do you ask?"

Timmen looked up and met Aurora's gaze, "I stole a jeweled dagger from three of her crew. The Shadow Wolf came upon me in their room and took it from me; that's when he gave me this," the thief motioned to his chin. The scab from the assassin's cut was beginning to break apart, revealing a fleshy pink scar that showed clearly on the halfling's soft and boyish face. "I entered Tavora Manor intent on either recovering the dagger or stealing something else of value. I followed the Shadow Wolf to your door, sir," he looked at Alishane Wyndam, "and the rest I believe you know." The nobleman nodded once and looked over at his servant, who had resumed sobbing at mention of the events in the Wyndams' room. "I do not know the extent or duration of our association, miss," the halfling continued as he turned back to Aurora, "but it would seem that at the moment we are working with common purpose. We've acquired the same enemies, and they are very powerful."

"Powerful indeed," Aurora answered. She closed her eyes and thought for a moment before continuing. "It seems clear that the Shadow Wolf had been sent to recover the dagger from the sailors. The Countess must have used it as payment for the *Wind Runner's* service, which was likely some form of smuggling, and the sailors stole it from the ship's hold." The elf's eyes were still closed and she again paused in thought before she continued. When she opened them, her eyes flashed with resolve and she got to her feet. "This may not have anything to do with the Scrolls, but for now it is our only lead." She had shed the leather armor of the Royal Guard and now pulled a dark green cape about her. "I am going to make contact with our spies here in the city. I must send word to my Jarl of what has happened and learn what I can about the *Wind Runner*. You all should remain here for the night," she looked over at Alishane Wyndam's pale and drawn face, "it looks as though you could use the rest." Alishane nodded and tried a feeble smile, which the elf did not return. "Stay together and set a watch. I will return before dawn." She buckled her sword belt and pack into place and turned to leave. As an afterthought, she added, "If you are discovered or anything should happen, make for the stable at the western end of town. I will find you from there."

Slipping through a window and out into the night, the elf quickly found the shadows and disappeared. But her passage did not go unnoticed. Two eyes blinked in the darkness of an overhanging loft. The Shadow Wolf waited until he knew she was gone and then moved quickly and silently to the open window.

* * * * * * *

Alishane Wyndam added a log to the coals of the fire and then stoked them to kindle the new wood. He huddled close to the pit with his left side to the flames to try to ease the stiffness in his wounded shoulder. Looking around the room, he found his servant Dunk asleep on the floor. The halfling was keeping watch and sat with his back to the fire pit. Timmen nodded to him briefly and then looked away into the dark recesses of the hall. It was an hour since the elf's departure and she had not returned.

Yawning, the cleric shook the sleep from his eyes and found that he had recovered enough strength during his brief rest to perform another healing spell on his wound. He placed his right hand on a stone inside the fire pit to warm his palm and fingers, then he closed his eyes and fell into a state of calm and focused concentration. When his hand was hot almost to the point of burning, he reached inside his cloak and tunic and put his thumb upon the puckered and tender flesh of the entry wound. Reaching under his arm, the cleric placed his middle finger on the exit wound.

The words of the spell swam in his subconscious until he found the core of his energy and placed the words at its base. Having been taught at Rue Mortelei that the core of his being was conical, the cleric sent the words of the spell swirling about its base until their spin reached such a speed and intensity that they started to rise inexorably up the cone toward its pinnacle. The spinning words picked up more and more speed and power as they rose. Alishane's lips began to move to form the words over and over and his core began to vibrate. When the words reached the very tip of his power, the cleric squeezed his right hand upon his wounds and voiced the spell aloud. *"Anno bueneth serra alleverace!"* White-hot energy flowed through his fingers and he felt a jolt run between them along the channel the blade had cleaved in his flesh. His body jerked and his right hand was thrown from its grip upon his shoulder. Having poured every ounce of his energy into the spell, Alishane slumped to the floor, utterly spent.

Dunk Worley awoke with a start when his lord voiced the spell and its energy crackled through the room. He looked up just in time to see Alishane slump to the floor and grope confusedly at the side of the fire pit. Dunk sprang to his feet and rushed to Alishane's side, supporting him and helping him to sit comfortably.

"Your power has grown considerably since last I saw you," Dunk said shyly. He kept his eyes down to the floor as he spoke.

"It does seem like a long time ago," Alishane answered wearily.

The porter straightened his lord's clothes, which had become disheveled during the spell, and retrieved some meat from their stores. "Here, my lord. You must eat and recover your strength," he said.

Alishane took the food but did not eat. He turned it over in his hands and frowned as he said, "Do not call me 'lord', Dunk. You were my father's porter, not mine."

The servant looked up in surprise. "But the title of Lord has passed to you, my lord… I mean, Master Wyndam. I am bound to you as I was bound to your father."

"I do not accept your fealty!" Alishane said loudly and threw the meat across the room. Timmen cleared his throat and shot a dark look at the cleric. Alishane lowered his voice and whispered hotly, "I have told you, Dunk. I do not desire lordship and I will not have servants attending to my needs."

Dunk felt as though he had been slapped in the face. Having watched helplessly as his beloved lord was murdered and being unable to stop it was bad enough. Now his new lord was rejecting his service and loyalty. Through a tight throat, Dunk choked, "What am I to do, then?"

"Do not ask me that!" Alishane spat tersely, struggling to keep his voice low. "Make your own decisions; live your own life. I am not your keeper and I am *not* your lord."

Dunk felt his lip tremble and he took a moment to compose himself before he spoke. "You would send me away, then?" he asked.

Alishane looked up at the porter and the answer was clear upon his face, but before he could voice it he saw a flicker of movement in the background.

Timmen saw it at the same moment and sprang to his feet. "Run!" he yelled and darted past the others. "Flee if you value your life!"

The cleric and porter got to their feet and followed after the halfling. They ran through the meeting hall, dodging between the tables with chairs. Timmen had already vanished from sight, but from a dark hallway ahead they heard him whisper urgently, "This way!"

The two men scrambled up some stairs and groped along in the dark. Behind them they heard a silky laugh that made their blood turn cold.

"Run," chuckled the Shadow Wolf. "Run and hide, little rats, for the Wolf is coming to hunt you."

Alishane and Dunk reached the end of the hallway and looked frantically about for somewhere to go. Just as they heard the Shadow Wolf's steps upon the stairs, they were grabbed and pulled into a dark room. Timmen eased the door closed and then crossed the room and opened the curtains. Soft starlight filtered through the window and illuminated his face as the two men crossed the room to join him.

"It's my fault," he said desperately. "I should not have brought us here."

"How do we get out?" Alishane asked.

Timmen was too distressed to answer immediately and in the void they heard the Shadow Wolf close a door down the hall and continue to walk toward them. "One room down and three to look," he called out, "there's no escape for Timmy the Crook." Again the assassin issued his silky laugh and they heard him open the door to the second of the hallway's four rooms.

The little thief was shaking horribly and his eyes were fixed on the door to the hall. "He's coming for me," he squeaked. The cleric put his hand upon Timmen's shoulder and the halfling looked up, "It's my fault," he said again. "He saw me in the Manor and knew I would hide here. This is all my fault."

"Timmen!" Alishane whispered urgently and shook the thief by the shoulders. "How do we get out?"

Timmen looked back to the window and said, "We can drop to the roof of the cellar from this window, but we must be quiet in opening it."

The door to the second room closed and the footsteps resumed down the hall. Again that wretched laugh. "Two rooms down and still you hide. A disgrace to your father who has recently died."

Alishane Wyndam tensed and turned to the door. His vision narrowed and his head was pounding with anger. He closed his eyes and tried to regain his composure, but all he saw was his father's death: the knife in his throat, the crimson flow, the last stricken look before he slumped to the floor. Alishane clenched his fists in rage, but they were closed upon nothing but air. He had no weapon. He would not get his revenge this night. He turned to the window and tried to open it as the Shadow Wolf opened the third door. They heard him walking through the room right next to their own.

Alishane tried again to open the window. It would not budge.

"It's stuck!" Timmen whispered desperately as he too struggled to open it.

The door to the third room closed and the Shadow Wolf laughed again. His voice had an air of victory as he spoke. "Now the rats are caught in a trap of their own design. The Wolf will have his sport and I shall have mine." His footsteps approached the door and they heard him try the handle, but they had locked it behind them. Alishane picked up a chair and heaved it toward the window. The glass exploded at the same moment that the assassin kicked in the door and entered the room. Timmen fled through the window, but Alishane and Dunk stood facing the Shadow Wolf.

"You cannot both make it through the window before my blade finds your back," the assassin sneered. "Will you flee, cleric, and bring final shame upon your house?" Again Alishane tensed, but none of the three men moved. Outside on the cellar roof, Timmen looked helplessly up at the empty window. "Your father's body remains in our possession, of course," the assassin continued. "If you turn and run, I will defile his corpse in ways you cannot possibly imagine."

Alishane's anger finally overcame him. He took a step forward, a swell of rage driving him, but the demonic howl that filled his ears did not come from his own mouth. Dunk Worley surged past the stunned Alishane Wyndam and threw himself upon the Shadow Wolf. The assassin had raised his blade in defense, but even as the steel pierced his body and ran him through, the servant rained blows into his murderer's face.

Alishane felt tears well in his eyes as he watched the death of the only man whose love for his father had rivaled his own. Again he started forward, thinking of nothing more than pummeling the assassin with his bare fists, but Dunk turned and with his last breath he said, "No, my lord! You must live to avenge your fa..." His words were cut off as the Shadow Wolf twisted his blade and jerked it upward, ripping it through the servant's body. Dunk's face contorted in pain and, unable to find breath to speak, he mouthed the words, "My lord...?"

Through the hot tears that were now streaming down his face, Alishane honored Dunk's sacrifice and turned and fled through the window. It took several moments for the assassin to shed himself of the servant's weight and dislodge his sword from Dunk's body. By the time the Shadow Wolf approached the window, all he saw was a fleeting glimpse of the halfling and the cleric as they turned a corner down the lane and disappeared into the night. Using the curtains of the window, the assassin wiped the blood from his blade and then he turned and strode from the room. He would find some sleep and then resume the hunt, he decided and smiled darkly. The hunt, after all, is what the hunter lives for.

__Chapter Nine__

~ The Vicious Cycle Turns ~

Aurora Daelin slipped into the shadows below a staircase on the outside of a decrepit old building off the docks. After looking all around her to insure she was not being watched, she took a small dagger from her boot and inserted the blade into a knot in the wooden wall of the ramshackle building. The blade slid in easily and she heard a 'click' from inside. She walked to the door and opened it and then stepped into the dank interior of the shack. Before her eyes could adjust to the dark, there was a rustle of sound and a croaking voice addressed her.

"What is an elf doing down on the docks at this hour of the night?" the voice asked.

"Perhaps I have come to rob you, old man," Aurora responded.

The warped floorboards of the old shack groaned as the man approached. "Then ye are a thief and a villain," he said. He was standing directly in front of her now; she could feel his sour breath upon her face. "And that would make ye no different from any other elvin scoundrel I've ever known."

"My father should have let you die in the road those many years ago," Aurora said.

There was a moment of silence as the elf's bright eyes bored into the old man's milky orbs. Then the old man threw back his head and laughed riotously. "Damn good to see ye, lass!" he roared as he put his hands upon her shoulders and pulled her into a rough bear hug.

"It is good to see you too, Ivan," Aurora choked and flashed a self-conscious smile.

"Sit down, sit down," he ushered her into a chair. "What brings ye by at this time o' night?"

"Don't pretend that I disturbed you, Ivan. We both know the hours you keep."

"Wouldn't be much use to ye otherwise, would I?" the old man asked.

Aurora laughed. "To business then," she said. "What do you know of a vessel named the *Wind Runner*?"

"Hmm... the *Wind Runner*, eh? She's a two-masted frigate with two big guns on her deck. She carries no armor so she's very light, and those guns are on rails so they slide down into a turn to help her catch the wind. The rails also absorb the recoil when the guns are fired." Ivan poured a draught of a smoking, acidic-smelling brew into a glass. He offered some to the elf, but she declined and he resumed speaking. "The *Runner* lives up to her name, as she can outrun pretty much anything out there, but if she turns and fights, any vessel that gets in the way of those guns will find itself on the bottom of the Andaluric in a big hurry. Why do you ask, Aurora?"

"I think she may have been commissioned by the Countess of Westbury to carry something of great importance."

"That wouldn't surprise me. The Countess has done business with Captain Eustacio in the past."

"Tell me of this Captain Eustacio," Aurora requested.

"Eustacio is a sea dog through and through. He don't care a squat for the politics of the Countess, but he'll do business with her because her pay is so good." Ivan spat a long stream of calambra root juice into an earthen jug near the table. Aurora looked with disgust at the jug; when she looked back at the old man, he gave her a crooked and root-stained smile.

Aurora smiled slightly and asked, "If Captain Eustacio's motives are monetary, do you think he would betray the Countess for a greater payoff?"

The old man thought for a moment and then answered, "I doubt it. That would mean that he can't do business with her anymore and he would have her for an enemy. Eustacio's too smart for that." A pause ensued while Aurora absorbed the information. Then Ivan made a connection, "The Captain was looking hard for three of his crew about a week back. Rumor had it they stole something off the ship. You thinkin' they stole the Countess's cargo?"

"That's what I'm trying to find out," Aurora answered. "Is there any way to learn what the *Runner* was carrying and for what payment, or what the destination was?"

"I don't dig too deep into the affairs of the Countess, lass. If you're smart, you won't either," Ivan answered.

Aurora gave the old man her most imploring look. "It is important, Ivan. My father sent me to personally look into this matter." She smiled sweetly and took the man's hand in her own. "I do not ask you to put yourself in harm's way, just point me in the right direction."

Ivan pulled his hand roughly from her grasp and got up to pace around the room. "Don't be givin' me those lovey eyes, you little minx!" the man stormed. "Ye don't need to endear yourself to me any more than ye already have." Ivan walked back to Aurora and knelt in front of her, putting his hands on her shoulders and shaking her slightly to accentuate his words. "Don't ye see? I don't want ye involved with those people. They're vicious, Aurora. And I wouldn't be repaying your father for saving my life if I sent ye anywhere near them."

Aurora smiled and put her hand gently upon the grizzled man's leathery face. "Ivan, you flatter me with your concern," she said, "but you need not worry. I am not underestimating them and I am being very careful. But I must know more about this business; it is of the utmost importance."

The old man hesitated, but he knew that he could not resist her. Still, he looked very troubled as he spoke, "You should go talk to Regent Darius Zannick at the university. Nobody knows for sure, but some believe that Zannick is the head of a thieves' guild called the Crystal Night. Why they're called that, I don't know, but…"

"The Crystal Night?" Aurora broke in. "I thought they were merely legend. The subject of tales that villains tell their children to scare them in the night, 'You better be good or the Crystal Night will come and take you away.'"

"Oh, they are very real, lass, and even the most villainous would do well to be scared of 'em. No one knows how many there are or anything about them." Ivan shivered in the darkness as he continued, "I can't tell you for sure that the Regent is their man or that he can help you, but rumors are starting to circle that he's ready to make a move against the Countess. He's letting people talk about him, and that means he's no longer scared. It's only a matter of time before the Countess hears of it. And then…"

"Yes," Aurora agreed. "There is going to be a war."

Alishane and Timmen ran from one alleyway to the next, darting in and out of shadows and zigzagging in different directions, but gradually making their way to the west end of the city. They came to a crossing of larger roads in the middle of town and scurried across it, feeling very vulnerable and expecting the Shadow Wolf to be hot on their trail. After crossing the large road they noticed a difference in the stature of the neighborhood. This end of Pilas Antum, being away from the coast and the docks and the industrial part of the city, was the more affluent part of town. The cobbling in the streets was even and the lamps more regularly spaced. The houses were large and some even had well-tended gardens. There were no back alleys in this part of town and so many lamps that skulking about was no longer possible, so the cleric and the halfling broke into a dead run. They covered a great distance before they stopped to catch their breath.

"What do you think we should do once we reach the stable?" Alishane panted.

They had taken shelter in a large garden behind a house and Timmen ate pilfered strawberries as he pondered the question. "I think we should get a horse and leave the city, avoiding the main road," he answered through a mouthful of berries. "The elf said she would find us from the stable, not at it, so I think she means to track us."

"The assassin will track us also," Alishane said bitterly as he too picked a handful of the fruit.

"Let us hope the elf finds us first," Timmen responded.

The cleric nodded and then let his head fall down to his chest. He was suddenly overcome with grief for his father and his faithful servant Dunk. He was still in shock over the tremendous losses he had suffered and he was aware only of a growing emptiness within him. He felt a great sob swell in his chest and wrack his body.

Timmen watched and felt sorry for the man. Pity was not an emotion he was used to and it made him uncomfortable. "What happened in the room?" he asked softly.

Alishane took a moment to compose himself before answering. He was proud and did not want his voice to waver. At last he looked up at the halfling and his face was calm, though his cheeks were wet with tears. "Dunk threw himself on the assassin's sword to give me time to escape," he answered. His lip trembled and indeed his voice faltered as he continued, "My last words to him were so hateful and bitter." The man's voice cracked. "I turned him away. He was so loyal and loved my father so much, and I turned him away in the hour of his grief." He hung his head and covered his face with his hands.

Timmen looked away so as not to embarrass the man by watching him cry. At last the halfling spoke in a consoling tone.

"We have much to avenge," he said and put his hand upon the cleric's shoulder. When Alishane looked up, Timmen continued, "And we shall have our revenge. We are part of a larger story now. We have been swept up in it and who knows where it will carry us. But we will not forget the personal loss. We will hold these people accountable for the pain they have caused, and we will revisit it upon them tenfold."

Alishane's face was dark. "I am supposed to be a holy man," he said through gritted teeth. "I swore an oath to follow a righteous path and I'm not supposed to feel such hatred and bloodlust." He looked to the east, where the first hints of pale blue told of the coming of day. "But I swear now in the waning moments of the night of my father's murder," he looked back at the halfling with a savage look in his eye, "before my life is spent I will have the Shadow Wolf's blood upon my hands."

Lord Garrett Finneran sat in the great meeting hall of Tavora Manor in the same seat he had occupied during the first meeting of the Council of the Eastern Province. The mood in the hall was very different today than it had been the day before. After all, much had happened in the night. After the public denouncement of Thrain Wyndam ended the first meeting and he was placed under arrest, many of the nobles in attendance retired to the several salons in the Manor to discuss what had happened and how they should proceed. Then the morning brought word of the battle in the

Wyndams' room, the death of Lord Wyndam and the escape of his son and, most startling of all, the murder of Lord Fence Winningham by the desperate and angry Alishane Wyndam.

Finneran had met with the Countess and knew the true manner in which Lord Winningham had died, but he was the only one in the room who knew the truth. As he now surveyed the gathered nobility, he saw uncertainty bordering on hysteria on their faces. This was his opportunity. Just as the Countess had promised, Garrett Finneran would be representing the Eastern Province at the Council of the Kingdom.

The hushed mutterings in the hall fell to silence when the Countess entered. She stood just inside the doorway and looked every person in the eyes. From one face to the next she glared at them, her gaze boring through their false bravado, their feigned adoration, their façade of calm. Before she swept up her gown and walked to her seat, everyone in the room felt secure in one unshakable truth: this was her meeting hall, it was her Manor in her city, she was the ruler of the Eastern Province and soon she would control the whole of the kingdom.

The Countess took her seat and waited. There were no prepared speeches or orchestrated arguments today; she knew they were not needed. She and her subjects sat perfectly still, waiting for one of Lord Wyndam's former allies to make the only move left to them.

After only a few moments had passed, Lord Danshing rose to his feet and cleared his throat. "My fellow lords and ladies," he began, "I believe I can adequately reflect the common sentiment by saying that I am shocked by what has transpired of late." The old nobleman paused and looked around the room. He was answered with nods of agreement. "You all know me," he continued. "I am an old and pious man. My service to the church and to the kingdom has been well documented. Perhaps it was my single-minded devotion to righteousness that left me blinded to the depths of depravity that lay festering among us." Again the old man paused and he looked truly pained. He glanced over at the empty seats where Lord and Master Wyndam had sat the previous day. "In any event, we all share the blame for our oversight and the burden of rectifying past misdeeds. Therefore, I urge us to put aside our petty differences and individual aspirations so that we might select a delegate to the Council of the Kingdom whose ties to politics and intrigue are minimal." Danshing looked over the crowd once more. "Lords and ladies," he concluded, "I nominate Lord Garrett Finneran."

As Lord Danshing took his seat and the eyes of the assembly turned from the aged man to the young lord from Anderton, Garrett Finneran found it more difficult than he had expected to hide his smile and wear a look of pleasant surprise.

Almost immediately, all heads in the hall turned to the Countess to see her reaction. She sat rigidly in her ornate chair and gave no clue as to her feelings. When at last she spoke, her voice carried an almost apologetic tone. "The events of last night left no one unscathed. My friend Lord Winningham died a terrible death at the hands of the renegade Alishane Wyndam. I feel personally responsible for his loss and I will be paying recompense to his family and sending a garrison of Guardsmen to maintain order in his lands until his son is old enough to assume control."

A murmur went through the assembly, the general nature of which was "She'll be taking control of his lands!"

The Countess waited for the muttering to die down and then she continued, "Lord Danshing spoke wisely when he urged us to put aside our differences and select a delegate whose reputation is not marred by rumor and insinuation, both of which seem to be linked inextricably to myself. Therefore, it is with a heart yearning for reconciliation and an eye toward a peaceable future that I second the nomination of Lord Garrett Finneran."

A gasp went up from the assembly. Lord Finneran was a supporter of Thrain Wyndam and had been openly contentious with the Countess the day before, but now she was supporting his nomination as the delegate from the Eastern Province to the Council of the Kingdom. This newfound agreement was very welcome, especially when contrasted to the deceit, intrigue and murder that had exploded of late and had been expected to continue. It seemed as though a huge weight had been lifted from the shoulders of every individual in the room. When Lord Finneran rose to his feet and his chair scraped upon the floor, every head turned toward him and a loud and raucous cheer erupted throughout the hall.

Finneran smiled widely and held up his hand to acknowledge the crowd and quiet the cheers. "My friends," he spoke above the dying clamor, "when I rode in from Anderton to attend this Council, it was not my intention to ride out of this city as our delegate at the Council of the Kingdom. I had hoped only to support Lord Wyndam, because I believed him to be an honest and worthy man. We have all of us been deceived, and we have all been wronged. I share in your shock and dismay at recent events, and I share in the guilt that you feel for allowing the misdeeds of one man to affect our province and the kingdom as a whole. As the rulers of this land, we bear the responsibility of maintaining the peace and preserving the highest quality of life for those under our charge. I have always strived to do that in Anderton, and now you look to me to do that for the kingdom of Coleraine. I am humbled by your faith, and I am driven to live up to it." Lord Finneran looked around the room at the people who were now his peers, but who would soon be nothing more than dust to be swept from his boots. He smiled, spread his arms out wide and said in a loud voice, "I accept your nomination as delegate for the Eastern Province."

"All those in favor?" the Countess's voice rang clearly through the hall.

"Aye!" the assembly voiced as one.

"Then it is decided," the Countess concluded. "Let us retire to our rooms or the salons for refreshment. Tea will be served in an hour." With that, the Countess of Westbury rose from her chair and left the hall, trailed by her long dress and several of her attendants. A buzz of excited chatter broke out behind her.

The Council of the Eastern Province had taken less than two days, and she had accomplished everything she desired. The woman frowned slightly as she climbed the stairs toward her office. It had almost been too easy. She thought Lord Wyndam would prove a worthier adversary. She was yet to learn the type of adversary his son would be.

Chapter Ten

~ Many Roads ~

Alishane and Timmen arrived at the stable shortly after dawn. The sun cut horizontally through an open door on the second level. Hay dust floated in the air and sparkled in the shaft of light. The elderly stableman heard their approach and raised his head from a stall halfway down one side of the barn. He had already been at his duties for a couple of hours so he was tired and in a surly mood. "Yeah?" he asked brusquely when the cleric and halfling walked into the dark interior of the barn.

"Let me handle this," Alishane whispered to Timmen.

"What if he recognizes you?" Timmen whispered back.

"Do you have enough money to buy the horse?"

"You handle this," the halfling replied with a quick nod.

Alishane approached the stableman casually; he raised both hands and waved slightly to show that he was unarmed and said, "Good morning."

"Morning it is, young man," the stableman replied, "but good or not I'll leave it to you if you'll leave me to my work."

Alishane stopped a few paces from the stall and turned to look at Timmen. The halfling shrugged and shook his head.

"We have no desire to inconvenience you, Mr..."

"Hobson," the man grunted.

"Well, it's a pleasure to meet you, Mr. Hobson," the cleric said and took a step closer. "My companion and I have need of a horse. Would any of these be for sale?"

"These five," the old man said, gesturing to the five animals on his side of the barn. He bent over and went back to his work of shoeing the horse in the stall.

Alishane walked the length of the barn, looking at each animal in great detail. Having been born into nobility, Alishane had been riding horses all his life. Though he didn't look after them directly, since there were servants for that, he still knew what qualities to look for in a horse and how to ensure its fitness for a particular task. To his estimation, all five of the animals for sale were comparable in breed, age and health. They were all large horses used more for labor than riding, but any of the five would suit their purpose.

"They seem to be quite similar. Are there any differences in price between them?" Alishane asked.

Hobson didn't look up from his work as he answered. "No. As you say, they're all the same."

"How much for a horse and gear?"

Now the stableman stood up. He looked at the cleric from head to foot, obviously assessing Alishane's wealth and deciding how much he could afford. The cleric's clothing was modest, as was usual for his profession, but was made of high-quality cloth and was cut to fit. "One hundred omani," demanded Hobson.

Alishane tried to look weary, which was extremely easy given the circumstances, and said, "Mr. Hobson, I am a traveler at the beginning of my journey. Would you accept seventy five?"

"Eighty," countered Hobson.

"That is fair," Alishane said and took out one of his coin purses. He counted out eight of the silver ten-omani coins and handed them over. The stableman accepted them and went back to his work without another word. Alishane looked at Timmen and again the halfling only shrugged at the old man's curt behavior. "Which horse shall I take?" asked Alishane.

The old man did not look up. "Take any horse you like," answered Hobson, "so long as it's the one closest to the door."

The halfling and cleric exchanged another look and then went to the stall near the door. They saddled the horse and secured the bit and bridle and then led the beast out into the rising heat of the day. Alishane helped Timmen onto the horse and then mounted behind him.

The city was stirring as they rode down the main street toward the western gate. Word of Alishane's escape and apparent murder of Lord Winningham would spread quickly over the next hour, but as yet it had not reached this part of town. Still, the halfling and the man drew a few curious looks as they rode along on their big horse.

"We should find a merchant and obtain a few provisions before we head out into the wild," Timmen suggested.

"And I would like to get a sword," Alishane said.

"It will do us little good if the Shadow Wolf finds us," Timmen put in. "We cannot afford to waste time."

"There are more dangers in the wild than assassins," Alishane argued.

"Very well," Timmen relented, "but let's wait until we're outside the gate; it would be better to find a store on the outskirts. They will be less likely to have heard of your escape and will probably have both food and weapons, that way we only have to make one stop."

Alishane agreed and before long they approached the western gate. A flash of fear passed through each of them, but there was nothing to do but keep riding and try to blend into the trickle of other travelers coming to and going from the city. The gate was open and sparsely manned since it was peacetime and there was little need for tighter security. Passing under the archway of stone and the raised metal bars of the gate, they felt the first tingles of relief. Then a guard turned and looked directly at them, his visage threatening. He looked at them for a long moment and terror rushed through them, but then he looked away and a moment later they were outside the city walls.

The sun was now fully risen and the morning dew was beginning to burn off, lifting the scent of growing things to their noses. The road changed from cobblestones to dirt and on either side of it there were grass, bushes and trees instead of houses and storefronts. Their hearts felt lighter. Out here in the open with the warm sun at their back they felt safe. There were no shadows to hide leering eyes and creeping death. Timmen began to sing in a high, lilting tenor:

> "In the dawn of darkest night
> She woke me with her hair upon my face.
> Stirring the tumult of my dreams
> With her locks of honeysuckle lace.
> She left me in the spring
> When everything was green.
> How much I loved her
> My Banderlee angel."

The tune was haunting and lolling; it reminded Alishane of the green moors of the Northern Province as it rolled and flowed through the sugared air of the early morning. Timmen hummed the tune for a few measures before he resumed singing:

> "I'm left now in the lee
> Of her departing grace
> To shelter my aching heart
> Behind a stranger's face
> To raise my glass alone
> Toward cold, gray, chiseled stone
> I drink this toast to you
> My Banderlee angel."

They rode in silence for awhile. Alishane was stunned by the grace of Timmen's singing. At last he said, "I'm glad to have you on the road with me."

Timmen laughed. "You'll truly appreciate me if we ever have need of disarming traps or opening chests."

The cleric's face became grave. In spite of the sun, he couldn't help but look behind him. "I have a feeling we will all need our unique talents soon," he mumbled and kicked the horse into a canter.

"'Ello, Aaron," the portly guard said to the other man, who had just arrived at the mid-shift exchange to relieve the guard with whom the fat man had started his watch.

"Oliver," the new guard nodded. They stood at the north gate of Tavora Manor, squinting out at the dusty lane as the midmorning sun baked the cobblestones. Both men had the sour smell one gets after a long night of drinking, the liquor oozing out through their pores and staining their undergarments with rings of sweat.

"Ah, these morning watches are going to be the death of me," the fat man said to his companion.

"Aye," said the other.

They stood in silence for awhile, shifting from one foot to the other to ease the discomfort and stiffness. "So Aaron," the fat man said, "James and me was talkin' before you arrived to relieve him and I was tellin' him about this chap I saw at the Copper Dram the other night."

"Aye," replied Aaron.

"And this chap was tellin' some mighty fine tales," Oliver went on. "A real dandy, this fellow was. Said his name was Sanguine, and he was tall and dark and he had a big, black moustache and a red and yellow bird settin' on his shoulder. And every so often the bird would talk, too. Only it wouldn't repeat what the man was sayin', like normal talking birds. This bird would finish the man's sentences for him, like they were of one mind. Strangest thing these eyes have ever seen."

"Aye," replied Aaron.

"So this chap and his bird were telling tales like nothing I ever heard. He would sing some parts of 'em too, with the bird clickin' and clackin' along, just a-bobbin' its head this way and that. And he told of faraway places and terrible creatures and odd people who carried magical weapons. I tell ye, Aaron, it felt like you was really there."

"Aye," replied Aaron.

"One of his stories was like a tale my Gam used to tell me, so I'm thinkin' that it might be true. But this fellow knew the names of people and the color of the leaves in the trees and how there was the smell of wood burning in the air, all the details that my Gam never knew." The fat guard Oliver pulled a flask from inside his coat and took a long swig. He corked the flask and returned it without offering any to the other guard. Aaron frowned a little but said nothing. Oliver continued:

"This tale was about a witch who came from a faraway land, and she was burned out of her own home and chased away from her country so that she had to fly on her broomstick all the way over the Andaluric Sea and it took her so long that she almost died from thirst while she was flying. And when she got to the coast away south of here she had to crawl into a cave and use her dark arts to bring herself back to health."

The fat guard scratched himself in a most undignified manner and Aaron looked down the lane at the heat shimmers rising off the stones. Then Oliver continued:

"When she came out of the cave she was so full of hate for people 'cause of what they done to her that she cooked up the most terrible curse that's ever been made. She put the curse in pine needles and then flew all over the land dropping the needles on villages and huts and people. And then do ye know what happened? People started growing extra fingers and toes, and their eyeballs fell out, and their ears got so big they could hardly walk. It took a whole army of paladins to catch her and they burned her on a stake and then a hundred monks went all around picking up the pine needles. And they took 'em up to their monastery and boiled 'em down to this goo that they pressed down into a clear, green ball. And the curse ball had strange magical powers that they didn't know how to control so they locked it away in their monastery and named it after the witch. Her name was Nivettrix so they called it the Orb of Nivettrix."

Aaron hadn't truly been listening, but he noticed that the fat man had stopped talking so he gave a grunt of acknowledgment.

"This chap what was tellin' the story said the witch's spirit still lives in the Orb and that every so often it lets out a terrible wail like her screams as she was gettin' burned. You believe that, eh?" the fat man elbowed his companion in the ribs.

"Aye," answered Aaron.

"Then the chap said that a few years back a vagabond went to this monastery and tricked the monks into giving him the Orb. Now he's out there with it and nobody knows what it does." The fat man sighed. "Yeah, I wonder what that Orb of Nivettrix can do," Oliver concluded. "I just love magic."

"Aye," Aaron responded.

The two men stood at their watch in silence as the sun climbed in the sky. Occasionally Oliver drew out his flask and drank from it, but he never offered any to his companion. They had both started to doze off when suddenly they realized that an old man was standing before them. He was wearing a tattered brown cloak and leaning on a tall staff that was so worn from his hands that it gleamed in the sunlight.

"Good morning," the man said and smiled warmly.

The two guards found themselves oddly afraid of the old man. They were not very worldly and knew nothing of wizards, but somehow they sensed great power in the bent figure before them. "What ye want?" asked Oliver.

"I am looking for the daughter of a very good friend of mine and I was told that she is here in the employ of the Royal Guard. Perhaps you fine gentlemen could assist me in finding her," answered the old man.

"Not many women in the Guard, actually. Not cut out for the life," stated the fat guard as he proudly thrust out his chest and held up all three of his chins.

"Quite," the old man stated simply with a wry smile. "Well then, if there are not many of them then she should be easier to find. She has very fair hair and features and is slight of build, but she is quite skilled with both blade and bow."

The two guards looked at each other as a cow might look at a sheep, then turned back to the old man.

"She is very attractive," he said. "Perhaps that will jog your memories."

A flicker of recognition flashed on both faces and Oliver said, "Gone. She's gone that one, and in a bit of trouble too."

The old man looked a little alarmed. In truth he was hiding the terrible fear that he felt inwardly. "Gone?" he asked. "When? And what kind of trouble?"

"Last night," answered Oliver, "with the outlaw Alishane Wyndam. And that will explain her trouble too."

"I see," the old man said and his thoughts drifted away from the two guards. They glanced at each other nervously and shifted on their feet. After a moment the old man snapped from his thoughts and looked back at them. They were startled by the intensity of his gaze and they jumped, but he merely smiled slightly and said 'thank you' and then he turned and was gone.

The two guards looked at each other again and then went back to watching the lane. "Strange old crupper," Oliver said after a few moments.

"Aye," said Aaron.

As the sun hovered near the apex of its journey across the sky and inflicted its heat upon the people of Pilas Antum, Aurora Daelin was climbing a tall staircase within the university. She had left a large foyer and now found herself looking down a long hallway with ornate wooden archways and classrooms on both sides. Inside the rooms were hundreds of students pursuing their education. It was the last place in the world one would expect to find a thieves' guild. Of course, that's exactly what made it the ideal place from which to operate one. Aurora looked around and tried to imagine what this same hallway would look like in the pall of moonlight: the nooks and crannies and doorways that would hold uneven shadows, the wood paneling that undoubtedly held doors to secret passages.

The university building was very old, with sharp, angular architecture that distinguished it from the rest of the city. It dated back to the middle of the Third Age when it was built by a reclusive band of druidic priests. The druids locked themselves away from the rest of humanity and then slowly went mad. They became obsessed with the purging of sin and made accusations against each other with a frequency and fervor that was matched only in the zealousness of their cleansing rituals. Their purification altars could be best compared to torture chambers and it was rumored that they were still in existence in the lower reaches of the university. Many adventurous students had sneaked out of the dormitories late at night to creep down stairwells and look for hidden doors. None had ever found anything, of course, but the adventure made for many great and exaggerated stories.

Just as Aurora was wondering what Timmen would find if he were set loose in the old building, a gong sounded and the hallway was suddenly filled with students. Aurora was wearing her hair down to cover her ears and she drew many stares from the male students and soft, indignant huffs from the girls. One girl, who was quite pretty and used to receiving the attention of the boys, made a snide comment about Aurora's green cape and dirty boots. The elf couldn't resist drawing back her cape to reveal the long sword sheathed at her waist. The girl gave a little squeak and skittered away with her friends.

The theatrics, though satisfying to Aurora, attracted the attention of an elderly male instructor who seemed very snobbish and entirely disinterested in the beautiful elf's feminine wiles. He walked up to her briskly and said, "May I help you, miss?"

"Yes, please," Aurora answered. "Would you kindly direct me to the administrative wing?"

The man's eyes narrowed and his lips pursed. "With whom do you have an appointment?" he asked.

"I desire to meet with Regent Zannick," the elf answered.

The man raised an eyebrow and his eyes passed quickly over her from head to foot and back up again. After taking measure of the woman and her request, he said, "Wait here, please," and turned on his heel and walked away. A few moments later another man came up behind her and Aurora turned to face him with her hand on the hilt of her sword.

"What business do you have with the Regent?" the man asked. He was younger than his predecessor and appeared to be very fit. Aurora did not see a weapon, but she was sure that he was not defenseless.

"I bring a message from Captain Eustacio," Aurora answered. A flicker of recognition flashed briefly across the man's face, and it did not go unnoticed by the astute elf.

"I'm afraid I don't know what you mean," the man said.

"Yes you do," Aurora countered. "Tell the Regent that I bring word of recent events within Tavora Manor. I'm sure he will grant me an audience."

The man looked her over one more time and then said, "Come with me, please." He stepped aside and held out his arm to indicate the direction in which she should walk. Aurora stepped forward and the two walked side-by-side down the hall, neither wanting the other at their back. The man indicated the turns and the doors through which they would go and Aurora soon found herself deep in the heart of the building and several floors below ground level.

"Wait here, please," the man said and disappeared through a door that had no handle and could not be distinguished from the rest of the wood paneling. Aurora looked around the room and found that it was perfectly square with no deviations in the wood on any of the walls. She couldn't even see the door they had used to enter the room. She looked toward the ceiling and saw viewing holes carved into the intricate wood trimming so as to be hardly noticeable in the shadows created by the graceful turns in the wood. She knew she was being watched.

After what felt to Aurora like quite a long time, her escort reappeared accompanied by a bent old man with one brown eye and one so white that at first glance it appeared as though there were no iris at all. The old man covered his normal eye with his hand and peered at her intently with the white one. Aurora suddenly felt very exposed, as if she were standing before this old man with no clothing on. He looked her over very carefully and then said, "The sword at her belt, a dagger sheathed at the small of her back, and another dagger in her right boot."

The younger man nodded and moved to open the door again, but the old man stood transfixed, his strange white eyeball locked on the elf. Then he lowered his hand and looked at her with both eyes. His mouth hung slightly open as though he were in terrible shock. That is when Aurora suddenly realized to her great horror that the man was not looking her in the eye, but rather was looking at her ears. The old man regained his composure and seemed on the verge of saying something, but then he thought better of it and remained silent. He looked at her in a way that was difficult to read and then he turned and left the room.

"Through here, please," the younger man said.

Aurora felt extremely nervous about the old man's behavior. She was certain that he had seen through the hair hiding her ears and the simple suggestive magic that she used on other humans. Clearly he knew she was an elf and she felt certain that he would tell his employer. What the Regent would do with that knowledge remained to be seen.

She entered the room and the younger man who had been her guide closed the door behind her without following her in. She was standing in a large, dimly lit office. At the far end was an oak desk with a thin, middle-aged man sitting behind it in a plush leather chair. He wore glasses and had gray hair at his temples. He looked composed and scholarly. The old man with the white eye was sitting in a chair against the wall.

The younger man looked at her for a few moments and then said, "Please come in, miss. May I have the pleasure of your name?"

Aurora walked into the room and stood before the desk. She looked carefully around the room and saw that there were no other people present, which surprised her greatly. Not only had she openly stated that she was coming from Tavora Manor, the home of the Regent's main rival, but she had also been allowed to enter the office with all of her weapons. Now she found the man sitting here with seemingly no protection. She looked at the man behind the desk, who sat coolly returning her gaze. Then, suddenly, three truths occurred to her at once. First, the Regent was not unprotected. Second, they knew she was not truly from Tavora Manor. And third, the man behind the desk was not Darius Zannick.

"You have asked for my name," Aurora addressed the younger man, "and I shall give it. But I came to speak with the Regent, not an imposter." She turned and looked squarely at the white-eyed man. "My name is Aurora Daelin, Mr. Zannick, and I have come in search of information."

Aurora felt the younger man tense, but the true Regent only smiled approvingly. "Very good, my dear. You are very perceptive," he said. "Let me pay you the courtesy of introducing myself properly." He stood and approached her with his hand outstretched. "My name is Darius Zannick, and I am very pleased to make your acquaintance." Aurora took his hand and shook it briefly, though the feeling of his skin and the way he looked probingly into her eyes made her uncomfortable.

Zannick then turned to the man behind the desk and said, "You may go now, Charles. I will speak to Miss Daelin in private." The man reluctantly got up from the desk and left the room. "You must forgive Charles, he is very protective of me," Zannick said and shook his head.

"He is your bodyguard," Aurora reasoned.

"Oh, he is much more than that," the Regent chuckled and moved to sit down at his desk. "Charles is one of the most dangerous men in the world." He wheezed slightly as he sat down. "He was trained in the hand-to-hand fighting style by the Mount Alcharist monks, in swordplay by Master Zen Shui from the island of Marsipol, and in the art of shadow stalking by, well, an assassin whose name no one would recognize since anyone who knew that he was an assassin did not live long enough to speak of it."

"That would explain why you didn't disarm me before our meeting," Aurora said.

"Oh, I probably still would have done if not for your heritage," Zannick replied. "Elves are not known as assassins." Again the old man laughed. "I must say," he continued, "it gave me quite a shock when I saw you for what you are."

"How are you able to see through my enchantment?" Aurora asked.

Zannick smiled. "I don't think I will be revealing the source of that power, my dear," he said. "Not today." A brief silence ensued and he continued to smile at her with that probing look, then he said, "You say you have come in search of information. Ask what you will and perhaps I will answer."

"I desire information about the *Wind Runner*."

"I do not have dealings with the *Wind Runner.*"

"But you know how the Countess is using her," Aurora insisted.

The Regent hesitated slightly. "Why would I know anything about the business of the Countess?" he asked.

Aurora responded curtly, "If you insist on repeatedly testing my power of perception, then this conversation will take much longer than necessary, and I'm sure you are a very busy man."

Darius Zannick laughed joyfully. "This is truly an enjoyable experience," he gushed. "I didn't even know there were elves still in existence, and here I find myself speaking to one. And what is more, you appear to be very well-informed."

"We have our sources," Aurora said dryly.

"Indeed," the Regent replied. He sat regarding the elf for a long time. She noted a sparkle of devious mirth in his expression. "Well then," he continued, "since you have passed all of my tests to this point, let me set you one more. If you pass it, then you will have proven yourself worthy of the information you are seeking."

Aurora looked back and forth between the man's two eyes. The white one was blank and revealed nothing; the brown one showed a fierce intensity that made Aurora slightly hesitant to voice her question, "What is your test?"

The man sat back in his chair and took a deep breath before he said, "The Crystal Night has been in existence for a very long time. But it fell virtually into extinction about three hundred years ago after an internal dispute led to mutiny and infighting. I have resurrected it, but some of its old power still escapes us. Our old sanctuary, a cave network in the Pandoran Mountains, remains inaccessible to us. I cannot tell you the layout of the caves, the reasons for our failure or the dangers held within. Your quest is to traverse the caves and bring me the treasure found at their core. It is said to be an item of great power and use. Should you prove successful, come back and tell me how to defeat the secrets of the caves. In return, you may keep the treasure and I will tell you everything you desire to know about the Countess."

Aurora huffed. "You ask much in return for simple information."

"If the information could be secured from any other source then you would not be here," the Regent said softly.

Aurora couldn't argue with his point. She thought about the implications of the quest. It was undoubtedly extraordinarily dangerous. And even if she succeeded, could she trust the Regent to be forthcoming with the information she needed? The answer seemed obvious: the Regent was preparing for war with the Countess and he wanted the caves as his base of operations. He would certainly give her the information she needed because they were allies by common enemy, at least where the Countess was concerned. The last issue was whether he would truly allow her to keep the treasure found in the heart of the caves. *I'll deal with that when the time comes,* she thought.

"I accept your terms," she told the Regent.

"Excellent!" He smiled widely and opened a drawer in his desk. He pulled out a folded map and held it out to her. "This will lead you to the mouth of the caves," he said as Aurora accepted the map. "Do not underestimate the Caverns of the Crystal Night, Miss Daelin," the Regent admonished. "To say that they are very dangerous is a gross understatement." He took a small bell out of the drawer and rang it. The young man who had brought her to the office entered immediately. "Please take our guest back to the front foyer and see her out," the Regent instructed. The man nodded and held the door open for Aurora.

"And Miss Daelin, one final bit of advice," Darius Zannick called out. Aurora stopped at the door and looked back. The old man was standing behind his desk, leaning forward tensely. "You may want to take a thief with you," he said with a smile and a gleam in his strangely colored eyes, "and a very good thief at that."

I think I know where to find one, the elf thought to herself as she turned and left the room.

Chapter Eleven

~ Branches Whip a Face Looking Back ~

Timmen O'Hook sat uncomfortably on the sweaty horse, teetering back and forth with the big animal's gait. The halfling was no longer singing but rather was stifling expletives under his breath as he struggled to stay in the saddle. He and Alishane Wyndam had ridden throughout the morning and noon hour, passing through a land of low hills and small farms. From time to time they came upon a stand of trees and rode off the road to give the trees a wide berth. They feared what might be waiting for them in the shadows and behind the boles of the trees.

The afternoon sun was beginning its slow descent toward the hills in the west when they came upon a small farming village on the outskirts of settled land. The squat buildings were huddled together in defense against the cold winters and the wild lands that began just past their doorsteps. The halfling and cleric were trail-sore and hungry as they dismounted the large horse and made their way into the village's only store.

The interior of the store was rustic, as one would expect on the borderlands. The proprietor of the store seemed to have gone to great lengths to advertise his prowess as a hunter. Heads from many beasts were hung upon the walls, their jaws snarling in a final rictus. Timmen looked at the glass eyeballs peering down at him from the heads and gulped; this was a bit too savage for his liking. Alishane looked around the room at its several occupants. Three were sitting around a fire and appeared to be frontiersmen: hunters, trappers, loggers or farmers. They were a bit hard to read, both because of the little light that entered through the dirty windows and also because of the full beards and bushy eyebrows that shrouded their grizzled faces. A fourth man, who was only slightly less dirty than these three, got up from a rickety chair and shuffled toward the newcomers. Alishane assumed he was the shopkeeper. The only other man in the room appeared to be a city dweller; he was clean-shaven and wore neat and fashionable clothing. Alishane thought the man looked very out of place, but he only reflected on the subject for a moment before the shopkeeper addressed him.

"What can I do for ye?" the man asked in a voice that was as cracked as his weathered lips.

"We need provisions," Alishane answered, "food for ten days, water jugs, bedrolls, an oiled skin for shelter, a small axe for cutting wood, a flint for starting fires, and I would like to see your stock of swords."

Timmen had turned his attention to the other people in the room when Alishane started speaking. The three dirty frontiersmen watched casually, each blowing smoke from long, hand-carved pipes. The neatly dressed man was listening to Alishane with keen interest. When the cleric mentioned buying a sword, the man flinched slightly and looked down at the halfling. Timmen saw recognition flash across the man's face and a chill ran down the halfling's spine. *He knows us,* Timmen thought. He wanted to tell Alishane so they could flee, but the cleric was following the shopkeeper into a back room to look at his wares.

Timmen was suddenly alone in the dark room with four strange men eyeing him suspiciously. The heads on the walls seemed to come alive in the flickering firelight, twitching and writhing and smiling in mockery at the scared halfling in their midst. The room began to spin and Timmen clutched at a chair to keep his balance. He was beginning to panic. Just as the thief gave thought to running from the room, the city dweller got up and moved to the door. He grabbed a cloak from the hook and pulled it around his shoulders, then he turned and looked quickly at the halfling before darting out the door.

Timmen's head began to throb. He didn't know what to do. If he went to Alishane immediately and they left, the other men would undoubtedly get suspicious and soon the whole village would be abuzz with talk of the two strangers. He thought it would be best to act calm and get their supplies and then get out of town and off the road as soon as possible. Perhaps the man from the city had been sent to inform the village of Alishane's escape, in which case he would have to ride back into town to inform the Guard. If he went by the main road, he could get there in half the time it had taken Alishane and Timmen to get to the village, with their wandering off the road to avoid other travelers and throw pursuers off their trail. If the man went straight back to town and reported the outlaws' whereabouts, then the Royal Guard would be riding hard to the village to capture them.

In all, Timmen thought they had a few hours' time to get away from the village and hide in the wild. What the thief couldn't have known, however, was that a regiment of Guardsmen had been riding up behind them throughout the morning and was now only minutes away.

Timmen took a chair in the common room of the store and sat down, trying to look calm even as he heard the clopping of the city dweller's horse growing faint in the distance.

Aurora Daelin had made only one stop after leaving Regent Darius Zannick at the university; she stopped by the small loft she was renting to pick up her supplies for the wild, including a gracefully powerful longbow. It was a standard elvish weapon with no enchantments or distinguishing marks cut into the shaft, although the grain in the yew was exquisite and the craftsmanship was of the highest quality.

Her pack for the wild was not much larger than the one she usually wore at the small of her back; she could find anything she needed for sustenance in the woods. All she brought with her was a bit more clothing and the tools she would need to cut wood, start fires, repair or cut new arrows, and any of the various other tasks that might be necessary.

She walked casually through town, using her elvish magic to appear inconspicuous and melt into the crowd. After meandering in its general direction for the better part of an hour, she finally approached the Wyvern's Tail Inn. The elf slowed her pace and looked around carefully for signs of trouble as she neared the building. She saw only the usual midday traffic milling about the lanes, alleyways and storefronts. Nobody gave her a second glance and none approached the inn, knowing of course that it was closed during the Tournament. Nothing appeared to be amiss, and yet she could not shake the feeling that something was wrong.

Aurora cautiously walked around the back of the building and tried to look into the windows without drawing attention to herself, but the glass was dirty and the interior dark so she could not see inside. She decided to crawl up to the second level so she could look around more freely and enter the building from an inconspicuous location. She stopped at a corner of the building and looked around. When she was sure no one was watching, the elf climbed nimbly up a drainpipe and pulled herself onto the roof of the lower level. She rolled away from the eave toward the middle of the building, but stopped when she felt the crunch of broken glass through her cloak.

They are dead, she thought to herself as a flash of fear ran through her.

Aurora lay unmoving for a long time. She was looking up at the clouds in the sky and she felt her heart beating very hard in her chest. There was an empty pit in her stomach. Her logical mind kept telling her that there were many reasons for there to be a broken window in a deserted inn, but the rest of her being knew that the broken glass was confirmation of the dread she had been feeling ever since she approached the Wyvern's Tail. She cursed herself for leaving them unprotected. She should have hidden them better before leaving to get the information she needed.

Aurora was laying there looking up at the sky and trying to master her fear when a bird flew onto the ledge near her hand. She lolled her head forlornly and looked at it. The bird was unlike any she had ever seen in her three hundred years of life. It was yellow with red wings and tail and a tuft of red feathers sticking up from its head. It resembled a finch in shape and size, but it was not skittish like a finch. This bird's movements were slow and measured. It walked toward her and then hopped up onto her chest. The bird approached her face, looking her directly in the eyes. She saw intelligence behind the bird's black, little eyes and she felt a swell of wonder and excitement. Aurora Daelin, like all elves, loved the natural world and all of the wondrous fauna it held.

Then the bird spoke.

"I bring a message for you, elf," the bird said in a throaty, croaking voice.

Aurora could not respond at first. After a moment, she stammered, "Who are you? What have you to tell me?"

"Your friends have fled, not three but two. Through yon window, the third waits for you."

"What has happened?" the elf asked.

"I know not, but go and look. Then to the road; find Timmen O'Hook."

Aurora was bewildered. "What do you know of our business? Why have you contacted me?"

"I see many things, Elf, and I may share them with you, but my motives for contacting you are my own," the bird said.

"Then how am I to judge your goodwill?" Aurora asked.

"Listen or not, it is up to you. Then judge for yourself what's best to do."

"Stop talking in riddles and tell me what has happened to my friends!" Aurora stormed.

The bird fluttered up from her chest. When again it settled, it landed on a shingle near her head and whispered into her ear, "I tell you all that a bird can know, dark as death is the pall of the Shadow."

Aurora felt an electric surge of fear rush through her. "The Shadow Wolf!" she exclaimed breathlessly. She jumped to her feet and rushed to the broken window. Looking in, it took her eyes a moment to adjust to the dark. The first thing she saw was the curtain, smeared with blood where the Wolf had wiped his blade. She was aware again of the horrible emptiness in her stomach. Then all at once her eyes adjusted and she was able to see the interior of the room. A broken body lay sprawled on the floor, soaking in a large pool of blood. Aurora looked at the man's face. There was no mistaking his identity: it was Dunk Worley, the cleric's servant.

Several emotions coursed through the elf, one on top of the other. First there was relief that the assassin's victim was not the halfling or the cleric. Then she felt guilt for the preference her relief revealed. She looked back to Dunk Worley's pale and pain-stricken face. She felt great pity and sadness. Clearly the servant had not been the assassin's main target. If Dunk was dead and the others were not, then it seemed probable that the servant had sacrificed himself to help the others escape. Aurora felt admiration for the humble man laying in his death pose before her. He did not deserve such a gruesome and violent demise.

The last emotion Aurora felt was anger, consuming and terrible. She spun around to face the little red and yellow bird, her ire flaming in her brilliant blue eyes. "Who are you and what is your involvement in this affair? Tell me now and speak plainly!"

The bird fluttered up to the eave overhanging the window and spoke to her at eye level. "My name is Huggins. I am the medium of a man who has great interest in your conflict with the Countess. His mind is mine, and my eyes are his."

"Zannick," Aurora guessed.

"No, not the regent," the bird answered. "My master will reveal himself in due time, for now you must rush to the aid of your two remaining friends. They escaped the Shadow Wolf for a time, but they are walking into more danger."

"Where are they?" the elf asked as she shifted her bow on her shoulder.

"They took the west road out of the city, but there are Guardsmen on their trail," the bird answered. Aurora nodded and started toward the ledge. The bird hopped down onto her shoulder. "There is something else," it said into her ear.

The elf crouched by the ledge and prepared to drop down to the alley. "Yes?" she whispered.

"Your father knows much, a wise man indeed. A new friend will show in your hour of need," the bird croaked.

"More riddles?" asked the elf. "I thought we had moved beyond that. Will you not just tell me what I need to know?"

But the bird only twittered merrily in true finch fashion and flew away. Aurora looked after it briefly and then dropped lightly to the ground. She had a long way to travel and much to consider, but the road is a wonderful place to think.

Zakarus Rinn awoke with a start. He had been dreaming about his days in training with the Mount Alcharist monks. He was nineteen and halfway through his training when he saw an older student return from his shinn-an jo, the mandatory seclusion in the Valley of Death that all students had to complete before they could graduate. Rinn had watched in fascination as the older student, Charles Bothan, was excommunicated from the Order of Alchary for his conduct while in seclusion.

The Valley of Death was aptly named, for it was filled with some of the most dangerous creatures in the natural world. Students were left in the Valley with no food, shelter or weapons. All they had was their training and the clothes on their back. During shinn-an jo, students were expected to survive through any means necessary, hunting their food and doing battle with the evil creatures whenever attacked. Bothan, however, had taken the survival edict too far. When a caravan of traders got lost in a blizzard and wandered into the Valley of Death, Charles Bothan had murdered every last one of them and took their supplies for his own. He led the carts and animals of the caravan back to the monastery and proclaimed his journey the most successful shinn-an jo in memory.

The monks did not respond favorably when they learned of Bothan's slaughter of innocent people. They publicly denounced him and removed him from the Order. Bothan accepted their decision without protest and quietly left the monastery. Zakarus Rinn, on the other hand, had been outraged. He was full of admiration for Charles Bothan and accused the monks of being hypocritical in their morals. When he challenged them on the subject, the monks accused him of sedition and punished him severely. He was whipped and put in isolation for six weeks with nothing to eat but bread and water. During that time, Zakarus Rinn was transformed. Whatever good and decent qualities he possessed upon entering Mount Alcharist dissolved into nothingness. All he felt was blackness as complete as the pitch dark of his isolation chamber. When at last the cell was opened, it was not Zakarus Rinn who emerged. It was not Zakarus Rinn who fell upon the monk who had opened the door. And it was not Zakarus Rinn who tore out the man's throat and then fled into the night. From the pits of this darkness was born an assassin, a man who in time would become known as the Shadow Wolf.

Now, eighteen years later, Rinn sat in his bed in Tavora Manor and wiped the sweat from his brow. He had just awoken from a dream in which he was back in that cell in the belly of the Mount Alcharist monastery. He opened the shades and looked at the clock. It was past midday. The assassin dressed and gathered his gear. He had just left his room and started down the hall toward a meeting with the Countess when one of his spies approached him.

"We have received word that the cleric and halfling were spotted in a small village on the western outskirts," the spy reported. Rinn nodded and sent the man to prepare his horse. The assassin felt the anxiety of his dream dissolve as he returned to the hunt. He would make his report to the Countess and then leave to find the outlaws. His step was light as he considered the impending confrontation, for he knew that the elf would be coming to find her friends. And the Shadow Wolf would be waiting.

Timmen O'Hook was nervous. Alishane had been in the back of the store for almost half an hour and had not emerged with their supplies. The halfling shifted in his seat. Every minute they remained in the village brought them closer to disaster. The three frontiersmen with whom he shared the room had begun a round of ballacord, a game played with ceramic tiles, and had not looked in his direction since he sat down. Still, he did not trust them. It was not in his nature to trust anybody.

Timmen was listening to their conversation as closely as he could without being obvious. Nothing they had said concerned him, but now they turned to a subject that made him listen more carefully.

"So ye think that dandy is Wyndam?" One of them asked the group.

"Seems odd that he could've murdered Lord Winningham and then be out here without a sword," another muttered.

"You really thinkin' he killed Winningham?" the third asked skeptically.

"Naw," the first answered, "I bet the Countess cooked that up to help her get him." The others grunted their agreement and all three looked over at Timmen and found him looking at them. "Well, none o' my business anyhow," the man said and they all turned back to their game.

The halfling got up from his seat and walked toward the back room. Entering, he heard the voices of two haggling men.

"I have told you that I don't need any more clothes," Alishane was saying. "What I still need is an axe for cutting wood and a sword."

"Are you sure you don't want to look at this larger shelter skin? It'll keep the rain off you twice as good as that one," the owner of the shop said.

"No, thank you. I'm quite satisfied with what I have selected already," Alishane answered. "All I need now is an axe and a sword."

"I could get you some more food," the owner insisted. "The smoked barrow rat is quite tasty, despite its name."

"You are beginning to try my patience now, sir," Alishane's voice was sharp with frustration, "kindly just show me what I have asked for: an axe and a sword."

Timmen spoke up. "Excuse me, might I have a word?" he asked Alishane.

The cleric hadn't heard Timmen enter and he spun around in surprise. After recognition lit his face, Alishane walked over and stooped down before the halfling. "What is it?" he asked.

"This man is stalling you because he knows who you are," Timmen whispered. Alishane's eyes widened and he started to turn around, but the halfling caught him by the arm and continued, "The city dweller left as soon as you came back here. I'm certain he was sent to this village to tell of your escape." Timmen looked past the cleric to the shop owner, whom he caught leaning toward them in an effort to overhear their whispered conversation, then he jerked his thumb behind him toward the outer room. "I overheard those men talking and it seems that Lord Winningham was murdered after we left." Alishane's eyes widened further as Timmen concluded, "And everyone thinks that you did it."

"Winningham?" Alishane asked, bewildered. "Who could have done that?"

"It can only be the Countess, but I can't understand her motives," the halfling answered. The shop owner tried to lean closer and nudged a hammer off a table. It crashed loudly to the floor. "We can discuss this further later," Timmen whispered urgently, "right now we must be away from here."

"I agree," Alishane said and turned to address the shopkeeper. "We have decided to postpone our journey and are heading back into town," he said. "Thank you very much for your time." The halfling and cleric left the protesting merchant and returned to the front room of the store, only to find it empty. They crossed the room quickly and went out the front door.

The companions' eyes were momentarily dazzled as they stepped out into the bright afternoon. Squinting against the light, they saw shadows move in around them. "Seize him!" someone yelled. Hands groped for Alishane and he began to fight them. Timmen's instinct was to flee, and he crouched and darted through the thrashing legs until he fell off the wooden porch of the store. Crawling in the dust, the halfling turned and squinted into the sun just in time to see the hilt of a sword crash into the back of

Alishane's head. The nobleman crumbled to the deck and the shadows fell upon him.

Timmen turned and scurried around the building and then ran to the shelter of the trees. He heard shouted orders and watched briefly as several of the Guardsmen hoisted the unconscious Alishane Wyndam and carried him to a nearby building while the rest spread out to look for the nobleman's halfling companion. Timmen swore at himself; he should have had them away sooner. He watched until Alishane disappeared into the building and then he turned and ran deeper into the forest, vowing as he went that he would find a way to rescue his newfound friend.

<u>Chapter Twelve</u>

~ Rescue ~

Timmen O'Hook picked his way carefully through the undergrowth of his deciduous refuge. Dusk was falling and the last golden rays of sunlight filtered through the top branches of the trees to dapple the bushes around him. A carpet of soft, damp leaves covered the ground, allowing him to move as quietly as a mouse over the musty earth. High in the canopy above him, an owl came awake and hooted softly before taking flight to hunt its evening meal.

With great care, Timmen approached the edge of the copse of trees. He pulled the shrouding foliage aside and peered into the deepening gloom. Off in the distance he could see the village. Townspeople and Guardsmen alike were milling about, seeing to the evening chores or standing at post. On the opposite side of the village from where the halfling crouched watching, the Guardsmen had set up a camp of tents and cooking fires. Timmen surmised that they had decided to stay the night near the village with their prisoner under guard in one of the buildings and then bring him into town the following morning. The logic seemed sound to the thief. If they left immediately, they may get caught out on the road when night fell. That would put them in a position of vulnerability to attack. This was much safer. Unknown to the Guardsmen or halfling, however, were the many other sets of eyes watching the village from various vantage points surrounding the clearing.

One such set of eyes, luminescent in the failing light, belonged to Zakarus Rinn. The assassin watched from a small hillock on the other side of the village from Timmen. After waking from his troubling dream, Rinn consulted with the Countess and then came straight to the village. The instructions he delivered to the captain of the Royal Guard regiment on behalf of the Countess were clear: keep Alishane Wyndam here for the night and set a watch, then be ready for an attack by the nobleman's accomplices. In truth, the assassin and Countess both had very little confidence in the watchfulness of the soldiers; this was not one of their elite units. In this trap, their presence served only the function of a net with a mesh left wide by design. Wyndam's friends could easily slip through the tendrils of the web, but that would only bring them into the jaws of the Shadow Wolf.

Rinn chewed on a thin cigar and sat back to watch the village and wait for the slow stalk of descending night. He scanned the woods and hills off in the distance and wondered if the beautiful elf was there, watching and waiting just as he was. He felt a thrill at the thought. She was close; he could feel it.

At that same moment, Aurora Daelin was indeed watching the village. She arrived after Alishane had been taken captive to find the village and surrounding area swarming with Guardsmen. Watching their movements, the elf quickly deduced that they were searching for something. She felt a flash of hope that her friends had escaped and fled, but those hopes were dashed a short while later when she saw an unconscious Alishane Wyndam being carried in bonds from one building to another in the village. She did not see

Timmen so it appeared that the halfling had escaped and was now the target of the soldiers' search. Aurora knew that the little thief would not be found.

Now she sat watching the village and waiting. She knew that Timmen would stay in the area and perhaps attempt to steal into the building to rescue Alishane. But the elf's senses told her that something was amiss, some other presence was in the area that she could feel but could not place. She decided to wait and see what transpired during the night, then perhaps she could help her friends while maintaining her advantage of surprise.

Meanwhile, one last set of eyes watched the calm before the impending storm. These eyes were the oldest by far, and they saw more and understood more than any others. From under the hood of his battered cloak, Arcanis Rhu watched not only the activity in the village, but also the inactivity, and from this he inferred the developing intentions of the others in the area. Throughout the course of his long life, the old man had learned enough about the ways of the world's creatures to make their actions predictable. As he sat and watched the village, the future unfolded before him.

Arcanis knew with clear certainty how each participant in this drama would act, and he knew the likely consequences of those actions. He knew that the impetuous halfling was going into the camp and there he would find trouble from which he could not escape. He knew that the elf-maiden he was sworn to protect would follow the halfling and find herself in the same trouble. And Arcanis knew that the only way they would escape was if he intervened.

The last light of day faded as the wizard sat under the bower of a majestic elm and closed his eyes. He attuned his senses to the rotation of the planet, the starlight on the leaves and the sliver of a waxing moon hanging above the western horizon. A gentle breeze tickled the hairs of his beard. Arcanis delved below the surface of his frail body and felt his spirit stir. The tide of his power surged, no longer ebbing away but flowing and swirling in a tumultuous, white-capped ocean in electric pale green. For the next several hours the wizard meditated, building his power for the moment he would need it. He had sworn what was left of his life in aid to the elf and soon she would be in danger, but Arcanis Rhu would be ready.

* * * * * * *

Night had fallen fully and the village was quiet. The smell of the earth and the sounds of the wild floated on the breeze and carried to the attentive senses of Timmen O'Hook. The thief looked up through the branches of the trees and saw the bright star Callumel with its three sister stars flanking it and knew that the time had come for him to act. Though the moon had set and the stars cast few shadows on the ground, he was still careful to keep his little frame low as he picked his way out of the trees and into the open. The halfling scurried across the wide meadow toward the dark buildings of the village.

Timmen came first to the corral. The horses silhouetted in the meager light looked like lonely sentinels guarding against the uncertainty of the frontier night. He climbed through the wooden fence and crept among the sleeping animals. The halfling peered from between the legs of one horse at the buildings nearby. The horse nickered and swished its tail. Timmen moved around the horse, stroking its flank along the way, to look the animal in the eye.

"Easy there, friend," he said. "I am not big enough to cause you concern." The horse blew softly and the halfling crouched and darted to the darkest shadows of the barn. Timmen took a moment to listen to the sounds of the night. All he heard was the breathing of the horses, the buzz of a few insects and the breeze stirring the leaves in the distant trees. Straining his ears and focusing his thought, the halfling could barely discern a muffled conversation mixed among the snores in the Guardsman camp.

Timmen edged out of the shadow of the barn and made his way quickly and quietly to the next building, which appeared to be a guesthouse to the main residence where Alishane was being held. Again the little thief paused to listen before easing to the corner of the building and looking around at the house. The windows were dark and all appeared peaceful. There were two guards standing outside the front door and, as Timmen watched, a third guard walked into view and continued his circuit of the house.

The thief watched the guards for a few minutes to learn their pattern. The two at the front door were relatively inattentive and looked to be concentrating all of their efforts on staying awake. The patrolling guard circled the house every three to four minutes and he was only slightly more attentive than his colleagues.

Timmen turned and went back the way he had come, rounding the guesthouse and darting to a shed on the other side of the barn. This position was a bit further away from the main house, but from here he could sneak up in the rear of the building away from the two guards in front. Timmen watched the patrolling guard make several more circuits, mastering the timing and inspecting the ground between himself and the house for weeds, loose rocks, holes, or anything that would make noise or cause him to stumble. When at last he felt he was ready, the halfling gathered his courage, took a deep breath and ran as quickly and silently as his skill would allow. He covered the distance like a cloud passing in front of the moon, a mere shadow and whisper over the grass.

Crouching in a nook behind a stack of firewood, Timmen struggled to keep his breathing measured, slow and silent. He felt as though the oxygen had been sucked out of the air. His chest burned fiercely and he had a stitch in his side. He knew that it was only his mind betraying him, but the more he tried to control his breathing, the less air he seemed to be getting. Just as he began to think that he should give in and take a few deep breaths, he heard the footsteps of the guard turn the corner and walk inexorably toward him. Closer and closer came the steps, and hotter and heavier did the thief's chest burn and heave. Timmen closed his eyes and focused all of his being on staying quiet and breathing slowly. His heart was pounding in his ears.

After a very long minute had passed, he opened his eyes and looked out from his shelter. The guard was not there. Timmen allowed himself to breathe more freely, and when the guard next came around the building toward him, he had regained his self-control. After the guard passed by, Timmen shimmied out of his hiding place and crept along behind him, matching the man's footfalls and staying right on his heels. At the corner of the building the man stopped and looked around. Timmen was close enough to touch him and could smell his sweaty uniform. When the man looked to the right, Timmen slid slightly to the left. When the guard turned around and looked behind him, Timmen moved too, staying directly behind the man and out of sight.

A moment later the guard continued his patrol of the building, oblivious to the halfling creeping along behind him. Soon the two of them turned the corner to the front of the house. Timmen did not fall back, however; he stayed right on the heels of the guard as the man approached his comrades. The two guards were standing in front of some steps that led to a large patio; neither looked in the direction of the patrol guard with the halfling shadow. About fifteen paces from the steps, the patrol guard veered out to pass in front of the patio and Timmen darted quickly to the juncture where the patio met the front wall of the building.

The thief crouched there, listening to the three men converse briefly before the patrol guard left to make another round of the house. Timmen quietly stood up and peered over the patio. The guards had resumed their lethargic stupor. Timmen pulled his thieving kit from his breast pocket and extracted three long, slender tools and a small, corked vial. He tucked his kit away in his vest pocket and put the lock-picking tools in his mouth while closing his hand over the vial. Casting another furtive glance at the guards, the lithe halfling pulled himself silently onto the patio and crept to the door.

First, he uncorked the vial and dropped some of the oil within onto the lower hinges of the door to keep them from squeaking. The halfling could not reach the upper hinge; he would just have to trust to luck on that one. He corked the vial and returned it to his pocket and then moved to the doorknob. He tried it once and found that it was indeed locked. The thief looked quickly back over his shoulder to be sure he had not been discovered, then inserted two of his tools into the lock, one pointing down on the lower tumblers and one pinning the uppers. His third tool resembled a small knife with grooves instead of blades that slid smoothly along the shafts of the first two tools. Once the third pick was in place, Timmen turned all three as one and felt the lock give way. He turned the knob, extracted his tools and put them back in his mouth. He looked back over his shoulder one last time and then opened the door.

The door opened quietly, much to the relief of the halfling thief. Timmen darted inside and closed the door behind him. This house, like many on the frontier, had a small room just inside the door where the inhabitants took off their coats and boots, both of which could be covered with copious amounts of mud or snow. The room was dark. The family who lived in the house was undoubtedly spending the night with friends while their cellar was being used as a jail. Timmen put his lock picking tools back in his thieving kit and closed his eyes to dilate his pupils as much as possible. He heard the patrol guard pass the front of the house and continue on his way.

When at last he opened his eyes again, the thief could see the shapes and figures of the furniture in the next room. He spent a long time looking into the darkness, trying to make out what he could in the feeble light coming in through the windows. Once he knew the layout of the room and was certain there were no other occupants, Timmen crawled slowly across the floor to the dining table, where again he paused before feeling his way to the hall. There was only one window in the hall and it was high at the far end. Underneath the window was a stairwell leading down to the cellar. There was another guard sitting in a chair at the top of the stairs.

Timmen's heart sank. He didn't know how he could get past the guard into the cellar. Just as he began to give thought to turning around and leaving, he heard a small snort from the guard. The man was snoring.

Timmen moved quickly. He scurried along the length of the hallway and peered down the stairs. Faint light from a single candle illuminated the cellar. The halfling worried that the stairs would creak even under his slight weight, but he certainly couldn't stay where he was so he tiptoed as lightly as he could down the first several steps. As the lower level came into view, the thief slid onto his belly and inched headfirst down the stairs. The scene that met his gaze made his blood turn cold. A squeak of surprise escaped him and he froze on the spot. He was looking into the leering eyes of the Shadow Wolf.

"Quite impressive, little one," Zakarus Rinn sneered. "Quite impressive indeed." The assassin was leaning casually against a table where several metal instruments glittered in the light from the room's lone candle. Timmen felt his stomach turn; these were instruments of torture. He looked past the assassin to find Alishane Wyndam tied to a chair and apparently unconscious. He was bleeding from many small incisions; some were in various stages of healing. It appeared that the assassin had been torturing Alishane and testing the cleric's healing abilities. Timmen's head began to swim.

"I'm glad you have chosen to join us," the Shadow Wolf said as he retrieved one of his bloody instruments and turned it over appraisingly. "I'm afraid Master, or rather, *Lord* Wyndam is no longer capable of providing decent sport." The Shadow Wolf looked up and smiled. Something in that smile unlocked the halfling's rigid body. He got to his feet and turned to run back up the stairs, but he ran headfirst into the guard, who had come up behind him.

Timmen fell backward down the stairs. He rolled over to find the guard towering over him.

"Take him to that chair and bind him," Rinn instructed.

The halfling felt himself being lifted from the ground and carried across the room where he was roughly dropped into a chair. Before the guard could tie him down, however, there came shouts of challenge from outside. Timmen heard the unmistakable sound of arrows knocking into the wooden frame of the house. Then came a clang of metal and the agonized wails of wounded and crippled men, followed closely by the sound of many running feet thundering from the direction of the Guardsman camp. Just as the running men reached the house, a flood of blinding light seared through the night sky and pierced through the cracks in the walls, sending narrow rays spilling into the cellar. As confused shouts issued from the soldiers, the front door of the house burst open and light footfalls could be heard running across the floor above them.

"Aurora!" Timmen yelled. "Down here, we are down here!"

The guard in the cellar made for the stairs, but he stopped at a shout from the Shadow Wolf. "No!" the assassin instructed. "Let her come."

Timmen looked in shock at Zakarus Rinn. Aurora had easily defeated the man in their previous encounter. What trick did he have in store for her this time? The halfling looked frantically around the room. Only then did he notice a regal old woman in flowing gowns sitting in a dark corner of the cellar. Timmen began to shake uncontrollably. "The... the... C... C...," he stuttered. "No! It cannot be!"

The Countess of Westbury looked at him coolly. When Aurora's footsteps could be heard descending the stairs, the Countess even smiled.

"Welcome!" said the Shadow Wolf when Aurora had reached the bottom few steps. "How splendid it is to see you again, my dear."

Aurora looked at him darkly, but then a slight smile lit her fair face. "I'm surprised to see you in such good spirits, assassin, after our last meeting. How is your head?" she asked.

"You flatter me with your concern," Rinn countered, "but truly you should be more concerned with the wellbeing of your friend." With these words, the assassin stepped aside to reveal the tortured and bleeding Alishane Wyndam.

Aurora's cheeks flushed hotly and her white hair blew away from her body as her ire swept through her. She reached for the hilt of her sword and pulled it free of its scabbard, but as she prepared to advance on the assassin and guard, an unfamiliar voice rang from the corner of the room. *"Impervio Solarum Adamenté!"* the voice said, and a globe of impenetrable darkness fell upon the elf. Aurora could no longer see her enemies or anything around her.

"I believe you have caused enough trouble for me, little girl," the Countess said as she rose from her chair.

Aurora ignited her bright magical energy, but it was devoured completely by the globe of darkness. She fell back upon the stairs, blind and totally defenseless.

The strange voice cackled and said, "Your magic will not avail you, elf!" The Countess moved toward the middle of the room as she continued speaking. "How fascinating!" she said breathlessly. "You were quite right, Zakarus, she is a fine specimen." As she reached the table, the Countess picked up one of the sharp instruments and looked at it lovingly. "I have heard," the old woman cooed, "that if done properly one can bleed the life-force of an elf and absorb the energy into one's own body." She picked up another grisly instrument and concluded, "I believe I should like to try that."

The Countess took a step toward the blind and helpless Aurora Daelin but then had to clutch at the table to keep herself from falling, for the very foundations of the building had been rocked by the force of a tremendous explosion. A huge fireball detonated above the house, incinerating everything in its path including the Guardsman camp, the barn and all of the soldiers. The top floor of the house was ablaze and the Countess and Shadow Wolf looked at each other in confusion. A moment later a tall, cloaked figure appeared silhouetted by the flames at the top of the stairs. The man was glowing faintly with a wavering blue outline that contrasted starkly with the red flames licking at his cloak. As the man descended the stairs, the guard dropped his sword and ran in fear to the back of the cellar. The Shadow Wolf pulled his sword and began to advance, but the wizard extended his staff and his voice boomed, *"Canterso Vot Statio!"* and the assassin froze in place, perfectly incapable of movement. The Countess finally shook free of her surprise and confusion and began to cast her own spell, but the wizard was faster. *"Annaoro Verbatum!"* he said forcefully and the Countess was rendered mute. Her spell fell away from Aurora and the elf got to her feet.

Aurora looked around in confusion for a moment, then she raised her sword and with wrathful eyes she made for Zakarus Rinn.

"No!" said the wizard and Aurora turned to look at him. He no longer looked like a wizard, but rather like a very old man. "I cannot hold off the flames much longer," he wheezed. "We must be away right now!"

Aurora nodded and went straight to Alishane. She cut his bonds and lifted him over her shoulder.

The old man looked at Timmen. "Come and help me, lad," he said. The halfling rushed to the old man's side and helped him walk back up the stairs. He turned to make sure that Aurora was following and saw that they were all now glowing with the same blue outline as the old man. When they got to the top of the stairs, they were enveloped in a roaring inferno. "Onward, now. Straight through the flames," the old man gasped. He had gone very pale. Timmen felt him shaking as they walked through what was left of the house. The halfling was worried that the old man would collapse.

At last they walked out of the burning structure and into a wasteland of smoke, ash and the charred remains of buildings and men. Two horses came galloping up to them and Aurora immediately slung Alishane over one of them and leaped up behind him. The other horse kneeled down beside the old man to make it easier for him to mount, and still Timmen had to help him up before climbing on, himself.

They rode through the rest of the village and into the night, leaving the smoldering ruins of the house behind. A short while later, Timmen looked into the night sky at the star Callumel with her sister stars beside her and he wondered at how very little of the world he understood.

"Thank you," he said to the wizard. The old man made no reply; his breathing was labored and ragged. They rode a bit longer before Timmen ventured to ask, "Who are you?"

"Arcanis," the old man wheezed and sank lower on the horse, "my name is Arcanis Rhu."

Part Three
~ *Sequela Villanorum* ~

Honor Among Thieves

Chapter Thirteen

~ A Turn in the Road ~

Darius Zannick sat behind his oak desk deep in the belly of the university and stroked the gnarled head of his pet galliwollup. The large lizard, which was thought to be a distant cousin to dragons, flicked her forked tongue from side to side and over her head, smelling the air as lizards do. Charles Bothan sat on a couch in the corner, casually peeling fruit with a slender blade. Neither man spoke. Zannick took the top off a canister on his desk and retrieved a fat, squirming insect from within. He dropped it in front of the galliwollup and the lizard's tongue shot out to snare the unfortunate bug and pull it into her mouth. The reptile's body heaved as it swallowed its prey.

"Enter," said the Regent after a knock at the door. A dirty, shifty-eyed thief walked in and gave a slight jump when the door slammed shut behind him. He recovered quickly and hurried into the room to stand in front of Zannick's desk. The Regent said nothing but only looked at the man for a long time, his pale white eye looking the man over very carefully. The thief began to sweat as he lost his struggle against looking nervous.

"I thought I told you to never enter my office when you're armed, Larons," the Regent said coolly.

"It's only a small blade, sir. I forgot I had it," Larons replied meekly.

"Forgot?" the Regent asked harshly and his eyes narrowed. The thief looked down at the floor. "Why would you feel it necessary to have a knife for this meeting?" Zannick pressed. Larons did not reply, but he cast a furtive glance at Charles Bothan reclining in the corner. "Perhaps," Zannick continued, "you felt the need to be armed because you fear my retribution."

"I've done no wrong, sir!" Larons said frantically as rancid sweat poured down his pale face to mingle with his dark whiskers.

"Do not insult my intelligence!" Zannick stormed. The Regent had grown very red in the face, but his voice lowered to a whisper and he smiled menacingly as he continued, "Did you think I would not discover your intentions and your true allegiance?"

"My only allegiance is to you and the Crystal Night, Mr. Zannick. If you would let me explain," the thief whimpered.

"Explain?" the Regent boomed and his voice echoed off the walls. "Yes, why don't you explain why you have been sneaking into Tavora Manor secretly and without my permission."

The thief opened his mouth as if to speak, but no words escaped his lips. He closed his mouth and shook his head, looking back at Charles Bothan who was now eating the apple he had peeled. Larons opened his mouth again and finally managed to croak, "A girl."

Zannick raised an eyebrow. "We have girls, Mr. Larons," he said skeptically.

"Oh not like Ellumen, sir. Not like her," Larons said fervently. "She's special. She's never given herself to anyone before me."

"Ha! Think you that?" the Regent scoffed.

Larons looked indignant. "Yes," he said. "She told me."

"Do not trust what a woman says by way of seduction, Mr. Larons; it is always poison and usually lethal." The Regent looked quickly at Charles Bothan, who picked up another apple and tossed it at the thief with his left hand. Before Larons could react, Bothan threw the knife with his right hand and punctured the apple in midair. The apple fell into the hands of the thief with the hilt of the dagger protruding from it. Larons dropped it as if it were a hot coal.

"But Mr. Larons," the Regent concluded, still stroking the head of his galliwollup, "the poisonous words of a woman will never hurt you as much as I can. Do what you feel you must to prove where your loyalty lies." The Regent rang a little bell and the door opened. A burly man entered and escorted the pasty-faced Larons out of the office. Zannick pulled another squirming insect from the canister and dropped it before his lizard, which snatched it up and gulped it down.

"Shall I have him followed?" Charles Bothan asked.

"No," answered the Regent, "but if the girl isn't dead by tomorrow night, then he had better be."

Aurora Daelin and Timmen O'Hook sat around their small campfire looking doleful. Though the elf had used her heritage and called upon the forest to help them hide, they were still uneasy and had spoken little. The cleric and wizard were sleeping, but both looked to be in bad shape. The old man's breathing was raspy and

Alishane looked feverish; he was mumbling and writhing in his delirium and sweating profusely.

"It's a dead man's luck that the cleric is ill, since he's the one with the power to heal," muttered Timmen.

"That is a terrible choice of words," scolded the elf, "but I do feel quite helpless." Aurora looked at Alishane with a concerned look on her face. A shadow of guilt passed over her. "And I feel somewhat responsible. I fear the assassin laid this trap to ensnare me."

"Rinn may have his own fascination with you," said the halfling, "but he's working for the Countess. She's the one who wanted to capture you."

"The Countess?" Aurora asked, her face showing her great surprise. "Is that who that was? I did not know she could command such magical power."

"Nor did I," said the thief, "and I've made it my business to know everything about Pilas Antum's criminal world. She has guarded that secret very well, and it explains a great deal about how she has grown so powerful."

"Indeed," Aurora whispered and then her voice trailed off. She wiped the sweat off Alishane's brow and then asked, "What happened in the Wyvern's Tail? How did the servant die?"

Timmen frowned. He did not want to recount the tale, so he simply said, "The Shadow Wolf." Aurora did not press any further.

After a few moments of uncomfortable silence, during which both felt sickened by the memory of Dunk Worley's demise, Timmen shook his head vigorously to chase away the images and asked, "Did you learn anything from your contacts?"

Aurora was a long time in answering; she was still deep in thought. At last she looked blankly at the halfling. "My what?" she asked.

"Your contacts," Timmen repeated. "Your spies."

"Oh," the elf seemed to come back from wherever she had been and focused her bright eyes on the halfling. "My source could not give me specific information about the *Wind Runner*, but he pointed me to Regent Darius Zannick. Do you know of him?"

"I know the man," Timmen answered. "I've seen him in various taverns with more security than one in his position should have occasion to need. And the type of security surrounding him was subtle and villainous. I doubt anyone who isn't in my line of work would even notice that his bodyguards were there. But I haven't tried to discover anything about his business. There are rumors he's trying to resurrect an old thieves' guild called the Crystal Night, but I don't believe any of it."

"It is true," Aurora stately flatly. "And what is more, he has apparently already succeeded." A brief wave of shock passed over the thief, but then his face registered a look of skepticism. "I have already met with the man," Aurora continued, "and he made no secret of his endeavors. I believe it is only a matter of time before he goes to war with the Countess."

Timmen was utterly speechless. He looked at the elf, radiant even under the dirt and dust of the road. *What have I got myself wrapped up in?* he thought to himself. *Elves, assassins, the Countess and the Crystal Night... I should have listened to Cane*

Shanney and never gotten involved in this. At last he managed to utter, "What did he say?"

"He said that he knows a great deal about the Countess and her business with the *Wind Runner*, but he will not tell us until we perform a service for him."

"And what is that service?" asked the halfling with trepidation.

"Well, that's where you come in," Aurora said with a conspiratorial grin. She saw the thief frown, but she pressed ahead anyway, "The Regent gave me this." She pulled the map to the Caverns of the Crystal Night out of her pack and gave it to Timmen. His eyes lit up immediately.

"A map!" he squeaked and inched closer to the fire.

Aurora watched the halfling's eyes roam over the parchment and saw his excitement begin to overmatch his misgivings. "The map leads to a cave complex called the Caverns of the Crystal Night," she said. "We must explore the Caverns and retrieve the treasure at their core." At these words the halfling's look of eagerness faded, and by the time she finished the sentence he was frowning and shaking his head.

"No," he stated flatly. "I will not go into those caves."

"We must if we want to have further dealings with the Regent," the elf countered, "and he is our only hope of gaining information about the Countess."

Timmen studied the map and the look of longing crept back onto his face. "What treasure is inside the Caverns?" he asked.

"Zannick would not say," Aurora answered, "he said only that it was a magical item of great value." She watched the thief for a bit longer and then added, "He also said we could keep it once we tell him how to master the Caverns, and I certainly have no need for human magic."

Timmen looked up quickly. "It would be mine, then?" he asked.

The elf nodded. "Yes," she said.

He considered this for a moment, then his eyes narrowed. "Don't think you can play upon my greed," he said. "This is all very tempting, but I will not risk the Caverns of the Crystal Night for riches or magic."

Aurora frowned and tilted her head. "For what would you risk it, then?" she asked.

Timmen looked at the cleric sweating and moaning in a fever-plagued sleep. "I will do it," he whispered, "for friendship."

* * * * * * *

Timmen and Aurora found sleep in the early morning. When they awoke, they decided that it would be best to stay in camp throughout the day and move on at nightfall. Late in the afternoon, the wizard woke up and took a little food. He was still pale and very weak. The elf and halfling sat in silence and watched him eat. When he had finished, the old man looked from one to the other and smiled warmly.

"I suppose you are looking for some answers," he said.

Aurora shook her head. "I will not ask any questions of you until I have thanked you for saving us," she responded. "We would not have made it out of there without you."

The wizard gave a small chuckle. "That is true," he said. "You entered the house without a full understanding of what you were facing." He gave Aurora a stern look. "I might have expected that of an impetuous halfling," he scolded, "but the daughter of the Jarl should know better."

Aurora was stunned. She felt heat rise in her cheeks, the blush bringing color into her pale face. "I think I will have those answers now," she said.

The old man laughed heartily until his breath caught and he gave a small, dignified cough. He cleared his throat and continued smiling. "I thought that would get your attention," he said. "Yes, I am here at the behest of your father. But don't worry, don't worry," he added hastily upon seeing the look on her face, "he has ultimate confidence in you. He just feels you might benefit from some advice from time to time."

"And a bit of magical assistance," Timmen put in.

The old man's eyes hardened. "Do not count on that," he said. "You see how long it has taken me to recover from last night." He shook his head resolutely. "No, I will not cast a single spell unless there is no other choice."

"What type of advice are you to give me?" Aurora asked hotly. "'Don't do that, you silly little girl?' Is that the advice you speak of?"

"It may have come in useful last night," countered the wizard.

"Then why did you not contact me before we went in?"

"For the same reason you did not contact the halfling," Arcanis nodded toward Timmen. "I didn't know exactly where you were and I could not have approached you in broad daylight." The old man looked at her down his long nose. "And would you have heeded my advice, had I endeavored to give it?" he asked. Aurora did not answer, but her cheeks were again ablaze with fury. "I thought not," he concluded simply.

"Regardless of what happened last night," Aurora said in a measured tone, "I do not yet trust you and I do not need a nursemaid."

"Alas for the arrogant precocity of youth!" the wizard lamented with a roll of his eyes. "Decide for yourself when I am worthy of your trust, but spare me your juvenile pride. I am not here to hold your hand, but rather to counsel you on the Sacred Scrolls."

Aurora and Timmen exchanged a startled look. "What do you know of the Scrolls?" she asked breathlessly. "Who *are* you?"

The smile returned to the old man's face. "My name is Arcanis Rhu, as I told your little friend there last night," he said, indicating Timmen, "and I know more about the Scrolls than anyone else alive. That is why your father sent me to you. Now, will you accept my counsel or shall I go back to Westwick and report your obstinacy?"

Aurora's cheeks flushed once more, but there could be no denying the usefulness of the old man's counsel. "Of course I will accept your help," she answered.

"Good," the wizard said, "then perhaps I could get a little more of that stew while it's still hot." The elf and the wizard stared at each other as Timmen ladled the stew into a bowl and handed it to Arcanis. The wizard blew on the steaming soup and asked, "So, what are your plans?"

"We are heading south at nightfall," Aurora answered before Timmen could speak. "We must make our way to the Pandoran Mountains."

Arcanis sipped the stew thoughtfully. Aurora expected him to ask questions and argue against their plan, but the wizard only nodded and said "Very well" and finished his supper. He gave the bowl back to Timmen and then lay down. "And now if you don't mind," he wheezed as he pulled his battered brown cloak about him, "I will try to get a bit more rest before we break camp." He rolled over and was soon fast asleep.

Aurora and Timmen cleaned their cooking utensils and set about tidying the camp, then they went to scout the perimeter of the woods to see if they would be able to leave when the sun went down.

They walked side by side, each making scarcely a sound as they tread lightly over the forest floor. Timmen looked sideways and found the elf frowning sourly. "Does this mean that I'm no longer your nursemaid?" he asked with a mischievous grin. Aurora shot him a scathing look but said nothing.

"Never before!" stormed the Countess. "Never before have I been bested in a magical duel." The woman paced to and fro behind her desk in Tavora Manor, having recently returned from the village. "And to be subjected to the disgrace of a silencing curse!" She spun around to face Zakarus Rinn, who was reclining on the divan beside the desk. "I want that man's head on a pike!" she spat and resumed her pacing. "Meddling in my affairs, killing an entire regiment of my guard..." She paused in her rant. "Unfathomable," she breathed. "Such power! Who could he be?" But Zakarus Rinn had no answer for her and merely sat returning her manic glare. Before the Countess could say anything more on the matter, there came a small knock on her office door. "Enter," she said.

The skinny, bespectacled man who scurried into the room looked thoroughly frightened. He started toward the Countess, then cowered from her stare and skittered toward her desk, but thought better of it and finally made his way before her and bowed in full obeisance as he presented a long piece of paper. She took it from him and scanned it quickly, then looked down at the man menacingly.

"Explain this, Gorvel," she commanded.

The man whimpered as he remained in his sycophantic bow. "We are losing our informants, my lady," he sniveled. "They either disappear or are found dead. And those who are still providing us with details about the shipping cargoes are giving us incorrect information. We show up to rob the ships and find the holds empty." Gorvel glanced up at the Countess and issued another whimper before continuing his report. "Our extortion ring is returning less gold as well. It seems the merchants are no longer afraid of us, or have secured protection elsewhere."

The Countess looked at Zakarus Rinn and the two exchanged a tense look. "Please continue," she instructed Gorvel through clenched teeth.

"Well," Gorvel said, "it seems the only part of our operation that is bringing in as much gold as usual is Madam Olivier's brothel in the Copper Dram, but that is a fairly small part of our business." He looked up pleadingly at the Countess and even took a small step backward before he concluded, "In all, my lady, our intake over the last two months has decreased by almost fifty percent. Over the same period, we have lost twenty-two of our thieves, four enforcers and thirty-seven informants." He returned his nose to the floor and began inching backward toward the door.

The Countess, who was already in a towering temper before the report on her troubled criminal empire, began to seethe with rage. The atmosphere in the room became charged. Glowering at the trembling Gorvel, the Countess slowly and deliberately removed one of her ornate rings and replaced it with another made of silver and possessing a pale blue stone. She extended her hand toward her quivering toady and hissed, *"Oodaaq Celsioso!"* A pulsing stream of blue energy poured from her outstretched fingers and struck Gorvel in the back. The man froze in place, a look of terror etched upon his face. When the Countess lowered her hand and ended the spell, Gorvel was frozen as solid as ice. He fell over upon the floor with a loud clang.

The Countess called to her servants. When they arrived, she instructed, "Take him to dungeon and wait for him to thaw, then bring him back to me." The servants nodded quickly and hurried to carry the rigid man out of the office. When they had gone, the Countess turned to Zakarus Rinn. "Tell me your thoughts," she instructed.

Rinn's response was smooth and casual, without the slightest hint of emotion. "It would seem that your syndicate is being undermined," he said.

"Clearly," the Countess replied. "But by whom?"

The assassin hesitated in thought. When at last he looked back to the woman to answer, his voice had lost some of its snakelike charm and had taken on a definite edge. "I do not yet know. I am an instrument of your designs and you have not bade me look into this matter yet." Though he was still reclined on the divan, both his body and voice were tense as he continued, "I believe you have been too focused on matters within Citadel Adbar and have grown complacent in your management here. As we have seen over the last few days, Tavora Manor is no longer impenetrable. Just this morning we discovered the body of a chambermaid strangled in her bed, and all indications point to a lover from outside the Manor. Such infiltrations may seem trivial, but they show vulnerability and weakness."

The Countess looked at Rinn for a long time, and he returned her gaze unwaveringly. She sat down at her desk and took a deep breath, sitting very tall and rigid. After a few moments of electric silence, she began shuffling papers on her desk. Without looking at him, she addressed the assassin. "I am now instructing you to cease your hunt for Wyndam, the elf and this... this *wizard*."

She spat out the last word with a tone of utmost contempt. "You are to find out who is assailing my organization and report back to me. Share this with no one; I trust no one but you." Rinn waited a moment to see if he would receive further instructions, but the Countess only scribbled furiously upon her papers. "That is all, leave me!" she snapped. The Shadow Wolf rose and departed without looking back.

Chapter Fourteen

~ All the World ~

The Council of the Eastern Province was over, as was the Tournament of Knighthood. Cane Shanney reopened the Wyvern's Tail Inn after arranging for the disposal of the body he found in one of the rooms. The sight had been grisly, but nothing the big barman wasn't used to. Over the years, Shanney had disposed of enough bodies out of the Tail that no one seemed surprised by it. In fact, his business had never been better. So much had happened over the last few weeks that folks were flocking to Pilas Antum's various drinking establishments to talk and speculate into the late hours of the night. Shanney was tired; he was getting little sleep and had worked very hard to tear down his tent on the Tournament grounds and get the Tail ready to reopen. Tired as he was, however, he could not forego the money he was making just so he could rest.

In his idle moments, few as they were, he worried endlessly about Timmen. From the patrons in his tavern Shanney overheard so many convoluted stories and rumors about what had happened in Tavora Manor that he couldn't feel certain about anything. Except, perhaps, that Timmen was in trouble; he felt quite certain of that. He wondered sometimes, when he was alone at night and subject to no distractions and faced with nothing but his conscience, whether he would help Timmen even if it were in his power to do so. After all, he didn't know what kind of help he would be able to render. And he didn't want to make any enemies. If only Timmen had heeded his advice and not gotten involved. But, he concluded, everyone has to be true to their calling; his was to tend bar, Timmen's was to get into trouble.

Shanney was standing behind his bar absently wiping a mug with his greasy towel and reflecting on these thoughts when a loud commotion erupted by the front doors. A murmur rippled through the establishment and soon most of the people were craning their necks to see the man who had just entered. Shanney didn't recognize him, but it appeared as though many of his customers did. The man was tall with piercing dark eyes, large hoop earrings and a shock of lustrous black hair. A red and yellow bird sat upon his shoulder.

"Who's that?" Cane Shanney asked his nearest patron, a rather large man with yellowish skin and eyes.

"Don't ya know? 'At's Sanguine," the big man said, "the bard."

"Bard?" Shanney repeated.

"So he says," replied the big man. "Don't know what that means, but he can sure spin ya a tale."

Shanney continued wiping the mug in his hand as he watched the mysterious stranger move through the crowd, talking and shaking hands. When the man smiled, Shanney saw the distinct glint of silver teeth.

"Play!" yelled a man near the bar.

"Aye, play!" answered another.

Sanguine held up his hands sheepishly. "Oh no, I couldn't," he mouthed, but the silvery smile was broader than ever. Soon a chorus of encouragement was swirling around the room. Sanguine allowed it to go on for a few moments and then at last nodded his consent. A cheer went up from the crowd. The little red and yellow bird flew from the bard's shoulder and fluttered up to the rafters of the hall.

Sanguine waved his hands in the air to quiet the crowd. When at last the clamor subsided, he bowed slightly and smiled. "My friends," he said in a deep, musical voice, "how nice it is to see you all again. You always make a humble traveler feel most welcome." A murmur of appreciation went through the crowd. "What shall we have tonight? A song? A story? Perhaps a soliloquy?" He hesitated and looked around the room. No one spoke. "Yes," he continued, "I believe I shall perform for you a scene from one of my favorite *coup de théatre*. A tale of pain, betrayal and retribution. A tale that I call *Woe Betide in Blood*."

A whisper of excitement raced through the crowd. Sanguine paced about, gathering his thoughts and falling into his character. When at last he stopped and looked around the room, his dark eyes appeared pained and slightly manic. The whispers in the crowd ceased and silence fell.

"Gone," the bard whispered in a tone of utter despair, "my love is gone." He looked around suddenly with a profoundly bestial glare and rushed at a well-to-do couple sitting at a table in the middle of the floor. They jumped in surprise and the woman issued a slight squeal as his hands thundered upon their table. "What know you of love?" the bard asked in a loud, accusatory voice. "What know you of death?" He straightened and turned upon the crowd. "For love *is* death, be certain of that, each of you."

He stalked around his small clearing in the middle of the room and glared at his assembled audience. They returned his look with utter amazement. "Know this!" he boomed. "If ever you truly loved, you will love until the end of your days. But if your love ends before your life is spent, then you will wither; you will die slowly yet certainly, begging for the mercy of a cold blade in your belly." Sanguine stopped in his pacing and towered over a young man whose false bravado melted under the bard's hot stare. "What know you of pain?" he whispered savagely. "Look upon it now, young one," Sanguine hissed, "for I am pain. I am pain in its misery standing before you."

He stared hard at the young man for a moment before turning once again upon the crowd. "Wherefore!" he yelled, his voice echoing off the walls of the meeting hall. "Wherefore this man who steals my love?"

Sanguine moved across the room, scowling darkly at the wide-eyed patrons. Not a sound could be heard but his boots upon the floor.

"And for what price, this recompense?" He threw up his arms in a great flourish and spun to face the other side of the room. "What offense brings payment dearer than blood?"

During the performance, the bard's red and yellow bird had changed form into a small, chestnut-colored monkey with a blonde face and quick, intelligent eyes. Once the crowd was wholly entranced by Sanguine's performance, the monkey crawled down from the rafters and made its way among the people in the dark recesses of the room, stealthily picking their pockets.

"For what price, this recompense?" Sanguine repeated, his voice rising in pitch to a tremulous tenor. "What offense have I wrought upon the gods in my youthful ignorance and arrogance? Whatever I have done, I meant it not! I am, after all, but only a man." He resumed his pacing about the room, looking all the more manic and crazed. "And that is the rub, is it not? I am but a man, fraught with weakness to temptation and greed for satisfaction. Can I be blamed for my transgressions? For living as I have been made? I think not!"

Sanguine stopped his pacing and pulled a dagger from his belt. His voice lowered from its high, frantic pitch to a slow, sinister drawl. "But if I am to suffer for my actions at the hands of this man, then let him also suffer! Let him feel the sting of love's labor lost! Let him experience the dawn of his happiness only to witness its extinction." He turned the blade over in his hand and made a quick stabbing motion. "I shall snuff it out, just as I snuff out his life." He looked back at the crowd and they wilted before him. "Love is death, I tell you. He has found his love in my own, and I shall have my vengeance!"

The bard gave an exaggerated heave with the blade and slumped upon the floor. A great cheer went up from the crowd. The red monkey sat in the rafters beside a small pile of treasure, swinging a golden watch by its fob. Cane Shanney had been wiping the same mug throughout the entirety of Sanguine's performance, and he now set it down upon the bar as his patrons turned to him and resumed drinking.

After a few moments, the bard uncoiled and rose from the floor. His silver teeth glistened in the torchlight as he accepted praise from the male patrons and eye-fluttering smiles from many flushed, female admirers. He kissed the hand of one young woman and she swooned so profoundly that nobody noticed as he slipped a jeweled ring from her finger. He made his way to a table in the corner and sat down, talking merrily and accepting the many free drinks being offered.

Cane Shanney poured ale, cleaned mugs and wiped down his bar as his bustling business continued. A simple man, Shanney didn't care much for the theater and he wasn't happy that it had invaded his tavern. But the people were euphoric and drinking his ale as fast as he could pour it, so he didn't dwell on the matter for long. Soon his mind returned to a familiar subject: where is Timmen O'Hook, and what is he doing?

Aurora Daelin guided her horse gingerly over the uneven footing of the dark forest floor. Alishane Wyndam sat behind her on the horse, his hands gripping her slender waist to help him stay balanced. The cleric had awoken shortly before they set out that evening. His fever broke and he was able to take some food, but he was still too weak to cast any healing spells for his many wounds.

It was now around midnight. They had been riding for several hours and Alishane was losing whatever strength he had recovered. When they first set out, he felt a rush of excitement at being in such close proximity to Aurora, particularly when his hands strayed down to the flair of her hips. He could feel her muscles flex as she used her legs to control and guide the horse. But his excitement ebbed with his energy. Now it was taking his full effort just to stay in the saddle.

Finally, after hours on the trail, his strength was gone. He slumped forward against her and she brought up the horse, whispering to the others to stop. In the brief moment before he lost consciousness and collapsed to the ground, Alishane found his face buried in the elf's long, white hair. He inhaled her scent and found in it something familiar, though he could not identify it. Something from his youth when he ran in the open fields under the sun. He smiled faintly before his mind went blank. He fell from the horse, but was unconscious before he hit the ground.

* * * * * *

"Jasper lily!" Alishane croaked as he woke with a start. He rubbed his temples and groaned; he had a pounding headache. The elf, the wizard and the halfling sat around their small campfire and watched as the cleric muttered something under his breath. When he finished whispering, a light blue wind flashed over him and some color returned to his face. Timmen looked at Arcanis and Aurora and found them both smiling.

"Your strength returns," Arcanis said warmly.

Alishane looked up at the old man, whom he had never seen before, and did not return the smile. "Who are you?" he asked.

"He's a wizard," Timmen said, moving over to sit by Alishane. The halfling began pulling the cleric's clothing aside to inspect his wounds. Alishane tried futilely to brush him away.

"A *retired* wizard," Arcanis corrected. "Now I suppose I am more of a sage."

"What does that mean?" Alishane asked testily, still trying to fend off the halfling who was busily looking him over.

"He's here to counsel us on the Scrolls," Aurora answered. She shot a dark look at Arcanis before she finished, "At the behest of my father."

The wizard and the elf looked at each other tensely. "Who is your father?" asked Alishane.

Aurora was still looking at Arcanis. "He is the Jarl," she answered, finally turning to look at the cleric, "the leader of my people."

Alishane looked at Aurora and noted the stubborn dislike she showed for the wizard. "I see," he said. He tried again to swat away the groping fingers of the halfling. "Will you please!" he erupted in exasperation.

Timmen returned to his seat and looked sulkily at Alishane. "Just trying to see if you're all right," he said.

"I'll be fine when I don't have you fretting over me like a mother hen," Alishane said acidly as he straightened his clothing.

"I'm not the one dreaming about jasper lilies," Timmen retorted.

A tense moment passed as they glowered at each other, then Arcanis Rhu burst out in riotous laughter. "Yes," he said, "a rather odd time to dream of flowers, I should think. Just what kind of dreams were you having, my boy?"

Aurora and Timmen started laughing as well, but Alishane blushed furiously and looked uneasily at the elf. "I don't remember," he muttered.

The laughter around the campfire rose into the night. When at last it died away, the smile on the elf's face lingered. She looked at Alishane, but the man refused to return her gaze. He sat looking stubbornly into the fire, and the heat in his cheeks wasn't only from the flames.

"Well, I'm glad to see we are all returning to health," Arcanis said. "Now we must decide our course."

"Our course has already been decided," Aurora said quickly and the smile melted from her face.

"Our general course, yes," the wizard agreed, "but there are many paths that would lead us to the Pandoran Mountains."

Alishane looked up in surprise. "The Pandoran...?" He turned to the halfling. "What is he talking about?"

Timmen looked from Alishane to Arcanis Rhu. He addressed the wizard. "We haven't fully explained this to you either, have we?" he asked.

"And I haven't asked," the wizard answered softly with a warm smile. Aurora bristled; she knew the insinuation had been directed at her.

"Well," Timmen continued, "Aurora's spy contact directed her to Regent Darius Zannick at the university in Pilas Antum. He claims to be resurrecting an old thieves' guild called the Crystal

Night and is preparing to make war against the Countess." Timmen paused at the incredulous look on the cleric's face. "If that's true then he is in a unique position to help us," Timmen went on, "but he won't until we retrieve a magical item for him."

"And this item is in the Pandoran Mountains?" prompted Alishane.

Timmen looked at the cleric and nodded gravely. "In the Caverns of the Crystal Night."

Alishane said nothing. He looked at his companions, from one to the next. Timmen looked determined and nodded slightly as if to say "We can do it." Aurora was watching the wizard from the corner of her eye to see how the old man would respond. When Alishane looked at Arcanis Rhu, the wizard was still smiling merrily. He gave the cleric a quick wink and continued to smile.

Alishane shook his head slightly. "And you think we can do this?" he asked the group.

"Yes," Aurora answered, "and we must. The Countess is involved in the disappearance of the Scrolls; we all believe that to be true. This is the only way for us to learn more about the extent and nature of her involvement, particularly where the *Wind Runner* is concerned."

Alishane was shaking his head more vigorously now. "I have more reason to visit pain upon that woman than any of you," he said, "but if there is to be a guild war between the Countess and the Crystal Night, then I don't want to be caught in the middle of it."

"One thing I have learned, young man, in all my long years," the wizard cut in, "is that violence and chaos serve only to breed further unrest. The fact that the Countess has been blind to the emergence of a rival guild in the heart of her own city is quite significant. It seems clear that her attention has been directed elsewhere. And now considering her skill with magic, of which none of us were aware until recently, it appears ever more likely that she is involved in the disappearance of the Scrolls." He looked at Alishane with his deep, black eyes for a long moment before he continued. "A journey into the Caverns of the Crystal Night is indeed perilous," he said, "and I would consider it folly if not for the gravity of our circumstances." The wizard looked at Aurora and the two exchanged a knowing glance before he concluded. "The two of you may as well know," he addressed Alishane and Timmen, "that recent events and my knowledge of the Scrolls have led me to one inescapable conclusion: the time of the Prophecy is at hand."

Silence fell. In the small halo of light that emanated from the campfire, the four of them looked at each other: the elf, the cleric, the halfling and the wizard. Nothing more was spoken, but in that moment the bond of their company was sealed. The only thing certain about their future was that it was filled with danger, but whatever came they would face it together.

Two nights after their escape from the village, the four companions abandoned riding overland through the bracken and little glens of the wild. They were unsure whether the Guardsmen were still on their trail, but they wanted to travel quickly and so took to the main road south out of Pilas Antum. As the dawn of their fourth day out of the village spread over the land, they came upon a large caravan also headed south.

The caravan was indeed a motley collection, with men of every creed and stature travelling together. There was even a contingent of dwarves stumping along beside their carts. The humans were careful to give a wide berth both in front of and behind their burly companions, being wisely cautious of the dwarves' notoriously quick temper.

As the companions approached the caravan, Aurora looked quickly to Arcanis Rhu. The wizard nodded and the elf led the party forward, pulling her hood up over her head to cover her ears and long, white hair. Alishane had been given a sword by Arcanis and he ran his fingers over its hilt to become accustomed to its feel.

They came first upon a group of gyptian humans. The gypsies were clearly poor, but they lived a nomadic life and were not daunted in the slightest to be living on the open road. Their possessions were meager but their packs were light; the children ran along the road gaily playing with their dogs and it seemed a smile was on every face.

Timmen, who was still riding behind the wizard, whispered to the others, "Let me talk to them. These are my kind of people." The others exchanged a quick glance and silently agreed. Arcanis nudged their horse forward and came alongside a dirty, yellow-haired man who was whistling a tune slightly off key.

"Ahoy," Timmen called out.

"Hoy hoy, little one," the man answered. "What brings ya to the road on such a fine morning?"

"Running from the Guard, I am," Timmen answered. "Been having too much fun in the city." Timmen felt the slightest flinch run through Arcanis Rhu, but the wizard's countenance remained impassive.

The gypsy's face brightened. "Ah, I'm sure of it. The Counsel and Tournament brought many 'a folk into the city. Too much for one such as yourself to resist, eh?"

"Aye," Timmen answered. "Like the dandies at the front of the column," he nodded ahead to where some wealthy families rode in luxurious carriages. "They left a lot of gold behind them, but maybe not as far behind them as they were thinking." The halfling jiggled his vest to make his coins jingle.

The gypsy laughed. "Ha! Serves 'em right, I say. They have more than they need and never think it's enough." The man glanced up at Arcanis and then around at Aurora and Alishane. "So what brings you folks over?" he asked. "Or did ya just like the sound of my whistling?"

"Wanted to know who's on the road," answered the halfling. "We thought we might join the group for awhile."

The man's face darkened slightly. "Tell ya the truth, mate," said the gypsy, leaning toward them and lowering his voice, "we might not be long for this crew ourselves. We don't care much for the way those rich folks treat their slaves. And travelling with dwarves ain't what I call a picnic."

"Slaves?" Arcanis Rhu spoke up. "Did I hear you correctly?"

The gypsy jumped slightly at the harsh tone in the wizard's voice. "Aye," he answered tentatively. "Several of those families have half-breeds. And they treat 'em just like…"

"Half-breeds?" The wizard's voice grew a little louder and somewhat threatening.

"Half-elves, aye," the man confirmed. "They treat 'em like dogs, as I was saying. Worse than dogs."

Timmen turned to look at Aurora, afraid of what she would do. The elf sat stoically on her horse; her face showed nothing of emotion. Alishane held her a bit tighter from his seat behind her on the horse.

Timmen turned back to the gypsy and made ready their departure. "We'll have to decide what we want to do as well. We thank you for your time."

"Fortune's smile on ya, mate," the gypsy said and waved. The companions stopped in the road and watched the caravan move slowly away. The gypsy resumed whistling his off-key tune.

Arcanis turned and looked at Aurora, his eyes smoldering in a way they had not seen since the night he had single-handedly destroyed half of the village. "What say you?" he demanded of Aurora.

The elf was a long time in answering. Her gaze continued to follow the caravan receding into the distance, yet she still showed no sign of emotion. At last, she took a deep breath and spoke in a measured tone. "It does not concern us. Our business is with the Countess." She turned her horse off the road and headed slowly for the trees. "Let us make our camp for the day. We will set out again at nightfall."

None of them spoke as they made their camp and ate a small meal. They were careful not to look too closely at Aurora, but whenever they stole a glance the elf sat in stony silence and stared into the fire. Alishane and Arcanis fell asleep first and as Timmen lay down his head and began to drift off to sleep, he looked one last time at the elf. Aurora hadn't shown the slightest hint of emotion since their meeting with the gypsy, but as Timmen's thoughts fluttered on the edge of consciousness he looked back into the elf's icy blue eyes and saw a single tear course down her pale cheek.

Chapter Fifteen

~ Hubris Humbled ~

Zakarus Rinn crouched in the shadows of a darkened house, peering out the window at the posh dwelling across the lane. From a room upstairs came the shuffling and muffled complaints of the family who owned the home in which he was sitting. Two adults and three children lay bound and gagged on the floor; the children were sobbing into their gags, the adults were struggling against their bonds. Rinn ignored them. If they became too much of a nuisance or threatened his objective, he would dispatch of them permanently. For now, he sat silently at the window, running a whetstone down the length of his dagger.

Three nights had passed since the Countess gave him the directive to investigate the mysterious threat to her empire. On each of those nights he paid a visit to one of the merchants who had stopped paying tribute to the Countess. His objective was twofold: first to gather information and second to send a message.

The Shadow Wolf's interrogation technique was simple and brutal. He would pose his question and then cut off a finger. He asked the question again and cut off another. After three fingers he felt certain that he had the truth. Then it was time to send his message. He slit his victim's throat, then placed a black orchid with the fingers and tied them together with a blue ribbon. The ribbon was distinctive; it matched the crest on the seal of Westbury. The orchid was the calling card of the Shadow Wolf. Taken together, these symbols sent a message that was clear: the Countess was dormant no longer.

Three nights and three murders later, the Shadow Wolf sat in a prosperous neighborhood on the north side of Pilas Antum, watching the house across the lane. Each of his victims had given him the same information, and each after only one finger; the second and third were simply confirmation. The merchants were paying tribute to another guild because the threat it posed seemed more immediate than what they felt from the distracted Countess. They had realized the error of their thinking too late, for once they looked into the eyes of the Shadow Wolf, only the gods could offer salvation.

What troubled the assassin was the second piece of information he had gathered from his torture of the merchants. This rival guild had assumed a name that would strike fear into the hearts of many. Though Zakarus Rinn was not among those who felt fear at mention of the name, still he found it somewhat disconcerting. *The Crystal Night,* he thought to himself. *Could it be?*

The last bit of information he had learned was the name of the Crystal Night's operative who was threatening the merchants. It hadn't taken the assassin long to find the man's house, it was the house he now sat watching from the shadows across the lane. Rinn didn't believe for a moment that the man had information worth extracting. He was undoubtedly a low-level enforcer in the Crystal Night's extortion crew and was kept largely ignorant of the inner workings of the guild. It was likely that he did not even know the true name of the superior to whom he reported. No, Rinn would not interrogate this man. He had left a clear message with the bodies of the merchants. Now he would sit and watch and let the Crystal Night make the next move. *Let them come to me,* thought the Shadow Wolf as he ran the stone down his blade and peered into the night, *and then it will begin.*

———————————————————

The companions broke camp and took to the road before the sun was fully set, though none of them had found much sleep. At various points during the day's rest, one of them would awaken and wander around the camp. Alishane found Aurora sleeping fitfully, tossing in the throes of a dream. Arcanis woke up to find her sitting with her back to the group, the hood of her cape pulled low over her eyes. When Timmen stirred and crept to their packs to sneak some more food, he looked around conspiratorially and was surprised to find that the elf was missing from camp. He slipped away and looked for her in the woods, finally finding her sitting on a rock with her eyes closed in apparent meditation.

The halfling sat watching her for a few moments. He wondered if he should try to talk to her, but he knew that there was nothing he could say to ease her suffering. His own folk had experienced their share of discrimination at the hands of the big people, but they never had to go into seclusion because of it. And they had never been subjected to slavery in the fashion of the half-elves. In the end, he crept back to camp and lay awake for a long time before succumbing to exhaustion and returning to sleep. He did not hear her return.

Now they sat in stoic silence, riding together down the southbound road into the gathering night. The uncomfortable tension that sprouted between them the night before was growing so Alishane looked at Timmen and implored him to try singing. Timmen, however, was not in a singing mood and shook his head. Alishane was insistent, but the halfling only shook his head more vehemently. Alishane scowled at him and the tension thickened.

"Did I tell you," Timmen addressed the group at large, "about the night our esteemed cleric and I ran from the Wyvern's Tail?" Aurora turned a look upon him that clearly warned against drudging up an unpleasant memory, but the halfling was undeterred. "We took shelter in the backyard garden of a large, fancy house," he continued. "There was a nice berry patch and clothes hanging on the line." The others were all listening intently now. "We ate some of the berries and they helped us feel a little better, though noble Master Wyndam was aghast at the thought of eating anything that hadn't been properly washed."

It now being clear that Timmen intended to poke fun at the cleric, Arcanis chuckled and Aurora smiled slightly. She felt Alishane tense as he sat behind her on the horse. Timmen looked over and saw that the man's scowl had deepened, but he continued with his story anyway. "As the night wore on, it got pretty cold. I was happy to find a child's coat hanging on the line, but poor noble Master Wyndam found nothing but the lady of the house's red dress and undergarments." Timmen paused for effect and then continued. "Now I tried to tell him that, circumstances being as they were, no one would judge him if he kept himself warm, but he refused to put on the gown. Finally, though, it just got too cold for noble Master Wyndam and he swallowed his pride and donned the dress."

"I did not! That never happened!" Alishane cut in.

"Don't be embarrassed, Al; it was a very nice party gown with pretty white frills around the hem," Timmen jabbed.

"Stop your lying, halfling!" Alishane threatened through gritted teeth while casting nervous glances at Aurora.

"Now no one's judging you for wearing the dress," Timmen consoled in his most placating voice. "Like I said, it was very cold." Again the halfling paused briefly before finishing the joke. "What I don't understand, though," he cast a sideways glance at the fuming cleric, "is why you insisted on putting on the undergarments too."

Aurora and Arcanis exploded in laughter. Alishane jumped from the horse and tried to run after Timmen, but the halfling kicked his horse in the haunches and he and the wizard went galloping down the road with the cleric running in pursuit. A few moments later, having given up his futile chase, Alishane waited in the road for Aurora to ride up to him on their horse. To her credit, the elf was no longer smiling, but her cheeks were flushed and her eyes twinkled with mirth.

Alishane got on the horse and said into her ear, "That never happened."

"Hmm," Aurora acknowledged. She bit her lip and won her battle against another burst of laughter.

The two continued up the road to where Arcanis and Timmen sat waiting. As they neared, the halfling stood on the horse's rump and bowed deeply. "My apologies, noble Master Wyndam," his high, clear voice rang out, "for clearly I was wrong," he winked at the wizard before concluding. "It appears as though we *have* judged you for wearing the dress."

This time, all four of them laughed. They turned their horses to the south and continued down the road. The sun had now set and the land was one big shadow, but their hearts were lighter and the tension was gone.

They passed over a hill and clip-clopped slowly down the other side. Alishane again whispered into Aurora's ear, "That never happened."

"I know," she whispered and continued to smile.

* * * * * * *

They rode throughout most of the night without any problems or further halfling shenanigans. Aurora told a little about the mysteries of Westwick Forest; Timmen spoke of loud, raucous nights in the Wyvern's Tail. Through all of it, Arcanis Rhu listened quietly with a slight smile and a faraway look in his eyes. When asked about his own adventures, by Timmen naturally, the old man simply held up his hand and said softly, "Some other time, perhaps."

Shortly before dawn, with a sliver of a moon hanging in the eastern sky, they came upon a split in the road and stopped to discuss their course.

Aurora dismounted her horse and inspected the tracks in the dirt. "The carriages of the wealthy continue down the main road on the left, along with the gypsies. The dwarves have taken this smaller road off to the right." She looked at the group. "Do any of you know where it leads?"

When none of the others spoke, Arcanis cleared his throat and said, "This is the juncture of the South Road, on which we now stand, and the Lodge Trail Pike. The Lodge Trail swings to the west, through the Anderton Vale to eventually merge with the Bourgan Road, which will in turn take us further south into the Pandoran Mountains."

"Would you say it is a straighter route to the mountains?" Aurora asked.

"Somewhat, but it is largely unused and would take us over Lodge Trail Pass, which is known to be fairly inhospitable."

"Inhospitable how?" Timmen asked.

"It is overrun with kobolds," the wizard answered, then added for good measure, "and the occasional band of goblins or wolves."

Timmen grimaced.

"The South Road will be more likely to have Guardsmen patrolling it, which makes it safer," Alishane put in.

"Not if you just killed a regiment of their friends," the wizard retorted dryly. They all chuckled.

"Let us move to the west and shorten our trip," Aurora decided. "I will take my chances with wolves or kobolds."

The group agreed and they set out once more.

Shortly after the day dawned they had begun looking for a place to camp when Aurora suddenly stopped and put an arrow to her bowstring.

"What is it?" Alishane asked. The elf did not answer, but sat taller on their horse and looked into the trees ahead.

"It is the dwarves," Arcanis stated. "Get down, Timmen," he said over his shoulder.

The halfling looked surprised but complied. "What do you intend to do?" he asked the wizard.

"Confirm my suspicions," the old man said. He nudged his horse forward, then whispered back at them. "Stay here, all of you."

The three of them looked at each other questioningly, but finding no answers, they turned back to watch the old man ride slowly forward. At last, after he had gone about a furlong down the road, a group of at least twenty dwarves swarmed out of the trees and surrounded him. Though the three friends could not hear what was being said, it was clear in watching that the dwarves were poised for battle. A moment later, however, their posture relaxed and a particularly swarthy dwarf stepped forward. He conversed briefly with the wizard and then became very agitated, waving his thick arms about and pounding the ground with the handle of his huge, double-headed axe. At last, the wizard's words apparently won out, for the dwarf stumped back into the trees and reappeared carrying his belongings. Together, the two of them turned and moved back toward the astonished companions.

Shortly thereafter, when they were close enough for the dwarf's features to become clear, Timmen gave a squeak and jumped back. "That's Dorak Shale!" he exclaimed.

Neither Alishane nor Aurora had heard the name before so they said nothing. When the wizard and the dwarf arrived, Arcanis attempted an introduction. "Dorak, may I introduce…"

"Bah! I'm not for carin' what their name's are," Dorak snorted. "I owe ye my axe, old man, not conversation." Arcanis smiled while the other three friends looked bewildered. "If ye're settin' camp for the day, then set it," the dwarf said and moved off the road into the forest. "I'll be sleeping under this tree," he said as he slumped down under a large elm. "And don't ye be wakin' me until we're ready to march!" With that, he pulled his helmet down over his eyes and was soon snoring.

The three friends looked back to Arcanis, who simply smiled and said, "The dwarf will be joining our party for awhile."

As they turned off the road to prepare their camp, Timmen poked Alishane and repeated, "That's Dorak Shale."

"I heard you the first time, Timmen," said the cleric.

The assassin moved silently through the shadows, over the cobblestones and around the puddles of filth that dotted the lanes even in this affluent section of the city. He was an artist, a bringer of death, and loyal to one master. His master was preparing for the first offensive of a war that would soon erupt in this city, and the deathbringer was the tip of his master's spear.

His assigned target tonight was a man in his master's criminal organization. Known as a shuffler, this man conducted business on behalf of the organization without ever knowing more about it than the person to whom he reported and the people whose services he filtered. Significant sums of gold passed through the man's possession, but he never stole a single coin. The shuffler was an asset, a strong and loyal worker who knew his place and never aspired to greater glory. He performed his duties flawlessly.

And tonight he would die.

Three merchants had been murdered, one on each of the previous three nights. One dealt in textiles, one sold fish and the third was a realtor who also bred horses. They had never met, but they had two things in common. They had all turned their back on the Countess of Westbury and accepted protection from another guild, and they all had the same shuffler.

The assassin slowed as he neared his target's home. He crouched in the shadows and surveyed the neighborhood. All of the houses were dark, the inhabitants surely asleep at this late hour. In one of them, however, was another bringer of death. The assassin was sure of it. He had followed the career of Zakarus Rinn with great interest and studied the man's habits. His mentor, who served as chief lieutenant in his master's guild, had even shared time with Rinn at Mount Alcharist. He knew the Shadow Wolf was behind the murders of the merchants; everyone knew that. But the assassin also knew that the grotesque manner in which the merchants had died, the message that had been sent, was brash and reckless and both were qualities seldom seen in Zakarus Rinn. It was a ploy designed to draw out the assailant to the Countess's empire, a ploy that a less experienced man might have fallen for. But the man who crouched now in the shadows was not short on experience. The Shadow Wolf had underestimated his quarry. It was a rare mistake, but in this business your first mistake was often your last.

Looking over the houses now the assassin zeroed in on one in particular. Like the others it was dark, all of its windows shuttered. All save one. The assassin placed an amethyst ring on his finger and touched his temple. His vision brightened and focused, the darkness of the night washed away by the ring's magic stone. Into the open window he gazed, through the slight parting in the curtains. The man squinted and leaned closer, his muscles tensed like a cat preparing to pounce. Then he saw him: the Shadow Wolf!

A target of opportunity.

The assassin removed the finger from his temple and waited for his vision to return to normal, then he set out for the rear of the Wolf's lair. He covered the ground swiftly, trusting to the element of surprise and the stealth he had spent years honing. How pleased his mentor would be when he returned with the Shadow Wolf's head! This kill would surely catapult him into infamy.

The assassin reached the yard behind the house and quickly scanned the area to make sure nothing was amiss. He saw what he expected to see: nothing to indicate that the Shadow Wolf feared an attack. The rear of the house was dominated by a large bay window off of the dining room. To one side, a door led from a landing into the kitchen. Beside that, a small window led to what was probably a pantry. The assassin made for the small window.

Again the man put the finger with the amethyst ring to his temple and peered into the house. The room was indeed a pantry. The assassin then reached into an inner pocket of his shirt and pulled forth the mightiest gift his mentor had ever lent him: the petrified eye of a Galvarian shaman.

The Galvarians were a primitive people native to the deep forests of the Galvary Basin. Small and somewhat bent in stature, they were believed to be distant cousins to halflings, though mixture of goblin blood was often rumored. Because their rituals involved sacrifices and bloody mutilations, "civilized" practitioners considered their dark magic to be taboo, but there could be no doubting its usefulness to those willing to use it.

The petrified eye that the assassin now held before the window possessed a powerful dweomer: it allowed its wielder to see any traps, glyphs or spells of warding within the immediate area. As the assassin whispered the incantation and held forth the eyeball between his thumb and forefinger, the gruesome orb twitched and jerked, the pupil dilating as the lens focused and looked about. There were no traps or protective glyphs, only the lock on the window that now glowed green in the mind of the assassin. He returned the eye to his pocket and quickly picked the lock.

Once inside the pantry, the assassin quietly pulled his blade and touched his ringed finger to his temple. Again his vision brightened. With perfect clarity of sight and agility honed by years of practice, the deathbringer crept from the pantry and turned right, slinking past the kitchen and into the dining room. An open door to the left of the room led to the front of the house, into the sitting room where the Shadow Wolf waited unsuspecting.

The assassin circled slightly to his right, around the chairs and table to look into the sitting room and find his quarry. The doorjamb slid slowly past his line of sight, revealing more of the room beyond and, finally, the cloaked form of Zakarus Rinn. The Shadow Wolf was still seated looking out the window, with his back toward the man who was even now rounding the table and entering the   room.

The deathbringer crept slowly and deliberately. He felt a tremendous urge to rush up behind his target and plunge his blade into the Shadow Wolf's back, but he ignored the urge and followed his training, moving silently across the final expanse. At last the moment came. He was standing directly behind the Shadow Wolf and Rinn had not stirred. The assassin watched the rise and fall of his target's shoulders as the Wolf breathed in and out. *Your last breaths, Zakarus Rinn* thought the assassin as he raised his blade and took aim to the left of the man's spine, where the Shadow Wolf's heart was pumping through its last moments of labor.

In that fleeting moment, with his blade poised and ready to strike, the assassin felt a pang of disappointment. *So this is how it ends for Zakarus Rinn?* He had grown up hearing tales of the man's exploits, studying him almost to the point of idolatry. And now he would die without a fight, stabbed in the back in the dead of night. *It is somewhat poetic*, the assassin thought. *So this is how it ends for Zakarus Rinn.*

The assassin struck hard, driving his blade straight through the Shadow Wolf's back, through the muscle and sinew and into his heart… through his heart and into the chair… *Wait! This cannot be!* The assassin's mind screamed the incongruity, but could not make sense of the information. He raised his hand again and drove it home again, straight through the image of the Shadow Wolf.

"You are not the only one with magic," said a voice behind him. The assassin raised his weapon and spun around, but it was too late. A vise-like hand held his wrist and a blade flashed before his eyes. Searing pain burned across his throat and he saw his own blood spray forth. His head felt heavy and his hands fell to his sides. Without the amethyst ring his vision darkened, but in the pale light that shone through the open window behind him an image materialized. His vision held long enough for him to lock eyes with the Shadow Wolf and see the man smile wickedly, and then everything went black.

Chapter Sixteen

~ Pandoran Passage ~

The companions slept for only a few hours before setting off again. They decided that it was no longer necessary to travel by night since they had left the South Road and were less likely to encounter pursuing Guardsmen. Travelling during the heat of the day on very little sleep discouraged conversation, however, and most of their time was passed simply trying to stay awake and atop their mounts. Aurora surrendered her seat on the horse with Alishane so that Dorak could ride. The cleric tried briefly to talk her out of it, but the elf insisted that she was the fleetest of foot and would not slow their progress. She was keen on moving with all possible speed. Alishane saw her logic and acquiesced, but he still wasn't too thrilled to be riding behind the smelly dwarf.

Around midday they came upon a stream and stopped to water the horses. Timmen led the animal he shared with Arcanis slightly upstream from the others so he could ask the questions that had stirred his curiosity all morning.

"How do you know Dorak Shale?" he asked as he watched the wizard stoop on the bank of the stream to run his hands in the cool water.

Arcanis took a deep breath and gathered his patience before answering. "I met Dorak shortly before my retirement," he said.

"Where?"

"The Argon Vale."

"What were you doing there?"

"I prefer not to answer that question."

"What was Dorak doing there?"

"Perhaps you should ask *him* that question."

"Did you help him?"

"In a way."

"Is that why he is indebted to you?"

"The nature of my relationship with Dorak Shale is none of your concern, Timmen O'Hook." The wizard's voice took on an irritated edge that gave the halfling pause.

After a few moments of chewing his lip, Timmen ventured one more question. "Can we trust him?" he asked quietly.

Arcanis dipped his hands in the water and splashed his face before walking to the halfling and dropping a hand on his shoulder. "Yes," the wizard answered with a warm smile; "we can trust him to be loyal to the party." He walked to the horse and checked the luggage. "Of course, he does not need to know what our overall objective is or why we are going to the Caverns. Not yet, anyway."

"But if he asks…" Timmen began.

"He won't," the wizard stated firmly and led the horse away. "Now come, let us rejoin the others."

Regent Darius Zannick huddled in conference with his top two lieutenants: Charles Bothan and a thick stump of a man named Kleet Olander. Kleet had slanted eyes, sparse black hair and a stubble beard that accentuated the long, shiny scar that ran down his left cheek. He had a huge barrel chest, thick arms and no identifiable neck supporting his large, bulbous head. The three men leaned over Zannick's desk, studying a large, intricate chart that showed with stunning detail the many facets of the Countess's criminal empire. The names on the paper were color-coded to show the various levels of importance attributed to the operatives. The chart was broad at its base and narrowed at the top to only one name: Morna De Lorraine, The Countess of Westbury. Under some of the names, written in red ink, were the words "Execute... Phase One".

"I believe we should send Kradjick after this one," Bothan said, pointing to the name "Cedric Knotting". Kleet Olander grunted, which was a clear sign of his agreement. The Regent said nothing, but merely rubbed his chin and continued scanning the chart with his off-colored eyes.

"And Smythe after this one," continued Charles Bothan, indicating the name "Dandrick Humple".

"We are not certain of Humple's affiliation with the Countess," said Zannick.

Bothan turned a look of slight surprise on the Regent. "Does that dissuade you?" he asked.

Darius Zannick looked at his lieutenant with a wide smile; a bit of spittle flecked the corner of his mouth. "Now Charles, I thought you knew me better than that. I don't care if the man lives or dies, but perhaps we shouldn't send an agent as skilled as Lon Smythe after a target of low priority. The boy *is* your top student, is he not?"

"He is," confirmed Bothan, "which is why I gave him the shuffler job last night and why I wish to send him to kill Dandrick Humple. The man's estate is well-guarded, which could cause delays in the execution. As we have agreed, the timing of the hits must be precisely coordinated."

"Yes, precisely…" the Regent drawled as he returned his eyes to the chart. He traced a gnarled finger slowly up the page, toward the apex of the pyramid. "I had thought perhaps," the old man said with a sideways look at Bothan, "you might grant the boy his exhaustive request and send him after…" The Regent let the words dangle in the air.

Charles Bothan followed the old man's gaze back to the very top of the chart, one spot below the Countess herself. The assassin exhaled a burst of air. "Smythe is not ready to face Zakarus Rinn."

"Then who do we send?" asked Zannick. "Would it not be prudent to take him on the first night, before our actions put him on his guard?"

Bothan shook his head, still looking down at the name "Zakarus Rinn" on the page before him. "The Shadow Wolf is always on his guard. There will be no moment that is better than any other."

The Regent's face was suddenly very serious as he looked at his lieutenant; his dark eye was black as coal and the white one narrowed probingly. He repeated the question, "Who, then, do we send?"

Before Bothan could answer there came a loud knock on the office door.

"Enter," called the Regent.

A flustered man entered carrying a wooden box. He rushed straight up to Darius Zannick and was quite startled when Kleet Olander seized him with a huge, meaty paw and held him back a respectful distance from the Regent.

"Sir," the panicked man said, "this was delivered to the back door of the kitchen a few minutes ago. It's addressed to you and nailed shut so it hasn't been opened, but it's dripping what appears to be..." the man swallowed down the knot in his throat and finished, "blood, sir."

"Put it on the chair and then leave," instructed Zannick. The man did as he was told and then ran from the room. The Regent looked at his two lieutenants and then raised his hand to cover his dark eye, opening wide the white one and staring at the box. A moment later, a shadow passed over the man's face and he dropped his hand to his side. "Kleet," he said and nodded toward the box. Olander stepped forward and ripped the lid off the box with a great cracking of wood and creaking of nails. The Regent stepped forward and reached inside. He looked directly at Charles Bothan and then pulled from within the box the severed head of Lon Smythe. There was a black orchid protruding from its mouth.

Kleet Olander issued his grunt and Charles Bothan closed his eyes and inhaled deeply. When he opened his eyes and looked back at Zannick, the Regent asked for the third time, "Whom will we send?"

Bothan's eyes returned to the chart on the table and the name inscribed at the top in elegant script: Zakarus Rinn. The assassin turned on his heel and strode to the door. He opened it and turned back to look at the Regent with a deadly zeal in his eyes. "I will do it myself," he said and left the room. The door slammed shut behind him.

The kobold commander issued the last of his orders in low grunts and short, sharp yips of excitement. His troop scurried off into the darkness, encircling the slumbering camp. Though primitive in their use of weapons and standing only three feet in height, the rat-like kobolds could be lethal when the pack fell upon a small band of weary travelers.

The commander emerged from the trees. His fangs glistened in the moonlight as his lips pursed in a snarl of carnal delight. Tonight they would have man-flesh and a small booty of gold!

Flash!

One of his troops loosed a tripwire and the small clearing was briefly illuminated in the pale, golden light of an apprentice's flare. The commander gave a loud, high-pitched bark and his troop moved into the camp, snarling and brandishing their short swords and daggers.

The figures of the slumbering men did not stir as the kobolds advanced. Doubt crept into the mind of the commander.

Surely the flare had awakened them. What were they waiting for? The hissing flare sputtered and extinguished. As darkness fell, the clearing exploded into a frenzied chorus of the sounds of battle. Blades were drawn and could be seen dancing in the moonlight. The deep twang of an Elven longbow could be heard on the left of the camp.

The kobold commander fled to the right, but tripped over debris and fell sprawling in the grass. Turning, the creature felt his hide rankle as he discovered that he had tripped over the severed head of one of his pack. A series of vulgarities shouted angrily in the Dwarvish tongue rained down upon the kobold commander and he turned to see a crazed dwarf in shining mail hewing wildly with a large battleaxe. Another headless kobold corpse fell to the ground and the dwarf turned, his eyes falling upon the prostrate kobold commander. A smile parted the dwarf's bushy, black beard as their eyes met. It was not a smile of friendship or mercy, however; it was bloodlust. The dwarf raised his axe, dripping blood and spattered with gore. The kobold squealed and soiled the ground beneath him.

"Hold!" commanded a booming voice. The dwarf hesitated for a moment, but the axe remained poised to strike. "Hold Dorak! We do not need to kill this one." A proud and ancient man strode forth, his white beard contrasted starkly by his deep, black eyes. The dwarf's crazed smile was replaced by a scowl of bitterness, but he dared not disobey Arcanis Rhu. He dropped his axe to his side and kicked one of the severed heads before stumping off into the gloom.

The wizard appeared to shrink as he leaned on his staff. When he pulled an old brown cloak around his shoulders, he seemed a road-weary old man. His dark eyes were filled with pity as he gazed down at the kobold.

"You may go now," he said. The kobold commander could not understand the man's words, but the intent behind them was clear. The creature rose and loped off into the night, leaving his slain troop behind him.

* * * * * * *

The following morning, as the sun rose and sent fingers of light reaching through the trees, the battle damage was unveiled by a shroud of rising mist. Timmen walked through the camp counting the carcasses. Dorak had exacted a heavy toll; there were twelve dead kobolds near his station, most of them missing their heads. Alishane took six with the sword Arcanis had given him and Aurora dispatched nine more, three by sword in the first moments and six with her bow after the kobolds scattered. Timmen had fled to the luggage when the battle started and Arcanis simply sat and watched, knowing that his help would not be necessary. None of the companions had been wounded.

While Arcanis and Alishane prepared the morning meal, Aurora left to scout the camp's perimeter and the road in preparation for their departure. Timmen was now going through the meager belongings of the dead creatures in search of anything valuable while Dorak piled the carcasses for burning.

"Not a bad morning's work, if ye ask me," the dwarf said to Timmen with a wide smile. He had not bothered to wash out the blood that matted his beard. Timmen grimaced and felt his stomach turn over. "I know ye, ye know," Dorak continued, looking down his fat nose at the halfling. "Seen ye in the Tail." Timmen's face turned white and his mind flew back over the last couple years in search of any slight he may have committed against the dwarf, but he could not remember any. Dorak seemed to recognize the look on the halfling's face and he laughed while heaving another body onto the pile. "Don't worry, wee Timmy, ye were never foolish enough to thieve from me."

Timmen gave a strained laugh and said, "That's good."

"If ye had, though," said the dwarf, moving closer and pointing menacingly with a thick finger, "I would 'a opened yer white belly like a fish." He lifted his double-headed axe and gave a great roar as he swung it down. The blade whistled past Timmen's head to cleave one of the kobold corpses in two. Timmen was too frightened to move; he stood stock-still with his eyes wide and his lip trembling.

Alishane gripped the hilt of his sword and started to rise, but Arcanis grabbed the cleric's wrist and held him back.

"Dorak," said the wizard in a bemused and patient voice, "I think that's enough sport for this morning. Would you agree?"

The dwarf slung his axe on his back and laughed. He reached out and tussled Timmen's hair before moving on to the next dead kobold and throwing it onto the pile. Timmen let out his breath and moved to sit down by the packs. Alishane muttered under his breath and returned to his work, but he continued to glare menacingly at the dwarf. Arcanis Rhu wiped the slight smile from his face and turned to his right, looking into the trees at the edge of the clearing. Though none of the others had noticed her presence, the wizard saw Aurora Daelin with her bow drawn and her head cocked, looking down the length of the arrow that was trained on Dorak Shale. The two briefly made eye contact, then the elf lowered her bow, returned the arrow to her quiver and moved away into the trees.

* * * * * * *

The party crested Trail Ridge Pass later that day and made their camp in the early evening. In the morning they set out once more and around midday they came to the Anderton Vale. The rocky hills opened up into a wide valley dense with trees. A stream meandered through the middle of the vale and at the far end sat the town of Anderton.

"Should we avoid the valley and move south over the mountains?" Alishane asked the group. "This territory is under the control of Lord Finneran. He has been an ally in the past and appeared to remain so during the Council, but I caught a strange look between him and the Countess shortly before my father was condemned. I don't know if we can still trust him."

"We can trust no one outside of this company," Arcanis stated.

"I agree," concurred Aurora. "Still, I should like to enter the town and get another horse. Our animals each carry two in addition to our baggage; I fear they will tire."

"I am known in the Vale," said Alishane, shaking his head. "It would be unwise for me to go down there. And we can't ignore the possibility that your descriptions have been circulated." He nodded to the rest of the group.

"That leaves only one of us," Arcanis said airily. They all turned and looked at Dorak Shale.

"Ho ho!" snorted the dwarf, "so ye think I'll be running yer errands for ye. Think again, wizard!" He thumbed his thick chest. "Dorak Shale is nobody's servant."

"No one is subjecting you to servitude, Dorak," said Arcanis, "but you are a party to this endeavor until our task is completed and right now we need you to buy us a horse."

A low growl rattled deep in the dwarf's throat. He glared at the wizard from under his bushy eyebrows and ground his teeth together. "Bah! Gimme the gold!" he finally shouted.

Alishane handed him a bag of coins and dismounted their horse. The four of them watched as Dorak cursed twice, once in Dwarvish and then once in the common tongue so they were sure to understand him, and then kicked the horse into motion.

"We'll never get a good price with a dwarf making the deal," Timmen complained.

"Shush, Timmen!" scolded Arcanis.

But dwarves hear better than the halfling thought. "Ha ha, I'd get a better deal if I were trading yer hide, halfling," Dorak called over his shoulder.

Timmen gulped and Arcanis gave him a reproachful look. Alishane and Aurora smiled at each other, then the four of them sat down to await Dorak's return.

* * * * * * *

The sun was halfway through its downward journey and still the dwarf had not returned. Timmen and Alishane made a game of thumbing rocks at each other and they sat in a small patch of dirt talking quietly and enjoying their leisure. Arcanis had been in meditation for most of the afternoon, sitting off to the side on a sunny rock. Aurora walked through the forest talking to the animals and feeling the mood of the trees. They were thirsty in the drought, but otherwise had no complaints.

The elf climbed onto a low branch of a large spruce and absently chewed a sprig, gnashing it between her teeth to raise the sweet fragrance to her nose. Her thoughts turned to her father; she wondered how he was fairing with the Jarlaeth.

"An elf in a tree. Who would have thought? We are happy to see you have not been caught."

Aurora recognized the high, croaking voice. She turned to regard the red and yellow finch perched on a nearby branch. "Verse from a bird, I am most impressed. Why, with your presence, has this elf been blessed?" she asked.

Huggins twittered and hooted excitedly, flapping his wings and shaking his tail feathers. Clearly he enjoyed this banter. "Strange company, you certainly keep. Befriending a dwarf! Your need must run deep."

Aurora smiled. "Necessity breeds that unusual alliance. Now answer my question and cease your defiance."

Again the bird warbled merrily and flapped its wings, hopping from one branch to another before returning to its original position. "Truly, we like you, Elf maiden fair! We come now to help you, your burden to share."

Aurora's eyes narrowed suspiciously. "Who? Who comes to help us? Who is your master?"

Huggins appeared doleful that she had ended their game. He turned his head sideways and looked at her through one black little eye. Finally he flew away. Aurora watched as the bird flew up out of the tree to circle high in the air then drop back down behind her and light on the shoulder of a man she had not heard approach. In a flash, the elf dropped lightly to the ground and faced the stranger with her sword drawn and at the ready.

"Please, please, lovely Aurora. You are in no danger. You may sheath your weapon," the man said with his arms outstretched and palms open.

Aurora was on her guard and her keen senses were searching for any possible threats, but still she was startled and slightly flustered by the man's appearance. He had dark, mysterious eyes and long, lustrous black hair. Golden hoop earrings dangled from his ears and his coat was long and flowing. When the man flashed his most disarming smile, she felt her ears burn.

"Who are you?" she asked.

"I'm the man you've been asking for," he answered and his smile widened. Again she felt a flush of heat rush through her cheeks to the tips of her pointed ears.

"I am in need of no man," she huffed indignantly. "You presume to know what I…"

The man held up his hand to stop her. "You misunderstand me," he said softly. "Certainly I would never presume to know the thoughts of such a beautiful creature, for I have no frame of reference. I am neither an elf nor a woman, or particularly beautiful for that matter," he chuckled. "No, I was simply referring to the questions you have repeatedly asked of my medium here," he pointed to the finch perched upon his shoulder.

Aurora's eyes narrowed. She was suspicious both of this stranger's intentions and of her own response to his presence. She had never felt this way before, and she was frightened.

"Why have you contacted me?" she asked. "What help could you offer?"

The man did not answer her questions. He looked haughtily into her eyes and flashed his smile. "I find your accent pleasing," he said. His gaze roamed over her body, from head to foot and then back again. When their eyes met, the smile lingered at the corners of his lips.

Aurora felt the fire in her cheeks flare and run down her spine. "Clearly that is not all you find pleasing," she blustered. "Master your roaming eyes, else you should lose them!"

The man took a step back and raised his hands defensively, but mirth still played upon his face. "My sincerest apologies for offending your virtue; it's not a quality I'm accustomed to seeing in beautiful women." He clasped his hands behind his back and assumed a placid tone of voice. "I'm afraid that, for now at least, I can't tell you why I wish to help you. Let us just say that I'll continue to watch your progress and offer what help I may when the time comes." He gave a deep, graceful bow but never removed his eyes from hers. "My name is Sanguine, Miss Daelin, and I am completely at your service."

Aurora was at a loss for words. She was trying to think of a retort when she heard a twig snap behind her. She spun around and brought her blade to bear, but there was nothing there. She turned quickly back to face the strange man only to find that he was gone. Through the trees in the distance she heard the receding chirruping of a finch.

The elf sheathed her sword and returned to camp. She sat down near the luggage with a flustered and confused look on her face. Alishane noticed and came to her.

"What is it?" he asked.

"Nothing," she said and shook her head. He was about to inquire further but was interrupted when Timmen gave a yell announcing the return of Dorak Shale. The dwarf was riding one horse and leading another. Alishane turned back to Aurora and started to say something, but she cut him off. "Let us load the baggage and be off. With any luck we'll make the Caverns by tomorrow night." Alishane still looked as though he wanted to speak, but she had made it clear that she wanted no further discussion.

They loaded the baggage onto the new horse, which Aurora was now riding, and set off over the mountains to the south. They would skirt the town of Anderton and pick up the Bourgan Road, then turn south once more until they reached the Caverns of the Crystal Night.

Chapter Seventeen

~ The Caverns of the Crystal Night ~

By the evening of the day after Sanguine's appearance, Aurora was feeling like herself again. She was still a little inwardly alarmed at the reaction the man had stirred in her, but nobody else knew of the encounter so it was easy for her to put it out of her mind. She went about her duties of scouting ahead of and around the party as they made their way south along the Bourgan Road. Once in a while, however, she caught herself listening, not to the general sounds of the forest, but rather searching for the warble of a finch. She looked into shadows or behind trees expecting to see the dark eyes and disarming smile of the mysterious stranger. At some point, she knew, she would have to look into her own heart and decide what these feelings meant. For now, she kept herself busy and alert and tried to prepare her mind for the challenges they would meet in the Caverns.

Alishane, meanwhile, respected her desire for privacy, even though he resented the distance that had sprung up between them and hated more than ever the fact that he now shared a horse, not with the beautiful elf who smelled like jasper lilies, but with the disagreeable dwarf who smelled like rancid wererat droppings.

Their passage through the upper reaches of the Pandoran Range was uneventful. Timmen hoarded the Regent's map with zeal and refused to allow anyone else to look at it or offer suggestions as to their course. His directions were true, however, and by the evening of the following day the party was within an hour's march of the mouth to the Caverns.

"Up there," Timmen said after studying the map carefully for a few moments. They had arrived at a small clearing in a heavily wooded area at the bottom of a narrow and steep ravine. There was not a distinguishable trail leading upward and large, jagged rocks jutted out intermittently from the sheer faces of the cliffs. The footing in the ravine was treacherous; the horses would not be able to make the climb.

"I believe we should camp here for the night and then enter the Caverns in the morning," Aurora suggested.

"When we have rested," Alishane agreed.

"And had a meal," Timmen put in.

So they set their camp and the following morning they gathered their materials to decide what they would bring into the caves. When they had finished, they repacked their bags with the necessities and started up the ravine. Timmen tried to lead the way, stating that he held the map and should therefore be the first in line. When Arcanis reminded him that wild creatures could be lying in wait behind the rocks and that the halfling was just about the perfect size for a morning snack, Timmen reluctantly allowed Dorak to take the lead. Aurora brought up the rear.

Arcanis found the climb quite taxing on his old body and he slowed their progress considerably. Dorak repeatedly grumbled his displeasure at being part of such a ragtag group, mixing in plenty of expletives to make the journey more colorful. Finally, after about an hour, they came to the top of the gorge. The cliffs rose unbroken on both sides to a great height. In front of them was a sheer face of rock that curved at the top like a wave, creating an overhang high above them.

"Ye've led us to a dead end, ye little runt!" barked Dorak.

Alishane, who felt he had unfinished business with the dwarf, put his hand to the hilt of his sword and stepped forward. "You will not speak to him in such a manner," said the cleric.

"Ye're too pretty to be challenging me, boy," answered the dwarf as he set his feet and faced off against the young man. His fingers flexed on the worn handle of his axe. "But if ye're feelin' feisty, I'll be happy to slap some ugly on ye."

Alishane simply smiled. *"Derma Impervius Stainen,"* he whispered and a great crackle went through the air as his skin thickened and turned slate gray. "Your axe cannot cleave stone, dwarf," the cleric said and took another step forward, pulling his sword from its scabbard.

Dorak's eyes lost all of their humor and narrowed dangerously. "Yer spell won't last forever you little whelp, and when it dies yer hide will be mine," he hissed and spit flew from his lips.

Aurora pulled back her cape with her right hand and her left grasped the hilt of her sword. There was no doubt in her mind for whom she would intercede if the two came to blows.

"Wait. No," Timmen squeaked in utter despair. He fidgeted from one foot to the other, his hands groping uselessly through his pockets for something that could stop what he was watching.

Arcanis was still laboring up the hill behind them. When he rounded a turn in the cliff and saw the cleric and dwarf facing off, his exhaustion left him and he ran the remaining distance to the group. "Look at me, both of you!" the wizard commanded. He was no longer leaning on his staff; rather he was standing tall and holding it in front of him. The group froze and all eyes turned to the wizard. "This foolishness cannot be allowed," Arcanis scolded. "Dorak," he addressed the dwarf, "you do not need to test the members of this party. I am here and that should be good enough for you. And Alishane," he turned to the cleric, "you cannot be so childish as to bristle every time he says something rude. He *is* a dwarf, after all."

"Eh?" Dorak asked in slight indignation. Arcanis turned to him and raised his eyebrows as if to say "Have I said something untrue?"

"Bah! Ye're right, as usual, wizard. I was testing the lad," Dorak admitted, "but ye didn't have to butt in before I got to see him play the blade." He looked over at Alishane with disdain. "He looks like a candy arse to me."

Arcanis exhaled deeply in his frustration, but Alishane merely bowed and said, "I shall let you have the last word, dwarf." The cleric sheathed his weapon and moved to inspect the cliff face. He released his stoneskin spell as he passed Dorak, a subtle reminder that he had been perfectly ready to accept the dwarf's test.

Aurora released her grip on her sword and let her cape fall around her. She, Timmen and Arcanis joined Alishane at the cliff to look for the opening to the cave. Dorak crossed his arms over his thick chest and watched.

"What does the map tell you, Timmen?" asked the wizard.

"Nothing," answered the thief. "It leads to this point but doesn't show how to find the cave."

"May I see it?" Arcanis asked. Timmen hesitated, but after looking around the apparent dead end one more time he reluctantly handed over the map. The wizard studied it for a few moments and looked around at the walls of the cliff. An idea sparked on his face and he turned the map on its side. "We have come too far," he said.

"What?" Timmen squawked, jumping up to take the map away from the wizard. "But the line clearly leads to this point," he said earnestly.

"It does indeed," agreed Arcanis. "Your map reading skills are admirable. But nothing requires us to follow the line all the way here. Turn the map on its side and look again. This time, see the line not as the path to our destination, but as the outline of a picture."

They all watched as Timmen followed the wizard's instructions. Suddenly the halfling's brow, which had been furrowed with doubt and confusion, lifted as he attained a new understanding. "Brilliant!" he exclaimed. The others crowded around him to see, even Dorak. Timmen held up the map to show them. "See, if you hold the map right-side-up, as you normally would, of course, the line just leads you through the mountains to the mouth of the ravine and then up to this point." He traced the path with his finger. "But if you turn the map on its side, the line as a whole shows the layout of the gorge. Look here," he pointed at a circle on the map, "when the map is held upright, this circle shows the contours of the land. A hill, probably. But from the side, it is clearly that tall outcropping of rock halfway up the trail. Remember it?" They all nodded, except for Arcanis who simply smiled. "Look at the small "X" on the back side of the circle," Timmen concluded.

They looked around at each other for a moment, too stunned to act. Finally the dwarf broke the silence. "Well what are ye waiting for, ye bunch of idgits? Let's go and get this over with."

The party made its way back down the path and soon came to the tall obelisk of stone marked on the map. At the base of the uphill side was a large boulder. Dorak, being eager for the opportunity to show his strength, made a big production out of insisting that they were not capable of moving it and should step out of his way. He set his shoulder against it and heaved with all his might, but the stone was hollow and slid to the side with such ease that the dwarf sprawled to the ground. They all laughed and when the dwarf arose and shook himself free of dirt he exclaimed sheepishly, "Don't know me own strength."

They turned as one and found that the boulder had been guarding a narrow stairwell. They inched to the edge and peered inside, but it was too dark within for them to see anything.

"I will go first," said Aurora and she began to move forward.

"No," stated Arcanis. "Do not forget: this is the hideout of the Crystal Night. There will surely be many traps and pitfalls." The wizard turned to the halfling thief. "Timmen," he said, "you must go first. And let us hope that your skill is as great as our need."

"Or greater," Dorak grumbled under his breath.

Alishane lit a torch and handed it to Timmen, who took a moment to steady his nerves before stooping low to inspect the mouth of the stairwell. Seeing nothing suspicious, he blew away some of the dust and looked again. Still nothing appeared amiss. Finally, the thief ran his fingers along the stone and then moved down into the hole, inspecting each step as he went.

After the halfling disappeared from sight, there was nothing for them to do but wait. Occasionally they heard Timmen shuffling around down in the darkness, but they knew they could do nothing to help and they didn't want to distract him from his work so they did not call out to him. Finally, after they were all quite nervous from being idle, the halfling poked his head out of the hole and said, "I've searched the first room and found only one trap. Do not step on the last stair."

The others looked at each other again and then, one by one, they descended into the hole. Each of them, as they came to the last stair, took great care not to step on it. Arcanis came down last. Rather than jumping over the last step, which would be hard on his old body, he uttered a small spell and floated over it. As he landed he winced slightly at the exertion. Aurora noticed and came to him. "Perhaps I should conserve my strength," the wizard said with a smile and a shake of his head.

Alishane stood in the center of the small room and looked around. He turned to the halfling. "Where now?" he asked.

"I should know?" Timmen responded curtly.

"Well…" the cleric began with a shrug.

"I will find the traps," the halfling retorted. "If I am to navigate as well then something will get missed. We can't afford that."

Dorak laughed. "Good boy, Timmy," he said. "Don't let the pretty boy boss ye around." Nobody paid any attention to the dwarf.

"Can you perform the scrying spell?" Arcanis asked Alishane.

"I can, though it tires me. It's an advanced spell," answered the cleric.

"So it is," agreed the wizard with an indulgent smile. "Will you try?"

The cleric nodded and looked around to get his bearings. There were three openings out of the first room, excluding the stairwell leading outside. The leftmost passage appeared to lead deeper into the heart of the mountain so Alishane decided to look there first. He closed his eyes and found his core, then sent the words of the spell spinning around its base to gain speed and power. His lips began to move and soon he was voicing the spell over and over, increasing in volume as he focused his strength. At last he took a deep breath and cried out, *"Decartem synesthesia!"*

The cleric's body went rigid and his eyes jerked open, unfocused and unseeing. His essence surged forward down the passageway. Though the tunnel was dark, he could still 'see,' for the spirit needs no reflected light to absorb information. He followed the tunnel around several twists and turns before discovering that it was a dead end. Soaring back the way he had come, his presence flew past the companions in the room and down the second tunnel. Aurora's white hair billowed as he passed.

The second passage was much like the first, with many twists and turns. He followed it further and further, exploring several side passages that turned out to be dead ends as well. He could feel his strength waning as he came to an obstruction. It was not stone, indeed the passage seemed to continue onward, but he could no longer move forward and his scrying revealed nothing. Believing that his blindness was the result of his failing strength, he retreated back toward his body. Only then did he discover that he had gone too far. The passage was long and he grew weaker by the second. Finally, he was utterly spent. His corporeal form began to shake violently. Aurora moved to help him just as the cleric's spirit slammed back into his body, throwing him to the ground. The elf caught him and gently laid him down. She wiped the hair off of his sweaty brow and he opened his eyes. He smiled faintly. Aurora leaned down and whispered in his ear; her hair fell down about his face.

"Hmph, Pretty Boy," Dorak grumbled.

Her presence and the words she whispered in his ear reinvigorated the cleric. He sat up and got shakily to his feet. "I didn't know you possessed healing magic," he said to her.

Aurora looked down and adjusted her clothing before answering. "I don't," she said softly.

"Oh," Alishane replied. He was embarrassed, but he gave a valiant effort at hiding it as he told them what he had seen in the two passages.

"What about the third?" asked Timmen.

"Let us worry about that if this one fails," said Arcanis as he stepped toward the middle passage and held forth his staff. *"Incandessom spherimon,"* he whispered and a small globe of light rose into the air and hovered glowing above them. "It is only a small bit of magic and may prove helpful if ever we decide to leave these caves," he said in response to their surprised looks. He then turned to the thief. "Timmen, if you please."

The halfling was still holding the torch and he stooped low to inspect the ground as he moved into the tunnel. The others started to follow him and he stopped and turned. "I will check the ground for traps as we go, but there may be some in the walls or rocks too. I'll try to check those as we come to them, but, well… just don't touch anything," he said testily. He returned to his work and the others exchanged looks of patient amusement.

Their progress was slow. Timmen insisted on going over every bit of ground by sight, stooping and holding the torch low, and then he would blow the dirt away and lightly run his fingers over the stone floor before moving on. The rest of the party waited patiently, talking little. Timmen discovered three traps in the floor and showed them where to walk. Whenever they came upon a branch in the tunnel, Alishane would tell him which ones were dead ends and Arcanis would float another globe of light to show the way out.

They had gone roughly halfway down the passage, and had spent most of the morning doing so, when Aurora heard a scraping and skittering sound behind them. She turned and pulled an arrow from her quiver. The movement got the attention of the rest of the party and Dorak and Alishane also turned and brought their weapons to bear. They stood in silent readiness, shoulder to shoulder in the narrow tunnel. Arcanis leaned on his staff and closed his eyes, meditating to gather his strength in case he was needed.

Long moments passed; the scraping drew closer. A faint red glow began to spread far down the passage, devouring the inky blackness. Alishane had recovered much of his magical power during the morning and he now sent his core swirling, readying himself so he could cast his spell quickly.

The red glow grew brighter and the skittering sounds became louder and more distinct; there was more than one creature approaching. Timmen turned to the forward passage where the oppressive darkness awaited. He felt the black void and shivered, then he crawled up behind Arcanis and huddled at the wizard's feet.

Suddenly, the red glow became flame. Three winged, reptilian creatures turned a corner in the tunnel and came into view. Each was about the size of Timmen and had green scales, a long muzzle filled with large, jagged teeth and was enveloped in a wreath of fire. One was advancing along each wall and the third along the roof of the chamber, their claws digging into the stone to create the scraping sound as the creatures came closer.

Arcanis opened his eyes. "Fire drakes," he muttered. He made no other move. Timmen clutched at the wizard's robes.

Alishane took several steps forward. Face to face with his enemy, he now knew what spell to cast. His core was already spinning fiercely as he sent the words into the vortex. *"Aeros Centé Enguardium!"* the cleric cried and with a great swooshing of power his form was now surrounded by a blue aura of cold. He rushed forward and the three creatures opened their hooked maws and screeched, shooting rolling flames through the cramped darkness of the tunnel. Two more drakes appeared in the corridor just as the first volley of fire was defeated by the cleric's protective spell. Alishane lunged forward and drove his sword through one creature as the other two leaped for the cleric's head. One never made it but fell to the ground, its flame extinguished by the Elvish arrow protruding from its side. The third creature pounced upon Alishane and slashed at his face and neck, but he quickly shook free of it and clove it with his blade.

The remaining two fire drakes screeched and spouted flames, then flew at the cleric with their claws outstretched. Dorak gave a great roar and surged past Alishane, who stood unmoving as the creatures flew at his face. At the last possible moment, the dwarf gave a mighty overhead swing of his axe and his blade split first one drake and then the other and the creatures fell to the ground.

With the flames of the fire drakes extinguished, the tunnel darkened to the feeble glow of the companions' lone torch.

Dorak turned to Alishane and jabbed him with the handle of his axe. "Not bad, boy... for a candy arse. Ha!" he laughed and moved to rejoin the others.

Alishane let go of his spell and also turned back to the group. "I guess we know what was in the third tunnel," he said.

Arcanis stooped to retrieve the torch and gave it to Timmen. "Back to work now, lad," he said.

"Oh, uh, yes," stuttered the halfling as he accepted the torch. He turned and resumed inspecting the floor of the passage.

Hours later, as the mid-afternoon sun was beating down upon the world above, the party came at last to the obstruction that had halted the scrying cleric. Timmen came to it first. He was still holding the torch and bent with his face to the ground when he felt a great void looming before him. He looked up and saw nothing but pitch black. Even the light of the torch was swallowed completely. The rest of the party came up behind him and they stood with mouths agape looking into darkness so oppressive it was like the beginning of time before the creation of the stars.

Arcanis approached and spoke softly to the thief, "Do not falter now, Tim. Finish searching the floor."

Timmen found that he was shaking too horribly to feel for traps and he could not proceed until the rest of the party came up and stood close behind him, ready to rescue him from whatever lay lurking in the yawning void. He discovered one more trap and its location made him pause uncomfortably before telling the others. "Here, at the end of the tunnel and into the darkness, lies a trap that I cannot disarm. It spans the whole width of the passage and I can't tell how far into the darkness it extends."

"What did you see when you came here during your scrying?" Arcanis asked Alishane.

"Nothing," said the cleric. "I got to this point but could go no further. I knew there was no physical obstruction and simply assumed that I stopped because I was at the end of my strength."

Arcanis frowned. "Where, exactly, does the trap start, Timmen?" he asked. The thief gathered handfuls of dirt and drew an outline on the floor. Arcanis then walked up to the edge of the trap and leaned out with his staff, poking at the empty air. *"Incandessom spherimon,"* he said and one of the little globes of light floated upward. The wizard sent it forward, but it was swallowed up completely when it met the wall of darkness. "There are other spells

I might venture," he said, "but I believe they would be pointless. This is a dead zone; no magic can be used beyond this point."

"That must be why I had to stop here while scrying," observed Alishane. Arcanis nodded his agreement.

"But why can light not enter?" asked Aurora.

The wizard was silent. He closed his eyes and searched through his expansive memory, but found no explanation. The answer was clear in his weathered eyes when he looked at her. "I do not know," he admitted.

The elf stepped forward and put an arrow to her bowstring. She fired straight into the void and they all stood listening. A moment later the arrow clattered to the ground far into the distance. She slung her bow over her back and looked at the others. "There is only one thing left to do," she concluded. "One of us must jump over the trap and explore the darkness. Since I can jump the farthest and land the lightest, I will be the one to do it." No one ventured to argue with her. Aurora stepped back and took a deep breath while the others cleared out of her way. Refusing to look into her friends' faces, for she didn't want to see their fear while struggling to master her own, she crouched and then sprang forward. A few running steps brought her to Timmen's line in the dirt and she leaped as far as she could. The elf soared through the air, suspended in time and space, and then tucked her head and rolled as she hit the ground.

Nothingness.

There was no light and no sound save for the beating of her heart. She turned and looked back toward her friends and saw them standing there. They appeared to be looking right at her but clearly they could not see her, for they each wore an expression of utter terror. "I am here. I am safe. Do you not see me?" she asked. Her voice echoed; she had entered a large chamber.

The fear eased from their faces but they each shook their heads. "No, we can't see you," answered Alishane. "Are you alright?"

"Yes, but I still cannot see anything on this side of the void. I can see your faces, but once the light crosses the threshold it is swallowed. Almost as if..." she looked around in thought for a moment, "as if the light cannot be reflected back into our eyes so that we might see." She groped along the ground until she found a large stone. Picking it up she discovered that it was not a stone at all, but rather what felt like a smooth, oblong crystal. "Here," she called, "I am throwing something to you. Tell me what you see."

She heaved the crystal through the opening to the cavern, narrowly missing Dorak's head, and it clattered to the ground behind them. Timmen scurried over to pick it up. When he brought it over and held it before their eyes, they all gave a collective gasp. Held in the halfling's outstretched hand was a shard of shadow, an embodiment of the void itself.

"I should have known," said the wizard.

"What is it?" asked Timmen, turning it over in his hand. It appeared black, but on closer inspection it looked more like a hole in the air.

"It is night crystal," replied Arcanis. "It absorbs light, rather than reflecting it. And if light cannot reflect off of it, then we cannot see it." The old man turned and looked into the cavern. "The entire structure must be made of it." He straightened and approached the threshold, holding his staff out into the darkness. "It also repels magic, which is why none of our spells can enter past this point."

Aurora had been listening to the conversation and she now stood up and addressed the vast emptiness. "If these crystals defeat ordinary light and magic," she said into the void, "then let us see what they make of me." With these words the elf blazed forth her innate power, the light that is unique to her alone among elves and men.

Her companions in the passageway stumbled backward, shielding their eyes from the blinding light. From within the cavern they heard the elf's high, windy laugh echoing far into the distance. "Perhaps a bit gentler would be best," she said and the light lessened. Then the elf turned to her companions with her arms outstretched and cried, "Come, my friends. Look and behold the Caverns of the Crystal Night!"

Chapter Eighteen

~ The Thief and the Crook ~

Aurora stood in the crystalline chamber with her arms outstretched and her inner light streaming forth from her spirit. When her companions opened their eyes and looked into the cavern, their gaze was met by a glittering luminosity none of them had ever imagined. The entire chamber was constructed of rose-hued crystal. The floor consisted of large slabs of it, inlaid like marble. Countless stalactites hung from the high ceiling of the chamber, giving it a rough and furry appearance. Around the outer walls, thick stalagmites towered like pillars into the air, buttressing the weight of the mountain overhead. Through all of this crystal passed Aurora's light. It refracted and reflected in radiance so brilliant that they had to squint against it.

Dorak Shale, being a dwarf and lover of caves, was mesmerized by the beauty of the cavern. He began to walk toward the entrance, forgetful of the trap that barred his way. At the last moment, Alishane noticed the dwarf's movement and held him back. "Oh, right," Dorak huffed and stepped back, but he offered no word of thanks.

Arcanis asked Timmen if he could outline the far side of the trap for them. "But how will I get over there?" the thief asked.

Without waiting for anyone else to respond, Dorak seized the halfling and cried, "Here ye go, Timmy!" He tossed the thief through the air and deep into the cavern.

Timmen landed with a thud and slid on his belly, his face and outstretched hands squeaking along the polished crystal floor. When he stood up, his eyes were wrathful, but Dorak was bent at the waist laughing heartily and paid the halfling no heed. Turning to his task, Timmen stooped and looked at the floor. The crystal slabs were transparent on top, then gradually grew cloudier and eventually became opaque. He didn't know how a trap could be laid in the crystal, but he didn't take any chances and looked carefully all the way back to the threshold of the chamber. As soon as he reached the stone of the passageway, he saw that the trap extended all the way to the crystal. It was a distance they could easily jump, however, and even Arcanis made the leap with Alishane waiting to catch him and ease his landing.

The group gathered around Aurora but could not look directly at her, even with her light somewhat subdued. Timmen scurried about checking the floor for traps in a widening circle while the others craned their necks to look around the chamber. They pointed out interesting formations or the way the light danced through certain crystals, but then the whole glittering spectacle would change when Aurora turned to look. Even Arcanis marveled at the kaleidoscopic beauty of the cavern. When Alishane asked him if he had ever seen anything like it, the wizard had to admit that he had not.

"I didn't find any traps in the floor of the main chamber," Timmen announced when he rejoined the group, "but I have no experience with this crystal so we should still be careful."

"Notice the alcoves around the outer wall," said Arcanis, holding out his staff to point at nine small, open rooms evenly spaced around the chamber. "And that looks to be a heavy iron door halfway down the left-hand side."

They went to the door first, but found it locked. The keyhole had an unusual design, was set deep into the door and was protected by multiple glyphs. Timmen knew at once that he would be unable to pick the lock. "This must lead deeper into the mountain," he said, "but I can't open it. Let's try the rooms."

The halfling led the way to the first alcove to the right of the entranceway. Aurora followed behind the others so the light was at their backs. As they approached the room, the party watched as their shadows were cast into the crystals before them to dance wraith-like through the surface of the wall. Timmen halted before entering the alcove and looked long and hard at the crystal archway that comprised the entrance to the room. Finding nothing suspicious, the thief crept forward and approached a small golden chest set in the middle of the floor. He squatted before the chest and studied it, then he asked Aurora to move forward and give him more light. Bending low to look through the crystal underneath the chest, the thief issued a low growl deep in his throat.

"What's wrong?" asked the elf.

"I see a shadow beneath it; I believe it is trapped."

"What will you do?" Aurora pressed.

Timmen looked at the lid and lock carefully and then sat back on his haunches and frowned, running his finger over the white scar on his chin. At last he stood and turned to his friends. "I cannot open this chest," he concluded.

"Hmph, some thief," snorted Dorak.

Timmen bristled. "I have brought you safely to the heart of the Crystal Night's ancient lair, Dorak, and still you question my skill?" he fumed. The others exchanged a look of surprise; Timmen had always cowered before the dwarf. "I could pick the lock and open it, of course, but not without setting off the trap, which is embedded in the crystal and can't be disarmed." The thief's eyes narrowed and he cocked his head to the side. "Unless you would like to volunteer to open it for us after I have picked the lock," he challenged.

Dorak looked around the group and they did well to hide their smiles. "Bah! It's yer job to open the dratted chests!" he stormed and walked back to the middle of the large chamber.

"Let me look in the other rooms," Timmen said and moved to the next alcove while the dwarf scowled at him from a distance.

Timmen went from one room to the next, with Aurora behind him to light the way, and found that in each of the nine alcoves there was an identical chest with a shadowed trap buried in the crystal. He sat in the middle of the main chamber and shook his head. "They are all identical and appear to be trapped in the same manner," he said to the group.

"We could always go explore the third passage from the outer entrance," offered Alishane.

"No, this is our goal," insisted Arcanis. "That iron door leads to the Cavern's inner sanctuary, and the key to the door must be in one of these chests."

"How terrible will be the traps if they are loosed?" Aurora asked of Timmen.

"I have no way to know," answered the thief, "but it's likely to be quite catastrophic. Perhaps the entire cavern will collapse." The party looked as one to the ceiling of the chamber and the stalactites that had looked so beautiful but now only looked like hanging lances waiting to run them through.

"There must be some clue," Timmen said in exasperation. He was fingering his scar again. He pulled out the map and studied it. He turned it all around and front to back, but could find nothing to indicate how to disarm the traps.

"Perhaps the Regent didn't tell you everything he knows," Alishane suggested to Aurora.

"No," she retorted, "he wants in here too badly to have withheld anything." Alishane started to respond when he was cut off by the halfling.

"Wait!" Timmen cried. "I think I have it!" He ran his finger over the bottom edge of the map and counted quietly to himself, then he got up and walked away from the group. They looked at each other for a moment and then followed. "This map is made of hide, not paper, so it hasn't become brittle, even with great age," the halfling explained. "Three of the edges are perfectly straight and smooth, but the edge along the bottom is rough. There are nicks taken out of it that are too symmetrical to be accidental. Look," he held it up for them to see. "Three in succession, then one, four, two and then one again." He walked to the entrance of the chamber and then turned on the others. "I think these numbers tell us which chest to open first."

"How so?" asked Arcanis.

"From the entrance, count the rooms using the numbers I just read, alternating moving forward and backward, and you will arrive at the alcove directly across from us." He pointed across the vast chamber.

"On which side of the entrance do we begin?" asked Alishane.

"It doesn't matter," answered the thief.

The group looked at him doubtfully. Alishane walked to the left of the entrance and Aurora to the right. "Call them out," the cleric instructed.

"Forward three," Timmen began, "now back one, forward four, back two and forward one." As he called out the instructions, Alishane and Aurora followed them from opposite sides of the chamber. True to the halfling's prediction, they both ended up in the same room directly across from the entrance hall. "It's too precise to be accidental," concluded Timmen.

"That's great, Timmy," Dorak drawled bitterly, "but who says ye read from the left of the page? What if ye start from the right? The numbers would be reversed and ye get us all killed."

Aurora and Alishane came back across the chamber and looked at the halfling. "It doesn't matter," Timmen replied with a smug smile. "Run the numbers forward or backward or from either side of the entrance, you will still arrive at the same room and the same chest."

"Let us be sure," said Alishane and he and Aurora returned to their starting points on either side of the entrance. "Read them backward, Timmen," he called.

The halfling complied. "Forward one, back two, forward four, back one and forward three." The elf and cleric followed the directions, walking from one room to the next around opposite sides of the chamber, and yet again they each ended up in the same room directly across from the entrance.

"Remarkable," whispered Arcanis. "Utterly remarkable."

Timmen strode across the chamber and straight into the appointed room. He kneeled before the chest, pulled out his thieving kit and a moment later the latch on the chest sprung open. Just before he lifted the lid, he looked back at his friends and saw them recoil slightly. He smiled and said, "Relax. This is why I'm here." Then he turned and opened the chest.

Darius Zannick decided to postpone the start of his offensive. The delivery of Lon Smythe's head was causing the old man considerable distress. It had been delivered to the university with the Regent's name on it. Clearly the Countess knew more than he had previously thought, a fact that made him very nervous. What bothered him the most, however, wasn't that the Countess knew his identity, which was bound to happen eventually anyway, but rather that he didn't know how she had gained the information. Could there be a leak in his organization? The Regent didn't think so. The truth was that the Crystal Night had never died, it had just splintered and gone underground. His faction had been operating in the southern province for years and he knew all of his subordinates better than they knew themselves. They would never betray him. So Zannick waited. He waited to see how Bothan faired with Zakarus Rinn. And he waited for the return of the elf. The Countess may have found him out sooner than he expected, but she would never find him again once he moved to the Caverns.

Meanwhile, several nights had passed since Charles Bothan began hunting the Shadow Wolf. He could sense that Darius Zannick wanted him to move more quickly, but the Regent knew better than to question Bothan about his methods. The assassin was an artist, and one does not rush an artist. These nights had been spent circling Tavora Manor, watching from rooftops and alleyways to find the best vantage points and observe movement patterns. Bothan had not yet seen his target, but that was to be expected; the Shadow Wolf was notoriously elusive. And, of course, stalking him had to be done carefully. If the Wolf sensed that he was being hunted he could turn upon his pursuer in the blink of an eye.

Bothan was now crawling out of a sewer drain several blocks from the Manor. He was exploring alternate exits from the compound that Rinn might use so he could plan his ambush. Though he had been alone in the sewer, his passage did not go unnoticed. The assassin disappeared into the shadows quickly and headed off toward the university to report to his superior. He did not notice the invisible presence breeze past him back to the east and the huge fortress on the Andaluric coast. Moments later, the Countess returned to her body and ended her scrying spell. Her vacant eyes blinked and then looked to her left where Zakarus Rinn reclined on the divan.

"You were right, Zakarus," she purred, "the man's snooping is getting closer to us." She stood and turned to look out the window behind her desk. "And you are sure that you recognize him?"

"Yes," answered the assassin, "and he is not to be trifled with. We must eliminate him immediately."

The Countess looked at him in the reflection of the window, her fiery eyes blazing from her porcelain face. "Well then, permission granted," she said and smiled wickedly. "Happy hunting."

Timmen opened the lid of the chest and a *click* resonated through the little alcove. The members of the party held their breath, but all that followed was silence. After a long, tense moment, Timmen reached into the chest and pulled out a rolled parchment and an ornate key. He unrolled the parchment and read aloud:

> *"If reading these words, our map you must hold*
> *And one of our order you surely must be.*
> *Move as the hand that makes one grow old*
> *Skip once and twice and open at three."*

"The hand that makes one grow old?" Aurora queried. "Can it mean the hand of a clock?"

"It must," Timmen declared. He got up and led them out of the room. "We move clockwise, skip two rooms and in the third we open the chest with this key. If we open them all in the right order, then the trap won't be loosed." He ran as fast as his little legs would carry him and the others came up just in time to see him open the second chest. A loud boom shivered through the crystal floor followed by the sound of falling rocks. Timmen retrieved the next key and parchment from the chest. Again he read it aloud:

> *"The trap is now moving; sand falls in the glass.*
> *Nine chests by nine keys is your time for the task.*
> *Move surely and swiftly or death be your doom*
> *Go back as you came to the very next room."*

The halfling sprinted from the alcove and pushed the others out of his way. "Eighty-one seconds," he panted as they turned to follow him. "We have eighty-one seconds to open them all." The thief fell to his knees in front of the next chest and inserted his key into the lock. The latch sprang open. Timmen reached in and extracted another key and parchment, which he unfurled and recited breathlessly.

> *"Continue this circuit until you reach four*
> *You've gone one too far if you get to the door."*

Five chests, five keys and exactly seventy-two seconds later, the companions were standing in the first room to the left of the entrance passage and Timmen was fitting the last key into the golden chest. He turned it and lifted the lid. Another loud boom rumbled throughout the cavernous chamber and a shudder ran through the walls and floor. The companions looked nervously at each other, but Timmen gave a victorious cry and pulled from within the chest a silver key and a final parchment. He held it up to Aurora's light and read aloud in a shaky voice:

> *"A race is not lost if one lives through the running*
> *And victory sweeter when tested in cunning.*
> *Into the sanctum you may now proceed.*
> *Good fortune befall you in treasure and deed."*

Timmen stood up on wobbly legs and walked to the big, iron door. The companions crowded around him as he slid the silver key into the lock. The halfling hesitated a moment before turning it. Looking over his shoulder, his rosy face smiled up at them, marred only by the white scar on his chin. Arcanis patted him on the head and they all returned his smile. The thief giggled, looked back to the door, and turned the key.

The door swung silently on its ancient hinges and they came into a dusty catacomb of offices and barracks. These rooms were constructed of wood and stone, not crystal, and Aurora's light was not necessary. Arcanis floated several balls of light and they looked through the rooms fairly quickly. Timmen looked for traps, but none were found within the sanctuary. At last they came to a large, plush central chamber with a vault behind the desk.

"This must be what we have come for," Aurora said and the others nodded their agreement. It took Timmen quite a while to open the vault; he drilled four different holes and finally managed to disengage the lock from the inside. When he opened the door, Aurora and Alishane frowned and Dorak growled.

"Bah, it's empty!" grumbled the dwarf.

But the thief's eyes sparkled. "No, it isn't," he said as he reached inside. Retracting his arms, the thief's hands seemed to have disappeared. "It's a shadow cloak," Timmen marveled as he held before the others a shifting drapery of darkness.

"Is this some form of magic?" Aurora asked the wizard. Arcanis gave no response, but stood smiling as he watched Timmen turning the cloak over in his hands.

"It must be the crystal," the halfling crooned. "The fabric is interwoven with shards of the crystal." He stood and donned the cloak, pulling the cowl low over his eyes. The others could see nothing but a halfling-sized hole in the air. "In a darkened room or at night, this will make me all but invisible," he said with excitement.

Alishane did not share the thief's giddiness. "With the crystal woven into the cloak, will it also repel magic?" he asked of Arcanis.

The wizard's bemused smile disappeared as he turned away from Timmen to address the cleric. "Yes," he answered. "It is a mighty artifact indeed, and *not* one to be used lightly." He looked at Aurora. "This could easily turn the tide in the Regent's war with the Countess."

"But he said we could keep it," Timmen squeaked and pulled back the hood so that only his head floated before them.

"Take the cursed thing off!" demanded Dorak. "I need only to see yer head to remove it from yer body."

Timmen frowned and removed the cloak. He folded it carefully and stowed it in his pack.

"We have what we came for," said Arcanis. "Let us be gone from this place."

They left the Caverns of the Crystal Night and began their northward journey with heavy hearts and busy minds. They had mastered the caves and left the iron door open, but the full protective measure of the Caverns was lost without closing the chests to reset the trap. And there was no way for the Crystal Night to gain access to their sanctuary if the trap were ever reset. Without Aurora's light, the companions could not have defeated the crystals, and without being able to see, opening the chests in sequence and in time was impossible. These facts led to only one conclusion: the Regent was not going to be happy. A dangerous confrontation was possible and would be even more likely if the whole party was present. In the end, they decided that Aurora would have to speak to the Regent alone, without the cloak and without her friends. This was her errand and her risk, and the information they needed justified that risk. But if the Regent went back on his word and sought to do her harm, then he would get a firsthand look at the power he sought to control.

Darius Zannick paced nervously behind his desk in the university. Charles Bothan had not returned when expected from his scouting of Zakarus Rinn. The Regent was finding it increasingly difficult to remain patiently idle while poised on the cusp of his war with the Countess. "The calm before the storm," he whispered and retrieved a glass of port from his desk. He swirled the thick, crimson liquid with a slight movement of his hand and stared hypnotically as the wine's legs grudgingly surrendered to gravity. "Or more like a besieged soldier looking out from the ramparts at the countless campfires of his foe, awaiting his doom with the coming of dawn." He stopped swirling the port and returned it to his desk without taking a sip.

"Ridiculous!" he stormed and resumed his pacing. "This waiting is making me as nervous as an old hen." He moved toward the corner where his coat hung on a hook. "Well, I refuse to cluck any longer!" He slung the long, wool coat over his shoulders and turned to the door, but just as he reached out for the handle the door opened, its frame darkened by the hulking form of Kleet Olander.

"You have a caller," Olander wheezed in his deep, gruff voice. "A woman."

"I am not accepting callers. Show her out and prepare to call a meeting of the guild. Our time of waiting is over."

Kleet Olander did not move. His dull eyes looked at the Regent and his lips moved silently as his mind organized words into a sentence. "Her message" he started at last, "she said you struck a bargain with her and she has fulfilled her end."

It took a moment for Zannick to make the connection. When he did, his eyes opened wide and he started to speak, then he caught himself and instead he asked, "She is alone?" Olander gave a quick nod and the Regent continued, "Show her in and then make sure we are not disturbed." When his lieutenant had gone, the Regent hung his coat on the hook and sat behind his desk. He picked up his glass of port and spent the next few moments mastering his appearance of calm and smug superiority.

Aurora entered and waited for the door to close behind her. She looked quickly around the room and then walked briskly before the desk. "Your bodyguard is not here this time," she observed.

"And yet I still granted you entrance. Do you think me foolish?" the old man asked with a wide smile that showed his yellow teeth.

"No," Aurora answered. "I have shown faith in coming here alone. Therefore, your show of faith is appropriate."

The Regent's smile widened. "My thoughts exactly," he beamed. He looked her over carefully with his probing gaze and then asked, "So, you were successful?"

"I breached the caves and retrieved your artifact, yes," she answered.

"And what was it?" he queried in a voice that showed he already knew the answer and was simply seeking confirmation of her claim.

"My thief kept the cloak," the elf declared impatiently, "as part of the payment you promised."

"Indeed I did make that promise," the Regent said and leaned forward in his chair. "The Cloak of the Crystal Night is a mighty gift, and it is yours to keep if you give me the information I need."

"You were also to tell me of the Countess," Aurora said firmly.

"I have already given you the cloak. It is your turn to..."

"I care nothing for the cloak," Aurora interrupted. "Our business with the Countess is to our mutual benefit. Tell me what you know of her affairs and I will tell you of the Caverns."

The Regent stared at her for a long moment and then gave her a smile that made her skin crawl. "Very well, elf maiden fair, I shall tell you." The Regent folded his hands on his desk and his lecherous smile evaporated. "You had asked me about the *Wind Runner*. I know that Captain Eustacio does not normally do business with the Countess, and that is precisely why she paid him a large sum of money to hire him on this occasion. Part of that small fortune, a jeweled dagger I believe, was stolen from the ship's hold by some of her crew. Their bodies turned up in an alley a fortnight ago." The Regent reached down to the floor behind his desk and pulled his pet galliwollup onto his lap. He stroked its gnarled head and it flicked its tongue. "I am afraid, however," Zannick continued, "that I cannot tell you what Eustacio was carrying for the Countess, because I honestly don't know. The *Wind Runner* has been at sea for weeks and has not yet returned. Perhaps you can learn more from Eustacio's mistress; I believe her name is Delila and she pours ale at the Copper Dram. What I *can* tell you, and this is the important part, my dear," the old man's smile returned briefly, "is that the Countess has invested great time and energy into infiltrating Citadel Adbar. She has agents inside the Brotherhood of Callamore. What is more, a great ritual took place three weeks ago within the Citadel and shortly thereafter a disturbance rippled through the Brotherhood. They have sequestered their entire Order within the fortress and have organized an inquisition. And all of this occurred within days of the *Wind Runner* taking to sea."

"So she has stolen from the Citadel," Aurora whispered.

"And now you see why I desire to begin my war immediately, while she is distracted, and why I must have the safety of my refuge before I do so. Now," the Regent leaned over his desk and looked at Aurora with great anticipation, "why don't you tell me what you learned of the Caverns?"

Aurora pulled the map from a pocket on the inside of her cape and opened it on the desk. "Your map was true," she said and pointed to a spot. "The entrance to the caves is here."

"Yes, yes I know," the Regent interrupted. "Tell me how to get into the dark chamber."

This was where Aurora expected to run into trouble. She shifted her body to appear more comfortable, but in truth she was making the dagger at the small of her back more accessible. "The dark chamber consists entirely of night crystal," she said. "Firelight will not reflect off it and magic is useless against it."

"I know this," the Regent spat; he was growing impatient. "How did you defeat it?"

"I do not know how your guild used to manage the feat, nor how you will do so now. For my purposes, I defeated the crystal myself." Aurora flashed her light briefly and the old man jerked backward and shielded his face.

When the light disappeared, Zannick rubbed his eyes and moaned. "Oh, you might have just *told* me how you did it," he groaned. Aurora allowed herself a brief smile. "Well now," the man said when again he looked at her a moment later, "how does this avail me? For I have no such power at my disposal."

Aurora pulled from her pouch the silver key that opened the door to the inner sanctuary. "You should not need to see to get through the chamber." She slid the key across the desk. "Be mindful of a trap in the floor at the end of the passage. Once past it, stay on the left-hand wall and pass two openings. You will come to a large door. This key will unlock it. Once inside, there is no crystal and torchlight will serve."

The Regent took the silver key and flung it into a drawer of his desk. "What are you not telling me?" he asked suspiciously.

Aurora took a deep breath and shifted her hand nearer the dagger on her belt. "The dark chamber is large and circular with nine rooms spaced evenly around its circumference. Each room has a chest set in the floor containing a key and a note leading to another chest. They must all be opened in the correct order and within eighty-one seconds to avoid setting off the trap." During her recitation, Aurora's eyes never left those of Darius Zannick, even as the old man's narrowed menacingly.

"This is not what I had hoped to hear," the Regent said tightly.

"That's not my problem," Aurora retorted.

"Hmm. Have you anything more to tell me?" asked Zannick.

Aurora shook her head. "Have you me?"

The old man broke their electric eye contact and looked down at his galliwollup, still stroking its head slowly. "Then I guess our business is concluded," he said. "You may wait in the anteroom and I will have someone show you out."

Aurora was still on her guard and she kept her hand on the hilt of her dagger as she left the office and waited in the square room with intricate carved wood around the ceiling and no doors. After waiting for several minutes, she began to get nervous. *This is taking too long*, she thought. *Something is wrong.*

Just then a small panel opened in the wall near the ceiling. Aurora recognized immediately the brown and white eyes of the Regent. "I am sorry, my dear, but I'm afraid I cannot let you leave," he said in a flat, emotionless voice.

"I am not an enemy you care to make, Zannick," Aurora responded.

The old man gave a caustic chuckle. "Please," he said, "cease your useless threats. Where you are going your friends will not find you."

"And where is that?"

"Where you cannot cause any trouble for me or divulge the information you possess. I will barter your life for the silence of your friends. Now please, sit down before you fall down. I do not want my prize damaged." With that, the panel closed and a green vapor began blowing into the room through tiny holes in the floor.

Aurora felt her head growing heavy and she fell to her knees. "Damn you, Zannick! You treacherous fool!" she cried. "You know not what you do!" She coughed on the poisonous air. "You know not what you do!"

"I take what is mine, elf maiden fair, I take what is mine," the old man called. Aurora crumpled to the floor, her mind swimming into unconsciousness. The last thing she heard before her world went black was the Regent's voice, hollow and distant, "Trust not in the honor of thieves, my dear. For I am the lord of this land, and the lord takes what he will."

Part Four
~ *Legem Amittere* ~

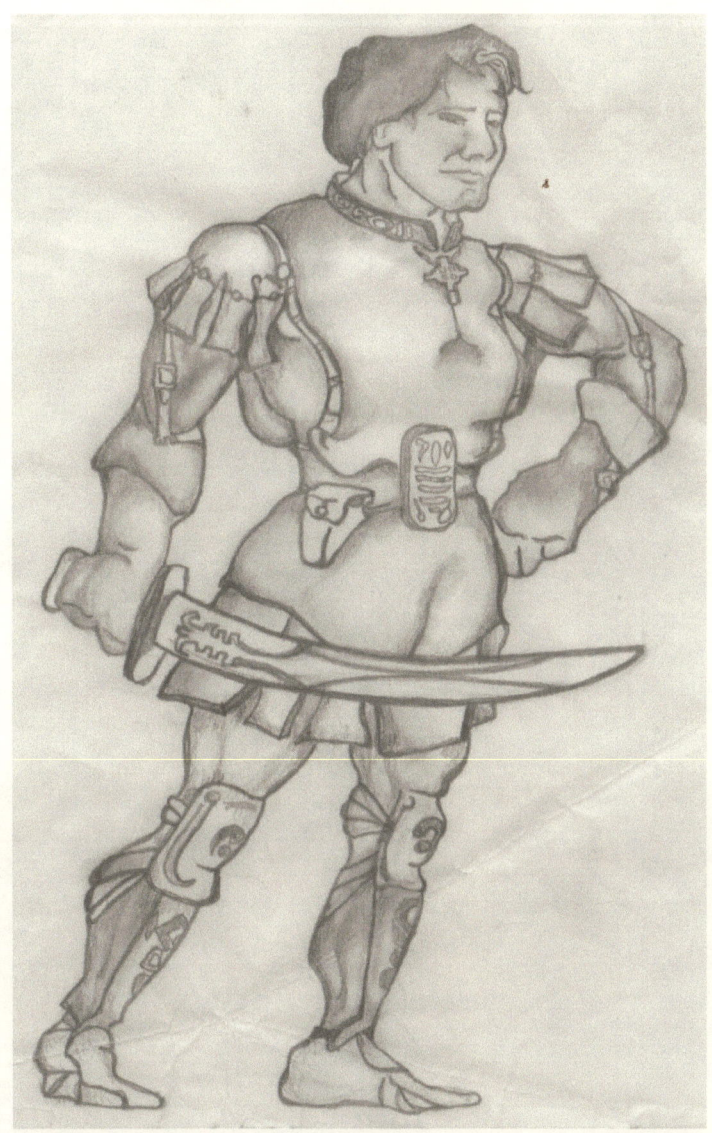

The Breaking of the Oath

Chapter Nineteen

~ Desperation ~

"I grow tired of hearing the same feeble answers, Sinjin; I had expected more cooperation from one so long and stalwart within the Brotherhood." The old man moved behind the seated Brother Sinjin and opened a door to the dark chamber buried deep in the bowels of Citadel Adbar. Two large, black-cloaked Brothers entered silently and stood with crossed arms behind Brother Sinjin.

"If my answers are repetitive," he responded in his deep voice, "perhaps you should cease asking questions to which you already know the answers." Brother Sinjin was tall and stoic, one of the few dark-skinned members of the Brotherhood of Callamore. Though his outward appearance remained calm, his bald head shone with perspiration.

The Inquisitor returned to his seat opposite Sinjin and folded his hands upon the table that separated the two men. The old man smiled warmly and asked in a kind voice, "Are you sure you can contribute nothing that may be helpful?"

Brother Sinjin took a deep breath and shook his head. "I've told you all that I know. The location of the crypt that held the Scrolls was a secret. I didn't even know..." The Inquisitor gave a slight nod and Sinjin was seized tightly around the throat, cutting him off in mid-sentence.

The old man leaned forward and his smile was replaced by a menacing glare. The candlelight flickered and his face looked sallow and lined, but his eyes reflected the glow with a sinister sparkle. "You are the Brotherhood's runic calligrapher," the Inquisitor growled. "You are responsible for laying the runes and glyphs that protect this fortress from magical intrusion. Do you think this theft could have taken place without the assistance of magic?"

The arm around his throat loosened and Sinjin gasped, "How am I supposed to know what magic they used? I have told you that I was not…" He choked again as the arm tightened and cut the wind to his lungs.

"So now it is 'they'?" the Inquisitor probed. "You know that it was more than one thief, obviously. Tell me, how many of your friends did it take to rob us of the Sacred Scrolls?"

Brother Sinjin opened his mouth to answer, but no sound and no air passed through the stranglehold on his throat. His façade of calm now cast aside, the dark man's eyes registered his utter terror and his hands pulled futilely at the arm under his chin.

"I shall ask this just one more time," the Inquisitor hissed, "what do you know about the disappearance of the Scrolls?"

Brother Sinjin did not answer; the powerful arm around his throat had crushed his larynx. His eyes rolled back into his head and his arms dropped limp to his sides. At a signal from the Inquisitor, the man holding Brother Sinjin released him and held him forward. The Inquisitor felt for a pulse and then grunted. "Take him out through the dungeons for burial and announce his death as another suicide," the old man instructed. The large, black-cloaked men dragged the corpse of Brother Sinjin out of the room. The Inquisitor rang a small bell and then began making notations in a leather book upon his desk. An attendant opened the door and awaited instructions. Without looking up from his writing, the old man said, "Bring in the next subject for questioning." The attendant nodded and closed the door with a boom that echoed forlornly down the halls of Citadel Adbar.

Zakarus Rinn went through the motions of shoeing the big, gray horse he had taken from the stables of Tavora Manor, but his attention was focused elsewhere. The street was abuzz with students entering and exiting the university and no one paid any heed to the assassin disguised in dirty clothes and long, greasy hair. Rinn kneeled in the dusty lane and peered at a small party of travelers talking discreetly under the awning of a street-front haberdashery. They kept their faces covered as best they could, all except for a dwarf who refused to cover his face and seemed incapable of discretion. Rinn also kept his senses attuned to the man crouching on the rooftop of the building behind him. Charles Bothan had been following him all day, and though he knew the man was there, the Shadow Wolf had given no indication of that knowledge.

Standing now to retrieve more nails from the pack atop the horse, Rinn watched the woman in the party leave her companions and climb the steps of the university. The rest of the group shuffled off into a dark alley. Though the matted hair of his wig fell down over his dirty face, the sharp eyes of the assassin gleamed as he watched Aurora Daelin walk through the institution's large front doors.

The Shadow Wolf had spent the morning prowling around the neighborhood, baiting Charles Bothan into a final confrontation. How surprised he had been when he saw the beautiful elf and her companions slipping quietly down the street! Rinn gave thoughts to abandoning his current objective to resume his hunt anew, but then his quarry stopped to talk just a few paces away from where the assassin crouched by his horse. He felt an odd mixture of emotion in those moments. He was apprehensive, but not afraid he convinced himself, to encounter the wizard again, and that apprehension drove him toward anger. In addition, the assassin felt an undeniable attraction toward the elf. He was drawn to her as a planet toward its star.

Rinn also noted carefully a new presence in the group. There were few in the land whom Zakarus Rinn deemed worthy of notice and regard, but Dorak Shale certainly qualified. The dwarf's presence raised new questions and he wondered what answers the Countess might provide.

All of these thoughts rumbled through the assassin's mind in the minutes after Aurora disappeared into the university. He watched as Alishane Wyndam stood against a wall in the dark alley with his arms outstretched, clearly in the process of spell-casting. The wizard and dwarf stood in front of the cleric to shield him from passersby on the street, but Rinn still noticed a white swooshing of energy flow over Wyndam's body as he completed his spell. Minutes passed. The cleric's arms were still outstretched as he maintained his prolonged invocation. Charles Bothan was creeping along the eave of the roof behind the Shadow Wolf, who was again kneeling by the horse with its front hoof in his lap. Rinn turned all of his focus behind him, listening to the slight scrapes of cloth and loose pebbles upon the eave. Bothan was getting into position; soon he would pounce. Seconds slipped away. The scraping stopped. The Shadow Wolf flexed the muscles in his legs, preparing to leap out of his crouched position.

Suddenly, across the lane, Alishane Wyndam cried out in an agonized wail. "No! Treachery! No!" the cleric howled and slumped to the ground. Zakarus Rinn leaned lower to look under the horse, but the animal screamed in pain and reared up violently. The Shadow Wolf rolled away from the beast and in one fluid motion removed the dirty cloak and wig of his disguise while pulling his sword and bringing it to bear. He looked quickly back at the horse to see a dagger protruding from its flank; blood poured down its side as it thrashed wildly and raised its voice in a frothing cacophony. Alishane Wyndam screamed once again across the lane, one word that Rinn heard clearly, "Aurora!"

Another dagger whistled past the assassin's head and he turned in time to see Charles Bothan leap from the roof and land lightly on the ground. Bothan pulled two more throwing knives from a bandoleer on his chest and sprang forward, his hands flashing as he let the daggers fly. In the same movement, Bothan's arms crossed his body at the waist and retrieved two stout short-swords. The two throwing knives, aimed expertly at the Shadow Wolf's throat, wavered in mid-flight and sailed past the assassin.

The two men came together in a clang of steel as Rinn parried three blows from the short-swords of Charles Bothan.

"Impossible!" growled Bothan as the men began circling. "Four throws and my aim was perfect."

The Shadow Wolf sneered and launched his own offensive: a thrust, feint, thrust. Bothan defeated it with ease. "I cannot be taken down by ranged attacks," taunted Zakarus Rinn. "Only a coward strikes from afar."

The two men continuted their lethal dance. The horse was now dead, its shrill cries replaced by the reek of its death. The street was almost deserted with only a few stragglers ducking into buildings to join their mates with their faces pressed against the windows.

"Your jeers betray you, Zakarus," Charles Bothan answered as the combatants circled in measured steps. "You cannot anger me to gain an edge, and you provide information."

The Shadow Wolf laughed. "I provide it freely," he said and raised his voice to the empty street. "Hear me villains, miscreants and challengers: Zakarus Rinn is invulnerable to your threats. I cannot be shot in the back; I cannot be defeated. All who attempt it will find my blade in their gullet." Rinn used his exaggerated bravado to disguise a new attack, but Bothan had not been lulled. As the Shadow Wolf leapt atop a railing near the street and sprang down upon his foe, the elder assassin deflected Rinn's plunging blade and stepped back.

The combatants resumed circling each other. Bothan looked carefully at Rinn's attire to try to discern what magical items the Wolf might be using. His clothing was shabby, consistent with his disguise. He wore two gauntlets upon his forearms; one made of gold and the other silver. Then Bothan noticed the Shadow Wolf's black leather boots. They were highly polished and had a faint shimmer about them. He looked up into the Shadow Wolf's leering eyes. "Boots of Displacement," Bothan stated rather than asked.

"I told you ranged attacks wouldn't work," Rinn boasted. "I knew you were behind me. I fear you not."

"You didn't complete your training at Mount Alcharist," Bothan responded. "You didn't learn to control your pride."

"Ha! And you seek to teach me?" Rinn scoffed.

"No," answered Bothan and it was his turn to smile, "I seek to end you." He pulled two pendants strung on a necklace from under his tunic and fit them together. They joined with a loud *click* and again Charles Bothan looked into the eyes of the Shadow Wolf and smiled. In the next moment, the elder assassin became a blur of movement. He advanced on Zakarus Rinn in the blink of an eye; the Wolf barely got his blade up in time to deflect one of the slashing short swords, but still took a wound to his left arm from Bothan's other blade.

Turning slightly to his left, Rinn again faced off against Charles Bothan, who was standing motionless and smiling wickedly. "The Amulet of Arthenor," Bothan answered the confused rage in the Shadow Wolf's eyes. "It gives me speed you cannot hope to counter. You are fast and skilled, young Zakarus, but you are overmatched. Today you will die." Bothan blurred past the Wolf again. A frantic clang of metal rang out and as it echoed down the street and the two stood facing each other once more, the Shadow Wolf was bleeding from a fresh wound to his stomach.

Zakarus Rinn was panting and pale from the exertion of the battle, the shock of his wounds and an emotion he had not felt in a very long time: desperation. He began retreating into a dark alley. "I admit that you have an advantage," he wheezed, "and you have forced me into something that I did not want to do."

Bothan flashed forward again. Rinn groaned in pain as he parried and continued to withdraw into the dark alley, a gash in his cheek oozing blood down his face.

"Enough of this!" Rinn shouted. "My mistress will be most displeased that I have done this, but you have forced your own demise." The assassin reached down and loosed the clasps on his silver gauntlet. As it fell to the ground, Bothan saw that ancient runes and script were inscribed upon it. The Shadow Wolf issued a groan that melted into a snarl. His body began to change, his muscles swelled and his bones cracked. The clothes ripped away from his body as he bent over on powerful haunches. When Charles Bothan looked up at Rinn's face he no longer saw a man, but rather the snarling and dripping maw of a werewolf.

"A lycanthrope," Bothan gasped in shock. "But it cannot be; the Order of Alchary would never admit your kind into the monastery."

The Shadow Wolf gnashed his teeth and clicked his claws together, then he spoke in a gravelly, growling voice. "You fool, I was not a lycanthrope when I entered the Order. This gift was given me by my mistress years after I left those pathetic monks on Alcharist."

"Who would accept such a curse?" Bothan wondered aloud. "To be forever servile to the animalistic urges of a beast... it is madness." The man was buying time now as he slowly backed toward the bright street at the end of the alley.

The Wolf stalked after the retreating assassin, pausing briefly to point with a long, curved claw at the runes inscribed into the golden gauntlet around his forearm:

"Gauntlet of light, of power and might
Silver keeps wolf at bay.
Gauntlet of gold, inscriptions of old
In losing the wolf will stay."

"Wh... What?" stammered Charles Bothan. The man was retreating faster now and sweat ran down his pallid face.

"The gauntlets allow me to change at will, when I have need," the Wolf answered; his lupine tongue licked the blood that was still dripping from the wound on his face. "You have given rise to my need, Bothan, and forced me to risk revealing the truth of my nature." He crouched and prepared to spring, the hair on his ridged back bristling. "But you won't live long enough to tell others."

The Shadow Wolf leaped forward with speed rivaling the Amulet of Arthenor, but his claws and power were far more lethal than Bothan's short-swords. The combatants came together in a spray of blood and sparks as claws met metal and fangs found bone. A moment later, it was over. The Shadow Wolf crouched over the limp body of Charles Bothan; the man hung with his throat clamped in the Wolf's jaws. The short swords fell from Bothan's hands and clattered to the ground. With his eyes gleaming red in the darkened lane, the Shadow Wolf surrendered to his bloodlust and shook his mighty head, tearing out his victim's throat and spattering the ground with blood.

The Wolf crouched over the broken body of Charles Bothan and gave a great coughing snarl, and then the red gleam faded from his eyes. The Wolf turned and retrieved his silver gauntlet. He placed it over his forearm and clasped the hooks. An agonized groan escaped him as the wolf was driven from his body. A moment later, a battered and bloody Zakarus Rinn limped to the body of his victim and took up the Amulet of Arthenor. He placed it in his pocket, turned back to the darkened lane, and disappeared into the shadows.

The companions moved into an alley adjacent to the university after Aurora left them for her meeting with the Regent. Alishane backed against the wall of a building and began a scrying spell; he intended to watch over her in the only way he could. Arcanis and Dorak stood guard in front of the cleric.

The wizard had the hood of his cloak pulled low over his face, but his deep, dark eyes surveyed the crowded street. "There will soon be trouble across the lane," he whispered to Dorak.

The dwarf looked up to see Charles Bothan creeping along the eave of a building and preparing to leap upon a disheveled man in the street. Looking closer, Dorak saw that the man was actually Zakarus Rinn and the Shadow Wolf was looking directly at him. For one long, fateful second, the dwarf and the assassin made eye contact. Dorak pulled his axe from the sling on his back and leaned upon it casually, but his hands gripped the handle tightly. "If trouble there will be," he said, "then let it come to me."

Arcanis smiled faintly. "I'm sure it will not come to that," he said, though his own hands roamed over the worn surface of his staff.

Timmen had been huddling near Alishane. When he heard the muted conversation between Arcanis and Dorak, the halfling quietly pulled the shadow cloak out of his pack, crawled a few feet away and disappeared.

The three of them watched Charles Bothan slither to the edge of the roof across the lane. He perched above the Shadow Wolf and seemed to hesitate, but a moment later they caught a glint of steel as the assassin pulled a throwing dagger from somewhere in his clothing. Bothan raised his right arm and took careful aim. Timmen held his breath.

At the same moment that Bothan's arm came down and let fly his dagger, Alishane gave a great, anguished cry that resounded over the clatter of the street. The companions looked to their friend to see the cleric's body slump to the ground, shaking uncontrollably as his spirit raced back to his physical form. A moment later, Alishane's eyes flew open and he looked around him frantically and tried to rise, but his friends held him down.

"Treachery! No!" he yelled.

"Hush," Arcanis instructed. "Come, Dorak. We must get him away from here." The wizard and dwarf hoisted Alishane between them, with Dorak shouldering most of the weight, and shuffled down the alley away from the commotion in the street. Feet thundered everywhere and women were screaming. Halfway down the alley, Arcanis looked around them and whispered loudly, "Timmen! Timmen, where are you?"

"Leave him be," grunted the dwarf. "That halfling can look after himself, that's for certain."

Back near the street, huddled invisible under his cloak, Timmen watched with wide-eyed fascination Rinn's transformation and murder of Charles Bothan. Long after Rinn returned to human form and disappeared down the alley, Timmen shivered under his cloak, scarcely able to breathe. Eventually, he found that his legs responded to his mind's instructions and he crawled down the alley, took off the cloak and ran to find his friends.

He found them a few blocks away. Alishane was huddled against the wall with Arcanis whispering quietly in his ear. Dorak was standing guard with his axe at the ready. "Who won?" the dwarf asked Timmen.

"Huh?"

"Who won the fight?" Dorak repeated.

Timmen swallowed. "Rinn," he answered, trying to find words to explain what he had seen.

"Hmph," grunted Dorak.

"No, you don't understand," Timmen whispered hoarsely. "He, he changed! I mean he..."

"Spit it out, boy!" shouted the dwarf.

"He's a werewolf," Timmen croaked.

Arcanis left Alishane's side and grabbed Timmen by the shoulders. "What did you say?" he demanded.

"I saw it," Timmen squeaked. "He tore out that other man's throat with his jaws."

The wizard closed his eyes. "I have not the strength for this fight," he wheezed.

"Don't say that," Timmen pleaded. "We need you. Who can help us if not you?"

"Bah!" stormed Dorak. "I knew the boy for a candy arse," the dwarf thumbed over his shoulder toward Alishane, "but I never figured *you* fer one too!"

Arcanis opened his eyes and fixed Dorak with a stare out of the depths of his power that made even the surly dwarf take pause.

"What happened to Aurora?" asked Timmen.

The wizard was still looking at Dorak as he answered. "She has been taken," he said. Timmen gave a little squeak and Arcanis looked down at him. "Zannick took her as a trophy."

"We must save her!" the halfling cried.

"Aurora knew the risks," Arcanis said sternly, "and she took them because our task is more important than any one of us." He nodded toward Alishane. "During his scrying he heard everything that Zannick told Aurora about the Countess." The wizard put his hand on Timmen's shoulder. "We must each gather our strength now, lad, for we will be separating."

"We'll do whatever we have to. Won't we?" Timmen looked to Dorak.

"Bet yer arse, boy!" bellowed the dwarf.

"Good," Arcanis smiled grimly. "Dorak and I will be going to the docks to find Captain Eustacio's mistress and learn more about the *Wind Runner's* plans. Alishane must go into hiding near the university and use scrying as much as his strength allows him to watch over Aurora. I do not think her health is in immediate danger, but we cannot abandon her altogether." That thought brought a smile to the halfling's face, but it was short-lived. "You, Timmen," Arcanis continued, "have the most dangerous and difficult task of any of us. You must use your new cloak and all of your skill to infiltrate Citadel Adbar." The wizard looked for a reaction from Timmen, but the thief gave none. Arcanis continued. "Zannick confirmed our belief that the Countess stole from the Brotherhood of Callamore, but we must discern with certitude whether it was the Sacred Scrolls or if something else is missing. We must also learn what the Brotherhood has uncovered during their Inquisition and what they are doing to retrieve their artifact. Can you do it?"

Timmen's face had gone a little white, but he stood as tall as he could and answered, "I got into Tavora Manor, didn't I? I can handle a bunch of withered old men." Dorak gave a shout of approval and clapped Timmen on the back so hard that the halfling stumbled. "Besides," Timmen concluded as he rubbed his back, "now I have the Cloak of the Crystal Night."

Aurora awakened in a small, dimly lit room. She was alone, cold and uncertain how long she had been lying unconscious upon the floor. Looking around her, she found that the room was finely furnished with a comfortable bed adorned in silk sheets, an oak armoire filled with expensive clothing, even a desk with paper, ink and a writing quill. There were no windows and three bare walls. A row of steel bars completed her enclosure. Venturing to the front of the room and looking through the bars, Aurora saw a long hallway with cells like her own along both walls. The only light came from a lone torch burning halfway down the corridor. Faint sounds of snoring and rhythmic breathing told her that the other cells were occupied, but the occupants were asleep. Aurora went to the bed and laid down. She stared into the dark and wondered how much Alishane had seen of her encounter with the Regent. Would they come for her? Could they reach her even if they tried? She didn't know enough about her captors or where she was to answer that question. It was likely that a battle with the Crystal Night would be cataclysmic; it would be the end of the party and possibly some of her companions. And it would surely end their quest against the Countess. Arcanis would never allow that. Thus, there was only one conclusion for her to reach: she would not be rescued anytime soon.

Aurora pulled her knees to her chest and despaired. She was not prone to self-pity and she knew this spell would pass; perhaps in the morning she would start thinking of ways to escape. But alone in the dark, lost and separated from her friends, she felt only a great, terrible sadness. The importance of her quest was oppressive and her distress at being unable to fulfill it was suffocating. She choked on her failure for several minutes before she realized she was sobbing. She did not cry often, but throughout that first night of her imprisonment the elf's cheeks ran with tears.

Chapter Twenty

~ Splinter ~

The Copper Dram was in its full, raucous splendor as Dorak
Shale ambled through its rickety front doors. No one spoke to
announce his arrival, but his presence did not go unnoticed. As the
thick dwarf walked across the packed floor toward the bar, the
crowd parted before him and squeezed shut behind to form a bubble
of caution. The drunken patrons of the shore-side alehouse kept a
safe distance from his famously quick temper and sharp axe.

Dorak climbed onto a stool at the bar and ordered a pint.
The man on the stool beside him scooted a bit further away. When
his ale arrived, Dorak took a long quaff and then belched loudly.
Wiping his dripping beard with his forearm, the dwarf turned and
surveyed the crowd. The usual array of sods jostled each other in the
cramped room. Through a heavy haze of smoke Dorak saw the man
he was looking for. He wore a weathered brown cloak, a tidy white
beard and had a long, wooden staff lain across his knees. As soon as
Dorak made eye contact with him, Arcanis Rhu nodded slightly and
turned to look at a plump, rosy-cheeked woman serving drinks
nearby.

"Come on, Delila," slurred a wretched man on reeking
breath, "yer man ain't even around."

Another drunk at the table piped up as the two men pawed
at the barmaid's rounded rump. "Yeah, Delila," the second man
said, "you know what they say: When the ship's at sea, the lasses
are free." A roar of laughter rolled from the neighboring tables. As

Delila pushed through the crowd, her behind was fondled with every step, though she showed no signs of noticing.

The woman moved to the bar to place her next order. Arcanis and Dorak again made eye contact and exchanged an understanding, then Dorak began looking through the crowd for the largest and drunkest man he could find. At the far end of the bar, seated near a roaring fireplace on the opposite side of the room from Arcanis, a huge bear of a man was bent over at the waist, laughing and being slapped on the back by several other large men. The big man's name was Dinford Delson and he was well known along the Andaluric Coast as a pit fighter of high ability.

Dorak watched as Delila hoisted her heavily laden tray up to her shoulder and made off through the crowd toward Arcanis and the table of free-fingered drunks. The dwarf retrieved his ale and drained his mug in one long gulp. After unleashing another loud belch, he hopped down from his stool and walked toward Dinford Delson and his group of toadies. A moment later, as Delila was plopping frothy mugs of ale on the table and the sods appreciatively patted her butt, Dorak shouldered into the ring of men encircling Dinford Delson.

The big man was just finishing another raunchy joke and his crew erupted in laughter. Dorak joined in and was guffawing merrily when Delson noticed the dwarf's presence. The man stopped laughing and the smile melted from his face. One by one the other men noticed their leader's silence and the group's jocularity trickled away. Soon Dorak was the only one laughing.

Dinford Delson was frowning and looked confused; his crew looked alternately from the pit fighter to the dwarf to see what would happen next. Dorak continued to laugh at the joke he had not heard. Most of the tavern was now silent, the people holding their breath as they watched with fascination the gathering storm. After several long moments the dwarf stopped laughing, but he was still smiling as he cocked his arm back and drove his fist straight into the face of Dinford Delson.

Utter chaos broke out. Dorak had the pit fighter on the floor and the two were grappling violently. Delson's friends fell into the melee and soon everyone in the Copper Dram was either scrambling to get out of the way or pushing forward to get a better look. The drunks at the table near Arcanis gave up fondling Delila and moved to watch the brawl at the other side of the room. The barmaid heaved a great sigh and began wiping down the table with a rag from her tray. Just as Dorak was heard shouting from under the pile, "Ha ha, got ye again, ye big lummox!" Delila felt a soft tap on her shoulder.

"Might I have a moment?" Arcanis asked with a gentle smile.

Delila looked at the crowd surrounding the brawl and brushed the hair out of her eyes. "Might as well," she said. "Looks like I'm free for awhile."

Arcanis led her out into the cold night air. "You are to be commended for your tolerance," he said as he showed her to a bench.

"Tolerance of what?" the woman asked blandly and took a seat near the old man.

"The roaming hands of your patrons," Arcanis clarified.

"Oh that," Delila gave a wave of her hand, "I wear a padded bustle. My butt starts far below this," she gave her rump a good smack, "so I don't even feel it when they grope me."

"I'm sure Mr. Eustacio is pleased by that."

"Horace? Oh," she giggled, "I already worked here when we met so he has no room to complain. He knew what he was getting." She blew her bangs out of her eyes. "Still, it's good that *I* don't complain or he would start trouble around here."

Arcanis looked around to be sure they were alone; a great roar went up inside the Copper Dram. "Please allow me to be blunt, miss," the wizard began, "it is Captain Eustacio I wish to discuss."

"Horace? What are you wanting with Horace?"

Arcanis looked the woman directly in the eyes for the first time and she flinched slightly. "I need to know where the *Wind Runner* has gone and anything you can tell me about her cargo."

"That's none of my business," the woman answered in a shrill voice and got up to leave, "nor yours, I would warrant." She stormed away, but as she approached the entrance to the Copper Dram the wizard gave a flick of his staff and the large doors swung inward and slammed shut. Delila turned and walked back in front of Arcanis. Her voice was angry, but her eyes showed that she was terrified. "Don't try to threaten me with your magic, old man!" she cried. "I've toted drinks in this bar long enough to see your kind and every other kind get what's coming to 'em. We all got it coming. So do what you're gonna do or leave me be!"

Arcanis put down his staff and held out his hands. "I did not mean to threaten you and I am very sorry to have alarmed you, but I have gone to great lengths to arrange this conversation and I cannot allow it to end just yet."

Delila looked through an open window into the Copper Dram. Dorak bellowed again, "No more fight left in ye, eh? Who's next, then?" Arcanis smiled.

"The dwarf is your friend?" Delila asked.

"This matter is gravely important," Arcanis persisted, "and may turn out to be very dangerous to Captain Eustacio."

"And you are seeking to help him?" She was skeptical.

"I cannot make that claim," answered the wizard. "I will pursue my own ends, but if I should fail in my endeavors then it will certainly be an ill turn for the Captain."

Delila's lip trembled and she returned to her seat near Arcanis. "I knew something was wrong with those people," she sniffled and wiped her nose on her dress. "Horace does business with some shady types, to be sure, but these were different. They were too wealthy, too clean and too cold. At least with rats you know what you're getting, but these people..."

"Who were they?" Arcanis pressed.

"I don't know," Delila's eyes were wet when she looked up at him. "They were not from this side of town, if you get my meaning. But one, the leader, I would remember if I saw him again, though I hope that I never do." She shuddered slightly to speak of it. "He was tall and thin with dark hair and these animal eyes; he looks like he drinks blood, that one."

"What else?" Arcanis asked urgently.

"Horace made me leave right after they arrived. There's nothing unusual in that, he always keeps me out of his business, but this time there was something different in his eyes when he told me to leave. When I came back, an hour or so later, he was almost done packing his bag. He said he was putting to sea right away and would not be back for five weeks, but when he returned we could leave this life and never work again. I asked how he could be leaving right away, since it usually takes a couple of days to load the ship with its freight, but he didn't answer. He just kept packing." Delila reached into her dress and pulled out a small pouch. "Before he left, he gave me this and told me that if he didn't come back in six weeks I should take it to Lord Wyndam with a message. Then he left," her voice cracked into a sob, "and Lord Wyndam was accused of those terrible things and got killed and I was so scared. Oh, Horace! What have you got mixed up in?"

"What was the message?" Arcanis asked as he took the pouch from her.

Delila wiped her eyes. "Um, let me make sure I get it right." She folded her hands in her lap and looked up at the stars. "He said, 'A pauper's prince may be a thief and into the fastness steal. Then fleeing toward a lonely dawn his true designs revealed.'" The wizard's deep, black eyes narrowed. "Do you know what it means?" Delila asked.

Arcanis knew perfectly well what the message meant, but he did not wish to share its meaning with the woman. "No," he answered, "but I mean to find out." He stood up to leave. "Thank you. You have been most helpful."

"Please look after Horace, if you can," Delila called after him.

The wizard did not answer but walked swiftly to the doors of the Copper Dram and entered. Half of the bar was in ruins. Dinford Delson's friends were all unconscious and sprawled on the floor. Dorak had Dinford's head in his arms and was squeezing the man into unconsciousness. "What do ye have to say now, eh? Young whippersnapper!" Dorak taunted. Arcanis thumped his staff upon the floor a few times and the dwarf looked up. Seeing the wizard, Dorak leaned in close to Dinford's face and whispered, "That's all the time I have for fun tonight, boy, but I'll be lookin' for ye the next time I come 'round." Dinford's face turned a darker shade of red as he tried to turn away from the stench of the dwarf's breath. Dorak slammed the man's face into the floor and then stood up. He stumped over to where Arcanis was waiting, then the two of them turned and left the Copper Dram.

Cane Shanney heaved a deep sigh as he closed the door to his bedchamber and hung his overcoat on a hook. He crossed the room and closed the heavy drapes on the window, shutting out the gray light of a pale dawn. He turned to his bed and stopped fast in his tracks.

"Hoy!" he exclaimed and gripped at his chest. The man reeled back on his heels for a moment, then his face darkened as his expression turned from shock to consternation. "You little villain!

What are ye doing sneaking into me room? And where have ye been? What trouble have ye been getting into?"

"It's nice to see you, too, Cane," Timmen O'Hook answered as he tucked his shadow cloak into a small pack. The halfling was seated on the bed; he looked tired and haggard.

"You've gone and stepped in it now, haven't ye?" Shanney persisted. "Sneaking in here like you've got the whole world on your tail, and it's likely as not that ye do! Let me thank you for bringing your trouble to my doorstep, while I'm at it." The man stood with his arms crossed, looking down upon the dirty halfling. After a moment his face softened and he sat on the bed next to his friend. "Why do ye always do it, Timmy? Ye can never just leave well enough alone."

"This isn't my usual trouble, Cane," Timmen answered softly with downcast eyes. "I've seen so much over the last few weeks. The whole world has changed for me." He looked up at his friend and his face showed profound fatigue and distress. "I won't tell you of it, for I don't want to lay the weight of knowledge upon you."

Shanney looked at the halfling and his heart was troubled. Timmen looked back at the floor and fingered the scar on his chin. "What can I do for ye, Tim?" the innkeeper asked.

"A little rest," Timmen answered; "that's what I need more than anything right now."

"Then ye shall have it," Shanney answered. "Sleep in me bed and worry not, wee friend; I will sit the watch." The man crossed the room and sat in a chair while Timmen lay down in the bed. As Cane Shanney leaned over to blow out the room's only candle, he saw that the halfling was already asleep.

* * * * * * *

Late in the afternoon, as the faltering sun cast slanting shadows on the world outside his windows, Cane Shanney awoke with a start. His body was stiff from sitting so long in the chair and he cursed himself for falling asleep when he had vowed to watch over his friend. He looked at the bed and found it empty.

"Ah, Timmy," he said mournfully. "May the wind be at your back and the grass before your feet, for I know not what darkness ye walk into." With that lament and a shake of his head the man took up his coat and left to find his supper. It would be a long night of worry for Cane Shanney as he tended his bar in the Wyvern's Tail Inn.

A deep gong resonated out from Citadel Adbar to announce the serving of supper for the Brotherhood of Callamore. Within the fortress, the cloaked men shuffled toward the central dining hall. A shroud of uneasy gloom hovered about the place and the shoulders of the Brethren slumped under the weight of it. The Inquisition was now three weeks old and all of the ninety-one Brothers had been subjected to at least one interview. Eleven had not survived their visit into the Inquisitor's dungeon. No one knew how long the Inquisition would last.

Timmen O'Hook had now been two days inside the fortress and he had learned nothing of the Scrolls and very little about the Inquisition. Large portions of the Citadel were guarded by magical glyphs that could not be disarmed and so were inaccessible to the thief. He had been relegated to skulking about the kitchens and common areas to pick up what little pieces of conversation that he could. He stole food and a few winks of sleep when opportunity allowed, but in most regards his time inside the Citadel had been miserable and fruitless.

He had, however, gained one potentially valuable piece of information: passing the glyph barriers required possession of certain magical stones. He had learned this while following one of the Brothers down a passageway that seemed to lead deep into the fortress. The man had a limp and a stooped posture that made him distinct from the rest of the Brethren, but he always kept his hood up so Timmen never saw his face. Due mostly to idle curiosity, the halfling decided to follow the limping man down the deep, dark passage. The man seemed to be concerned about being followed, for he repeatedly turned to look behind him. When he reached an archway of rune-engraved stones, the stooped figure fumbled through his pockets and then pulled out a jewel, which he then held up to the light of his lantern to be sure it was the one he desired. Peering out from under his shadow cloak, Timmen saw the jewel glitter in the lamplight before the man returned it to his pocket and disappeared down the passage. Timmen had spent the rest of the evening devising a plan to steal the jewel.

Now the halfling huddled in the shadows of the corridor outside the dining hall, watching for the limping Brother. He didn't have long to wait. While most of the Brethren were still taking their seats and beginning their meal, the stooped man shuffled out of the hall and started down a narrow side passage. Timmen followed behind him, sliding silently through the shadows under the protection of his cloak.

After a few twists and turns of the passage, the rumble of conversation in the dining hall was lost and the halfling and the man were alone in the dark. Again the man seemed nervous; he looked around repeatedly and walked as fast as his limp allowed. They walked a little further into the heart of the mountain and then came suddenly to another archway of rune-inscribed stone. The man stopped and looked back into the dark while fumbling through his clothing to find his jewel. Timmen pulled a toxin-tipped dart from a vial in his pack and shrugged off the shadow cloak so he could make his throw. He edged forward slightly and cocked his arm.

"Stand where you are and don't move," the halfling instructed. The cloaked man obeyed. "Turn around."

Very slowly the man held his hands out to his sides and turned. He still wore his hood low over his eyes so Timmen could not see his face in the dark tunnel, but as they faced each other the man seemed to relax and spoke in a high, clear voice.

"Timmen O'Hook?" the man queried. "Are you Timmen O'Hook?" The halfling's breath caught in his throat and the man gave a little laugh. "You gave me quite a fright. Life is dangerous around here nowadays." The man let his arms fall to his sides and took a step forward; Timmen held the dart up higher and reached behind him for his shadow cloak. The man laughed again. "Don't worry, Timmen, I am no threat to you. We have friends in common, you and I. How else would I have known your name?" Timmen still did not answer. "Come now," the man said in his soft voice, "step out of the shadows so we can discuss the purpose of your visit."

Timmen retreated further into the darkness. "You ask much," he whispered, "for one who himself hides beneath his hood."

The man grunted. "Hmph, a fair point." He seemed to ponder for a moment and then conceded. "Very well, I will satisfy your curiosity." With one hand holding the jewel and the lamp, the man drew back his hood and uncovered his face. Timmen couldn't stifle a little squeak of surprise. The man's face was heavily scarred. It appeared as though he had been badly burned; there was no hair upon his head and his ears were no more than tiny nubs of flesh.

The man's deformed lip curled in his fashion of a smile and he chuckled, "I suppose that's one more lesson in being careful what you ask for." Timmen made no response but continued to slink backward down the passage. The man looked around nervously again. "Come now, Timmen, we cannot linger in the open. I have already said that it's dangerous now in the Citadel."

Timmen was hesitant. "You ask me to trust you without giving me cause to do so. You have said that we have friends in common, but you don't name them or reveal how you knew that I was coming."

The man looked around once more and lowered his voice to a mere whisper, "I cannot speak more of this in the open, but I'll give you this final show of faith: the friends of whom I speak are Jarl Talos Daelin of Westwick and his daughter Aurora."

"You know Aurora?" asked Timmen breathlessly.

"Yes. Now please, come with me."

Timmen put the dart in his pack and moved to stand next to the man under the archway. They walked together through the glyph-ward and proceeded down the tunnel. Timmen wondered if this man knew that Aurora had been taken. He felt sullen thinking of Aurora alone in the dungeons of the Crystal Night, being subjected to unknown horrors, but he also felt determined to complete his task so they might sooner be able to rescue her.

They passed several doors in the tunnel before the man stopped at one and entered a small room. Timmen followed him inside. The room appeared to be the man's living quarters. He went to a desk and turned the chair so he could sit facing Timmen. "So," he said, "where shall we begin?"

"You can start by telling me your name," the halfling answered, "and then tell me how you knew I was coming."

"My name is Corliss Landen. I work for the Jarl and that's how I know of your companionship with Aurora. In truth, I did not know you were coming here; I saw a halfling and made a guess. It happened to be correct."

"If you work for the Jarl, are you also elven?" Timmen asked.

Landen smiled slightly. "You are kind to ask," he whispered. He looked down at his hands in his lap and appeared embarrassed when he continued. "Actually, I do have some elvish blood."

"Some?" Timmen echoed. "So you're a half-elf."

"Yes," answered Corliss Landen and his voice cracked. "Though I hear in your tone that you see nothing of the fairer race in me." Timmen gave no response and the half-elf continued in an animated and slightly bitter tone. "I *am* a half-elf and I was born into slavery because of it, I was tortured and burned as a child because of it, and I have given myself to the service of the Jarl because of it." He paused and lifted his deformed head to lock eyes with the halfling. "I was rescued from my torment and torture by the elves of Westwick. They raised me as one of their own. Aurora was particularly nice to me in those first years; she helped bring me out of the darkness and discover the elvish part of my nature. I owe them more than my life; I owe them for the salvation of my soul. That is why I now serve them as a spy within the Brotherhood of Callamore. Because one cannot tell by looking at me that I have elvish blood, I pass now as a wretched and deformed human. Here in the Citadel I am known as Brother Vayne. I am the keeper of the Citadel library and learned in all of their lore. I can tell you everything you need to know."

"Please continue," Timmen prompted.

Corliss Landen leaned forward and looked intently at the halfling. "First, the Sacred Scrolls were not the only artifact stolen from our vaults. We keep also, in the library, a full history of Coleraine, including a chronology of the half-elf eradication efforts, in which I have taken a personal interest, and the events surrounding the writing of the Sacred Scrolls. Now, where do those two subjects converge?" Timmen shrugged his shoulders and Corliss Landen gave his deformed smile. "I will tell you," he chirped in his high, windy voice. "The eradication movement and resultant cataloguing of heritage happened about eight hundred years ago, twelve hundred years *after* the War of the Haunted Isle and the writing of the Scrolls."

Landen paused for effect and his eyes sparkled, a thin smile playing at the corners of his lips. Timmen wondered how long the half-elf had been waiting to tell this story. "Well now," Landen continued, "twelve hundred years is a long time and one might think that a family's lineage couldn't be traced back that far. For most human families that might be true, but those with royal blood can often be traced back to antiquity so it's not surprising that a catalogue taken eight hundred years ago would reveal noble ancestry from the era of the Scrolls. One of those catalogues was the other artifact that was stolen."

"Why was it stolen? What did it reveal?" Timmen asked.

Again Corliss Landen gave his deformed smile before answering. When he spoke, his scarred face was beaming with the joy of revelation. "The House of Westbury descends directly from Kendrid the Red."

"The Countess?" Timmen asked in shock.

"The Countess indeed," confirmed Corliss Landen.

Timmen was dumbfounded. When at last he found his voice he asked, "What has the Inquisition uncovered of this?"

"Nothing," answered the spy. "I have told them nothing. And I will continue to tell them nothing until I receive instructions from the Jarl. Unfortunately, the Citadel has been locked down during the questioning; my connections have been sundered." He leaned forward and locked Timmen with a look of desperate urgency. "You are now my voice, Timmen. No one else in all the world knows this vital piece of information. You must take word of it to Aurora; she will know how to contact her father."

But Aurora has been taken! Timmen's mind screamed at him, but he said nothing of it aloud. "Have you anything more to tell me?" he asked.

"Only this," the half-elf replied, "I do not know how the Scrolls or the catalogue were taken, but it seems clear that I am not the only spy in the Brotherhood. My position here is tenuous. I feel more clearly every day that my life is in danger. If possible, pass along to the Jarl my request for clear instructions. I await his bidding."

"I'll do what I can," Timmen answered as he got to his feet. "Do I need the jewel to pass under the arch?"

"Yes, I'll take you out." Timmen took the shadow cloak out of his pack and slipped it on. Corliss Landen gave a sort of whistle, but his deformed lips couldn't quite make the sound. "That's an amazing garment. You must be a thief of high ability." Timmen shrugged at the compliment but he smiled inwardly. "Well, that's good," the half-elf concluded. "I like to think that Mistress Daelin is keeping good company."

Timmen pulled the hood of his cloak low over his eyes and Landen cut the light of the lamp to a low flicker. They edged out of his room and crept down the passage; Landen already held the glyph-jewel in his hand.

Suddenly there came the soft *snick* of several crossbows being loosed and the whine of the bolts flying through the air. Timmen jumped back as the bolts thudded into the body of Corliss Landen. The spy gave an agonized groan and slumped to the ground. The sound of approaching feet came from behind him as Timmen swung his pack and crushed the lamp that had rolled away from the dying half-elf.

"What the…?"

"There must be more than one."

"Give us some light."

Timmen sprang forward and grabbed the glyph-jewel from Corliss Landen's hand just as several magical globes of light drifted through the passage. The thief's shadow cloak absorbed the magical light, but there were no more shadows in which to hide. He could now be seen as a moving hole in the air.

"There he is!"

"Where?"

"The dark shade. Get him!"

Timmen ran up the passage as fast as his little legs could carry him. His unknown attacker cast another spell and a bolt of lightning slammed into him from behind. The crystals in his cloak absorbed most of the magical energy but the force of the blast still knocked him to the ground. Several more crossbow bolts whistled over his head.

Timmen got to his feet and ran on. Soon he was beyond the illumination of the magical globes and he disappeared into the darkness. He darted around corners and past several side passages and soon the sounds of pursuit faded behind him. Clutching the jewel in his hand he ran breathlessly through the arch and along the tunnel out into the wide corridor. Several of the Brotherhood noticed the fleeting shadow as it rushed past them into the night.

The Inquisition resumed with renewed vigor the next day. The Inquisitor now had new questions to ask, and the gloom around Citadel Adbar deepened.

<u>Chapter Twenty One</u>

~ The Forgotten Menagerie ~

Aurora awoke to the familiar, dull glow from the lone torch burning halfway down the prison chamber. It was the only light she had known for the last several days. At least she thought it had been days; it was impossible for her to tell time without the rising and setting of the sun. She went to the bars of her cell and peered out. The view was the same as it had been since her arrival: other cells, one torch, the sounds of breathing, and nothing else. No one spoke. No one cried out in anguish. She wondered how long the other occupants had been here to be so crushed of spirit that they didn't try to talk or communicate in any way.

"Hello?" she called out. The word echoed off the dingy stone walls, but when the sound of her voice died away there was nothing but silence. Even the sound of breathing from the other cells was gone. Perhaps she had awakened them, perhaps she had frightened them, but they all held their breath as if waiting for some swift and terrible punishment to swoop down upon them.

Aurora retreated to the back of her cell and looked into the mirror on the armoire. She could barely see her reflection in the dim light, yet knew that she looked dirty and ragged. She had not changed from her travel clothes into any of the fancy and frilly clothing that hung in the armoire. She did not want to lose her sense of self, despite the oppressive vacancy around her that threatened to suck her individuality right out of her soul. She picked up the writing quill and dipped it in the inkwell then carefully marked a sixth line on the top sheet of paper. Six days she had been here, to the best of her reckoning. She had been provided food and water on the first four days by an imp-like creature that wore a hood over its head, but for the past two days nothing had been provided to any of the prisoners.

As Aurora stood looking into the mirror, she caught a flicker of movement behind her in the dark passageway. She spun around and saw a small figure fluttering by on tiny wings. Running to the front of her cell, the elf gripped the bars and peered down the corridor. She saw a small, red and yellow finch flying through the torchlight.

"Huggins!" she called out. "Sanguine, is that you?"

Seven floors above the dungeon, the bard was in the middle of a grand performance in the university auditorium. Nearly all of the institution's students were assembled there to watch. At the sound of the elf calling his name through his medium, the bard stumbled in his dance routine and forgot the next verse in his song. The audience watched him in stunned silence. Sanguine looked around at them for a long, ridiculous moment.

"I am sorry, dear friends," the bard bowed low as he spoke, "but I have just remembered something that requires my attention." His words were met by grumbles of complaint. "Nay, I do not have another or better appointment, but I'm afraid a friend of mine is in need and I must leave to see what aid I can render." He strode across the stage and retrieved a small, silver harp from his belongings. "I will end with a soothing adagio, so that you might forgive my departure." The bard began to pluck the gossamer strings of his silver harp and the crowd fell instantly silent. He sang in a strange tongue and his mesmerizing baritone voice filled the room. The crowd began to sway back and forth in time with his tune. Suddenly the bard ceased his song and commanded in a loud voice, "Stay! Converse amongst yourselves. Do not leave. I will return shortly." The crowd began chattering amiably; no one got up to leave.

Sanguine gathered his belongings and left the hall. Once he closed the doors behind him and shut out the noise within, he could hear faint sounds of battle emanating from distant corridors of the university and rising from the dungeons below. The bard sent a mental command to his medium to fly through the dungeons and find his quickest route to Aurora's cell, then he crossed to a stairwell and descended into the depths of the building.

Sanguine had gone down three flights of stairs and was hurrying around a corner to the next stairwell when he was seized savagely and thrust up against the wall. "And just where do you think you're going?" hissed the seething voice of the Shadow Wolf.

Sanguine looked into the assassin's eyes and saw a faint red glow that pulsed with the energy of pure evil. "I'm going to the lower reaches," answered the bard.

"For what purpose?"

"My employment with the Countess extends only so far as the task I was hired to perform," Sanguine replied coolly, "beyond that my ends are my own."

"And you would abandon your task so easily?" retorted Zakarus Rinn. "Perhaps the Countess should rescind your employment," the assassin drew his dagger and pressed it against the bard's stomach. "And that would leave you without her protection."

Sanguine was not phased. He dared not move a muscle, but he looked unwaveringly into the eyes of the Wolf as he spoke. "My task is being performed just as I promised. The university faculty and student body are still in the auditorium, and there they will remain until I release them from my spell." The Shadow Wolf's leering smile turned into a snarl and he pressed his knife a bit harder into the bard's stomach. Sanguine held his breath and his voice was tense as he continued, "Of course, knives make me nervous, and I find it difficult to maintain my spells when I feel one pricking me."

The Shadow Wolf locked the bard with a long, cold glare and then released him, flinging him off of the wall and toward the stairs. "Go, then," the assassin cried, "but do not make mischief for me. Tonight the blood of the Crystal Night flows as a river, and if you cross the Countess or fail in her service, then your blood will join the flood ere the new day dawns."

Sanguine turned toward the stairs and took a step in that direction. He looked back to see if the assassin was still staring after him, but the Wolf was already gone. Skipping down stairs, darting through hidden doorways and following the mental directions of his medium, Sanguine soon found himself in the secret dungeons below the university. After several more minutes of walking through the dank and musty tunnels, the bard came to the prison ward where Aurora was being held. Huggins flew up to him and lit upon his shoulder. Sanguine walked directly to the elf's cell and found her waiting, gripping the bars and looking out at him through the dim light.

"Sanguine, I thought that was you," Aurora sighed her relief. "Can you get me out of here?"

"Hmm," the bard rubbed his chin and looked around. "I don't see a guard station where I might find some keys, and I cannot pick the lock. I'm an artist, dear Aurora, not a thief."

"So you're not going to help me?" Aurora was exasperated. "You promised a few weeks ago, that day in the Pandoran forest, that you would help me if ever you could."

"Aye, when I could," Sanguine answered, "but this is beyond my abilities to alter. Would you ask the painter to trade his brush for an anvil, or the flutist to chop wood? I cannot sing a song or write a poem that will make the lock fall open."

Aurora slammed the bars in frustration and screamed an elvish word of profanity, of which there were very few. She took a moment to regain her composure and then looked up at the bard, wiping her white hair out of her eyes. "Why are you here?" she asked.

"To see if I could help you, of course. I cannot at present, unfortunately, but if a guard happens by I might persuade him to open the cell."

"Persuade?" Aurora asked and Sanguine flashed a devious and glistening smile. "Well," the elf huffed as she sat on the dirty floor of her cell, "there are no guards, so I suppose you are back to being completely useless."

Sanguine looked genuinely hurt. "Do not say that, my beautiful one," he sat down in the dirt beside her with only the bars between them. "I am good company, at the least. I'll sit with you, and perhaps we'll find a solution to this problem yet."

Aurora heaved a great sigh and her voice was quiet as she spoke. "Do not call me beautiful," she said. "I am too tired and upset to be wooed."

"I would not seek to woo one whom I could not embrace," Sanguine replied, "for there could be no reward for my efforts." He reached through the bars and stroked her soft hair. "No, fair one, when I call you beautiful it is simply an honest compliment."

"You are incapable of honesty," the elf countered, but she did not pull away from his touch.

"You presume to know much about me, though we have met only once before."

"I know your type," Aurora responded with a wry grin, "smooth of word and soft in hand, but full of pride and vanity, and wholly incapable of loving anyone as much as you love yourself."

Sanguine smiled and his hand ventured from her head to her slender yet muscular shoulders. "Full of pride and vanity, aye; you know me better than I had thought. But I am capable of love. Indeed, I am well acquainted with it. Most of the odes, dramas and tragedies that are the ply of my trade focus on the subject of love. I have studied the joy and the anguish of my characters as they labor in the blissful, bittersweet agony of love's undulating tides. I have meditated on it. I know it to my marrow. Yet never have I felt it so alive within me as I do right now, sitting beside you in the dust and stink of this hole beneath the earth. My hand is afire where you allow me to touch you."

Aurora smiled and her pointed ears blushed beneath her hair. "Yes, well, do not get used to it; I only allow it because you are the first person I have spoken to in six days, and you are better than nothing."

Sanguine blew a dramatic sigh. "She fills her sails with my wasted breath and slips away over the cold, black waters of regret."

Aurora threw her head back and let loose a high, lilting laugh that echoed off the walls of the dungeon. "You are impossible!" she said and turned to him. Their eyes met, hers icy blue and his dark as coals. Aurora inclined her head and began leaning toward him.

Suddenly a loud crash rang out in the distance, followed by shouts of pain and death. Aurora leaped to her feet and groped at her belt, searching for a sword that was not there. Sanguine remained seated, reclining casually against the bars of the cell. Huggins flew up from his shoulder and fluttered down the hall in the opposite direction from the noise.

Pounding footsteps preceded the appearance of five black-clothed men who swept into the prison and hurried down the corridor. Three of them wielded long swords and two held crossbows. Next appeared a tall, thin man in a dark purple cloak. He carried a staff and was clearly a wizard. Finally, the doorway darkened and in walked Zakarus Rinn. The assassin strode purposefully into the corridor and his cold, gleaming eyes narrowed on Sanguine.

The Shadow Wolf walked toward the seated bard, his sword held low and dripping with blood. "What are you doing here?" he asked and pointed his blade menacingly. As he approached

Sanguine, Rinn looked into the cell and caught sight of its occupant. His step faltered and his mouth hung open in shock. "You? What?" he breathed. Aurora did not respond. The Wolf looked alternately from the bard to the elf, then a lecherous smile curled his lips. He turned to his men and called out in mockery, "It would appear that we have interrupted their courtship. Forgive us, Sanguine, for this conquest would surely have added to your legacy."

Sanguine did not respond, but Aurora stiffened and looked sharply at the bard. "What is he talking about?" she whispered. "You two know each other?"

The Shadow Wolf's predatory instincts flared and he moved in for the kill. "Yes, elf maiden, we know each other. We are allies in this endeavor. You will be glad to know, Sanguine, that our mission has proved successful; the rest of my men are routing the Crystal Night as we speak."

Aurora gasped and flushed red in anger; her white hair flared away from her body. "You venomous, treacherous snake!" she cried and sprang forward, punching and kicking through the bars of her cell. Sanguine rolled away and got to his feet.

The Shadow Wolf laughed. "She *is* a feisty one!" he cried and patted Sanguine on the shoulder. "Again, my apologies for interrupting your work; she would have been a marvelous distraction."

Sanguine brushed the assassin's hand off his shoulder and stepped forward. "Aurora, you can't believe that I'm part of their organization. I simply go where the money is; I am in league with no one but myself."

"And yet here you are, helping them in their work," the elf retorted bitterly.

"Why should I not contract with them against another criminal organization?" the bard asked. "One that imprisoned you, I should add."

"You speak of allegiance as though it has no bearing on morality!" Aurora countered. "Your actions do not exist only unto themselves; all things are connected."

"Not to me," Sanguine stormed. "I am independent."

"You are a mercenary," Aurora shouted, "and though you might delude yourself into believing otherwise, your actions reveal you for what you are: a coward. You are too afraid to align yourself with the righteous or the evil so you tarry between them and call it independence. I call it pathetic."

Sanguine's dark eyes were ablaze and Aurora's resolve almost faltered. "Very well," he said, "since I am nothing but a pathetic mercenary I will fulfill your expectations and pursue my own interests." He turned to Zakarus Rinn, who was smiling broadly. "Our business is concluded, assassin," said the bard. "I shall return to the auditorium and release the audience from my spell. The halls will be full of people in a few moments. Find your own way out of the building; I care not." He brushed past the Shadow Wolf and walked briskly out of the dungeon. He did not look back.

"Well," said Zakarus Rinn, turning back to Aurora, "that was quite dramatic." The elf did not answer, but merely glared at him with intense hatred in her eyes. "Now we must decide what to do with you," the assassin continued. "Should we leave you here to rot in that cell? The Crystal Night has abandoned this post; there was only a remnant of their guild still here when we came in to destroy them, so I wouldn't count on any food or water any time soon." Rinn paced back and forth in front of the cell, gesturing dramatically with his sword. "On the other hand," he continued, "I could take you back to the Countess and let her bleed you like she wanted to in the village a few weeks ago." He stopped his pacing and walked up to the bars of the cell, looking her directly in the eyes. "Or I could turn you over to my men and let them use you for sport." He held his sword out in front of him in a lewd gesture, the blood-smeared blade protruding through the bars. Aurora spat on the ground at his feet.

"Give her to us, Rinn," said one of his men, "we will tame her."

The Wolf and the elf stared directly into each other's eyes. Rinn smiled. "No," he said slowly, "I will take her for myself."

The assassin spun and seized a crossbow from one of his men. "Away, all of you," he ordered. "Finish the sweep of this level and then begin our withdrawal." He looked to the wizard. "You are in charge now," he said and then turned to Aurora. "It is time for the victor to claim his spoils."

Rinn sheathed his sword and took out a small tool, which he used to pick the lock on the cell, and then he pointed the crossbow at Aurora and opened the door. "None of your tricks this time, my dear," he said. "Turn around." Aurora had no choice but to comply. Her mind was racing through the odds of trying to escape when she felt the Wolf press up against her. She heard the clatter of the crossbow hitting the floor and then felt the cold edge of a knife press against her throat. "Follow my directions, please," the Wolf breathed into her ear, "it would be a shame to have to kill you now."

He led her through winding passages into the sewer that ran beneath the city and eventually out into the cool air of early evening. Aurora breathed the open air for the first time in days, but her heart was not lightened. Now her friends would not know where she was. She had been spared the slow death of starvation, but what horrors awaited her at the hands of the Wolf? She felt his breath upon her neck and shuddered with revulsion and fear. Perhaps she was moving toward a fate worse than death.

Alishane Wyndam had spent the majority of the last week either using his scrying spell to watch over Aurora or in meditation recovering his strength. It took him the better part of the first day to locate her in the dungeon. He found it extremely frustrating that he could not perform the spell for longer than a few minutes at a time. As the days passed, however, his skill with the spell grew considerably. He had hardly slept or eaten and by the third day he grew light-headed and delirious; the lines between the tangible world and the surreal nature of the spell became intertwined. His fasting, combined with utter fatigue, made it easier to detach from his body and stay in the spell for longer periods. By the fifth day, when Arcanis and Dorak joined him, Alishane could perform the spell for upwards of an hour at a time.

Arcanis was deeply worried about the cleric's wellbeing. He watched over Alishane fretfully while the younger man mumbled and swayed in the throes of the spell. When Alishane came back to his body and collapsed, the wizard would wipe down his sweaty brow and force him to take water and food. Then Alishane would enter his meditation until he could cast the spell anew. Through all of this, Dorak sat dolefully in the corner and watched. The dwarf understood nothing of spellcasting, but he could see clearly the sheer force of Alishane's will and the strain he was putting on his body. Dorak Shale gave respect grudgingly, but over the course of their association the dwarf found that he could not help but respect the cleric, and from that respect grew fondness.

The sixth day since Aurora's capture by the Regent was waning; the sun had dipped below the horizon to kindle a low line of clouds and make them glow like embers burning in a hearth. Alishane was in the midst of the scrying spell, mumbling incoherently with his face drawn and pale. Arcanis knelt over him with grave concern etched in his features. Suddenly Dorak gave a shout of surprise and the wizard turned to see Timmen O'Hook emerge from a shadow near an open window.

"You little rascal!" bellowed the dwarf. "Don't ye be using that thing around me, lest ye want to be buried with it." Dorak pointed a thick finger at the shadow cloak Timmen was stuffing into his pack.

"I guess that's all the greeting one can expect from a dwarf," Timmen answered and winked at Arcanis.

"It is a relief to see you, my little friend," the wizard said as he stood to address the halfling. As he did so, Timmen caught sight of Alishane for the first time. He dropped his pack and rushed toward the cleric, but Arcanis held him back. "He is the middle of his spell, Timmen; you must not disturb him."

"But what's wrong with him?" cried the halfling. "He looks half dead! How could you let this happen?" Timmen turned an accusatory glare on the wizard.

"He could not be dissuaded from watching over Aurora," answered Arcanis. "Besides, his magical power has grown immensely with this exercise; I want to see how far he can go." Timmen looked with consternation at the wizard. His concern for Alishane was obvious. "Do not worry," Arcanis soothed, "I am watching over him. He will not suffer any permanent harm."

"Oh, well, as long as it's not permanent," the halfling scoffed. "That makes me feel *much* better."

The three of them sat down in a circle around Alishane. "What did ye learn in the Citadel?" asked Dorak.

"Aurora's father, who is the leader of their people," Timmen clarified for the dwarf, "had a spy in the Brotherhood of Callamore. His name was Corliss Landen."

"Was?" Arcanis broke in.

"Yes," Timmen confirmed. "He's dead now."

Dorak's thick brow knotted as he eyed the thief. "You didn't kill him, did ye?" he asked suspiciously.

Timmen shot the dwarf an exasperated look. "No, I didn't. He was killed in front of me, but at least it didn't happen until after I spoke with him because he gave me vital information." Timmen looked at each of them to be sure he had their full attention; Arcanis and Dorak leaned in attentively. The halfling took a deep breath. "Two things were stolen from the Citadel. One was the Sacred Scrolls." Arcanis closed his eyes and sighed deeply. Dorak's eyes went wide in surprise. "The other was a catalogue of family bloodlines written during the half-elf eradication efforts." Arcanis opened his eyes again and fixed Timmen with a sharp look of concern. The halfling faltered briefly before concluding. "The missing catalogue traces the house of Westbury back to Kendrid the Red."

The group was silent for a long moment. At last, Dorak got up in a huff and shook his fist at the wizard. "A fine mess ye've got me mixed up in!" he stormed and then thumped over to the corner and sat down.

Arcanis thought in silence for a bit longer, then he turned to Timmen and asked, "Does the Jarl know of this?"

The halfling shook his head. "No," he answered. "The Inquisition has kept the Citadel sealed up too tightly for Corliss Landen to get word out. And, of course, now he's dead, so we're the only ones who know."

The wizard stroked his beard and brooded. Timmen began looking through the packs for some food. Suddenly, Alishane moaned and slumped over. The wizard, thief and dwarf rushed to his side. It was several minutes before the cleric came back to his body and opened his eyes.

"Worse," he whispered and coughed. "Matters are worse."

"What happened? What did you see?" asked Arcanis.

Alishane tried to rise but the others held him down. "Shadow Wolf," he sputtered. "Killed everybody."

"Calm down, son," Arcanis urged. "Breathe first, then speak."

Alishane took several long breaths before continuing. "The Shadow Wolf and his men went in to destroy the Crystal Night, but the Regent and most of his people were already gone. To the Caverns, presumably." He tried to rise again, clutching at the clothes of his friends who tried to control him. "He found her!" he cried frantically. "Rinn found Aurora!"

"So, she's dead?" asked Dorak.

"No," answered Alishane and he finally succeeded in sitting upright. "He hasn't killed her yet."

"What did he do?" asked Timmen in a small voice.

"He *took* her!" cried Alishane. "And I couldn't follow. I was too weak. I couldn't hold onto the spell and now I don't know where they've gone." He began to weep. "Oh, I have failed her," he sobbed and then his fatigue overtook him and he fell unconscious. Dorak laid him gently on the floor and retrieved some cloaks for a pillow and blanket.

Timmen looked to Arcanis and asked in a barely audible whisper, "What does this mean?"

Arcanis got to his feet and snatched up his staff. "It means, Timmen O'Hook," the wizard answered, "that the burden falls upon you and Alishane to use all of your skills to find where the assassin has taken Aurora."

"What about you?" Timmen queried.

Arcanis walked to the door and opened it. "I am going to the Haunted Isle," he answered and then he closed the door behind him.

Chapter Twenty Two

~ Taking the Poison for the Cure ~

Arcanis Rhu sat hunched over at the end of a pier with his cloak pulled tightly about his shoulders. The wind was howling off the Andaluric Sea and the cold spray peppered his face and clung to the white bristles of his beard. In making ready for his journey, the wizard had commissioned a light and fast-running schooner to take him to the island of Banthus, or as it was more commonly known, the Haunted Isle. The crew of the schooner had made it clear that they would not go within a mile of the island, but they would give him a small sailboat to take him the rest of the way in. The ship would be putting to sea shortly.

After securing passage on the schooner, Arcanis had returned to the party's hideout to find Alishane awake. The cleric tried vehemently to talk the wizard out of going to Banthus. His years of schooling at Rue Mortelei gave him vast knowledge of the undead, as it is one of the primary areas of expertise for a cleric.

"I know better than anyone else here, perhaps even better than you, Arcanis, the dangers of going to the Haunted Isle," Alishane said. "That island is infected with death and the living cannot set foot upon its soil without being tainted. The disease is still there and there is no cure. If you go," the cleric warned, "you will die."

"I will die anyway," retorted the wizard. "I am at the end of my life and if I do *not* go then many more will suffer their demise prematurely."

"But we need you!" Timmen pleaded. "You are our leader and you're the one who knows all about the Scrolls."

"And the Scrolls have gone to the island, Timmen," Arcanis answered. "I must learn what has become of them."

"Bah! 'Tis a disgraceful way fer ye to die," grumbled Dorak. "After all that ye've done, all the power that ye have, to just waste away from some stinkin' infection…"

"I may contract the disease," Arcanis began.

"You will," insisted Alishane.

"But that does not mean that I will die from it," finished the wizard.

"I have told you," the cleric said with a shake of his head, "there is no cure."

Arcanis thumped his staff against the floor and the curt tone of his voice told them that this was the final word in their conversation. "My power is waning, it is true, but it is still greater than any of you know," stated the wizard, "and I may long hold out against the disease." He stood up to leave, hoisting his staff and a small bag of supplies. "Besides," he concluded as he headed for the door, "I swore an oath to the Jarl that I would protect Aurora and I will not be leaving this world until I have rescued her." He turned and shot a simmering glare down the length of his angular nose. "The two of you had better find her before I return." Alishane and Timmen exchanged an uneasy look, but they said no more.

Arcanis had, however, bowed to their concern in one way: he was no longer going to Banthus alone. While Alishane and Timmen were looking for Aurora, Dorak would accompany Arcanis on the schooner. When they reached the Haunted Isle, the dwarf would remain aboard the ship to make sure her crew didn't change their minds about the venture and leave the wizard stranded.

"I've said it before and I'll say it again," came the gruff voice of Dorak Shale as the dwarf thumped along the pier to stand behind the wizard, "this is a fine mess ye've got us into." Arcanis did not respond. The two of them waited at the end of the pier listening to the cry of the gulls and the creaking of the ships as they rolled on the churning tide.

When at last their vessel was laden with its supplies and the captain signaled for them to board, the wizard stood up and shook the water from his cloak. "A long time I have wandered this world," Arcanis said quietly, his voice thick in the salty air, "and many things I have seen. It is strange to think that this will be my last journey."

"It is not yer last," growled Dorak. "This jaunt to the Haunted Isle may be a fool's errand, but yer not making it alone. There's one more fool going with ye, and I intend to make sure ye come back."

* * * * * * *

The waters around Pilas Antum were notoriously violent. Sudden squalls or pirates often appeared out of nowhere to wreak havoc upon the unwary or unfortunate. While some merchants chose to protect themselves with large armadas and cannons to return fire against marauders, others, including the vessel Arcanis and Dorak had employed, chose to run fast and light to outpace any trouble they might encounter. Such a vessel did not make its living off of large shipments of cargo, but rather small caches of valuable and dangerous commodities. Thus the crew was used to secrecy and knew better than to ask any questions of their two passengers. The wizard and the dwarf kept to themselves and spoke little. Arcanis spent a lot of his time in meditation preparing for his upcoming trials.

Six days out from Pilas Antum the sailor in the crow's nest gave a shout. "Land ahead!" he called down from his perch. "Ahoy, land ahead! Two miles and off the starboard bow."

The ship's captain emerged from his quarters and ordered the mainsail lowered. "Prepare the skiff," he shouted to his crew and turned to Arcanis. "Get ye ready, old man; we'll not be getting much closer."

"This will be fine," answered the wizard with a smile. "I can make my way from here." Leaning heavily on his staff to negotiate the rolling deck, Arcanis went into the ship's lower hold and retrieved the small pack of food, water and clothes he had brought for his time on the island. When he emerged onto the deck, he saw that Dorak already had his axe in his hands and was casting dark looks over the sailors as they went about their work. Arcanis walked up to him. "Don't threaten them before I have even departed," he whispered. "They will most likely be true to our agreement." He took a few steps toward the waiting skiff before he looked back over his shoulder. "Of course," he concluded, "if it should prove necessary then, by all means, threaten them."

"Ha!" Dorak laughed. "The ship will be here when ye return, wizard," he said. "Ye just watch yer arse and bring it back in one piece."

Arcanis nodded and walked to the skiff, where the captain was waiting. "'Tis small but serviceable, as we agreed," the captain said.

"I'm sure it will be fine," answered the wizard.

"Ye'll have a hard time rowing against the waves at first," the captain continued as he pointed out over the water, "but closer to the island the tide will slacken."

Arcanis gave a small smile and tossed his bag into the boat. "You may stow the oars," he said. "I will not be rowing." The captain looked confused but did as the wizard asked and told his crew to stow the oars. Using his staff for support, Arcanis lowered himself into the skiff. He checked the sail to make sure the riggings were tied securely then he sat down at the tiller and closed his eyes.

The crew of the schooner watched with fascination as the wizard held forth his staff and mumbled under his breath. Suddenly a swirl of wind swept up from the sea and enveloped the skiff in a torrent of spray. The wizard finished his spell with a wave of his staff and the wind surged forward, filling the sail and propelling the little craft over the water at a quick pace.

"Mage wind," the captain whispered incredulously. "I have heard of it but never before seen it in use." He turned to Dorak. "I held out little hope before, but perhaps your friend *is* powerful enough to return from the Haunted Isle."

"Aye, he'll be returning," answered the dwarf and his fingers flexed on the handle of his axe, "so ye best be sure the ship is ready to sail when he does."

The captain swallowed hard and turned back toward the island of Banthus, where the skiff was already growing small in the distance.

* * * * * * *

Arcanis put to shore in a tiny cove of murky green water and sparse, sickly vegetation. Large stone facades and crumbling walls bore witness to the ancient fortifications that once dominated the island. Arcanis tied the skiff to a large rock and began picking his way gingerly over the uneven footing of the beach. As he walked through a low draw between two ridgelines, the wizard was struck by the absolute stillness that seemed to shroud the entire island and permeate the rocks, the bushes and the stunted trees. There were no animals peeking out of the shadows; no birds chirped in the cracks and eaves of the battlements. Not even insects seemed to be immune to the plague of death.

Making his way toward the center of the island, Arcanis came upon the remains of a road. The cobbles were split, broken and overgrown with weeds, but the path gave some sense of direction to his wandering. A feeling of foreboding swelled in the wizard as he hobbled along the road. His hands played over the familiar ridges and knots in the wood of his staff and his eyes darted in all directions looking for a threat he could feel but could not see.

Here and there along the way, the rocky hills of the island ceded small parcels of open land and in these places Arcanis saw the skeletal remains of an expired civilization. From the rubble of collapsed houses, stone chimneys stood stark against the cold, gray sky.

After walking through the barren landscape of Banthus for nearly an hour, Arcanis began to have difficulty breathing. He sat down on a rock and drank some water. Squinting up at the sun he asked aloud, "What are you looking at? Haven't you seen an old fool lose his breath before?" He wiped some sweat from his brow and laughed at himself. "I know what you're thinking," he said as he looked back at the sun. "You're thinking that I'm already losing my mind to the illness, but you're wrong. I didn't have much mind left to begin with. Why else would I have come here?" He laughed out loud and took another sip of water. "And now, if you will permit me, I must get going. I would prefer that our next conversation take place over different ground." He put his water jug back in his pack and resumed walking.

A short distance later, Arcanis was rounding a rocky knoll when he caught his first glimpse of Banthus Castle. Unlike the rest of the buildings and walls on the island, the castle had resisted the erosive forces of weather and time. The fortress was not in ruins, but rather was stalwart and strong. All of the doors and window shutters were gone, but the stone was not chipped or cracked. The castle looked every bit the bastion of death it was rumored to be. Arcanis felt a surge of energy run through his body as he approached the imposing edifice before him. He had not faced such a challenge since his youth, and this challenge was to be one of the last of his life. He walked to the front of the castle and stood before the yawning entranceway.

"Be warned, sentinels of darkness and captains of the dead," he cried into the cavernous interior of the fortress, "you shall not assail me or you will be destroyed. I will not suffer your insolence! I have come for a purpose and to my purpose I will see. I will not suffer your interference! Flee and report to whatever master you serve. Shrink and hide in whatever shadow you choose. Arcanis Rhu has come." The wizard's voice echoed off the walls within. As it diminished into silence, it was answered by a gust of wind blowing through the many open portals in the stonework. The howl of the wind running through the empty halls of the castle sounded like hideous laughter answering the wizard's threats. Arcanis was undaunted. He held forth his staff and strode into the darkness.

* * * * * * *

Banthus Castle was a large and very old structure. It had been abandoned even before the arrival of Kendrid the Red and very little remained within its expansive halls and chambers. Above ground, it consisted of seven floors, four towers and one hundred thirty six rooms. There were also five subterranean levels with winding passages, dungeons, and various other drainage tunnels and sewers. An unskilled explorer could spend weeks in the structure and still not know half of its secrets. Arcanis Rhu did not have that kind of time, but he was not an unskilled explorer. The aged wizard quickly surveyed the general layout of the building. He saw where the servants had lived and where the pantries had been. Arcanis also knew quite a bit about the undead and deduced that their foci of power were likely to be underground. He planned on moving quickly through the upper floors of the castle before conducting a more careful and thorough search of the lower levels.

Arcanis began his search of the upper floors. As he moved quickly through the rooms around the perimeter of the castle, he found that the light of the setting sun filtered in through the open windows. He used a torch to light his way through the interior of the building. The rooms were largely empty, with only a few scattered and rotting articles to show that the castle had once been inhabited. Tattered tapestries were clumped at the base of various walls. Broken furniture cluttered the corners of the rooms. The wizard moved through the upper floors with efficient speed and found nothing of interest.

Returning to the first level of the castle, Arcanis discovered that there were five stairwells leading down into the lower reaches: one from each of the four towers and a small spiral staircase hidden in the back of what was once a large bedroom. The aura of evil rising out of this hidden stairwell was so strong that it had a palpable presence, a cold and forbidding force resentful of the wizard's arrival. Arcanis decided to make it his point of entry into the lower reaches. After taking a few moments to meditate and recover some of his spent strength, the wizard retrieved his torch and staff and took his first steps into the darkness under Banthus Castle.

Arcanis followed the stairs to an earthen tunnel that had not been exposed to light for millennia. He expected to hear the sound of thousands of tiny insects skittering away from the intrusive light of his torch, but there was only ancient dust, the smell of decay and oppressive silence. Arcanis followed the tunnel through several twists and turns and the feeling of evil in the air increased. Soon he began to sense another presence in the tunnel. It loomed ahead of him in the darkness, just beyond the reach of the torchlight. There was a discernible malice emanating from the presence, a hatred that was pure, unwavering and completely devoid of reason or prejudice.

"Incandessom aratasse!" barked the wizard suddenly and a flash of light blazed from his staff. For a brief moment, the whole passage was illuminated and Arcanis saw the hulking frame and sallow, featureless face of an afreet djinni.

The afreeti were specters of incredible destructive power. Their origins were unknown, but they were believed to be planar aberrations: shadows from a dark plane of existence that could be summoned through a fissure between worlds to protect an area or object with their indiscriminate destruction. Only a dark wizard of fantastic power could summon an afreet djinni; Arcanis had a strong suspicion of who had summoned this one.

"Warden for the dead and wizard's bane, stand aside!" Arcanis commanded. "Kendrid the Red may have summoned you, but Arcanis Rhu shall destroy you. Aratasse!" Again the light flashed from his staff and the wizard confronted the pale, flat face and dead, black eyes of the djinni. The creature issued a low, resonant moan and a wave of poisonous fumes flowed over the wizard.

Arcanis gasped and choked through a counterspell, *"Erumpere aeros!"* A green fog immediately exploded in the tunnel and saturated the poisonous fumes.

"Incandessom spherimonia!" the wizard followed his last spell with another and several globes of light soared through the tunnel.

"Speré Akuban!" Arcanis growled his third spell in succession and a magical red spear flew from his staff and pierced the evil creature through the chest. The djinni bellowed in pain and fled back down the tunnel with Arcanis following in pursuit.

Ushering his globes of magical light ahead of him, Arcanis turned a corner and found that the tunnel opened into a small room. There were chests overflowing with gold and jewels; this had obviously been a treasury. There were also two more afreeti in addition to the one he had already wounded.

"Scildori afflélo!" shouted the wizard as he slammed the base of his staff upon the ground. A glittering blue globe erupted from the floor to envelop him just as two afreeti launched waves of magic missiles. A dozen red darts of energy struck the wizard's protective barrier and sent shockwaves rippling through the globe, but the barrier held.

Arcanis swayed and his knees nearly buckled; his energy was fading fast. Searching back into his memory, the wizard recalled a spell that was said to be very useful against planar creatures. Named for the mage who invented it, Sorrick's Wilting Age could suck the life force out of an earthly being. Though planar creatures could not be harmed by it directly, the spell was useful against them because it covered the area in powerful earthly magic and isolated the planar creature from the fissure that tied it to its own world. Thus weakened, a planar creature became vulnerable to the basic elements of the earthly plane.

"*Welken Plantari il Gaea,*" Arcanis wheezed and pointed his staff at the afreeti. A sickly yellow mist spat from the end of his staff and hung in a shroud about the djinn. The afreeti issued a gasping wail and tried to conjure their own magic, but the wizard was already voicing his next spell.

"*Fyrima Völ Nast!*" Arcanis boomed the command for the most powerful spell in his arsenal. A ball of fire flew from the end of his staff and exploded at the feet of the djinn. This same spell had leveled nearly half of a village several weeks prior and it was equally devastating to the earth-locked afreeti. Severed from their home plane by Sorrick's Wilting Age, the creatures could not retreat, nor could they withstand the inferno that now raged in the treasury. The djinn shrieked as they burned, experiencing for the first time, and for the last, the anguish that exists on the earthly plane.

Arcanis held onto his magical shield as long as he could. After a few long moments, having consumed everything in the treasury that could burn, the flames died out. Arcanis collapsed to the floor. The room swirled around him in a haze of smoke and melted gold. Just before he lost consciousness, his head lolled to the side and he saw into an alcove on the far side of the room. His breath caught in his throat and he struggled to raise his head. There on a pedestal, shining of its own brilliance, was the item the djinn had been guarding. Arcanis breathed a word of amazement, and then his head fell to the floor and he knew no more.

*   *   *   *   *   *   *

The djinn had not been guarding the Sacred Scrolls. Arcanis knew that from the very beginning. The Scrolls had only recently arrived on Banthus and the afreeti had been there for a very long time, since the days of Kendrid the Red. But for what purpose had the dark wizard summoned them? What were they guarding? Those were the first thoughts that came into Arcanis Rhu's mind when he regained consciousness.

As he looked around to gather his bearings, he noted that the torch he had dropped outside the entrance to the treasury was still burning faintly. His knees wobbled as he staggered over to retrieve it. He held the torch aloft and surveyed the room. There was nothing left of the afreeti. Once locked onto the earthly plane, they had been consumed completely by the fire. Much of the gold was melted and the chests were reduced to ash. Then the wizard saw it again: the glittering object on the pedestal within the alcove. Using his staff to aid his aching body, Arcanis hobbled across the room.

"Amazing," he marveled, his face radiant with the torchlight reflecting off of a silver rapier. The leather wrapping upon the hilt was singed, but the blade was otherwise unharmed by the inferno of his spell. Arcanis lifted the sword and found that it was extremely light. The blade was strong but very thin and there were words inscribed upon the crossguard:

Raderé Y Occamo

"I know this weapon," the wizard whispered. He turned and slashed it from side to side; the thin blade made hardly a sound as it cut the air. Arcanis lifted the rapier over his head and turned back to the pedestal. He heaved with all his might and brought the sword slicing downward as hard as his frail body would allow; a moment later the stone pedestal tumbled to the floor, cloven in two. The wizard gave a wheezing laugh and held the shining silver blade before his eyes. There wasn't a scratch on it.

"Occam's Razor," Arcanis said with great reverence. "No wonder Kendrid hid you here with afreeti guards." On an impulse, he put the edge of the blade to the palm of his hand and drew it across his flesh. The wizard laughed as he held his hand up in the torchlight; there was no incision. "I guess I pass the test," he chuckled and flexed his fingers. He looked around and found a scabbard hanging on the wall. Like the rapier, the enchanted scabbard had survived the inferno of his spell. After sheathing the sword and tying the scabbard to his belt, Arcanis picked up the torch and his staff and turned to leave the treasury. "Alishane is going to love this," he said with a smile as he limped into the darkness of the tunnel.

* * * * * * *

Arcanis had barely ascended the stairwell to the first level of the castle when a dark figure rushed at him from the shadows.

"*Vinum Tangilen,*" he said quickly and stepped back in a defensive posture. Writhing black vines sprouted from the floor and shot upward to ensnare the attacker. The dark figure hung suspended in midair and did not move. It issued a pathetic noise that sounded like a sniffle and Arcanis poked it with his staff.

"Ah! Why are you poking me, you wretched old man?" the figure cried and shielded its face with its hands. It appeared to be a human.

"Who are you?" demanded the wizard. "Speak!"

"No more porridge, Mother, please. I don't want any more," the man wailed. Arcanis poked again with his staff. "No, I won't go to school; the teacher hates me! Please don't make me go, Mother, please," the man whimpered pitifully.

Arcanis gave a wave of his staff and the vines tightened around the man's midsection. He howled in pain and dropped his hands from his face to try to loosen the vines' grip. "Captain Eustacio?" Arcanis inquired in a dismayed whisper. The man did not answer but only sniffled and continued to struggle with the vines. "Horace Eustacio, answer me!" Arcanis commanded.

The man looked up and his eyes were bloodshot and crazed. "Delila? Delila is that you?" Arcanis did not answer, but only watched with great pity etched on his face as Eustacio returned to frantically pulling at the vines. "I'm coming back for you, Delila, just as I said I would," the deranged man grunted.

Arcanis loosened the vines and Eustacio sagged within them, then went back to sobbing into his hands. "I don't want to be here anymore," he whimpered. "Mother, don't leave me! Don't leave me here alone!"

Arcanis shook his head. He knew that Captain Eustacio had lost his mind to the illness and that he would soon die. "Horace, I want you to listen to me now," the wizard said in his most soothing voice. Eustacio stopped sobbing and looked up. His eyes were vacant and unfocused. "What happened to your ship?" Arcanis asked.

Eustacio reached for Arcanis as he answered. "Take me with you, Mother, please. Don't leave me like they did. I promise to be good."

"Did your crew abandon you?" asked the wizard.

Eustacio covered his face with his hands again. "I don't know why they hate me, Mother, I try to be nice like you tell me to."

"Where are the Scrolls?" Arcanis persisted.

A vicious change came over the Captain. "I'll never tell you," he hissed and spat at the wizard. "You want all the credit for yourself. If I tell you then you'll sail away and leave me here like the others did. Oh, Delila, I'm coming back for you my darling!" he wailed and resumed pulling at his bonds.

"You will not be leaving this island, Horace, we both know that," Arcanis reasoned.

"You want the treasure for yourself," Eustacio stormed as he gnawed at the vines.

"Delila can have the treasure if you tell me what you did with the Scrolls," insisted the wizard.

Eustacio stopped struggling and his eyes focused on Arcanis for the first time. "Do you mean it?" he asked. "You'll take it to her?"

Arcanis presented the pouch he had taken from Delila and held it aloft before the wild eyes of Horace Eustacio. Upon one side of the pouch was stitched the insignia and creed of the *Wind Runner.* "I will fill it with jewels from the hoard downstairs," the wizard promised. "She will never need to work again."

The Captain's lips trembled. "Please, you must. I couldn't get to it and now I can't take care of her like I promised."

"Where are the Scrolls?"

Eustacio closed his eyes and took a deep breath. He seemed to have recovered some clarity of mind when he resumed speaking. "The northern stairwell. Descend three flights and take the passage on your right. You will find the room where I took them. But they are beyond your reach now. They are beyond anyone's reach but The One."

"What do you mean?" Arcanis asked with narrowed eyes.

"I took them in there and laid them upon the sarcophagus as I was instructed, but then the doors began to close. I barely had time to run out before they slammed shut."

"Sarcophagus?" Arcanis repeated with trepidation.

He started to walk by but the Captain called out desperately, "Wait! You can't leave me like this!"

"I cannot have you following me when you are not in your right mind," answered the wizard. "But fear not. The spell will not last much longer."

"No, you can't leave me here to slowly go mad and die. You must end my suffering."

The wizard's face softened, but his voice was firm. "I will not kill you, Horace. I am not a murderer."

"Please," Eustacio begged, "you must."

Arcanis closed his eyes and struggled with an inner torment. When again he looked up at the imploring face of Horace Eustacio, his gaze was full of pity. He gave a flick of his staff and one of the vines curled into a noose. "Worry not for Delila," he said and walked away, "she will have the treasure, just as I promised."

He walked to the northern stairwell and followed Eustacio's directions until he came to two huge, stone doors. He tried to open them, but found that he could not. It was then that he noticed the words inscribed upon them:

> "From humble beginnings the scourge shall spring.
> From lowest man will come Man's doom.
> A drought, a plague, a childless king,
> Only The One can enter this tomb."

"Tomb?" the wizard wondered aloud. "You are in there, aren't you Kendrid?" He shook his head sadly. "And now so are the Scrolls." Arcanis gave one more shove at the doors and then turned and hobbled back the way he had come.

He returned to the spot where Eustacio hung in the vines. The Captain was already dead. Arcanis hurried past and descended the stairs to the treasury. He rummaged through the charred remains of the chests until he had enough jewels to fill the pouch and then he went back up the stairs. Pausing briefly before the hanging corpse of Horace Eustacio, Arcanis jiggled the bag of jewels and affirmed his promise with only two words, "For Delila." Then he tucked the pouch into his bag and turned to leave the Haunted Isle.

__Chapter Twenty Three__

~ Panacea ~

"Tell me of the Crystal Night," the Countess demanded of her trio of subordinates.

A tall and shifty-eyed man named Chartrand stepped forward. "They have retreated to a hideout in the Pandoran Mountains," he said, "but we haven't been able to locate it." The Countess narrowed her merciless eyes and Chartrand hastened to add, "They're completely isolated, your Excellency; their threat to your empire is ended."

"I don't want the threat ended; I want their lives ended!" the woman stormed. "I want the Regent's head on my mantle."

Chartrand couldn't help but cast a furtive glance at the shelf above the fireplace. It was devoid of heads. "We'll continue to scour the area," he said. "I'm sure we'll have results by my next report."

"See that you do," the Countess replied, "or it will be your head that decorates my office." She dismissed them with a wave of her hand. When they were gone, she turned to the dark figure reclining in the corner of the room. "Zakarus, how is our guest?"

"Delectable," answered the assassin, who couldn't keep the smile from his face. "Just as we knew she would be."

The Countess surveyed him appraisingly. "You are sure that your affection for her will not cloud your judgment when the time comes?" she asked.

"She is a toy," the man answered, "a way to release some of my more feral urges, but that's all. I care nothing for her." The

Shadow Wolf's eyes flashed red. "We'll be rid of them soon, Highness. The teeth of the trap are in place. When the elf's friends come to rescue her, they will all meet their doom."

It took Timmen O'Hook twelve days to locate the Shadow Wolf.

Alishane tried using his scrying spell to look through Tavora Manor, but the building was completely invulnerable to magical intrusion. The cleric resorted to searching other buildings owned or controlled by the Countess. There were many of these, however, and his search proved fruitless. Timmen's work was done largely at night so he could utilize the shadow cloak. He did not try to get into the manor.

After the first few days of frantic searching, the two settled into a schedule of the cleric using his spell to search by day and the thief using the cloak to search at night. For twelve days their work had been in vain, then Timmen finally caught the break he was waiting for.

The shroud of darkness was falling as the halfling crouched atop a building overlooking the walls of Tavora Manor. Behind him, the city languished through a few more hours of life before its people retreated to their slumber. Timmen waited fitfully, trying to resist the pull of sleep.

Sometime past midnight, he jerked awake. He had fallen asleep, and it wasn't until a voice called out to him in his dreams that he realized his mistake and fought his way back to consciousness. The city seemed unusually dark. Light from the lamps along the streets was unable to dispel the inky blackness, creating small halos around themselves but surrendering the rest of the city to the shadows.

Timmen huddled beneath his cloak, fighting to keep a watchful eye in spite of the despondency that choked his heart. Throughout the long hours of waiting, the same irrepressible question kept swimming in his mind: what horror was Aurora enduring at the hands of the Shadow Wolf? He wondered if it had been the elf who had cried out to him in his dream. The halfling shuddered and tried to push the thought away. So much had changed since the night of his first encounter with the assassin in the Wyvern's Tail Inn. Timmen had wanted revenge against the Wolf for the cut on his chin, but now he was part of something larger. His concern for his friends outweighed his own desires and wrought in him a gnawing fear. He was afraid that he would not be able to help his friends when they needed him most.

Timmen shivered as a cold breeze swept across the rooftop. He closed his eyes against it and in that moment his mind registered a shift in the shadows. He opened his eyes and looked again. Where was it? Perhaps he had just imagined it. He peered into the blackness at the dim outline of the manor walls. Once more his eyes moved past the shadow before his mind noted its presence. He looked back at the dark form just as it moved and slithered down the outside of the wall. Timmen knew at once that it was the Wolf, but why was the assassin slipping out of the manor secretly? Could he be going to see Aurora?

Timmen moved quickly. He got to his feet and skittered to the edge of the roof and then dropped lightly to the ground and hurried down the lane to where the Wolf had exited the manor. Timmen stopped and tied the collar of the cloak around his face so only his eyes were uncovered as they peered out from beneath his hood. He paused to slow his racing heart and to keep his breathing measured and quiet. His ears strained to hear a sound from the Wolf, but the assassin was as silent as the surrounding gloom.

Suddenly, the hair on the back of Timmen's neck stood on end. The halfling crouched to make himself as small as possible. In the next moment, the Shadow Wolf materialized next to him. Timmen held his breath. The Wolf was dressed all in black and his leather boots were silent as he crept down the lane. Timmen followed close on his heels.

The assassin walked deep into the heart of Pilas Antum, pausing briefly to sniff the air and listen to the muted sounds of the night. Timmen stayed behind him, sliding occasionally to the left or right to stay downwind from the dangerous man. At last they came to a large cemetery in the middle of the city. The assassin slid over the metal railings of the fence just as the clouds relinquished their concealment of the full moon, which cast the headstones and naked trees of the cemetery in silver-green light.

Timmen did not enter the cemetery. He hid behind a tree near the fence and watched as the Shadow Wolf picked his way between the headstones and then entered the stairwell housing of an underground mausoleum. The thief was too far away to read the lettering over the mausoleum door, but it did not look inviting.

Timmen waited for a few minutes to make sure the Shadow Wolf did not reappear and then he turned and ran across the city to the hideout where Alishane lay sleeping. He did not wake the cleric, but he could get no sleep for himself. Instead, he sat restlessly through the remaining hours of the night, worrying about Aurora and wishing for the return of Dorak and Arcanis.

* * * * * * *

Timmen told Alishane what he had seen as soon as the cleric awoke. Alishane asked for the location of the cemetery and then fell immediately into his scrying spell. Timmen waited next to the cleric's vacant body for what felt like an eternity. When at last Alishane shuddered and opened his eyes, there was a deadly zeal in them that Timmen had never seen in the cleric, even after the murders of Lord Wyndam and Dunk Worley.

"What did you see? Is she there?" the halfling asked urgently.

Alishane did not answer at first, but sat staring at the wall with such intensity that it made the thief's skin turn cold.

"She's there," the man stated simply.

"Is she all right? What's happened to her?" Timmen asked in a meek voice.

Alishane turned his dark gaze upon the halfling. "She's there," he repeated. "Don't ask me more."

Timmen did not ask. He was afraid of what he would hear and, he realized to his astonishment, he was also afraid of what he saw in Alishane Wyndam. The man sitting before him no longer looked like his friend, whom Timmen had only known as a man with a righteous heart and infused with the nobility he tried so hard to reject. Now, sitting on the floor in the dusty room and staring at the wall through the slanting early-morning sun, Alishane no longer looked righteous or noble. Indeed, he no longer looked like a cleric at all.

* * * * * * *

Arcanis and Dorak returned later that same day, the thirteenth since their departure. Alishane and Timmen had spoken very little, but when their friends walked through the door they both jumped to their feet and relayed what they had learned. Timmen told of the long hours of waiting and how he had finally spotted the assassin and followed him to the cemetery. Alishane confirmed that Aurora was in the mausoleum, but he would not discuss what he had seen, saying simply "We must go and get her immediately. This very night!" The others agreed and they huddled together to make their plans.

Arcanis issued a wheezing cough and stumbled slightly when he moved to sit down. Alishane rushed to his side and helped the wizard to sit comfortably while instructing Timmen to fetch some water from their packs.

"You're sick," the cleric observed. Timmen returned with a water jug and handed it to Arcanis; concern was etched on the halfling's face.

"Yes," confirmed the wizard. "You were quite right about the Haunted Isle, my friend. It is infested with death and it seems to have affected me." He chuckled weakly and sipped some of the water. "But I was also correct about the necessity of the journey," he continued, "for I have confirmed that the Sacred Scrolls are there."

Alishane placed his hands on either side of the old man's face and examined the wizard's eyes. Arcanis brushed him away and continued speaking.

"Captain Eustacio was abandoned by his crew. The madness took him and he has perished, but not before he took the Scrolls into Kendrid's tomb." Timmen looked up uncomfortably and Alishane paused briefly in his examination of the wizard. "Yes, he is there," nodded Arcanis, "and now the Scrolls are there with him. The tomb cannot be opened, but the inscription upon its doors confirms that we read the Scrolls correctly. The foretold events are occurring; the prophecy is at hand."

"What was the inscription?" asked Timmen.

Alishane was still stooping over the wizard and looking him over carefully. Arcanis tried unsuccessfully to push him away, but the cleric would not budge until Arcanis swung his staff in a wide arc and walloped the young man squarely on his rump.

"Are you trying to heal me of the incurable disease?" the wizard asked.

"I cannot cure the disease," Alishane said crossly as he rubbed his rear, "but I can address the symptoms and try to keep you alive a bit longer."

"And to what symptoms are you referring?" asked the wizard with a trace of a smile.

"Fatigue and dementia," Alishane answered, "though the latter may be confused with senility in a man of your age and temperament."

Arcanis used the end of his staff to push the cleric away. "Then leave me to my senility," he said and his smile broadened. "It is oddly liberating to be unfettered by the restrictions of logical thought and proper behavior." Alishane looked uneasily at the end of the wizard's staff leveled directly at his midsection. Arcanis hesitated for a moment and his eyes sparkled, then he lowered his staff and turned to Timmen. "Now, where was I? Oh yes, the inscription on the tomb. It said:

> "From humble beginnings the scourge shall spring.
> From lowest man will come Man's doom.
> A drought, a plague, a childless king,
> Only The One can enter this tomb."

"So you see," the wizard concluded, "we were right about the Scrolls and, it would seem, about the intentions of the Countess. She is trying to aid the fulfillment of the prophecy."

"So what are we going to do?" asked Timmen.

"We are going to rest for what's left of the day," answered the wizard, "because when night falls we are going to the cemetery to retrieve Aurora from her torment. We will deal with the Countess later."

A shadow seemed to pass over the group at the mention of their friend's suffering. Timmen crawled over to Dorak and the two sat in whispered conversation, discussing the details of the past two weeks. Arcanis sat in silence and studied Alishane. The cleric was staring into the corner with a deeply troubled scowl upon his face.

Arcanis took a deep breath and closed his eyes. In the last few moments of tumultuous thought before he fell into his meditative trance, the wizard worried for Alishane. The young man had been through so much in the last several weeks; he had suffered through tragedy and great loss. And he had clearly witnessed something terrible during his scrying. *How much hatred,* the wizard wondered, *can his soul endure before it is twisted into the very thing it despises?*

* * * * * * *

With the coming of dusk, the party rose and began silently making preparations for the night's work. Timmen checked his thieving kit and then set out some food. Dorak sharpened his axe. Alishane looked through their gear from time to time, but mostly he paced the floor restlessly and stared out the window. Arcanis awoke from his meditation and watched Alishane for a few moments before getting laboriously to his feet and approaching the cleric. He reached out and put his hand upon the young man's shoulder.

"I have something for you," he said, "a gift from the Haunted Isle."

"The disease isn't contagious," Alishane answered sarcastically, "if that's the 'gift' you mean to give me."

Arcanis smiled slightly. "I have never known you to be humorous," he observed.

Alishane snorted. "We haven't had much occasion for humor during our time together."

"Too true," the wizard agreed somberly. "Well, maybe this will brighten your mood." He stepped back and pulled Occam's Razor from the scabbard at his belt. The silver rapier sang as it was drawn and sparkled in the meager light coming through the window. Dorak and Timmen noticed and came closer to get a better look. Alishane only lifted an eyebrow in slight curiosity.

Arcanis noted the cleric's stubborn melancholy and decided that a demonstration was in order. The wizard turned to the nearest wall, took one step forward, and drove the blade straight through the thick, wooden planks. Timmen gasped and Dorak's mouth fell open. Alishane opened both eyes in astonishment; his attention was captured. Arcanis withdrew the Razor and put the edge of the blade to the palm of his hand, then he pulled the sword down in one long, fluid motion. The entire length of the blade passed easily over the wizard's flesh, but at the end of the stroke there was no wound left behind. Arcanis held his hand up and wiggled his fingers, his eyes twinkling merrily.

"How is that possible?" Alishane whispered hoarsely.

Arcanis turned the weapon and presented its hilt to the cleric. "A gift from the Haunted Isle, as I said," the wizard chortled. Alishane reached out and grasped the hilt of the sword. "This," said the wizard with relish, "is Occam's Razor."

Alishane lifted the rapier and inspected its flawless surface. He tested the sharpness of the edge with his thumb and then looked back at Arcanis, his face full of wonder.

"That is the finest weapon a cleric could ever hope to wield," the wizard stated. "The blade is strong and its edge is sharp, but it will never cause harm to those with a righteous heart."

"You old rascal!" Dorak bellowed. "Six days we were on that ship coming back from the Isle and you never showed me any of this!"

"You saw that I had it," the wizard answered indignantly. "I did not hide it from you."

"You… but you," the dwarf blustered. "You told me it was just an antique!"

"It *is* an antique," insisted Arcanis. "It just happens to be a very fine one."

Dorak huffed and balled up his fists. His face turned a dark crimson. At last, unable to find the words to express himself, he crossed his arms over his thick chest and turned his back on the wizard.

Arcanis turned to Alishane and the smile melted from his face. "That is a cleric's weapon, son," he said seriously. "It holds an enchantment that renders it especially devastating to the undead but, as I said before, it will never cause harm to one with a righteous heart. If your aims are true and your spirit pure, that weapon is a powerful extension of your goodwill. It can remove the doubt from your mind; it will show you the straightest path." He untied the scabbard from his belt and handed it to Alishane, who accepted it and sheathed the sword. "When you find that you doubt the loyalty of those around you," Arcanis concluded, "put your trust in Occam's Razor; it will show you the truth of their hearts."

Alishane nodded and strapped the Razor to his belt then he turned to look out the window. "The sun has set," he observed. "The city grows dark." He turned and looked back to his friends. "It's time," he said in a steely voice. "Time to go get Aurora."

* * * * * * *

The party took no provisions with them when they left the loft that had served as their hideout for the last few weeks; they carried only what they would need for battle. Dorak carried his double-headed axe and wore plate mail armor under a dirty purple cape. Iron greaves covered his stout legs, bronze gauntlets his forearms, and an open-faced helmet contained his mop of bushy, black hair. Alishane wore no armor, but the cleric's determined stare and the blade at his belt showed that he was ready for the night's work. Timmen carried his thieving kit in his vest pocket and the shadow cloak in a small pack around his waist. Arcanis wore his battered brown cloak and leaned heavily upon his staff, looking for all the world like a helpless old man. When he coughed hoarsely and stumbled, the others tried to aid him, but he pushed them away.

"Keep your minds on the task at hand," he instructed. "I am not as feeble as I appear."

They moved in silence through the Pilas Antum night, stopping briefly at the Copper Dram. Arcanis told them to wait outside and entered the tavern alone. Alishane and Timmen turned inquisitive looks upon Dorak, but the dwarf only threw up his arms and yelled, "Don't be lookin' at me! That old villain keeps his own secrets."

When Arcanis emerged and rejoined the group, Timmen started to ask him what his business in the tavern had been, but the wizard was not in the mood for questions.

"Never you mind, Timmen O'Hook!" Arcanis snapped. "I have already told you to focus on your own tasks. Now, don your cloak and run ahead to scout the cemetery. We will meet you at the eastern gate."

Timmen saw clearly that it was not a time to argue with the old wizard, so he did as he was told and soon disappeared into the shadows.

When the others approached the cemetery a short while later, they did so slowly and with caution. The moon was slightly past full and was hanging large and orange on the eastern horizon as they crept up to the gate.

"I am here," came the halfling's quiet whisper from some bushes near the path. A moment later, Timmen pulled back the cloak's hood and his head appeared before them. "I've walked along the fence on this side and I see nothing amiss," the thief reported. "I already picked the lock on the gate; we can proceed whenever we're ready."

Arcanis looked each of his companions in the eye. Timmen was scared but determined; Dorak wore the crazed smile of a dwarf on the verge of battle; Alishane's face was stoic, but his eyes were a smoldering furnace of anger.

"We are ready," stated the cleric and he started to move forward, but Arcanis caught him by the arm and held the group together. The wizard was shaking slightly as he spoke.

"Whatever happens on the other side of that gate," he said and tried to stifle a cough, "whatever may befall any one of us, the party *must* survive. We four are the only ones who know the truth and location of the Scrolls. We four are the only ones who know the heritage of the Countess and the aim of her designs." Again the old man had to pause to stifle a cough. His eyes were watery when he looked back at them, clutching their cloaks tighter with his shaking hands. "We are going in there now and we are bringing Aurora out, that much I swear. But I fear that this may be my last battle and I need…" Timmen and Dorak began to protest his statement but the wizard shook them into silence. "I need you all to promise me now that this party will endure. That you will hold true to our purpose and persevere to the end."

Alishane reached up to his shoulder and took the wizard's hand, holding it between them in a strong grasp. Dorak seized their clasped hands in one of his meaty paws and Timmen reached up and held on too.

Alishane then drew Occam's Razor from its scabbard and placed the sword between their hands, each of them accepting the blade into their unified grip.

"It will be done," the cleric stated firmly and pulled the blade down through the entwined fingers of his friends. The rapier passed quickly across their flesh, but there was no blood upon its silver blade when the cleric held it up in the moonlight.

Arcanis held the hands of his friends for a moment longer and gave a firm shake, then he released them and turned to the gate. He closed his eyes and muttered a spell under his breath. A crackle of energy rent the air and the wizard stood up straight, no longer leaning on his staff for support but wielding it before him. His battered, brown cloak fell off his shoulders and pooled around his feet, leaving him garbed in pale white breeches and a silver tunic. "It is time," he said and stepped forward to open the gate.

The others followed the wizard into the cemetery and then Dorak and Alishane surged past him to take up the forward positions. They had just passed the first few rows of graves when the cemetery came to life and the battle began. A dozen skeleton warriors wielding broad swords and cudgels emerged from behind headstones and trees. The undead creatures advanced on the party. Dorak cursed through a loud dwarvish challenge and rushed forward to meet them. Alishane swung the Razor easily in front of him and moved forward as well.

"Derma Impervius Stainen," the cleric voiced the stoneskin spell and his features thickened and turned slate gray.

Dorak hewed from side to side with his double-headed axe and within seconds had felled three of the skeletons. A fourth bore down upon him from the side and scored a hit with its cudgel, but Dorak's iron helmet turned the blow and the dwarf swung around with a growl to face his attacker.

"Oh, no ye didn't!" he bellowed and kicked out with his leg, breaking the femur of the skeleton warrior and sending the creature crumbling to the ground. Dorak lifted his axe over his head and brought it crashing down into the skeleton's ribs, then he swung again and severed its neck, and finally he hacked a third time and broke its skull in two. Dorak spat upon the wreckage and laughed, then he turned to find more victims.

After casting his spell of stoneskin, Alishane strode straight into the fray. His fingers flexed upon the hilt of his sword, but he did not bring it to bear. He came to a halt and stood perfectly still as six skeleton warriors encircled him. All at once, the creatures began their attack. Two swords and four cudgels rained blows upon the cleric's spell, but the stoneskin turned them all. Though the blows caused him no damage other than a gradual weakening of his spell, Alishane felt them land. Each strike rocked his body and stirred his anger, and still he stood motionless while holding the Razor at his side. At last, just as his spell was about to expire, an image of Aurora's torment flashed in his mind and the dam restraining his anger burst.

Alishane exploded into motion. He hewed wildly and lustfully, his modest skill with the sword more than compensated for by the power of his strokes and the keen edge of the enchanted blade. In a matter of moments, it was over. All six of his attackers lay in ruins at his feet. With his chest heaving and his head pounding, Alishane looked over the battlefield to find that Dorak had dispatched of the last two skeletons.

"Why don't ye save some of that fer later, pretty boy?" Dorak asked in a gruff voice. "The fight's just gettin' started."

Alishane relaxed his stance and lowered his sword. "Let's get on with it, then," he said and started for the door to the mausoleum.

"Wait!" Timmen called out. "I should go first to check for traps." The rest of the group looked around but could not find the halfling.

"Well what are ye waiting for, you little...?" Dorak blustered.

"Shh," Timmen hushed from the direction of the door. Dorak leaned on his axe and grumbled something about the indignity of being shushed by a halfling. A few moments later, Timmen whispered that the door had been left unlocked and there were no traps around it.

"Unlocked?" Arcanis wondered aloud, but he gave no more thought to the issue, as Alishane was already through the door and descending the steps to the mausoleum. Dorak and Arcanis hurried to catch up; they still could not see Timmen.

The flight of stairs was long and straight. A golden light spread from the room below to guide their way. Alishane waited for them halfway down and they cautiously descended the final length together.

The mausoleum was a single room made of stone and illuminated by oil lamps running along two walls. The room was empty except for three large sarcophagi that were spaced evenly down the center of the floor. At the far end was a raised platform set against the back wall. A figure was laying on the platform with its arms shackled to the wall behind it. The party recognized her immediately and gave a collective gasp: it was Aurora.

Alishane called out to her, but she did not respond.

Timmen took off his cloak, it was almost useless in the well-lit mausoleum, and held out his arms to keep his friends behind him. He stooped to the floor and began looking for traps. The floor was made of large slabs of stone so the halfling's pace was swift as he led them across the room.

When they passed by the second sarcophagus, Alishane again called out to Aurora. The elf groaned and lifted her head. She stared at them blankly for a moment and then her head fall back to the floor.

"Faster!" Alishane barked at Timmen.

As they passed the third sarcophagus, he pushed the halfling out of the way and rushed to Aurora's side. Dorak turned and set his feet, his axe at the ready to protect their rear.

"Aurora," Alishane whispered urgently and stroked the hair from her face. "Come back to us, Aurora. Look at me." He shook her slightly and she turned toward him. Her sky-blue eyes were dilated and vacant. "Fight it, Aurora," Alishane urged. "We're here for you now. Come back to us!"

Timmen picked the lock on the shackles and Aurora's arms fell to the floor. A loud *boom* shivered through the walls as the trap was loosed and the sarcophagus nearest the stairs exploded. From out of the smoke and dust of the sundered stone coffin poured a swarm of poisonous snaga spiders. Dozens of the barrel-sized creatures crawled up through a hole in the floor and began skittering toward the party, their red eyes glowing and pincers dripping with venom.

"Get over here, boy! I can't do this on me own," Dorak called over his shoulder. Alishane looked quickly to Timmen and then turned from Aurora's side, lifting the Razor as he rose.

Arcanis stepped to the front of the dais and sent a wave of magic missiles into the advancing horde. Ten bright red darts of energy flew forward and struck their targets. Ten spiders screeched and began to retreat, but twenty more replaced them and the swarm surged closer.

Alishane leaped from the platform just as the first wave of spiders reached Dorak. "Come and get it, then!" the dwarf snarled and swung his axe, splitting the first spider's head right between its pincers and through its gaping maw. Alishane smote two more with the Razor just as Dorak scored his second and third.

Suddenly, the second sarcophagus opened with a deep, grating moan. Though pitched in battle, the party hesitated and then gaped in shock as two massive stone behemoths appeared.

Dorak swore loudly and continued hacking violently with his axe; its blades were now smeared with the green blood of the snaga spiders. Alishane kept his sword dancing in front of him while he began a slow retreat. Timmen redoubled his efforts to get Aurora to her feet.

"*Welken Plantari il Gaea!*" boomed the wizard's voice from above them and they glanced up briefly to see Arcanis standing on the third sarcophagus, the yellow mist of Sorrick's Wilting Age pouring from his staff. Alishane and Dorak stepped back as the mist enveloped the arachnid swarm. The snaga spiders twitched and slowed as the spell sucked their life force. Those that were already injured by the wizard's first volley flopped over on their backs with legs folded together in their death pose. Many of the rest tried to retreat, but a few continued to advance.

The stone behemoths, however, were only slightly weakened by the mist of the Wilting Age and they charged forward, swinging their huge fists and shaking the room with their footfalls. Dorak stepped forward and presented a target. When the first troll swung at him, the dwarf dove forward and to the side, avoiding the thundering blow and rolling to his feet. A mighty, backhanded chop of his axe crippled the creature's leg and brought it crashing to the ground. Dorak turned to deliver the deathblow, but one of the remaining spiders leaped onto his back and drove its pincers into his neck. The dwarf yelled and tried to reach behind him, but that moment of distraction proved his undoing. The second behemoth gave a vicious swipe and the force of the blow took Dorak full in the chest and sent him flying across the room. He struck the wall near Alishane and crumpled to the floor.

Arcanis acted quickly and sent two globes of light floating across the room in an effort to distract the creature. The ploy worked, as the ignorant beast swatted at the globes with its fists. Those few moments were all Alishane needed. The cleric rushed to Dorak's side and placed one hand on the dwarf's forehead and the other over his heart. *"Anno bueneth serra alleverace,"* the cleric breathed and the blue energy of the healing spell flowed down his arms and spread through Dorak's body.

Slowly, Dorak opened his eyes and sat up. He shook his head to clear his mind and then looked at Alishane and smiled. "Thanks, boy," he grunted. "I knew there was a reason to like ye."

"Now's our chance," Timmen said from the platform behind them. "We must make a run for it!"

The party turned to see Aurora standing next to the halfling. She looked ill and somewhat foreign to them, but her eyes had regained some clarity. "I can make it," she said, "if you show me the way."

Alishane helped Dorak to his feet and they all began running for the stairwell. The crippled behemoth noticed their movement and issued a thunderous roar, which got the attention of its mate and the creature began to move toward the stairs to cut them off.

At that moment, the third sarcophagus scraped open and a great rush of putrid air swept through the mausoleum. Everybody and everything stopped moving. The party stood near the hole in the floor where the first sarcophagus had been. The stone behemoth stood on the other side of it, looking back at where the third sarcophagus was now opened. They followed its gaze and all but Arcanis shrank back against the wall. The wizard did not cower, but simply closed his eyes and hung his head. A moment later, Arcanis opened his ancient eyes and they reflected a resigned determination. He held his staff in front of him and stepped forward to face the lich.

The creature hovered above its stone coffin with its hands folded in front of it and its cold, black eyes surveying the room. Liches were the rarest and perhaps the most powerful magic users the world had ever known. Created during the darkness of the Second Age, they had once been human wizards. But driven by their lust for more knowledge and heedless to the dangers of the dark arts, they gave their souls to the pursuit of power and immortality. Tied now to the mortal plane and vengeful toward the living, a lich was the pure embodiment of evil and hatred.

The room was eerily silent for a long moment as the specter chose its first victim. The crippled behemoth was closest and it started crawling away desperately when the black eyes of the lich fell upon it. The undead wizard slowly extended its hand and whispered a few words from a forgotten language. The behemoth stopped crawling and went rigidly still, then it exploded in a shower of pebbles and dust.

The remaining behemoth roared in blind rage and started to charge.

Arcanis turned to his friends and told them to run. They obeyed and he began backing out behind them, keeping his staff pointed at his enemy.

The lich lifted its other hand and repeated its spell, destroying the second behemoth in a single thought and with a few whispered words. Then it turned its merciless gaze upon the fleeing companions.

Arcanis knew that he no longer possessed the power to defeat this foe, but he also knew that he must face it if his friends were to escape.

"*Scildori affélo,*" he muttered and evoked his blue globe of protection. Weakened as he was, the wizard's barrier was not strong enough to defeat the lich's spells, but it would draw the specter's attention away from his friends.

"Bodigae nas Manig," the wizard growled his second spell and his form immediately blurred into five identical images, the four false embodiments mirroring the movements of his true form.

The lich cast a spell in its strange tongue and one of the fake images disintegrated. Arcanis' plan was working; the lich was focused upon him. The wizard looked over his shoulder to see that his friends had made it to the bottom of the staircase. He only needed a few more seconds.

The lich cast another spell and blue flames spouted from its fingers to devour another of Arcanis' fake images. Only two false ones remained. Again the wizard glanced over his shoulder. The party was halfway up the stairs now and out of the specter's line of sight; soon it would not be able to reach them with its spells.

Arcanis continued to edge backward toward the stairs. He started to entertain thoughts of escape, but the lich's next spell was a red bolt of negative energy that ripped through one of his fake images and exploded into the stairwell behind him. The stairs crumbled in a mass of broken stone and dust.

Arcanis was cut off. There would be no escape.

From the top of the stairs, his friends turned and watched in horrible dismay as the wizard looked up at them through the dust and the truth registered on his face. In that one, long moment, he said goodbye and then he smiled.

The party stood in stunned silence as they watched their friend turn and draw himself up to his full height. Arcanis slammed his staff upon the floor and strengthened his magical barrier and then he let loose a bolt of lightning and followed it with a fireball. From away in the crypt, the lich wailed in agony and anger, but the reprieve was short-lived. The creature's next spell crushed Arcanis' barrier and sent him sprawling to the ground. The aged wizard struggled to rise, but his power was too far spent. With his last effort, Arcanis rolled over onto his back, gave one last look at his friends and then he broke his staff over his knee.

A great blast of energy erupted as the wizard's life-force broke free of his body. The companions struggled through the door and out into the Pilas Antum night just as the roof of the mausoleum crumbled and the entire structure collapsed. A huge depression sank into the earth where the mausoleum had been.

The companions held onto each other and staggered out of the cemetery. Whether the lich had been destroyed in the blast or not, they would never know. And they didn't care. All they knew and cared about was that Arcanis was gone and that he had died so that they could live. Deep in their hearts, they knew that the wizard had been dying anyway. Not only from old age, but also from the sickness of the Haunted Isle. But Arcanis did not die of old age or disease. He died in battle, fighting evil and saving his friends. That thought gave them all strength, and they resolved to carry on.

<u>Chapter Twenty Four</u>

~ Gainsay ~

The citizens of Pilas Antum scrambled out of the way as an ornate carriage and its mounted entourage thundered down the crowded lane. Inside, the Countess of Westbury held her pallid chin in the curl of her delicate fingers. The woman looked with little interest at the open mouths and shaking fists of the people she had forced off the road. Her thoughts were far away in the wooded vale of Anderton and in the huge capital city of Coleraine: Vardiz. The Council of the Kingdom was now only four weeks away and the Countess was going to Anderton to coach Lord Garrett Finneran in the subtleties of Kingdom politics.

A high-pitched squeal came up from the road and was followed by two bumps of the carriage as a small child fell under the wheels. The Countess instructed her driver not to slow. These peasants mattered not at all. She had her eyes on loftier goals than human compassion; she would not allow these vermin to stand in her way.

"You would do well not to bring attention to the fact that you're leaving," offered Zakarus Rinn from the seat opposite her.

The Countess turned very slowly to regard him with one of her thin eyebrows raised. "You would have me sneak out of my own city in the dead of night?" she scoffed.

"Secrecy has its advantages, Highness," retorted the assassin.

"Secrecy of allegiance, perhaps," the Countess agreed, "and secrecy of intent, always. But never secrecy in presence, Zakarus. One who has attained my station in life does not skulk about in the shadows. I will leave that to my underlings."

Rinn did not flinch at the insult. "And to what further use shall you put my skulking talents?" he asked with a straight face.

The Countess looked out the window of the carriage. "What of this elf and her troublesome friends?" she asked.

"I believe they were destroyed," the Wolf answered.

The Countess turned her cold, gray eyes upon the assassin once more and her voice took on a steely edge, "You *believe* they were destroyed?"

Now it was Rinn's turn to look out the carriage window. His inability to meet her gaze told the Countess more than the words of his answer. "They could not have escaped from the lich," he said with forced certainty. "Besides, the entire mausoleum collapsed. There's no way they made it out of there alive."

"It is not the way of a lich to destroy itself with its own magic," the Countess said dryly. "No, that seems more the work of that wretched wizard," she spat the last two words with disgust. Rinn noted a flush of anger come to her pale cheeks at the memory of her encounter with Arcanis Rhu. He struggled to conceal his bemused smile. "I want you to confirm that they are dead," the Countess instructed. "That they are *all* dead," she clarified. "Use whatever means you find necessary. I want this done before you join me in Vardiz." She called to her driver to stop the carriage as Rinn gave his customary small bow of consent.

"Bring up the horse," the Countess commanded when the carriage rolled to a stop. A moment later, one of the soldiers of her entourage came forward with Rinn's black gelding, which the soldier had been leading since they left Tavora Manor.

"Do you know how you will find them, if indeed they are alive?" the Countess asked of the assassin.

"I'll use the bard," Rinn answered. "He knows the elf, and I know his price."

"Do not fail in this, Zakarus," the Countess instructed as she opened the door to the carriage. Rinn thought to ask her if he had ever failed her in the past, which of course he had not, but he held his tongue and jumped down into the dirt.

The Countess closed the door and called to her driver to continue. A moment later, the carriage and soldiers were gone, leaving the assassin to brush the dust from his clothing and black leather boots. He tightened the gold and silver gauntlets upon his forearms and mounted his steed.

"The price one pays for power," he sighed to himself and turned back toward the center of Pilas Antum. He kicked the horse into motion and galloped off down the lane to arrange his meeting with Sanguine.

After returning to the hideout on the night of Aurora's rescue, the companions split off from one another to grieve their loss in the manner that seemed best to them. Dorak accepted Alishane's offer of another healing spell and then he went out into the city to pick a fight. Timmen sat sullenly in a corner and watched as Alishane tried unsuccessfully to engage Aurora in conversation. Eventually, the elf simply rolled onto her side, pulled her knees up to her chest and started to cry. Alishane covered her with a blanket and lit a fire in the hearth.

They sat in silence for a very long time. Timmen drifted in and out of sleep. Sometimes when he woke up, Aurora would be sobbing gently; sometimes she was still. But every time the halfling looked at Alishane, the man was sitting next to Aurora and staring into the flames of the fire. He tried once to comfort her when she first started crying, but she shrank away from his touch and cried all the harder. After that he just sat next to her, his frustration growing at being unable to help.

Dorak returned with the rising of the sun. He was covered with blood, and very little of it was his own. He sat in a lump next to Alishane and the cleric dropped his hand upon the dwarf's shoulder. Alishane whispered the words of the healing spell and the electric-blue energy flowed through his hand and into the dwarf. Dorak sucked in a deep breath as if he felt better but, when he exhaled, the air came out in shudders and the dwarf's thick body quaked. Alishane left his hand on his friend's shoulder. A few minutes later, Dorak wiped his face with his beard and moved off into a corner to sleep. Nothing more was said of the matter.

By midmorning, all of the companions were awake and sitting around the rekindled fire. Alishane tried again to talk to Aurora, but the elf ignored him. When he persisted, she turned her cold, blue eyes upon him and her anger flared.

"Leave me alone!" she seethed. Alishane rocked back in surprise.

"We only want to know if you're all right," Timmen put in.

"You seek to satisfy your own curiosity and appease your sense of guilt," Aurora spat venomously. "You will do neither at my expense."

"But Aurora," Alishane began, "we only…"

"Can you not see?" the elf stormed and got to her feet. "I have had enough of satisfying the whims of others. I have had enough of being dominated!" She pushed through them and went to the opposite corner of the room where she slumped to the floor and began beating her thigh with her fist, unable to stop the flow of tears that were once again streaming down her face.

Timmen, Dorak and Alishane sat together in muted frustration. They wanted to help her, but knew that they could not. Aurora would have to heal her wounds in her own way and in her own time.

After a few moments of silence, they turned their attention to their current predicament. "What are we to do now?" Timmen asked.

Alishane sighed. "I suppose we had better try to find this 'Chosen One' spoken of in the Scrolls and on Kendrid's tomb."

"Bah, and how are we to do that?" grumbled Dorak. "We know naught that will lead us to him."

"We know two things," corrected Alishane. "We know that he is about sixteen years old and he has a crescent moon birthmark on his back."

"Oh, well why didn't ye say so?" scoffed the dwarf. "That clears it right up! When are we leaving?"

"Do you have any better suggestions?" Alishane retorted acidly.

"Aye, I do, since ye're asking," Dorak growled. "I say we hunt down this Shadow Wolf and remove the wart from our arse before he gives us more trouble."

Aurora sat up on her haunches and began listening intently at Dorak's mention of the Wolf.

Alishane noticed the movement and looked over at her. Her white hair was disheveled and her eyes red with spent tears. An image flashed through his mind of what he had seen during his scrying spell and his best intentions toward the fulfillment of their mission waned. "Yes," he said slowly. "We cannot have him dogging our trail wherever we go. It's time we took the initiative. It's time to make him pay for what he's done."

"Yes! Ha ha!" agreed Dorak boisterously.

"So we go back to the endless nights of watching the manor walls in the hope of spotting him?" Timmen asked in exasperation.

"No," Aurora answered. The others looked at each other in confusion for a moment before realizing it was the elf who had spoken and turning to regard her. "No," she repeated, "I know a better way to find him."

The others exchanged another confused look before Timmen voiced their collective question. "How?" he asked.

"I believe I can arrange a meeting, but I will need to find a vagabond bard named Sanguine."

"I know of this 'Sanguine' character," Timmen piped up. "He is said to have magical abilities that he bends toward the wooing of women." The halfling gave a wry grin and looked sideways at the elf. "How do *you* know him, Aurora?"

"Stuff it in your hat, Timmen," Aurora said and pulled her knees to her chest to hide the blush that flared through her cheeks.

Alishane noted the color that came to her face and felt a bolt of jealously surge through him. "How do we know that we can trust this lecherous bard?" he asked icily.

"What difference does it make?" Dorak huffed. "Either he leads us to the assassin or he doesn't. If he betrays us, then we kill 'em both."

"We can worry about that when the time comes," said Aurora. "For now we must focus on how to contact him."

"You mean you don't know?" Alishane asked and his jealousy lent a terse tone to his voice.

Aurora turned her reddened eyes on him. "No, I don't," she answered defensively.

"Then how do you know he can lead us to the Shadow Wolf?" the cleric persisted. "Just what *is* your relationship to this great wooer of women?"

Aurora sat up straight and the color in her cheeks now showed her anger. "My love life is not now, nor will it ever be, any concern of yours, Alishane Wyndam!" she declared.

Alishane stood up and his voice raised in tenor and volume. "When it stands to endanger the rest of this party then it most certainly *does* concern me!" he yelled back.

Now it was Aurora who got to her feet. "You are not the leader of this party, Alishane," she countered. "Arcanis did not bequeath that title to you."

Alishane started to answer, but Dorak reached up and gave a tug on his arm. "Let it go, boy," the dwarf instructed.

"I, I think I know how to find him," Timmen squeaked. "The bard, I mean."

Aurora and Alishane stood fuming at each other; Dorak turned to the halfling. "How's that, Timmy?" he asked.

Timmen looked nervously from the elf to the cleric before swallowing and answering, "Sanguine plies his trade in taverns and inns, so it is said."

"His trade?" Alishane said coldly while still staring at Aurora, prompting the elf to bristle and Dorak to elbow him in the thigh.

"Yes," answered Timmen quietly. "Such as it is." He looked back and forth between Alishane and Aurora before continuing. "I have connections at most of the taverns in Pilas Antum. If Sanguine is still in the area, I'll hear about it."

"Well, that's it, then," said Dorak, who began pulling Alishane toward the door. "Come on, boy. We need to get more food 'afore the markets close and the lass here needs another sword. Timmen, ye start making the rounds o' the taverns and spread the word about the bard."

Alishane gave a last, spiteful glance at Aurora before turning and following Dorak out of the loft. Timmen turned at the door and gave Aurora a sheepish grin before closing the door behind him. Aurora watched them go and then closed her eyes and breathed deeply to regain her composure. At last, she went to the water basin and began to cleanse herself of the stain of the Wolf.

Cane Shanney stood behind his bar and wiped mugs while his eyes scoured the crowd. It had been several hours since Timmen O'Hook had paid him a visit, and the big barman was getting more jumpy with each passing minute. *Curse that halfling for the trouble he gets into*, he thought, but then his scowl was replaced by a faint smile. *And bless him for his ability to get out of it.* Shanney thought back over the last several weeks and the many times he had wondered whether he would be able or willing to help the halfling if Timmen ever asked. Now the time had come, and Shanney did not quail. "If that is what ye need of me, Tim, then that is what I'll do," he had said when the thief asked for his help. Shanney did not regret his decision now, but that did nothing to lessen the queasiness growing in his stomach. *Curse that halfling for the trouble he gets into*, the barman thought again.

Just then, a red and yellow finch fluttered up to the counter and landed near Shanney's hand. It held a tiny scrap of paper clenched in its beak. Shanney looked around, but none of his drunken patrons seemed to have noticed the bird's appearance. The finch warbled softly and hopped closer, then it dropped the paper and flew away. Again Shanney scanned the crowd; nobody was looking at him. He picked up the paper and saw words written on it but, being unable to read, he simply turned it over in his hands and then looked around the room once more.

After allowing the man a few moments of torturous confusion, the finch returned and landed on his shoulder. It warbled once and then croaked into his ear:

> "To measure a man, ask not if he reads,
> But whether he helps when friends are in need."

Shanney's eyes went wide in surprise, but otherwise he didn't know how to respond. The finch continued:

> "A friend you have made in Timmen O'Hook
> And help him you can, if you will just look."

With that, the bird jumped from his shoulder and fluttered up into the rafters of the room before twirling down to land on someone's shoulder. The man had dark eyes, large hoop earrings and flowing black hair. When he gave a toothy smile that glinted with silver, Shanney knew instantly it was the bard. He looked around and marveled that no one else seemed to have noticed Sanguine's arrival, but then he realized that he, himself, had not noticed until the bird led his eyes to its host. Giving one last glance around the room, the barman wiped his hands on his rag and ambled across the tavern to address the mysterious bard.

"Sanguine, is it?" Shanney asked and presented his hand.

"Aye, barmaster, Sanguine I am and very pleased to make your acquaintance," the bard answered and shook Shanney's hand with a great flourish and another flash of his glistening smile.

Shanney retracted his hand and regarded his guest with suspicious distaste. "What are ye doing in me bar?" he asked. "And what can ye do for Timmen?"

"As to the former, why, I'm looking for you, Mr. Shanney," Sanguine chuckled, "and as to the latter, I would advise against looking too deeply into the affairs of halflings."

"Or bards, I would warrant," Shanney retorted.

Sanguine laughed. "Well said and too true, I'll grant you," he acknowledged. "Let's just say that you would be fulfilling your friendly obligations to Timmen if you arranged a meeting for me with him and his friends. Tell them to be here at the tolling of midnight." Sanguine stood up and straightened his shirt and long coat. "And, Mr. Shanney," he concluded, "see to it that your establishment is empty of both patrons and yourself."

Cane Shanney went very red in the face at the indignity of being told what to do with his own tavern, but before he could say anything Sanguine had slipped through the crowd and disappeared through the Tail's large double doors.

After sitting for a few moments and worrying about what it meant that it had been the bard who initiated contact, Shanney concluded that the matter was too big for him. He got to his feet, called to his waitress to tend the bar, and then left to find Timmen and arrange the meeting.

The party arrived to find the Wyvern's Tail dark and deserted, just as Cane Shanney promised it would be. The barman had also made sure to lock all of the doors, knowing that the locks would prove small obstacle to his halfling friend but would probably keep out idle trespassers. Once inside, the companions huddled together in the middle of the meeting hall while Timmen traveled the perimeter and set small warning traps to alert them of intruders. He joined his friends in the middle of the room a short while later.

Throughout the day, Dorak had repeatedly warned Alishane against starting in on Aurora about her relationship with the mysterious bard. The cleric answered these warnings with either a simple grunt or by ignoring the dwarf altogether, but when they returned to the loft he said nothing to Aurora. For her part, Aurora seemed very much like her old self when they returned. She had washed and brushed the tangles out of her gleaming white hair and her eyes had recovered a glimmer of their former sparkle. She was still short on conversation, however, and very little was said as they prepared for their meeting with Sanguine.

"Do you know what you'll say when he arrives?" Timmen asked as they waited in the middle of the meeting hall.

"No," Aurora answered. "It would be of little use to prepare a speech or scripted questions." She turned her new sword over in her hands. "Sanguine has a way of dictating the terms of conversation."

Alishane's face darkened, but nobody noticed in the feeble light coming through the windows.

"That's a rather cryptic observation, my lady lithe," Sanguine's voice announced his approach from the back of the hall. "I hardly know if it's complimentary or critical."

The group turned as one to regard him. Alishane put his hand to the hilt of the Razor.

"How long have you been here?" Aurora asked.

"Since long before the barman closed up shop for the evening," the bard replied. "I can go unnoticed when I want to." He moved to join them in the middle of the room. "Though I seldom want to," he added with a flash of his smile.

Aurora went straight to business. "We have arranged this meeting because we need to employ your services," she said brusquely.

"Really?" Sanguine responded with a raise of his eyebrows. "I was under the impression that *I* had arranged this meeting."

"You did?" Aurora asked suspiciously. "Why would you have done so?"

"Oh my fair forest fawn! Have I not always said that I would help you if ever I could?" Sanguine asked with an exaggerated bow.

"Ha, ha!" Dorak laughed and poked his elbow at Alishane. "My apologies, lad, for ever calling ye a pretty boy. For I clearly missed me mark now that I've seen this one!" Alishane only frowned.

Sanguine turned his smile upon the dwarf. "Ah, the renowned Dorak Shale," the bard cooed. "Your reputation precedes you, sir. As does your odor."

Timmen laughed riotously at the barb and was soon joined by Dorak, who was not offended but rather proud of the observation. Even Aurora managed a slight chuckle. Alishane continued to frown.

"There is still the question of trust," the cleric interjected. "How do we know that you will be true to your word?"

Suddenly, one of Timmen's warning flares erupted and the spitting flames silhouetted an advancing shadow.

"Yes, how indeed?" came the sinister drawl of Zakarus Rinn. "How can they ever trust you after you have led me straight to them?" The assassin pulled his sword and continued toward them through the jumping shadows from the flickering flare.

Dorak gave a yell and rushed forward. Aurora pulled her sword and looked from Rinn to Sanguine, her doubt locking her into immobility. Timmen shrank into the shadows and began looking for a way to help.

"You!" Alishane yelled at Sanguine and suddenly the Razor was free of its scabbard. "You treacherous, damnable filth!" he cried and took a step toward the bard.

Sanguine raised his hands and began in protest. "I, I didn't..." he stammered, but his sentence was cut off as the Razor flashed forward, piercing his upraised hand and diving deep into his chest. For one long, fateful moment, Alishane, Aurora and Sanguine all stood rooted to the ground, transfixed by the sight of Occam's Razor buried to its hilt in the bard's chest. Suddenly, one remarkable truth occurred to all of them at once: there was no blood, no wound. The rapier had run him through, but the bard was still standing. Alishane retracted the sword and held it before his disbelieving eyes. There was still no blood on the sparkling silver blade. The truth of Sanguine's heart had been revealed.

A loud ringing of steel shook them all from their stupor and they turned to see Dorak hacking at the Shadow Wolf with his huge double-headed axe. The assassin was backpedaling and appeared to be on the defensive but for the wicked smile upon his face.

"Just as I suspected," the Wolf sneered, "all bluster and blubber but very little skill." As he spoke, the assassin reached up to his chest with his off hand and snapped together the two halves of the Amulet of Arthenor. In the blink of an eye, he was gone.

Dorak stood motionless. Slowly, he turned to his friends with a disbelieving look on his face. Another of Timmen's flares ignited as the Wolf skirted the outside of the room. His hideous laughter resonated off the walls. In the pale, sickly light of the flares, the companions followed Dorak's eyes down to his chest, where a thick flow of blood was oozing out of a wound near his armpit. The assassin's blade had gone in where there was no armor and stabbed horizontally through Dorak's chest. The dwarf's thick legs wobbled as he tried to walk back to his friends, but he only got a few steps before he fell to his knees. He crawled a bit further, then collapsed and fell facedown in the dust.

"No!" came Timmen's high-pitched wail from the back of the room.

"Stay there, little one!" instructed Sanguine as he reached out to Aurora and Alishane. "Here, stay near me, both of you," the bard implored. He pulled them together and then turned to Alishane. "I know not what enchantment is on that blade," he said with a quick glance over his shoulder, where the Wolf again laughed and set off another of the flares, "but I swear to you now that I did not bring the assassin here on purpose. If he followed me, I knew it not."

"Save your oaths and affirmations, for they are useless," said Alishane. "Whatever else may be said of you, your heart is true. The blade does not lie."

Aurora turned to where the Shadow Wolf stalked toward them and set her feet. "You swore to help me, Sanguine," she said as she raised her blade. "If ever you are going to keep your word, now is the time."

"Yes, my love," said the bard with relish as he moved past her, "now is the time when Sanguine shows his worth."

With his right hand, he reached into the neck of his shirt and pulled forth a glowing green orb on a silver chain. With his left hand extended toward the Shadow Wolf, Sanguine delved into the depths of the Orb of Nivettrix and with a high, sonorous cry pulled forth its power.

"Colstairth-en!"

A stream of pulsing green energy exploded from the bard's outstretched hand and the spell of slowing caught the Shadow Wolf full in the chest. The Wolf hesitated in his advance and looked down at his limbs, which were now moving with ordinary speed. The bard's spell had countered the Amulet of Arthenor.

The Shadow Wolf's air of calm superiority was now gone and his visage darkened to a hideous snarl. With a great roar, he came on. Aurora and Alishane moved to meet him, the cleric's deep voice booming through the stoneskin spell as he advanced.

The combatants came together with a flash of power and a clash of steel. Aurora and Alishane fought side-by-side in perfect harmony. The elf, lacking armor, fought defensively and waited for an opening in the Wolf's defenses. Alishane possessed the least skill with his sword of any of the three, but his stoneskin spell allowed him to accept hits from the Wolf and so he pressed his attack. The clang of blade meeting blade rang off the walls, interrupted occasionally by a dull thud as the Wolf scored a hit on Alishane's stoneskin.

Suddenly, the air was rent by the piercing cry of a streaking red osprey. Huggins had changed form and now dove at the Shadow Wolf's head, clawing at the assassin's eyes. Rinn swatted at the bird with his left hand and gave Alishane an opening that the cleric did not miss. Lunging forward and slashing with the Razor, Alishane connected with the Wolf's left elbow just above the silver gauntlet. The rapier's keen edge cut easily through the Wolf's flesh and bone and his lifeless arm fell to the floor. Rinn reacted too late to avoid the blow, but he still scored a devastating counter-thrust that crumbled the remainder of Alishane's stoneskin. The dazed cleric stumbled back, leaving Aurora to face the Wolf alone.

But the elf could not attack. She stood transfixed by the gruesome glory of the spectacle before her. For the severed arm was not the only thing that fell to the floor in the wake of Alishane's attack. The silver gauntlet was now gone as well and the Shadow Wolf was starting to transform. His hideous cries of pain became spitting, frothing snarls as the Wolf took hold. A moment later, Aurora stood face to face with the crippled and very angry werewolf.

The two confronted each other: the elf and the Wolf, the woman and her defiler. Aurora now looked into the same red eyes that had surfaced in the assassin whenever he used her during her imprisonment. She began to shake with rage. The Wolf, seeing the recognition on her face, gave a rasping, snarling laugh and his lupine tongue escaped his teeth to lick his snout. The indignity, the shame, the pain, the pit of despair that had filled Aurora all of those long days became a boiling cauldron of red-hot hatred. Her white hair flew away from her body and she raised her sword, narrowed her crystal-blue eyes and attacked.

Aurora's hatred drove her. She embraced it, used it, rode the crest of its rising swell like an ocean wave until it broke, bubbling and thunderous, upon the shoals of her enemy. She drove the Wolf back. His dripping maw was no longer leering but rather was contorted in anguished disbelief as he fought feverishly to parry the blows from her spinning blade. Behind her, Alishane shook the dizziness from his head and got to his feet.

Backward, ever backward, the elf drove the Wolf. Another flare ignited as they approached the far wall. Suddenly, a large barrel exploded over the Wolf's head and he crumbled to the floor. Aurora looked up to see Timmen O'Hook perched on a high shelf, his face pale and frightened in the flickering light.

Alishane and Sanguine walked up and they all stood looking down upon the unconscious Shadow Wolf. Already the lycanthrope's regenerative powers were at work upon his wounded arm: stanching the flow of blood, regrowing bone, knitting together muscle and sinew.

"What should we do with him?" asked Timmen.

Aurora was still shaking with anger. She stepped forward and placed the tip of her sword over the Wolf's heart. She stood there, her blade poised, for several long moments. At last, her shoulders slumped and she looked up at her friends.

"I cannot," she said helplessly. "My people believe it is murder to kill an unconscious foe."

"What, then?" asked Sanguine. "Take him captive? Turn him over to the authorities?"

"What authorities?" asked Timmen.

Alishane looked down at the creature that had murdered his father and Dunk Worley, the creature that had tortured him and caused the death of Arcanis Rhu, the creature that had violated the woman he loved throughout weeks of torment. A pounding in his ears began to drown out the voices of his friends. He thought back to his training at Rue Mortelei and his oath as a cleric to always follow the righteous path. The pounding in his ears grew louder. A vision of his father's stricken face appeared in his mind, the blood, the knife in his throat. The pounding grew louder. Dunk, Arcanis, his father, his oath... the pounding grew louder. Then he saw Aurora in her anguish, as clearly as he had seen it during his scrying spell: she's on the dais, the animal atop her, her eyes clenched shut and streaming while she pulls futilely at the chains binding her to the wall... the pounding grew louder.

Finally, he snapped.

Stepping forward, Alishane drove Occam's Razor straight through the heart of the unconscious monstrosity that was Zakarus

Rinn. A slight shiver and a last rush of air escaping the lungs, and it was over. The Shadow Wolf was dead.

Alishane retracted his blade and turned to Aurora. He was surprised to see tears of sadness filling her eyes.

"Unconscious or not," said the cleric, "murder or not, I care nothing for the distinction." He sheathed his sword and turned and walked away, leaving his righteousness and his oath as a cleric behind him.

Epilogue

"Bah, bring yer arse, boy. I want to be on the road 'afore the day's half spent."

"I've told you already not to rush me," Alishane Wyndam answered as he sauntered up to his horse and added more baggage. "And yet you persist in doing so. This is the thanks I get for saving your life... again?"

"You little whelp!" Dorak Shale blustered. "That's what yer here for, to heal. Every party needs a cleric and yer as close as we could get. Gods know yer no good with that fancy blade hanging on yer belt."

"Just don't call me pretty boy, okay?" Alishane whispered with a wink as he bent down near the dwarf's head.

"Ha! Never can again with that one around," Dorak laughed and bobbed his head toward the next horse, where Sanguine was reclining and picking his silvery teeth.

"Maybe we'll both get a chance to slap some ugly on him," Alishane quipped as he finished cinching his baggage and climbed atop his mount.

The clatter of hooves and skidding dirt made them all turn toward the road and regard Aurora Daelin, who sat atop her own horse with her gleaming hair pulled back and a hood over her head to hide her elvish features.

"Come along, all of you," she said. "The road is clear of Guardsmen and Vardiz is a long way off."

"Yes," cried Sanguine as he kicked his horse into motion. "To the road and the wild, my sweet! We will lay the mountains low if they stand in our way!"

Alishane and Dorak exchanged a look and then the cleric nudged his horse forward while Aurora helped the dwarf climb into the saddle behind her. They moved down the road into the rising heat of the Pilas Antum morning. They had not gone far, however, before Alishane pulled his horse to a halt and turned around.

"Come on, Timmen," he hollered, "or you'll be walking to the Council of the Kingdom." The halfling burst out of the building and ran as fast as his little legs could carry him. When he reached the horse, Alishane scooped the thief up into his lap.

"I couldn't find my hat," Timmen wheezed as he squashed the felt cap, complete with feather, onto his head.

Alishane laughed. "Just bring your thieving kit, Timmy the Crook. That's all you need." He kicked the horse into a canter to catch up with the others and together they road south toward the main road.

A short while later, the huge compound of Tavora Manor passed by on their left. The companions said nothing, but each looked out of the corners of their eyes at the courtyard where earlier that morning Cane Shanney had unceremoniously dumped the body of Zakarus Rinn.

Hours later, as the party made their leisurely way down the road south of Pilas Antum, a messenger of the Royal Guard thundered past them on his lathered mount. He was on his way to Anderton to inform the Countess of Westbury as to the fate of her trusted lieutenant. The Countess would have to cut short her trip and return to Tavora Manor. The Shadow Wolf was dead, but death is not permanent in the eyes of a necromancer.

End of Book One

The story continues in

Mark of the Crescent Moon

Book Two in the Sacred Scrolls Saga

Prologue for *Mark of the Crescent Moon*

Four wagons descended the hill with a slow sucking noise as their wheels cut grooves into the muddy forest road. Slick from their labor despite the bitter cold, the oxen blew clouds of steam into the crisp autumn air. With a shout and a crack of his whip, the drover pulled hard on the reins and stopped the column.

"Hoy, Garrick! What passes?" called a large, yellow-bearded man as he galloped forward on his snorting steed. The bronze buckler slung over his shoulder clattered against his mail shirt as it was brought to bear. The scout's other hand gripped the hilt of the broadsword strapped to his waist.

"The air is evil," the driver answered in a gravelly voice. From under tangled brows, his eyes darted into the trees on either side of the road. "Forest is quiet," he growled, "animals gone."

The scout pulled his sword free of its scabbard; its blade was notched with the tale of heavy use. Riding slowly forward, the bearded man squinted his eyes and held his breath as he listened to the vacancy of the surrounding gloom. Utter silence greeted his straining ears. No flutter of feather. No scamper of squirrel. Air that had been sweet with the smell of autumn's slow decay now turned sour with the pungent reek of death.

"What seems to be the problem?" asked a soft voice from within the dark interior of the wagon.

"No problem, Master O'Hook, none at all. We'll be along shortly," the scout answered as he squinted unseeing into the darkness.

"And I suppose you'll be runnin' the wagons, then?" the drover snarled under his breath.

"You'll run the wagons as we've agreed, Garrick, or you won't get paid," the yellow-haired scout retorted.

"Nay; I'll not!" insisted the old drover, his face ruddy and nostrils flared. "I run the West Road, the main pike, not this backwoods lane leading deeper into the hills. This is too dangerous."

"You worry about the ox and the box, Garrick, and leave the danger to me," stormed the scout.

"Gentlemen, please," interjected the soft voice from within the wagon as a small figure emerged from the darkness. "You have brought us farther out of your way than reason could have hoped for. This will do nicely." Timmen O'Hook dropped lightly to the ground and then turned and extended his hand. Pale, delicate fingers accepted the halfling's grasp and a veiled young woman emerged from the wagon. She stepped tentatively to the ground and then pulled her long, black cloak tightly around her neck.

"The Withywindle is around the bend and down the slope," the girl whispered. "This forest may be quiet, but it still has eyes." Overhead, a hawk issued a long screech that echoed off of the low-lying clouds. The bird circled once and then disappeared over the black treetops.

"Yes, this will do nicely," Timmen repeated. "Master Jachin, come along, now. We must continue from here on foot."

The veiled young woman stepped aside and a boy of fifteen years emerged from the wagon. "Excuse me, Kami," Jachin muttered as he stepped into the mud. He looked down as his feet sank to his ankles in the muck; a low growl resonated deep in his chest.

Kami giggled. "I believe he is displeased with your guide service, Timmen," the girl teased.

Jachin pulled his foot from the mud with a dripping pop. "This journey had better prove fruitful," he said and began slogging down the path.

Timmen took Kami's hand and led her into the young man's wake. Behind them, the drover cracked his whip and whistled to his team. The wagon train turned and made its plodding way back up the hill, leaving the three dark figures to struggle along in the mud and failing light.

* * * * * * *

Night had fallen cold and hard as the halfling and his two young companions rounded a hill and found before them a wide clearing illuminated by dozens of campfires. The Withywindle River bubbled over a stone bed and wound its way through the clearing.

"The gypsies have made their camp on both sides of the river," Timmen observed, "though I've never known them to be so quiet."

"We've come to the camp?" Kami inquired incredulously. "I can hear nothing but the sound of the water."

Jachin started forward with a determined stride. "It is here," he whispered so softly that the others barely heard. "My answer is here."

Timmen, with Kami still in tow, hurried after the young man as quickly as he dared. "It is dark," he whispered over his shoulder. "I'm nearly as blind as you."

Kami's thin lips curled into a grin. "More so, in some respects," she chided. Timmen didn't answer. A few stumbling steps more and they came upon Jachin. The young man had stopped in the shadows a stone's throw from the outer rim of the camp.

"How should we do this, Timmen," he asked.

"We had best be careful," the halfling answered. "They're sure to be guarding their camp this deep into the forest." Timmen put Kami's hand onto Jachin's shoulder and then dug into the pouch he wore at his hip. Extracting and unfolding a long cloak, the halfling drew it about his shoulders and disappeared. "Wait here," he instructed. "I will find the one we desire and the best path to her."

He reappeared half an hour later, folding his shadow cloak and stowing it safely in his pouch. "Follow me," he whispered. "Be quick and quiet."

Timmen led them partway into the camp, then veered away from the river into the outlying tents. Far to the rear of the camp, off to the side and behind a stand of willows, a solitary tent huddled near the foot of the hills. Its canvas walls were heavily patched, their frayed ends blowing softly in the breeze. As they approached it, Kami shuddered violently and nearly tripped.

"Oh yes, she is here," the girl wheezed. "I can feel the power in this place. She is here."

Timmen stooped and picked up a small stone, preparing to throw it against the side of the tent in his fashion of a knock on the door.

"Go away!" called a cold, high voice from within the structure. "I am not accepting callers or visitors."

Timmen turned and looked at his companions. Jachin wore a frustrated frown; Kami's veil hid her eyes, but could not conceal her bemused smile. "We desire to employ…" he began, but the cold voice cut him off.

"No visitors. No exceptions."

Now it was Timmen's turn to frown and, with a determined shake of his head, the halfling set his stubborn chin and walked through the flap that served as the tent's door. No sooner had the flap closed behind him than a loud *thunk* was followed closely by Timmen's cry of surprise.

"Well that's hardly necessary…"

Thunk!

"Hey!"

"No visitors, I said. No visitors."

The sound of a struggle ensued. Kami giggled. Jachin's frown deepened. A moment later, a high-pitched squawk was followed by another, though subdued, battle. Shortly thereafter, a bedraggled Timmen O'Hook emerged through the flap in the tent and bowed graciously.

"Our host awaits your company, Master Jachin," he panted as he swept his felt cap through the air.

The halfling held the tent flap open as the young man led Kami inside. Once within, Jachin gasped as he saw a thin, middle-aged woman sitting on a chair with her hands tied behind her back and a scalding look upon her face.

The woman seemed to swell as she took a deep breath, then she let loose with a high-pitched tirade. "You have no right invading my home after I expressly told you not to," she spat at Jachin and then turned to Timmen, who had followed his companions into the tent. "And you," her eyes were murderous as they fell upon the halfling, "you... you mop-headed little rascal. You..." but Timmen held up his hand and cut her off.

"We," he nodded toward the others, "are not leaving until our business is concluded. So you can either extend our stay by continuing with your rant, or you can simply perform the service we have come all this way to commission."

"Commission?" the woman asked in a voice so shrill that it awakened a hound on the other side of the camp. "You mean extort!" Her face contorted and flushed red as she pulled against her bonds. Timmen and Jachin exchanged a look. Kami leaned forward, listening intently. At last, the woman's frail form slumped and her shoulders heaved as she tried to catch her breath. "Very well," she wheezed. "You have come for a reading and you shall have one, so long as you promise to leave immediately thereafter."

"Agreed," Timmen slapped his thigh and pulled the abode's only other chair in front of the woman, signaling for Jachin to sit. The young man complied as Timmen untied the woman's hands. She rubbed her wrists and scowled at the halfling, then she reached out and seized Jachin's hands. She turned them palm-upward and closed her eyes, then she began circling his palms with the tips of her fingers. A moment later, the woman frowned and her head jerked to the side as a pained moan escaped her lips.

"I feel the earth in you," she rasped as her circling intensified. "Yes... yes the earth is hard; it is unyielding; it is timeless. It is moved only by great catastrophe." The woman's shoulders swayed as her hands moved feverishly over the upturned palms of the sweating young man. "The earth will be moved, oh yes, it will be moved. Whispers of plague will sweep across the countryside on the very same winds that herald the coming of winter. Rumors will breed fear and mistrust. City gates will be closed, shutters boarded and doors locked. You are the coming of woe."

Suddenly, the woman's eyes flew open and she screeched, pulling her hands away from Jachin. "Out! Out!" she screamed. "No! Kill me if you must but get out!"

"Finish it!" Jachin yelled and seized her hands again. She struggled to pull away but his grasp was too strong. "Please, I must know. You must finish it! Finish it now!"

Their struggle ended in the woman's agonized wail as Kami suddenly lunged forward, ripping off her veil and seizing the seer by the head. As the woman's painful scream died away, Kami's eyelids opened, exposing two blackened pits where her eyes should have been. The seer was shaking violently with her mouth agape as Kami invaded her mind and channeled her gift. With the pits of her unseeing eyes wide open, Kami delivered the seer's doom in a low, monotonous voice:

> *"The Revelation shall be born on the fifth day, and in the ninth hour the birds will awaken and sing a new song. For you are the Chosen One and have been deemed worthy. By your blood shall the Scrolls be opened, the tomb sundered, and the Prophecy fulfilled."*

One long, dark moment later, Kami's eyelids fluttered and closed. With shaking fingers she replaced her veil and groped toward Timmen, who took her by the hand and pulled her to him, holding her tight against his small body. Jachin was ashen-faced as he shakily got to his feet and turned to his friends.

"I… I…" he stammered, then he shook his head and ran from the tent. Timmen took Kami's cold fingers in his and followed, leaving the unconscious seer slumped in her chair.